ELAF
Winds of Change

To Margaret

A new adventure begins - enjoy!

Jack

Contents

Prologue 3

Chapter One 14

Chapter Two 24

Chapter Three 48

Chapter Four 62

Chapter Five 84

Chapter Six 136

Chapter Seven 150

Chapter Eight 182

Chapter Nine 203

Chapter Ten 230

Epilogue 240

Prologue

Caesia glanced up from her book as the silence was shattered by the crack of vibrant arcane fire overhead. She peered out the window of the carriage, where the colossal, looming gate of Aldreichen gave way to the starry night sky. Another firework exploded above them, flooding the sky with magical red fire. The glorious splashes of vibrant colours were more than just mesmerising - they were inspiring to a young mage such as herself, who could barely shoot sparks from her fingers. One day, she would light up the sky.

The journey, as usual, had been one of total silence. Her mother and father had sat as always at opposite ends of the carriage, barely a word between them. Caesia didn't really care, in fact she preferred the silence as it helped her read. Gerard on the other hand, had been left behind after being grounded for playing with one of the servant girls. Thank God, she hated her brother with a passion.

"Caesia," her father snarled. "Stop kicking your feet, it's childish."

"Sorry, father," Caesia mumbled, tightening her tiny legs against the seat and staring down at her knees.

"Come, Edmund," Amelie sighed. "It's Unity Day, let the girl be herself for a bit."

"That is exactly why she must be on her *absolute* best behaviour!" Edmund insisted. "This is the last day on which I wish to be made a mockery of."

Caesia zoned out once again as her parents began to argue. She closed her book and went to place it on her lap, only to freeze in fear of creasing her pretty, violet dress. Scared to fail in her presentation, she planted it beside her and shifted her glowing, pale green eyes to the window once again.

Today was the 32nd of Aldris, or Unity Day to the Kingdom of Verdenheld. The celebrations were in full swing - peasants sang and danced in droves, confetti polluted the main roads, fireworks set the skies alight and the ground trembled at the passing of vast military parades. Caesia wished she could be out there, having fun like everyone else. Instead, she was being dragged along to the palace, so she could watch her parents mingle with grown-ups that they didn't even like.

"Mother?" Caesia asked quietly, garnering no response from her mother who still argued with her father.

Amelie's attention was caught as Caesia tugged gently at the her sleeve. "Yes, darling?"

"Caesia," Edmund snapped. "Do not pull at-"

"Calm down, Edmund." Amelie groaned. "Go on, dear."

Caesia struggled to produce her words under the burning eyes of her father. His very presence terrified her. "W-why can't we go outside?"

Amelie smirked. "Because, darling, the commonfolk would eat you alive."

Caesia's eyes fluttered in confusion. "But they're having fun… and the colours…"

"Those people out there are filthy, diminutive and would happily take advantage of you should you give them the chance." Amelie said with a casual smile. "We don't belong with them."

"They look so happy," Caesia mumbled, overcome with envy.

"Yes, happy rolling in the mud," Amelie sneered.

Caesia sighed and withdrew from the window. The outside world was making her sad again, as it had always done. Her parents were always so mean when they talked about it, like everybody there was evil. She could never understand why…

She sat quietly through the journey into the city centre. The carriage took them around Victory Plaza in an attempt to avoid the marching columns of red-cloaked soldiers, weaving from the beautiful golden brown houses of the city centre to the aged stone buildings that surrounded it. Where was once dazzling colours and feverous celebration, there was now eerie silence and drab grey structures.

Edmund glanced curiously out of the window, watching a battalion of House Verden soldiers marching a few blocks away, a frown on his face that screamed superiority.

"It never ceases to amuse me how it is House Verden who flexes their might on these days, despite being the weakest of us all," he muttered.

"You say that every year," Amelie sighed. "And every time I tell you - there's more to power than how hard you can hit."

"Which I why I have you," Edmund smirked.

Amelie chuckled quietly, almost mockingly. "Of course," she smiled sweetly.

"As I was saying…" Edmund continued, earning a subtle roll of Amelie's eyes. "The parades here should be unified - more representative of the glue that binds this kingdom together, rather than those who sit on top."

"You sound jealous, Edmund."

"Do not mistake discontent for envy." Edmund sneered. "House Verden has no right to take the credit of other houses!"

"Maybe you should hold your own parade," Amelie smugly suggested. "Get the College of Arcana involved and blow Friedrich's out of the water."

Edmund lay back in his seat with a sigh. He knew when his wife was mocking him and had no intention to fuel it. Then again, that wasn't so bad of an idea...

"What do you think, Caesia?" Amelie asked, dragging her daughter's attention back to the conversation. "What do you make of Unity Day?"

"It, er... it is very pretty," Caesia mumbled with a nervous smile.

She shrank into her seat as her father rolled his eyes. Amelie smirked at the sight of it, never ceasing to enjoy her husband's displeasure.

"No, darling," she smiled. "What do *you* think?"

Caesia looked back and forth at her parents anxiously. It wasn't often they gave her the privilege of freedom of speech. Now she feared that she would say something wrong.

"I-I don't like the soldiers..." she mumbled.

"Why ever not?" Amelie asked with intrigue.

"Soldiers are mean... and scary. I don't like them," Caesia sighed. "They kill people..."

"So, you think Unity Day should be less militarised, to convey a less authoritarian message?" Amelie smiled, gaining only a blank expression from Caesia before turning to Edmund. "Clever girl."

"She didn't mean that at all!" Edmund snapped, prompting Caesia to bury herself further into her seat.

"Perhaps she didn't say it directly, but her answer certainly implied what she would rather see in a Unity Day celebration," Amelie insisted, taking a great deal of pleasure in putting Edmund down. "Caesia is right. With the Republic spouting messages of freedom and democracy, I fear Verdenheld will struggle to maintain its grip on the world should it continue these authoritarian practices."

"And what would you have me do?" Edmund scoffed. "Ask Friedrich to abolish the monarchy?"

"Monarchy is not tyranny. We needn't change our government, we must simply be... well, a little bit nicer."

"You know that your criticisms would fall on deaf ears, even mine would! Nobody cares to change the kingdom, only to continue on its current course."

"That course being straight to the grave, should nothing change," Amelie warned. "The world is not as it was a hundred years ago - Norskar and Thyresia are growing exponentially in power and House Arrenni's little foray across the ocean has only revealed more competitors. I'd hazard to say it's only a matter of time before the world we think to rule comes down on our heads."

"I'll... I'll bring it up," Edmund sighed. "But I expect that it will be dismissed within seconds."

"We have to try," Amelie urged. "We may be the only ones who see the bigger picture."

The golden gates of the Palace Gardens were flung open ahead of the carriage. Caesia watched excitedly from the window as they passed through the Gardens. It was a paradise of flowing, crystalline water and lush, vibrant plants of every colour. Her eyes darted around, mesmerized, as the carriage trundled into the courtyard.

It ground to halt beside four other carriages, with the Ironhands running late as usual. Caesia took a deep breath as their driver moved to open the door. There was nothing more intimidating than one's first formal visit to the palace, especially considering what her father might have done should she make a fool out of them in front of the king. She never knew what to expect from a man who would strike his daughter over a poorly executed curtsey, but she rightfully feared the worst.

Edmund and Amelie stepped out from the carriage, followed closely by Caesia who emerged cradling her book in her arms. She stared up apprehensively at the colossal, golden palace looming over her, a sight that did not particularly help her nerves.

Edmund glanced up at the moon and shot a glare at their driver. "We are late."

"Only by a few minutes, sir," The carriage driver smiled nervously. "I'm sure-"

"Once we are returned to Abenfurt, you are relieved," Edmund snarled, taking off angrily towards the towering throne room door.

Amelie looked the speechless driver up and down with a smirk as he sagged defeatedly. "Say, how would like a new job?" She smiled, watching Edmund closely with a cunning grin.

"Um… very much, ma'am."

"Wonderful. You will transport people to and from Abenfurt by cart. For every piece of intrigue you can bring me, I shall give you five gold coins."

"Five?!" The driver gasped.

"Shall I consider that a yes?" Amelie smiled.

"Yes, yes, thank you, my lady!"

"No," Amelie grinned sinisterly. "Thank *you*."

Edmund came storming back, an impatient scowl on his face. "What is the holdup?" He growled, narrowing his eyes at the driver. "Is this man harassing you, Amelie?"

"Apologies, dear," Amelie smiled sweetly. "I was just offering our friend here my condolences."

"He deserves no such words," Edmund hissed. "Come, the Council is waiting."

Amelie followed slowly as Edmund rushed off again. She tugged Caesia along and leaned in closely.

"Do not speak a word of what you just saw," she whispered.

"Yes, mother," Caesia mumbled.

Amelie looked into Caesia hypnotic green eyes with a smile. "Good girl."

The massive throne room doors ground open and they stepped into the magnificent hall ahead. Caesia looked around in awe at the colossal white pillars and golden statues that lay at the room's edge. The crimson eagle banners of House Verden fell from every pillar, flanking a massive banner of the Kingdom of Verdenheld, which bore the image of a golden phoenix rising from flame. It hung above the glorious golden throne of the King, a shimmering marvel encompassed by a phoenix, wrapping its wings around it.

Stood before the throne conversing amongst one another were the house patriarchs. At the centre was King Friedrich Verden, a fossil of a man with a trimmed grey beard and a gammy leg. Laughing by his side was Alvus Severin, a young man, barely twenty, with his favourite scar down the side of his face and the beginnings of a beard cluttering his chin. Dwelling nearby was Ilias Barethia, eavesdropping being an act not well suited to someone so incredibly large and equally bald. Finally, Jonas Arrenni stood brooding off to the side, likely considering how much money he could make from melting down the throne, the scrawny cretin he was.

These were the most powerful men in Verdenheld - a king on death's door, a hot headed man-child, an obese holy man and a conniving little creature. No wonder the realm was in decline.

"Edmund!" called Alvus. "Better late than Kranik, I guess!"

"Are the Ironhands not gracing us with their musk?" Edmund sneered.

His fellow lords chuckled heartily amongst themselves. Caesia could never understand why the other houses made fun of the Ironhands - she thought they were nice.

"I'm afraid not," Friedrich sighed. "I'm told Anvilport is being raided again by that 'Ashen Fleet', as I believe the Thyresians call it."

"Any excuse…" Alvus chuckled.

"You've left Kranik to fight the Ashen Fleet?" Edmund scoffed. "If any of us should be out dealing with that, it should be Jonas!"

"Why me?" Jonas hissed.

"I don't know, maybe because you control the *entire* navy?" Ilias laughed.

"Yes, but I don't command it!"

"My point still stands," Edmund groaned. "House Ironhand has no naval capabilities!"

"Kranik's smart, he'll figure something out," Alvus said dismissively. "Besides, what's even the point of attacking an Ironhand port anyway? What can you get there that you can't get at an Arrenni port?"

"Certainly not defences…" Ilias muttered.

"Enough!" Friedrich barked. "We haven't come here to waffle about Kranik, we're here to celebrate!"

"Yes, to celebrate unity and cooperation while our allies are left to die alone!" Alvus chuckled. "Here's to Verdenheld!"

Friedrich glared at Alvus, who smiled smugly as he took a sip of wine from his silvered goblet.

Caesia stared blankly into the distance while the lords conversed. She was never sure why she had to come to these affairs. What did she have to contribute?

As her gaze drifted lazily around the room, it became snagged on something. Her eyes came to rest on the glistening golden throne at the centre of the room. Yet, it was not the throne that had her attention, but rather what lay beyond - something that she could not see, yet she knew was there.

Caesia glanced up at her mother, who was busy conversing with Lady Arrenni. She looked back across the throne room, to an alcove that wrapped behind the throne. With her parents both locked in conversation, she edged slowly towards it. As she drew closer, her mind began to itch. At least, that was the only way she could describe it. A scratching in her mind drowned her thoughts and her skin grew cold. She moved cautiously into the alcove, the scratching becoming a whisper - a harsh, unintelligible voice in the back of her mind.

"Hello?" She whispered as she anxiously rounded the corner.

Behind the throne lay a huge door, guarded on either side by a pair of the King's golden armoured Phoenix Guard, menacing behemoths of men in ornate, tricinium plate. One of them looked at her curiously through his winged helmet as she slipped out from behind the wall and approached the door. She knew she shouldn't, she barely even wanted to, but she felt implored to do so. She supposed it couldn't hurt - the guards didn't seem to care, why would they?

The whispering grew louder as she stepped up to the door. It called out to her, it wanted her to come closer. It needed her to come closer.

Caesia looked up at the door. It was enormous, several tonnes of pure gold condensed into a pair of colossal slabs. She could never open that, no matter how much she wanted to meet the voice.

"Give me your hand," urged the voice, clearer than ever.

Caesia gasped, startled but nonetheless intrigued. She couldn't help but feed her curiosity.

She outstretched her arm, quivering in anticipation. As her hand drew close to the door, her hand began to tingle, a sensation the likes of which she had never felt before - it was kind of painful, but also satisfying in a strange way. A tendril of green light jumped from her hand before it pressed firmly against the door. She closed her eyes and breathed deeply, the tingling intensifying and spreading down her arm.

To the guards, it seemed like nothing - simply a girl touching a door. To Caesia, it was so much more. In her mind, through a shifting green lens, she could see what lay beyond. There was a large room, empty and barren, yet still decorated like the rest. There was something there, only metres from her. It was an orb, filled with writhing, black energy. She couldn't take her eyes off it. It called to her, urged her to simply step forwards, to help it finally be free.

"You lost, little one?"

Caesia's eyes snapped open, the image vanishing from her mind. She turned in a daze away from the door, eyes fluttering in confusion.

A man approached her, smiling amidst a fledgling brown beard. He knelt down beside her and looked curiously into her eyes, which hummed more intensely than ever with green light.

"You must be Caesia," he said gently.

Caesia stared at him for a moment, before shuffling around and placing her book delicately on the ground. She took her dress in either hand an executed a flawless curtsey.

"A pleasure to meet you, Lord Arrenni," Caesia said slowly, a long rehearsed greeting.

"Not quite," the man chuckled. "I'm Lord Severin."

Caesia gasped, her tiny eyes widening in terror. "I'm sorry!" she sobbed, burying her face in her hands as her cheeks were flushed with red.

Alvus tilted his head in confusion. "It's okay, accidents happen."

"Are you going to tell father?" Caesia mumbled behind her hands.

Alvus smirked at the teary eyed girl. So this was how Edmund treated his girl, by scaring her into submission. It was certainly effective, but no way to nurture a gift.

"No, I won't," Alvus said, smiling warmly.

Caesia withdrew her hands with a reassured smile, while Alvus scraped her book off the ground and grinned as he read the title.

"A History of Verdenheld?" he laughed. That was quite an advanced book for a nine year old. "My, you are a smart-"

Alvus paused as he flicked to a random page. Where he had expected to find a page of fanatical drivel about the glory of Verdenheld, he instead found a series of complex diagrams and symbols. Upon a quick skim read he realised what he was holding was not a history book at all, but rather an electromancy spellbook.

Caesia looked at him blankly, stiff with distress. Her mouth quivered as she tried to produce an excuse. Her father only allowed her to read histories and arcane theory, he would not let her anywhere near a spellbook.

The silence between them was broken as Alvus began to chuckle heartily. "How on Elaria did you pull this off?" he laughed, handing the book back to her. "Don't worry, your secret's safe with me."

"Th-thank you, Lord Severin," Caesia smiled, wrapping her arms around her book once again.

"Call me Alvus. What are you doing back here anyway?"

Caesia glanced back at the door, a raspy whisper still hissing at the back of her mind. She wanted to see what was back there, but she knew that she would get in trouble if she did.

"I was exploring. I… like this door," she mumbled, fearful to expose herself.

"Do you now?" Alvus smirked. "Yeah, I guess it's a pretty nice door."

"Can I go in?" Caesia asked. It was worth a try.

"No! No, definitely not!" Alvus stammered. "There… there's something back there that you're not allowed to see."

"An orb?"

Alvus' eyes widened in terror and his skin grew pale. He glanced up at the phoenix guardsman beside him, who was staring at her with equal shock. They looked at each other for a moment, before Alvus anxiously signalled for the guards to leave. He turned back to Caesia and pulled her close.

"Who told you that?" he hissed.

Caesia shrank back against the door. "I saw it…"

"You what?!" Alvus gasped.

"Am I in trouble?" Caesia mumbled into her book.

Alvus looked for a moment at the girl. She knew information reserved solely for the Phoenix Guard and the house patriarchs, too dangerous to be kept in the hands of a little girl. If the Council found out, it would mean her immediate death.

"No…" Alvus whispered. "Not yet, at least. Look, just explain to me exactly what it was you saw."

"Um, okay…" Caesia murmured. "It was black… and angry. It wanted to get out. It-"

"Wait, wait!" Alvus hissed. "What do you mean, it wanted to get out?"

"It asked me to open the door, but I couldn't," Caesia sighed, looking back at the colossal golden slabs. "It's too big."

"You mean to say the orb talked to you?"

Caesia nodded her head slowly. Alvus ran his hands through his hair in distress. That was impossible - it didn't matter how much black essence was pumped into that thing, it shouldn't have been able to communicate! It had to be her green essence, there was no other explanation. Even so, how would an abnormal essence colour allow her to communicate with an inanimate object?

"I... I see," Alvus stammered. "Caesia, I need you to listen to me *very* carefully."

She nodded obediently with an attentive smile. Alvus couldn't let such a sweet girl get tied up in this.

"Alright. What you saw in that room... nobody can ever know about it. Forget it ever existed if you can, just promise me that you will *never* speak a word of this to anyone. Can you do that?"

"Why?"

Alvus sighed impatiently. The girl was too smart for her own good. "Because that orb is very, very bad and hurt a lot of good people."

"Okay. I won't tell..." Caesia sighed.

"Promise?" Alvus smiled.

"Promise."

The quiet was broken as Edmund's booming voice echoed throughout the throne room, Caesia nearly leaving the ground at the sound of it.

"Where is my daughter?!" He bellowed.

Alvus watched with a sympathetic smile as Caesia froze and stiffened in terror. "Don't worry, I'll cover for you," he grinned, springing to his feet. "Come on."

Caesia followed Alvus cautiously back into the hall, taking one last glance back at the door. She winced as the whisper became harsh and contemptuous. It was furious, screaming after her as she backed away. She shook her head erratically, she would not help it! It was bad and hurt good people. The voice subsided as she stepped back into the main hall, flinching as her father's gaze snapped immediately to her.

"Caesia-"

"Apologies, Edmund," Alvus smiled. "I was just showing the little one around."

Edmund glared down at Caesia for a moment, visibly drifting in and out of various intense emotions. His response was drowned out however, as the doors to the throne room ground open.

Into the hall stormed Kranik Ironhand, the old man wielding a furious glare, his teeth gritted in the midst of his long grey mess of a beard. A silence fell over the other lords as he advanced upon them.

"Kranik!" Friedrich called in manufactured merriment. "I, er... didn't expect to see you here!"

"No thanks to this band of pricks!" Kranik hissed, flinging his finger at Jonas. "Where the bloody hell were you?!"

"I... was here," Jonas mumbled.

"And your fleet? The one that is supposed to protect the damned ports?!"

"Kranik, calm down!" Alvus urged. "It's-"

"Shut your trap, boy!" Kranik hissed. "I tolerate plenty of jokes at my expense, but this goes well beyond the line!"

"Is the situation not dealt with?" Edmund asked.

"It is, a fleet from Thisavros came in and scared 'em off," Kranik sighed. "But the port's nought but rubble."

"Ha! Trust the Thyresians to do half a job." Jonas laughed.

"At least you can trust 'em do it in the first place!" Kranik snarled. "Slimy bastard."

"Okay!" Alvus shouted over them. "With that out of the way, what are we getting up to tonight?"

"I believe the main article of tonight will be the Strausian frontier," Ilias grinned.

"That it will," Friedrich declared. "It's high time House Arrenni got its reinforcements!"

"High time indeed!" Jonas concurred. "The savages would sooner burn than quit."

"Then burn it is!" Alvus laughed merrily. "I'm sure I can shift a few thousand soldiers out of Jordenholm. What's the worst that could happen?"

"Then at that, gentlemen, let us begin," Friedrich announced, waving the other lords along.

Caesia watched as the patriarchs departed. As they left through the hallway, Alvus turned around and pressed his finger against his smiling lips. Caesia imitated his gestured before withdrawing her hand and waving him goodbye. Amelie watched the exchange with amusement.

"It seems you've made a friend," she smirked. "You're going to be a natural diplomat."

As usual, Caesia couldn't tell if her mother was being mocking or sincere. It didn't matter, she supposed. She would take it as a compliment.

"You will learn quickly that friends in high places are the only friends worth having," Amelie muttered "So, good start."

Caesia wondered if that was the reason her parents didn't let her have friends.

"Come, darling," Amelie commanded. "Let's go meet some boys. I hear Geldus Verden is growing up to be quite the handsome young man."

Caesia sighed as Amelie took her hand and dragged her along. As she departed the throne room, she recited once more in her head her promise to Lord Severin. She would never speak of the orb to anyone. She wouldn't let it hurt people ever again.

Chapter One - Abenfurt Bound

Caesia slumped back in the chair and buried her face in her notebook. Another failed attempt, another hour's work wasted. She had been trying for a six days now to wrap her head around this translocation nonsense, but to no avail. It was beginning to take its toll, to irritate her more and more by the day. It was so infuriating having this revolutionary power, but not knowing a damned thing about it.

She scowled at herself in the scuffed mirror that lay on her desk, her ghostly green eyes glaring back amidst a sea of deathly white skin. Seeing her reflection glare at her with contempt served only to multiply that which she already felt.

"Stupid green essence…" she muttered, casting her notebook onto her bed and readjusting her wavy brown bob. "Why couldn't you have been born normal?"

She slid unenthusiastically from her chair and trudged over to the opposite wall. She had procured one of the walls as a 'notes wall', having cluttered the pristine white wallpaper with diagrams, symbols and crazed ramblings. Writing on walls helped her think, it laid everything out in front of her to consider all at once.

"You could've had friends, maybe a loving family…" she sighed as she scrubbed a block of text from the wall. "But no, you had to go and be born with some stupid essence like the stupid girl you are!"

In a fit of self-loathing, Caesia flung out her arms, sending a vase toppling from her desk with a spine chilling crash.

"Ow!" she hissed, withdrawing her bandaged fingers as they shot with pain. "Aw, crap…"

She looked down at the shattered vase, wringing her sickly yellow fingers nervously. The soggy purple flowers looked about as sad as her, lying there helplessly as the water seeped through the floorboards.

"Ugh, why did you do that?" she groaned, throwing herself back onto her bed. "Idiot!"

With a tiresome huff, Caesia looked up blankly at the ceiling. She couldn't take it anymore - being cooped up in her room, trying aimlessly to understand something impossible. She needed some air, but there was so much left to do!

Her heart skipped a beat as the door thundered suddenly with a vigorous knock that shook the walls around it. That could have only been one person.

"Come in..." she moaned, attempting for a moment to peel herself from the bed but giving up almost instantly.

Eris poked her head around the door with her usual insufferable grin plastered on her pasty freckled face. Caesia had desperately hoped that the scar across her cheek would have stopped her from smiling so much, but alas...

"What, er... what happened to the vase?" Eris smirked, the broken pottery being glaringly obvious in such an otherwise immaculate room.

Caesia would have glared at Eris had she the strength to do so, but instead she simply stared at her. Eris was a far healthier specimen than her, not particularly muscular but extremely athletic in her build, a far cry from Caesia's practically skeletal frame. Her dull hazel hair highlighted her pretty blue eyes and the slender red scar that stretched across her cheek from her nose to her jaw. That wasn't to say she was perfect - her skin was awash with freckles and rosy spots, and her teeth were not exactly pristine. Even so, her healthy glow served only to sour Caesia's already foul mood.

"Shut up," Caesia sighed, shuffling upright. "I just lost my cool a bit..."

"That's like, the twelfth time this week!" Eris laughed.

"Sixth," Caesia spat. "Anyway, can you blame me?! It's so close, yet so painfully far!"

"Maybe you ought to have a break," Eris suggested. "Stars know you need one."

"I-I can't!" Caesia stammered, springing up from her bed and pacing up the length of the room. "I mean, I want to... but my brain won't let me! I need to do this, I-"

"Caesia, calm down!" Eris giggled. The girl was going crazy in here, Eris had to get her outside fast. "I think it's time to get going."

"Get- no! I mean, yeah... Look, I just want to try one more thing."

"How long will it take...?"

"Just a few minutes, I promise!" Caesia smiled.

Eris could see the crazy in her eyes. It felt like Caesia was about to ask to dissect her.

"Okay..." Eris mumbled.

"Cool! I mean, thank you," Caesia mumbled, taking a quick moment to compose herself. "Okay... so, I've concluded that translocation, or as I intend to refer to it - blinking, is triggered by incoming threats. Thus, I need you to throw something at me."

"Anything?" Eris grinned deviously.

"Preferably something that won't hurt all that much."

Eris picked up one of Caesia's new books, 'Magical Translocation: Theories and Hypotheses'. Albert had been incredibly resourceful in tending to Caesia's needs, having provided her with all sorts of magical

15

texts for her obsessive research. Eris hurled the book at Caesia, who clumsily strafed to the side. The book thudded off Caesia' forehead and onto the floor, leaving her clutching her forehead in pain.

Eris blurted with laughter. "That was really impressive," she giggled. "Do I need to throw another?"

Caesia glared at her and returned to her wall, rubbing her head glumly. "Well, that's another hypothesis off the list…"

Eris had a thought, a smile growing across her face as she silently unbuckled her sheath.

"Damn, I thought I was so close with that one! Yet once again-"

"Hey, think fast!" Eris yelled.

Caesia span around to see Eris' battered steel sword spiralling towards her. She screamed in terror and threw up her hands as pale green light burst around her and swallowed her up in but a split second. The sword sprang off the wall and fell to the ground with a rattle, while Caesia exploded into reality on the other side of the room and stumbled into the dresser.

"There you go!" Eris smiled, picking up her sword.

"Are you mad?!" Caesia spat, splayed out across the dresser. "You could have killed me!"

"But I didn't," Eris rebuked with a cheeky grin.

Caesia knew there was little point in shouting at Eris, so instead she shuffled back to her wall muttering under her breath. She grabbed a stick of chalk and scrawled the words 'immediate danger' onto the wall.

"Immediate danger?" Eris asked. "Then how do you explain the snowball fight?"

Caesia paused her writing and thought. "Hm… perhaps not danger then, but rather desperation. Whether it be desperation to live or to win."

"That makes more sense," Eris agreed. "How're your arms?"

Caesia's arms were still bandaged, but Eris could see by her uncovered fingers that the bruising had gone a sickly yellow now, which she believed must be better than throbbing and purple.

"Still sore, but better," Caesia sighed. "As you can see, I can move my fingers now, which is a start… I guess."

"Think you'll be ready to hit the road soon?"

Caesia lifted up her hands and inspected what little of her skin she could see. Her arms still hurt when she moved them, but it was becoming far more bearable. She believed that she could probably start casting spells again, although it may hurt a little.

"I suppose…" Caesia muttered. "I doubt I'd be at my best."

"Long as it means getting out of here sooner, that's fine by me."

"You don't like it?" Caesia smiled. "I think it's a lovely place."

Caesia felt quite at home within the finely maintained white walls of a Thyresian house. It was almost like being back home, only without the issue of her parents.

"I mean, yeah... but I've only got a year, you know?"

Caesia chuckled quietly and shook her head. It was amusing how eager Eris was to get back to facing certain death. It seemed in the tomb like Eris would be changed by her experience, that she would learn to become less reckless and to pick her battles rather than charge headfirst into danger. That certainly didn't come to pass, though Eris had at least been practicing her defence as a result.

"You know what? I think it's high time I got some fresh air," Caesia smiled.

"You mean it?" Eris gasped with childish glee.

"Yeah, I think I'll go insane looking at this wall much longer," Caesia smirked. "Grab your stuff, we'll leave for Abenfurt promptly."

Eris smiled with relief. Thank the stars, she could finally get back to doing what she came here for. She sped off back into her room and began rummaging around feverously for her armour.

Caesia sighed as she picked up a stack of books and hauled them from her desk. She now knew the circumstances required to activate the power instinctively, but she desired more than that. She wished to control it, to learn how to use it at will. Assuming that the ability was linked to her essence, she believed that once she knew how to control it, she would be able to do so with ease. It was an exciting prospect, learning what made her unique after so many years in the dark, yet that only made it more infuriating when her work was getting her nowhere.

She crammed a few of the books into her shoulder bag and as she slung it over her shoulder, found herself suddenly stiff with anxiety. She was to return to Abenfurt, the place of which she had only terrible memories, where she had lived a secluded life of loneliness and misery. She had intended never to see her parents again, to run as far and as fast as she could, yet now she found herself walking right into their clutches. She hoped to God that this would be worth it.

Caesia stepped out of her room and into Eris', where Eris was finishing suiting up in her armour. Unlike Caesia, who wore a completely new brown jerkin after disposing of the old one, Eris had refused to change her old leather armour and rather had it professionally cleaned. Clean as it was, it still bore the lingering, metallic scent of dragon blood, much to Caesia's dismay.

"God, this place is a mess," Caesia muttered at the sight of Eris' upturned room.

The room was littered with dirty plates, unwashed clothes and various items of rotting food and garbage. Most of the furniture was halfway across the room from where she remembered and the curtains had several gashes cleaved through them.

"I prefer to call it… creative design," Eris smiled, strapping on her last bracer and slinging her backpack onto her back, rammed with food and money.

"Call it what you want, I've seen animals living in cleaner conditions!"

"Oh yeah?" Eris smirked. "Name one animal you've stood within a metre of."

"Um… shut up," Caesia hissed. "It's not my fault I didn't live in a mud hut!"

"Mud hut?" Eris asked, an eyebrow raised. "What're you trying to say?"

"Nothing…" Caesia mumbled. She really needed to stop insulting people's cultures. "Ready?"

"Oh yeah, I've a week's worth of readiness to get out my system!" Eris declared, throwing her arms out in excitement.

"When we get back, you're giving this place a clean," Caesia insisted as they made for the stairwell.

"In your dreams…"

"If this room isn't spotless in two days of us getting back, I will… I'll beat you up!"

Eris smirked and looked Caesia's scrawny frame up and down. "Please, I could snap you like a twig!" she laughed. "Stars, if this is what having a mum is like, I'm sorta glad I missed out."

"Hey, I'm just trying to teach you some responsibility. Albert let us stay here and I intend to look after the place."

Eris sighed in defeat. She supposed Caesia was right, they owed Albert that much. "Okay, fine. I'll get it cleaned up."

"See, was that so hard?" Caesia sneered. "Don't worry, I'll give you a hand."

"You even know how to clean a room?" Eris laughed. "I figured you had people doing that for you."

"I did, but I'm not a moron. It's not exactly advanced alchemy, you know."

The pair headed downstairs and into Albert Bexley's store. The middle aged wellspring of class and chivalry stood behind the counter having a debate with another man, grinding his magnificent, curled moustache furiously in his fingers.

"And I say to you, sir…" Albert bellowed. "That lettuce is a far superior produce to cabbage!"

"You old fool!" The other man hissed. "The cabbage has far more utility in the kitchen!"

"Ha! It's not about the usage, boy," Albert sneered. "Lettuce is simply superior in of itself, vastly more succulent and watery!"

"I will hear this blasphemy no longer! Good day to you, sir." The other man spat, storming out the front door and slamming it with a furious crash.

"That must have been quite the gripping conversation," Caesia smirked. "Morning, Albert."

"Ah, Casey!" Albert boomed. "Apologies, that was an old rival of mine, Ernest - a younger fellow who sells his own produce down the street. The bloody fool came to convince me once and for all that cabbage is the superior vegetable over lettuce! Can you believe it?!"

"Oh, lettuce is clearly better," Eris laughed. "Cabbage is just…"

"A bit crap, really." Caesia muttered.

"Really?" Eris sneered, an eyebrow raised. "You struck me as a cabbage girl."

"Believe me - the amount of cabbages I've been fed, I don't want to see another in my life. I swear, they were in every damned dish!"

"Well, I'm glad to see we're all level headed individuals here!" Albert smiled. "Anyhow, it looks to me like you ladies are off, no?"

"Yep!" Eris exclaimed. "We're gonna go save the world from an evil warlord, so we might be a while."

"Ah, in that case I'll have celebratory pie ready for your victorious return!" Albert declared excitedly.

"Leave my notes, would you?" Caesia asked.

"Of course, of course." Albert mumbled. "Well, you girls be sure to have fun. And Erin, do be more careful this time!"

Eris smirked and subconsciously scratched at her scar. Anytime somebody brought it up, it seemed to become itchy.

"I'll try…" she sighed. "No promises."

"You can say that again," Caesia muttered. "I'll try to make sure she gets back in one piece."

"Capital," Albert smiled. "On that, I'd best let you ladies go. Be seeing you!"

Eris and Caesia stepped out of Albert's shop and into the streets of Tryzantopol. The streets of the Acropolis District were often quiet in the mornings, with most residents attending brunch or pampering themselves for the day ahead. Outside of the district however, the streets were always bustling with peasants going about their lives.

Caesia smiled and took a deep breath as the soothing summer air washed over her, staring up with satisfaction at the cloudless blue sky.

"God, you spend so long cooped up inside and you forget how great it is out here!" she said with newfound merriment.

"Yeah, it never gets this warm back in Norskar," Eris smiled. "It's nice."

Eris was still in many ways blown away by Verdenheld's beauty. The skies were bluer, the grass was greener and the flowers were a variety of mesmerising colours that she had barely even seen before. The gardens of the acropolis were the first place that she had seen purple or pink in her life! She had spent at least three hours staring at plants that first day, time she considered well spent.

"That it is," Caesia chirped. "Dare I say, there are places even more beautiful. Even more so than Abenfurt."

"Really?" Eris gasped, grabbing Caesia by her arm and yanking her closer. "Where? I wanna go!"

"Well, let's see... there's Apilistia over in Thyresia, Loftenheim in Norskar... Oh, and they say there's nothing more humbling than watching the sunrise over Unity Bay."

"Guess we can put all those on the to-do list!" Eris declared.

"I hope you're writing these down," Caesia laughed. "I swear, you come up with a new addition every few hours."

"What can I say? There's a lot to do!"

"You really think you can do it all in a year?" Caesia asked, an eyebrow raised in doubt.

"Eh, probably not. Doesn't mean I'm not gonna try though!"

"There's that enthusiasm," Caesia chuckled. "Let's hope it doesn't get you hurt this time."

The near silence of the Acropolis District was gradually overtaken by thunderous marching as they neared the district gate. Over the past week, House Severin had been mobilising vast amounts of troops in a panic to retain control of their territory and keep law and order.

"You know, every day I think 'ah, that must be the last of those damned troops'," Eris muttered. "And every day I'm wrong."

"Unbelievable isn't it? You wouldn't think there were enough people in the world to fill House Severin's army!"

A cohort of Severin soldiers came into view around the corner, passing through the gate and into the outer city. House Severin's forces were as terrifying in appearance as they were in number - their heavy, enclosed armour plating was dull and scuffed from years of conflict, complemented by burning orange tabards that asserted an air of power. Many of their blades were tinted red by layer after layer of blood, while their shields were battered and dented to the extreme of appearing a fraction of their original size. They were the sword and shield of Verdenheld, and they oozed war in every way.

"Those guys look like they've done a fair bit of fighting," Eris observed, finding herself on edge in their mere presence. "What do they fight?"

"House Severin mostly deals with peacekeeping nowadays - uprisings, abhumans, bandits, that sort of stuff. We haven't had a proper war in a good... hundred and thirty years?"

"Then why do they look so beaten up?"

"Because Verdenheld has to do *a lot* of peacekeeping," Caesia smirked. "I imagine things are only getting worse now that Jordenholm has gone up in flames, what with Severin's grip slipping from the western heartland."

They turned onto the street leading to the district gate, the wide, open road lined with lush flora by which they had entered a week prior. Near the gate was a gathering of finely dressed nobles and merchants, all unfolding their newspapers as the last of the troops passed by. A young boy stood atop a crate in their midst, ringing a tiny bell.

"This just in!" he cried. "Dragon destroys Jordenholm!"

"Speaking of which..." Caesia smirked, starting towards the crowd.

"What are these people reading?" Eris asked.

"Newspapers, they contain information on the latest goings on in the world. They're mass produced in Abenfurt using illusion magic."

Caesia approached the boy, who immediately shoved a newspaper in her face. "Hey lady! Want a copy? One silver!"

Caesia sifted through her pockets and presented the child with a silver coin. He took the coin happily and forked over the newspaper before turning to his next patron. Caesia slipped from amidst the crowd and unravelled the newspaper to read it aloud.

"Jordenholm razed!" she announced. "Jordenholm... dragon... ah, here we are! The dragon responsible for the attack is reported as having been hunted down and slain by-"

Caesia scowled at the newspaper and Eris peered over her shoulders to investigate.

"House Severin?!" Eris scoffed at the sight of an illustration depicting heroic Severin knights standing over a dragon's bloody corpse. "But we... I don't-"

"I wouldn't take it to heart," Caesia groaned, thrusting the newspaper shut. "There was no way we would get even a slither of public credit."

Eris huffed angrily. It seemed that she would have to one-up killing a dragon if she wanted to be a hero. So be it.

"On the bright side, we won't be stopped by every passer-by," Caesia sighed. "Admittedly, I detest the idea of fame. I could never handle having an audience."

"Speak for yourself!" Eris hissed. "How am I meant to be a hero if I don't get any credit?!"

"Guess you'll have to do something more public."

"Then that's what I'll do!" Eris declared. "Or my name isn't Erisian Myra Hestia!"

Caesia shook her head in amusement at Eris' obsessive drive. They wandered through the gate with a nod of approval from a guard and into the streets of the outer city, where the streets swelled with hordes of dirty commonfolk. Caesia detested cities, nothing more than dense masses of filthy, plague ridden and starving people, all inhumanely crammed together like cattle. Avoiding places like this was one of the many perks of living in Abenfurt.

"Anything else interesting in there?" Eris asked, peering again at the newspaper.

"Wha?" Caesia slurred, waking up from her trance of thought. "Oh, well let's see."

She unfolded the newspaper as she walked and flicked quickly through the pages, reading the headlines faster than Eris could read a single word.

"Nothing much of note, it seems," Caesia sighed, coming to the last page.

"Well, at least now I know that the price of grain has gone up!" Eris chirped.

It was a few seconds before Caesia processed Eris' response. She looked up suddenly from the newspaper and gave Eris a confused double take.

"Wait, you can read this?" Caesia scoffed. "I thought you couldn't read Common!"

"That's not Common, that's Nordic!" Eris insisted. "That looks nothing like Common, *your* stupid alphabet is all squiggly and stuff."

Caesia glanced down in confusion at the newspaper. "So... I see Common, but you see Nordic." she mused. "Must be a new generation spell, I've never heard of any sort of adaptive illusions. Fascinating..."

"I guess," Eris muttered. "Well, I think this thing has to be the biggest waste of a silver ever."

"Perhaps to you, but I learnt something new," Caesia said proudly. "And knowledge has no price!"

"Nerd."

Caesia nodded in total agreement and promptly homed in on the first homeless peasant she saw.

"You there," she called to a filthy woman in rags sat cross-legged in the mud. "Here, um… use this as toilet paper or something."

"Thank ye, Miss!" the peasant cried, taking the newspaper excitedly in her hands.

"Toilet paper?" Eris smirked.

"Oh, don't tell me you've never heard of toilet paper." Caesia muttered, receiving a blank look from Eris. "You absolute barbarian…"

As Eris glanced up from the woman, she was suddenly struck by the view. From atop the colossal central hill of Tryzantopol, past the drab grey walls ahead, she could see for miles. The snow capped mountains towered over the city in the north, giving way further south to the familiar rolling grasslands and the Minaachen River, which wrapped around Tryzantopol and trailed off into the distance. It was a view similar to those before it, yet Eris could never get tired of it.

"Damn," she sighed. "All that time we were climbing this hill and I never turned around once."

"You know, I find it nothing short of impressive how unobservant you are," Caesia sneered.

"I find it impressive how much of a dick you are…" Eris muttered with a faint smirk.

"That… is fair," Caesia smiled. Abusing each other's shortcomings had become something of a tradition between her and Eris. It kept them amused.

Eris watched down the hillside as units of House Severin soldiers barrelled up and down the road, barging aside peasants in a panic. The city was in complete disarray, she figured it was probably a good thing that they were leaving before things could get any crazier.

"Alright, I guess we've got places to be," Eris declared. "Shall we?"

Caesia's eyes twitched at the reminder of what was in store for her. After a moment of internal screaming, she took a deep breath and plastered on a pained smile.

"Indeed. Let's be off."

Chapter Two - The Serpent's Lair

Eris and Caesia headed out of Tryzantopol, down the western road by which they had arrived and paid the driver of a horse drawn cart to let them ride along in the back. The road took them back past the Tomb of the Dragonslayer, the Norskar Gate and the still smouldering ruins of Jordenholm, where early reconstruction had already begun. The journey was uneventful, mostly a lot of laughing and reminiscing about the various locations they passed, such as Eris recounting her displeasurable encounter with the Norskar Gate guards.

Eventually, they passed into the forest in which they had once met, quickly recognised by Eris for the ominous darkness cast by the canopy. The dense forest was a cluttered mass of trees that blotted out the sun in all but a few places. Luckily, the trees split in wake of the road, casting some light upon the otherwise eerie path.

"Stars, this place is no less creepy than last time..." Eris muttered.

Caesia watched in confusion as Eris' eyes lit up. Eris scrambled eagerly to the other end of the cart and glanced with a grin over the edge.

"Look, up ahead!" She chirped. "Isn't this where we met?"

Caesia peered over to Eris' side of the cart, seeing the familiar tree behind which she had quite poorly hidden from Eris. Eris sniggered at the sight of the Caesia shaped indentation in the mud where she had fallen flat on her face as she ran away.

"Oh, shut it. I was tired!" Caesia laughed, relaxing back in her seat. "I'd been running for a good two hours, and that's about a hundred and nineteen minutes more than I can normally manage."

"I have every right to laugh, you nearly tried to kill me here!"

"Oh, piss off," Caesia chuckled. "That's like saying you desire compensation for someone deciding not to break your leg!"

"You know, you've started swearing a lot lately," Eris observed in a motherly tone. "You angry or something?"

"Well, mask it as I may, I am in constant pain," Caesia sighed, nodding her head towards her arms. "But I think it's more of a simple bi-product of not having to be polite all the time. It's rather refreshing."

"I guess in that case I'd probably swear a lot too," Eris muttered. "You're sure its that though? I mean, you 've been looking pretty stressed and-"

"I'm fine," Caesia snapped, crossing her arms in defiance.

"Right..."

Eris didn't believe that for a moment. Caesia was visibly freaked out by the idea of going home. Eris could see the fear and uncertainty in her vacant eyes whenever she gazed off into the distance, something she had been doing often throughout the journey's course. She clearly couldn't take her mind off it.

"We ought to reach Abenfurt within the hour," Caesia said, looking ahead and trying to remember her bearings. "Of course, we'll have to pass through border control."

"Border control?" Eris scoffed. "We didn't have to do that for the last city."

"No, we didn't," Caesia sighed. "You see, Abenfurt is completely exclusive to the rich and the poor must remain outside of city limits in farms and hamlets."

"Isn't that just like Tryzantopol?"

"No. House Tarantis tightly controls the flow of peasants in and out of their territory. They make certain to maintain exactly enough peasants to sustain Abenfurt, no more, no less. The poor are less than even servants to House Tarantis, they're tools - a means to an end."

"That's... awful!" Eris gasped.

"It is. Luckily for us, House Lacroix is particularly close to House Tarantis and thus I should be able to get us through no problem."

"You don't sound all too confident about that," Eris muttered.

"Oh, I'm confident we'll get through," Caesia said darkly. "I'm just worried about what comes after."

The cart approached the border checkpoint connecting Tarantis and Severin lands. The checkpoint appeared pointless from afar, with no kind of border wall or fence connected to it. However, as their cart drew closer, Eris realised that the forest beyond the checkpoint was somewhat distorted.

"What's going on with the forest?" Eris asked Caesia, who was looking ahead anxiously.

Caesia completely blanked Eris, distracted in her own little bubble, going over every possible, terrible outcome of the coming scenario in her head.

"Caesia!" Eris hissed.

"Huh?" Caesia mumbled, staring at her friend vacant expression.

"What's the deal with the forest?"

"Oh, the distortion? It's a magical barrier, made transparent using illusion magic - border control Tarantis style."

The cart pulled up at the border gate and Caesia hopped from the back. A guard came around the cart to meet her. The border guards were different from the guards they had seen so far, these wore pristine silver armour over turquoise hooded robes. They must have been the battlemages Caesia had mentioned in the tomb.

"Papers," the battlemage demanded.

"I believe you misunderstand, mage," Caesia said confidently. "I am Lady-"

"Papers."

Caesia screwed up her face in annoyance. "I do not need papers, do I look like a commoner to you?"

"She does," the battlemage replied, gesturing to Eris. "She needs papers too."

"Look, you don't seem to understand who I am-"

Another battlemage approached and tapped the other on the back. The first mage turned to his comrade, who handed him a slip of paper and whispered something unintelligible.

"Sorry for the misunderstanding ma'am," The battlemage muttered, swivelling back to Caesia. "We have only now received word."

"Great…" Caesia smiled, utterly confused.

Caesia hopped onto the back of the cart and they started unimpeded into House Tarantis lands.

"What was that?" Eris whispered.

"It seems I'm expected," Caesia muttered darkly.

She could feel her mother's hand in this, it was just her style. Really, it was her father that concerned her - she knew he would not be merciful were she brought before him. She could only hope that her mother found her first.

The cart rolled along the smooth dirt road up to Abenfurt. Even the area surrounding the city was pristine, the grass and trees flawlessly trimmed, the roads neat and well maintained. The whole place felt somewhat fake in its perfection, achieved with ease through the use of magic.

"This place is weirdly spotless," Eris observed, looking curiously around in a hope to pick out the slightest imperfection.

"Creepy, isn't it?" Caesia chuckled. "Most look to the school of biomancy for its healing power, but its gardening potential is quite often overlooked."

"Healing?" Eris mused.

"What, looking to get rid of that scar?"

Like that was going to happen. Since it had stopped hurting all that much, the scar across Eris' cheek had begun to grow on her. She thought it made her look far cooler and since it wasn't really a problem, she was quite happy to keep it.

"Never!" Eris laughed. "But your arms on the other hand…"

"I doubt that would work," Caesia sighed. "Only a master of biomancy could heal damage through skin. So, unless you want to head back and haul every coin we have over here to pay for a master, we're out of luck because there is *no* way I'm letting someone cut my arms open to heal my bruising."

"Point taken," Eris muttered.

The tree coverage began to disperse and the sun pierced the sinister canopy of the forest. They came to the edge of a man-made clearing and as the trees subsided, the city came into view.

From behind the trees emerged the flawless spires of Abenfurt. The city, split in two by a glistening blue canal, was a magnificent spectacle. The city sported hundreds of towers, grey brick with slanted, red rooftops accented with gold and each utterly spotless. Amidst them, one colossal tower broke the skyline and rose to touch the clouds, from which hung a myriad of fluttering turquoise banners. The walls on the other hand were carved and pillared, as much a piece of art as they were defence. The whole place looked perfect. Too perfect.

"Well..." Caesia sighed anxiously. "I never thought I'd be back here again."

"You alright?" Eris asked with a comforting smile.

"I'll live. I'm just... well, nervous would be quite the understatement."

"You'll be fine." Eris smiled. "I won't let anything happen to you."

Caesia smirked at Eris' cheesy chivalrousness. It was quite befitting of someone who thought they were in a storybook. She may have been stupid and naive in many regards, but Eris rarely failed to force a smile onto Caesia's face, no matter how hard she resisted.

"So, what's the plan?" Eris asked eagerly "I assume you've got a plan."

"Not really," Caesia sighed. "I was just going to walk in and see if anyone stops me."

"And what do I do?"

"You wait," Caesia said bluntly. "They won't allow you into the Citadel."

Eris frowned in frustration. How would she protect Caesia if she couldn't be with her? "Fine, but if you don't come back, I'm coming in after you!"

"That'd be a sight," Caesia giggled. "But seriously, don't get killed. Please."

"Fine..." Eris groaned. She was lying, of course. It would take more than death to stop her from protecting her friend.

The cart trundled along the road and over the intricate, marble canal bridge. It ground to a halt just ahead of the city gates. The cart driver looked back over his shoulder at his passengers.

"End of the line, ladies."

Eris hopped from the back and Caesia leaned over to the driver with a handful of silver coins. "Thanks," she said, handing him the half of his pay not paid in advance.

"You ready?" Eris asked as Caesia hopped down from the cart beside her.

"Nope!" Caesia sighed. "Let's get this over with."

They departed the cart and headed towards the city gate. Unlike the usual grated metal gates of other cities, Abenfurt sported a finely carved, reinforced set of massive wooden doors. However, as many a foolish attacker had fatefully discovered, the city gate was protected with a powerful magical shield. Posted outside the gate were four battlemages, one of which eyed Caesia and immediately signalled for the gate to be opened.

"Welcome back, my lady," he smiled, stepping aside to let Caesia pass.

"Good to be back," Caesia smiled painfully. Those very words made her scream inside.

They passed through the gates and Caesia immediately exchanged her smile for a frown once they were in the clear.

"That was weird," Caesia muttered.

"They not normally that nice?"

"Oh no, the battlemages would happily wipe my arse should I ask them," Caesia smirked. What concerns me is they acted as if I'd never been gone."

"Is that not a good thing?"

"Well, it could mean one of three things. One, my father kept my disappearance quiet to avoid embarrassment. Two, my mother paid the guards to look the other way. Three, it's a trap."

"Right…" Eris murmured, shifting her hand closer to her sword.

They headed past the gate and into the streets of Abenfurt. Just like outside of the city, the interior was completely spotless, from the pavements to the spires. Despite all the terrible things Eris had heard of this place from Caesia, it was incredible. The flawless brick streets were laden with perfectly trimmed, cherry pink trees and accented with streams of water, out of which shot arches that criss-crossed over the streets like ribbons. The streetlights hummed with magical, throbbing orbs like shimmering stars, which she could only imagine to look utterly beautiful at night. It was like a place from a dream, so alien yet so jaw droppingly magnificent.

"This place is amazing!" Eris laughed, marvelling at the city's beauty.

"As I said, it's a beautiful place," Caesia replied, still stiff with anxiety. "On the outside…"

Eris felt as if she was in a wonderland. Her head was spinning and her mind was swamped with so many thoughts and feelings - from curiosity and excitement to anxiety and uncertainty.

"Can we look around?" She asked giddily.

"I think have more pressing matters to-"

"Come on!" Eris urged. "We won't be long…"

Caesia took a moment to reconsider. As much as she was here for serious matters, she had never been allowed to explore the city and enjoy the many wonders of her childhood home. Suddenly filled with hungering curiosity, her mind began to turn on itself. Someone was bound to notice her eventually, but she might as well have tried to enjoy herself for a bit. Maybe it would even help to relieve some of the pressure.

"Go on then," she sighed with a quivering smile. "Why not?"

"That's the spirit!" Eris gushed. "So, where to?"

Caesia completely drew a blank. She barely had any idea of what the city had to offer. Before her time at the College, she had been able to count the amount of times she had been outside on her hands.

"I don't know…" she mumbled. "I didn't get out much."

"Just take us somewhere!" Eris chirped, practically bouncing up and down. "Anywhere!"

"I guess I can to that… Follow me."

Caesia waved Eris along, who followed in a fit of excitement. They passed through the streets, bustling with the rich and noble, into the heart of the city. Unnerving as being back in Abenfurt was for Caesia, it was nice finally being able to navigate the city on her own accord. It was a wonderful place, perhaps now she could finally enjoy it for what it was.

At least, that was what she had hoped before Eris began bombarding her with questions. It was easy to forget that Eris had never seen many things one would consider normal - something that Caesia was quickly reminded of when Eris pointed with overwhelming enthusiasm to a bin and asked her what it was.

"Ah! I always wanted to go here!" Caesia gushed, rushing ahead as they rounded another corner. "Mind if I take a look?"

Eris snapped out of her awe stricken daze and looked the building up and down. Eris scowled as she read the carved words strewn above the door.

"Museum of History?" Eris groaned. "Stars, you're boring."

"Oh, shush!" Caesia hissed. "History is a discipline that all can enjoy! Epic battles, legendary heroes, clashes of good and evil!"

Eris wasn't going to fall for Caesia's dramatization - she knew that they were to spend an age learning about politics. She grumbled angrily under her breath as Caesia hurried up the steps. She yanked the door handle, which barely shifted in response, earning a pleasurable smirk from Eris.

"Ah. It's still closed…" Caesia sighed, withdrawing into a sulk.

"You knew it was closed?" Eris laughed.

"It had a temporary closure about two years ago, something about an exhibit being stolen, I think. Not a word has been said about it since."

"Then why did you think it would be open?"

"It was just a hope…" Caesia muttered, descending the steps.

"Well, it sure doesn't look like it's been closed that long. It's cleaner than half of the other buildings here!"

"Don't let that fool you," Caesia smirked. "Everything in this city is coated with illusion magic, even some of the people. Peel it away, this place would look like a damned sewer."

"You mean I could be standing in a turd right now?"

"Yep," Caesia chirped. "I'll leave you with that thought."

Caesia led Eris around the city block and down a long, open street towards a towering arch built purely of glistening arkansteel. The arch, displaying the words 'College of Arcana' across blue tinted silver, accommodated a swarm of students, young and old, passing in and out of the College grounds.

"Welcome to the College," Caesia smiled. "Only place I've really been in this city."

"I thought you hated it here…"

"I… hated a fair few things about it," Caesia sighed. "The tutors, the people, the incessant probing… the place itself however is rather exciting. Come!"

They passed under the arch and onto College grounds. The place was not dissimilar from the rest of the city - mind bending water features, a technicolour assortment of trees and flowers ripped from foreign shores, all surrounded by slender grey spires tipped with black roofs accented with gold. The streets were cluttered with masses of people, many rushed between buildings while many more stood conversing and laughing with friends. Eris had always imagined the College to simply be a load of rich kids shooting spells about, yet there was barely a spell in sight.

"What do people actually do here?" She asked.

"A lot," Caesia smirked. "Too much to cover in the time we've got, that's for sure."

"Okay, well let's cut it down. What did you do?"

"You know that - abjuration and electromancy."

"Yeah, but what did you actually *do*?"

"Ah. Well, it was mostly studying," Caesia muttered unenthusiastically. "Very little time was spent actually performing spells."

"Huh, that's a lot less fun than I imagined." Eris sighed.

"Indeed, and don't even get me started on the arcane theory essays." Caesia sighed. "I mean, I like the theory side of magic, but twenty thousand words in my first year was... draining, to say the least."

"So, you never had any cool wizard battles?" Eris asked, utterly disappointed.

Caesia grinned in amusement. "I wouldn't say never... there was a tournament at the start of the summer which had a combat round."

"Meaning you never bothered with it?" Eris sneered.

"Actually, I did, though it was purely for research purposes."

Eris chuckled at the thought it. "Sounds to me like you just got your ass handed to you."

"Well, I... did nearly get knocked out... but I got what I wanted out of it!" Caesia smiled. "I joined in purely for the sake of analysing the other mages, took a load of notes on how they handled themselves and applied it to my own studies. It's how I picked up abjuration so quickly."

"So, all you ever did here was study?" Eris smirked.

"In my case, yes. There's this whole 'social life' aspect that they really like to push, but it wasn't exactly for me. I... don't really enjoy people."

"What about me?"

"Oh, you're fine. Thing is, you're not from around here," Caesia sighed. "Most people I've met in Abenfurt have been several feet up their own arses."

"Like you?" Eris sneered.

"I am not!" Caesia laughed, Eris narrowly dodging her elbow.

"You are a bit."

"I... okay, maybe a bit," Caesia chuckled. "But these people are *leagues* beyond me."

"Stars... there's no way you hated everyone here. You're cold, but not that cold."

"Well, maybe not everyone." Caesia mused. "There were a few exceptions I think, but I never really got to know anyone. Maybe I would have, had I not run away... But enough about me and my poor social skills. Let's go have some fun!" She declared. "The square is just down there."

Eris followed Caesia's gaze down the road, where lights flashed and distant music hummed.

"Now we're talking!" Eris grinned. "Race ya!"

Caesia watched as Eris bolted down the road, garnering a fair few looks of confusion or disgust from passing students. She rolled her eyes and walked after her. She wasn't about to waste her energy in a futile and childish race.

While Caesia caught up, Eris found herself in the midst of the bustling square lost in a world of her own. She simply stood and looked around in a wondrous daze, infatuated by the beauty of the square. The atmosphere was incredible, upbeat acoustic rhythms echoing from the golden bandstand at its edge as many a performer displayed their own unique spectacles. Eris surveyed them all, from fire jugglers and sword swallowers to adept mages showing off dazzling ribbons of light.

Eris ran up to one performer, Caesia in distant tow. The performer revealed a jug of water and presented it to the crowd. He put his hand on the base of the jug and cast the water into the air. Many of the surrounding students jumped and wailed in fear of the water, only to laugh as it rushed out of the jug as a funnel of snow.

Eris giggled with delight as the snow settled on her skin. "Why can't you do that?" she yelled over the din of music.

"Because I don't deal in novelties," Caesia laughed. "We're not just going to gawk at performers are we?"

"For my next trick, I will need a volunteer!" announced the performer.

Caesia froze as Eris glanced at her with a devious grin. "Don't you-"

"Over here!" Eris yelled, shoving Caesia towards the performer.

Caesia's breath fell short, blood rushing to her head as a deeply ingrained fear of publicity took hold.

"Step right up, miss!" The performer called, extending his hand.

Caesia stood for a moment rooted to the spot, her mind burning with anxiety as the eyes of the crowd fell upon her. What if she did something wrong, made a fool out of herself? Her father had made it quite clear that she had a talent for public embarrassment, mainly through the medium of the back of his hand. Crowds terrified her, struck her with an overwhelming fear of terrible consequences that she had no real reason to feel anymore. Her body locked up, her mind aflame with different scenarios of utter failure. This was *not* funny, this was torture.

She took a careful step towards the performer, raising her quaking hand slowly to meet him. She could hear Eris sniggering to herself at the expense of her terror. While Eris had no idea just how petrifying an experience this was for her, Caesia would nonetheless reap a terrible vengeance for this.

The performer took a double take as Caesia stepped anxiously up to him. "Your eyes…"

"I, er- it's a disorder!" Caesia stammered. "Yes, I was born with… weird eyes."

"Right… you just get up on the stand, ma'am," he smiled. "Nothing to be afraid of."

Caesia sighed with what little relief she could feel in this situation. It had become something of a reflex for her to deflect comments on her eye colour. She just hoped people would keep buying it.

She stepped up onto the stand and turned to face the piercing eyes of the crowd. Eris gave her a cheeky smile and raised her thumbs, working only to add to the intense hatred for her that Caesia was feeling. It also worked to distract her from the water oozing from the central fountain and pooling around her feet. As Eris glanced down, Caesia followed her gaze and stared blankly for a moment at the pool of water below her. Terror gripped her, even more so than before.

"Ladies and gentlemen, prepare to experience a glorious feat of hydromantic skill!" the performer declared. "I give you, the water slide!"

Eris barely got to see Caesia's eyes widen in horror before a jet of water exploded from the ground and sent her flying several metres into the air. She watched, mouth ajar as Caesia vanished amidst a towering column of water, her terrified shriek trailing into the distance. This was far beyond what Eris had expected. It was hilarious, but she could not laugh in fear of the consequences. And for her life.

"Oh... she's gonna kill me," she mumbled to herself.

The rippling column suddenly convulsed, bending and stretching into a rushing spiral, all the way down into the fountain below. Eris grinned as Caesia's screams drew back into earshot, getting ever closer and as she reached the bottom, gradually calming into panicked breaths. She snorted with laughter as Caesia floated gently from the end of the spiral and was deposited in the fountain, drenched head to toe and quivering in fear.

The performer took a bow as applause roared from his audience, while Eris, her mouth teetering between an amused smirk and a wrath-fearing frown, edged over to the fountain. Caesia simply lay there, her hair floating like tendrils around her head as she stared blankly into the sky.

"So... some performance, huh?" Eris mumbled, leaning over the fountain's edge with a wobbly smile.

Caesia spat a mouthful of water into Eris' eyes. "Bitch," she growled.

"Look, I'm sorry, I didn't think he'd shoot you miles into the sky," Eris smirked, reaching out with her hand. "Come on, let's get you outta here."

Caesia glared for a moment before reluctantly taking Eris' hand. Eris pulled her from the water and helped her out of the fountain, only to immediately come face to face with the back of Caesia's hand. A chilling crack punctuated the collision and as Eris stumbled back, Caesia threw herself at her and barged her into the side of the fountain. She watched with a spiteful grin as Eris staggered over the edge and toppled into the fountain with a great splash.

Caesia cackled hysterically at the sight of Eris splayed out on her back in the fountain, a look of complete surprise still on her face as she squirted water from her nose.

"Cheeky prick!" Caesia laughed, steam beginning to below from her clothes as she heated herself.

Eris lay there for a moment in contemplation of her likely well deserved fate, while Caesia giggled away. That was an unexpected reaction, to say the least. She had never seen Caesia, usually so cynical and sarcastic, so genuinely happy.

"Well played…" Eris croaked, rolling over and heaving herself out of the water.

Caesia was elated by her bit of vengeance. This is what she had missed out on all her life, not the festivities that she had so jealousy watched from her window, but simple friendship. It felt like she was living the childhood she should have had.

As Eris scrambled up out of the fountain, Caesia's eye was caught by a man across the square. She grinned deviously and yanked Eris aside.

"Eris?" she smiled. "How do you feel about practical jokes?"

Eris made a wide smirk. Caesia had entered some kind of childish frenzy, much to Eris' enjoyment. It was about time the girl loosened up and enjoyed her life and Eris was happy to accommodate.

"I'm all ears," she smiled, leaning in intently.

"See that man over there?" Caesia whispered, pointing out a middle aged, black haired man in a turquoise robe. "That is Gunther Von Hirsch, one of the administrative staff. He's the one responsible for segregating me to a corner during meals and making me live in a bloody cleaning cupboard. What do you say we ruin his day?"

"Ah, a bit of vengeance!" Eris grinned sinisterly. "What's the plan, Miss La- Lacroy?"

"Lacroix!" Caesia laughed. "I imagine you're more of an expert in this manner of foolery, so I'll leave the plan to you."

"You know me too well," Eris smiled. "You're talking to the girl who replaced a religious text with eighty-four drawings of her ass!"

"Isn't that sacrilege?"

"Wouldn't be the first time," Eris said with pride. "Luckily, I have never once been caught!"

"Do I even want to know the rest?"

"Um… probably best not," Eris mumbled. "Anyways, prank time."

Eris analysed her surroundings with the perception of a master, picking out every little thing that could be used to her advantage. She only wished that she could be so cunning all of the time.

"Alright, I got a plan," Eris whispered.

"That was fast."

"I'm good at what I do," Eris grinned. "Now, first things first - what is that stuff?"

Caesia tracked Eris' gaze to another performer. He presented an apple in his hand, while his other was slick with a viscous, transparent liquid. He raised his hand to the apple and rubbed it, the apple vanishing as his hand swept over it.

"I believe that is vanishment gel - slime enchanted with illusionary magic to turn things-"

"Perfect!" Eris declared. "See those buckets behind his stand? I need one."

"A whole bucket?" Caesia scoffed.

"Yes."

"And you want *me* to get it."

"Yes."

"This had better be good…" Caesia groaned. "And what will you be doing?"

"You'll see…" Eris smiled cheekily.

Caesia sighed and sauntered off towards the performer. Perhaps she had gotten ahead of herself in her excitement. What was Eris about to get her into?

She watched the performer carefully, racking her brain for ideas as to how she would pull off this theft. That thought made her terribly tense - the idea of breaking the law. For the longest time, the concept of defying authority as a whole had terrified her. Even so, she couldn't seem to resist the idea of doing it, the temptation to break the rules. Scary as it was, it was equally exhilarating.

Taking a deep breath, she headed past the stands and slipped into cover behind the red accommodation tower. The stand was but a few metres away, no cover between them. She would have to be quick.

Caesia jumped from cover and crept slowly towards the stand, the performer distracted by a small audience. As his apple reappeared and the audience turned their backs, Caesia leapt for the bucket. As she wrapped her hands around its rim, the performer stepped back and turned to his buckets, coming face to face with nought but grass.

In a burst of green light, Caesia staggered back into cover, green sparks trailing in her wake. She stumbled into the wall behind her and squeezed shut her eyes as transparent goo sloshed from the bucket and onto her jerkin. She peeled her eyes open to see that her jerkin had been split down the middle by the gel, exposing the shirt below. That was going to look rather suspect, though she was thankful that none had touched her shirt.

"Bloody brilliant," she groaned as she placed the bucket at her feet and peered cautiously around the corner.

Across the square stood Eris, nonchalantly stuffing a wire into her backpack and discarding a stack of multi-coloured flags into a bin. Caesia was truly astonished that Eris had managed to take those without anybody seeing. She waved to Eris, who glanced up with a confused smirk.

Eris giggled quietly to herself as her distant friend presented her half-invisible jerkin. In return, she thrust her hands up and down her body.

"What?" Caesia mouthed.

"Gel!" Eris mouthed back impatiently.

Caesia looked down at the bucket with a sigh. She retreated back around the corner and reluctantly reached down to the bucket. She shuddered at the touch of the gel before pulling her hands out and slathering it up and down her jerkin, rendering it completely invisible. She seriously hoped that vanishment gel washed out, else she would have to buy a second jerkin in the space of one week.

Eris chuckled as Caesia approached, her shirt still compressed down the middle by the invisible jerkin. "You had one job!" she laughed.

"I got the bucket, didn't I?" Caesia hissed. "Besides, I didn't ask to teleport!"

"You did it again? What was it this time?"

"He was about to catch me when I found myself behind that building again."

"Damn, you're the peak of thief evolution!" Eris declared excitedly.

"Shut up," Caesia smirked. "Are we doing this or not?"

"We are indeed!" Eris smiled, yanking the wire from her bag.

"How in the world did you get that?" Caesia asked.

"I bet a pyromancer that he couldn't burn through it, then I bet another one that he couldn't do the same to the other end."

"Using their egos to your advantage!" Caesia laughed, surprisingly impressed. "That's… actually pretty brilliant."

"Yeah, if only I was this smart all the time!" Eris chuckled. "Now, prepare to see a master at work!"

Eris plunged one of her hands into the gel, yanked it out and slid the wire through her grip. The wire gradually disappeared until Eris' hand reached the end, where she stopped just short of the end.

"Here, take this end and tie it around that metal stick," Eris commanded, gesturing to a lamppost across the square.

"Couldn't this cause, you know… collateral damage?"

"Civilian casualties?" Eris smirked. "Worry not, this end's staying down until the time is right."

"Okay…"

Caesia handed Eris the bucket and wandered to the lamppost with the wire. Eris discarded her end of the wire and hauled the bucket over to a nearby stand, where she waved to the performer behind it.

"Hey!" she smiled. "Mind if I leave this here?"

The performer looked at her with a great deal of confusion. "Um... why?"

"My friend and I are gonna set up a stand just here. I'm just helping her bring some stuff down so she can get set up quicker."

"Huh, you don't look like a mage."

"She is," Eris insisted. "She's an... abjurator."

"Oh, what's her act?" the performer asked with a curious smile.

"Oh, it's um... she draws pictures on barriers!" Eris stammered. "Yeah, it's pretty cool. She's a really good drawer, makes some real nice... stuff."

"Hm, not bad," the performer smiled. "Go ahead."

"Thanks!" Eris chirped, placing the bucket carefully to loom over the edge of a table and stepping away with a cute smile.

"Wire's set," Caesia whispered as she approached. "Are we ready?"

"Yep! Why don't we take a seat?"

Eris grabbed her end of the wire and skipped giddily over to a bench. The setup was always fun, but watching her handiwork come to life was always the best part. It gave her a certain sense of gratification that even her training could never give her. She kicked back casually on the bench and Caesia perched herself on its edge, stiff as a broom.

"Hey, relax!" Eris laughed. "Aren't you having fun?"

"I am..." Caesia sighed. "I'm just concerned that we might be a making a mistake."

"I find it's best not to think about these things until *after* the prank," Eris smiled. "Oh! Here he comes."

Eris watched with a sinister grin as Von Hirsch moved away from a performer and began to head across the square. Caesia tensed as Eris readied the wire, she wasn't used to the looming possibility of consequence.

With a powerful tug from Eris, the invisible wire jolted up. Caesia cupped her mouth in suspense as she watched Von Hirsch's foot catch on thin air. He stumbled forwards, his shoulder catching the bucket positioned expertly on the table's edge. As he crumpled to the ground, the bucket toppled after him, a torrent of transparent gel rushing from within and drenching him completely. Most of his robes vanished in an instant, the rest following as the gel seeped over him. He scrambled angrily to his feet, only to realise that naught but his underwear remained.

Fingers pointing and students laughing, Von Hirsch retreated hastily from the square under a hail of ridicule. Caesia wheezed hysterically with laughter, while Eris steepled her fingers in embrace of her success - another target crushed by her unrivalled pranking skills.

"Okay, I take everything back!" Caesia giggled. "That was brilliant!"

"I know," Eris smiled smugly. "It's a gift, some say."

"Some gift," Caesia chuckled as a slender shadow crept over her from behind.

"Enjoying the festivities, Miss Tarantis?" asked a voice all too familiar to her.

Caesia's face dropped and her laughter subsided, everything swept suddenly away as she froze with anxiety. Eris' eyes fluttered, confused as to what she had just heard.

"Tarantis?" she asked, narrowing her eyes.

Caesia glanced at Eris apologetically and turned away. "Grom! Fancy seeing you here!" she gushed, pulling a wide smile and springing up from the bench. "It's been a while, hasn't it?"

"Glazed apple, my lady?" smiled the tall, pasty man, waving a sticky brown apple at her.

"Thank you!" Caesia chirped, taking the apple with a warm, welcoming smile.

"You needn't hide your displeasure in seeing me, my lady," Grom smiled unnervingly. "Reading people is part of my job, after all."

Caesia dropped the smile immediately, contorting her face to an irritated frown.

"Who is this, 'Miss Tarantis'?" Eris hissed.

Caesia closed her eyes and took a deep breath as she fought through how terrible she felt. She had hoped to keep this under wraps, a foolish notion in hindsight.

"This is Grom, my mother's toadie," she sighed. "Easily mistaken for a lizard of some variety."

Grom smiled warmly, an expression that did not suit his face. "You must be Erisian. I have heard much about you."

That was extremely unnerving, especially coming from such a creepy man. His pale skin and dark features left him a ghastly sight indeed.

"Enough of the niceties, Grom," Caesia demanded. "I know you don't deal in coincidences."

"Right you are, ma'am," Grom grinned. "Your mother has been awaiting your arrival eagerly and I would not keep her waiting."

Just as she had suspected. No doubt she'd been under her mother's gaze ever since she left the College. She had to wonder why Grom did not snap her up sooner.

"Of course she has," Caesia muttered, turning to Eris. "We'll talk about this when... *if* I return. I promise, I'll explain everything."

Caesia turned back to Grom, who smiled and waved her along. They departed back down the road from which they had came, Caesia exchanging one more apologetic look with Eris' betrayed glare.

Caesia followed Grom closely as they weaved through the bustling streets. She was nervous to be sure, but she was at least given some solace in that her mother had sent Grom, meaning she had found her before her father had.

"Why'd you have to call me that?" Caesia hissed.

"Is that not your name, my lady?"

"Well, yes... but you saw how she looked at me! That was sheer betrayal on her face!"

"If she is truly your friend, surely it would take more than a name to break that bond."

"Yeah... I guess so," Caesia sighed. "But that doesn't mean she isn't going to slate me about it."

"I am sure you will live, my lady," Grom smirked.

Grom was probably right, ever the font of cold logic. There was no doubt that Eris would overreact, but there was also no doubt that she would get over it. Such was always the case with her.

"You seemed like you were having fun," Grom smiled. "Not a common sight at all - that girl has changed you."

"You needn't make small talk," Caesia muttered.

"Oh, but I will. I always did enjoy your company."

"Why?"

"You offer an outlook on the world that the rest of your household cannot offer. It intrigues me."

"You mean to say you *enjoy* my constant pessimism?" Caesia scoffed.

"Realism, my lady," Grom said. " You see the world for what it is, rather than what the kingdom wants it to be. It is refreshing."

Caesia glanced up as they approached the colossal Arcana Citadel, the towering spire at the centre of the city from which House Tarantis ruled. The Citadel dwarfed the surrounding city and dominated the skyline. Designed after the six-pointed star of House Tarantis, six smaller towers were connected by enormous bridges to the central spire. From each of those protruding towers hung banners depicting one of the recognised schools of magic, while the central spire was decked from top to bottom with the turquoise banner and six pointed star of House Tarantis.

As they drew close to the Arcana Citadel, Grom quickly stepped into a nearby alleyway and gestured for Caesia to follow.

"Let me guess," Caesia muttered. "We're going to use a magically hidden secret entrance?"

Grom chuckled quietly. "It seems I am becoming predictable..."

Grom stepped up to one of the alley walls and pressed up his hands against two of the bricks. Part of the wall was engulfed with shimmering yellow light before vanishing completely. Grom and his men loved illusions, they were a key part of their jobs.

The gap in the wall led straight through into the empty hallways of the Arcana Citadel. The interior of the Citadel could only be described as egotistical - the marble walls were a flawless white, not real but rather an illusion, and they were carved in all kinds of patterns and styles, the designs of some going back a thousand years. The floors were glossy and spotless, strewn with various murals depicting the many glories of House Tarantis. Expensive paintings and statues cluttered the corridors, imported from all across the continent. The whole place reeked of perfectionism, it was a terrible reminder of the unattainable heights she had always been expected to reach.

"Welcome home, my lady," Grom smiled.

Home. The very mention of the word sent shivers down her spine. In these walls were held hundreds of terrible memories, each room a contributor to her tortured existence, each a reminder of the tragic life she had lived.

"Why the deception?" Caesia asked. "Why sneak in rather than use the front door?"

"Your mother wishes to keep your arrival... discreet."

"Meaning my father doesn't know?"

"Not yet. Whether that remains the case depends upon your mother."

That was just like her mother. Amelie and Edmund often had competing agendas, only Edmund never suspected it. He had no idea how in the dark he truly was.

"You mean she hasn't shared her devious plans with you?" Caesia sneered.

"The hammer need not know why it strikes the metal, only what metal it must strike," Grom grinned. He always had a soft spot for philosophy.

Grom led Caesia through the halls and up several flights of stairs. The Citadel always felt more like a prison than it did a home, the endless maze of corridors had a way of making all hopes of escape seem bleak. Had she not been sent to the College, there was no way she could have fled this place.

"I understand you've been busy," Grom said with a knowing smirk.

Caesia knew he would know about the dragon. Nothing escaped Grom's eyes, even halfway up a mountain.

"We have," Caesia sighed.

"Your mother was quite impressed to hear of your achievement," Grom smiled. "I think I may have even detected a hint of pride."

"You must have imagined it," Caesia hissed. "She doesn't have emotions."

"You are too hard on her," Grom sighed. "She truly does care about you, even if she struggles to show it."

"I find that rather hard to believe."

"What if I told you that on the night you escaped the College, the guards may have been given paid leave by a generous benefactor?"

Caesia paused, taken completely aback. It made sense as to how she managed to escape, but she could not fathom the idea of her mother doing that. Why would she?

"You're lying."

"If I was lying, my lady, you would not know it."

"Why would she do that?" Caesia snapped. "Am I not integral to her 'grand scheme'?"

"You'll have to ask her yourself. As I said, I am but the tool."

Caesia sighed and withdrew to silent contemplation. Her mother was never as cruel as her father, but was equally as cold. She thought it impossible that Amelie could care about her daughter. It simply didn't add up.

Grom came to a stop at a large, ornately carved double door and smiled another of his creepy smiles before dramatically pushing both open, unveiling an extravagant bedchamber.

"Your daughter, my lady!" Grom announced.

Amelie Tarantis stood, a silvered goblet of fine red wine in hand, on a balcony across the room. Her elegant blue dress fluttered in the breeze as she gazed out upon the spires of the city, impatiently curling her short grey hair with her finger.

"Thank you Grom," she smiled, waving him off with her back still turned.

Grom bowed dutifully and departed, the huge double doors slamming behind him.

"What do you want?" Caesia spat, trying to make her displeasure in being there crystal clear.

Amelie smirked, turning away from the balcony and striding back indoors. "You can lose the attitude, darling. I don't intend to keep you for long."

Caesia's mind surged with hate at the sight of her mother's creased, round face, ever plastered with that same demeaning smile that took nobody seriously. In this moment, all that Caesia could think about was the endless criticism, belittlement and ridicule she had constantly received at her mother's hands.

"I find that hard to believe," Caesia hissed. "What would your plans be without your precious little puppet?"

"Plans change," Amelie sighed. "Well, mine do. Your father insisted that Grom hunt you down, drag you back in chains."

"So why didn't he?"

"Because Grom does not answer to Lord Tarantis, or any Tarantis for that matter," Amelie sneered. "Grom serves House Lacroix and will do so always."

"And what does House Lacroix want with me?" Caesia muttered.

"Patience, darling," Amelie smiled. "I believe there is some catching up to be done."

"No, there isn't," Caesia demanded. "Just tell me what you want so I can leave and never see this damned place again!"

Amelie smirked and approached Caesia slowly. "Look at you," she smiled, looking Caesia up and down with pride. "When you left for the College, you were pathetic. You were weak, gutless, barely able to stand on your own two feet, let alone stand up for yourself."

Caesia scowled and batted her mother's hand away as it approached her cheek.

"And look at you now - you're strong, charismatic... everything I wanted you to be and more."

"That's bloody rich!" Caesia scoffed. "You belittled me at every turn, never said one nice thing about me! Father made my life hell, but all you did was kick me while I was down!"

Amelie sighed and took a delicate sip of her wine. "I was harsh, yes, but I did it to make you stronger. I did it because I wanted you to defy your father's authority, so that House Lacroix could finally break from the trap that was my marriage."

"So, this wasn't about me at all!" Caesia spat. "Of course it wasn't. Like always, I was a tool! I was a means to fulfil your stupid plans!"

"You were... but then we got a letter from the College. They told us how you threw yourself from that window, how you tried to poison yourself in the alchemical labs. Then I realised just what we had done to you, how broken you really were... so I let you go."

"It took you *nineteen years*," Caesia hissed. "Nineteen years of neglect and I had to attempt suicide twice to get your attention!"

"I never realised just how severe it was," Amelie sighed. "I'd always passed you off as overreacting or simply being a teenager. I should have known better."

"Yes, you should have!" Caesia snapped, her voice becoming shaken and rough. "All I ever wanted to hear was 'well done' or 'you can do it', just once! Yet I was never good enough, was I? I was never the picture of perfection you always dreamed of!"

"I... I'm sorry, Caesia," Amelie mumbled. "I only ever wanted what was best for you."

Caesia's face was glowing red now, tears beginning to trickle from her eyes. "Best for me?!" she cried, furiously wiping the tears from her face. "Y-you know what would've been best for me? Having a family who loved me! Being told I was worth something! Not having my dreams crushed and spat on at every turn!"

Amelie was silent, trying not to let her demeanour waver. She had no excuse for what she had done, no matter how well she meant.

"This past week has been the best of my life. Not because of the adventure, my powers, my freedom - because I've finally come to know someone who cares about me," Caesia sobbed. "Eris has done in the week I've known her everything you've failed to do all my life. She comforts me when I'm sad, holds me when I'm scared, listens when I cry and most of all, she helped me believe that I can be something more!"

"What can I say, Caesia?" Amelie asked. "What is it you want to hear from me?"

"I- I... nothing," Caesia mumbled. "There's nothing you could say that would change a thing. I guess... I guess I just needed to get that off my chest."

"Well, in that case... in that case I think it best we wrap this up," Amelie muttered. "And that we never see each other again..."

"I-I think so," Caesia sighed, snivelling as she wiped down her face.

"So tell me, what do you know about this alleged return of the Oppressor?" Amelie asked, reverting quickly back to her calm, emotionless tone.

With such a rapid shift of tone, Caesia had to wonder how much of that argument was genuine. Her mother was a manipulator, she could have simply been playing her... yet it seemed so real. She didn't know what to believe.

"Nothing really," Caesia sighed. "We only know he's back and that he was probably behind Jordenholm."

"Interesting..." Amelie mused. "That adds up, though it poses grave tidings."

"I was hoping you would have a lead or-"

"I do. I have it right here," Amelie smiled, gesturing to a roll of parchment on the table beside her.

"Wait… have you been spying on us?!" Caesia hissed. "What am I saying? Of course you have! Why am I bloody surprised?"

"I assure you, I was-"

"Oh no, you're not worming your way out of this!" Caesia snapped.

Amelie sighed defeatedly. "I will repeal the order. I promise."

"Said the spider to the fly…" Caesia muttered. "So, what's the angle?"

"Excuse me?"

"What do you gain from helping me?" Caesia asked. "Go on, what's the ulterior motive?"

"You will be surprised to know that there isn't one," Amelie smirked. "You may find it hard to believe, but I simply wish to help."

"I bet that's what you tell everyone," Caesia muttered.

"It is… but this time it is true."

Caesia glared at her mother with narrow eyes. She didn't trust a word that came out of the woman's mouth. Lying was as natural as breathing for House Lacroix.

"But I digress," Amelie smiled. "The lead is of… loose connection, but it is the best I can find. This Valkyr leaves few tracks."

"I guess I'll take what I can get," Caesia sighed.

Amelie handed Caesia the parchment with an apologetic smile. "I have all the information you need on this parchment, but allow me to summarise. A group of inquisitors recently disappeared in the sewers of Aldreichen while investigating what they believed to be 'anomalous magical activity'. You will meet one of Grom's agents at the address specified on the parchment, he will fill you in on the details of your investigation."

"What's stopping this agent from doing this himself?"

"Grom and his men are ill suited to conflict. It is likely that pursuing this lead may bring you to blows with this mysterious attacker, so I need someone more capable in that field."

"And how do you know this links to Valkyr?"

"Because it adds up with previous reports," Amelie smiled.

That was extremely vague, but Caesia knew her mother - when it came to intrigue she was never misinformed. Deep down, she trusted that her mother meant well, but simply didn't want to believe it. It was an incredibly difficult reality to stomach.

"So, I'm to go to Aldreichen and investigate?"

"Yes. You may leave out the front gate, your father is out of the city on business so you shouldn't worry about being seen. I assure you, the guards will not say a word."

"Right…" Caesia murmured, heading for the door.

"And Caesia?" Amelie called.

"What?" Caesia sighed impatiently.

"I love you," Amelie smiled. "And I couldn't be more proud of what you've become."

Caesia took a deep breath and continued walking without a word. She couldn't take any of her mother's words at face value. For all she knew, Amelie could simply have been trying to twist her for some scheme of hers. Either way, Caesia didn't care for her mother's words.

Eris stood with a perpetual scowl outside the gates of the Arcana Citadel. Her head was spinning, combing through each and every interaction she'd had with Caesia. It made no sense, why would Caesia lie to her about who she was? What did she have to hide?

Caesia emerged from the gate, her eyes red and raw. Even so, she seemed quite calm - almost too calm considering the big deal she had made of her father. She approached Eris with a roll of parchment in hand.

"Look, I know I-"

Without warning, Eris slapped Caesia hard across the face, planting a glowing white mark on her scarlet cheek. Every guard outside the Citadel jumped suddenly into action, grabbing the silvered hilts of their swords and igniting their hands with a multitude of colours. As Eris looked around anxiously, Caesia shook herself off and waved her hand, signalling the guards to stand down.

"You lied to me!" Eris snapped.

"I know... you must understand," she urged. "I lied about nothing but my family. Everything else is as I explained it."

"How can I believe that?" Eris hissed. "How am I meant to believe any of this?!"

"Look, you know me, so believe me when I say that I promise you, I swear on my freedom that am telling you the truth!"

Eris wanted to be mad, yet she couldn't bring herself to distrust Caesia. After all they had been through, she knew Caesia had no reason not to be sincere. She knew that Caesia must have had good cause to hide true her name.

"I took my mother's maiden name as my own because I wanted to disassociate myself with House Tarantis," Caesia explained. "All I wanted was to run from my past and never look back."

"But why bother if you just changed it to another house's name?" Eris sighed.

"Because I can't exactly hide that I'm a noble. I just had to get away from House Tarantis - being the second born in my family carries a lot of responsibility. While my brother was groomed as heir to the house, I was prepared for a different path. Tradition holds that House Tarantis always provides the royal magical advisor."

"You would have been advisor to the King?" Eris scoffed. "Why pass that up?"

"Because I didn't want it!" Caesia moaned. "You've no idea how depressing it was, the idea that my whole purpose in life was to be some walking encyclopedia... I tried to end my life *twice*, because I preferred death over being the king's slave."

Eris was speechless. She had never quite understood why Caesia wanted so badly to escape her privileged, luxurious life, but now she realised just how terrible it truly was for her.

"I wanted to tell you," Caesia sobbed. "But I'd hoped I could just forget it, push that part of my life deep into the depths of my mind and live like it never happened... but there's no running from who I am."

Eris sighed, put on a smile and wrapped her hand gently around Caesia's wrist. "I was always scared of my responsibilities. I got upset about it all the time, but every time my dad would come to me and say 'Erisian, the only way to overcome your fears is to accept them into your life'."

"I am not making up with my parents," Caesia growled.

"Okay, bad example," Eris sighed. "What I'm trying to say is you should just own it! You're Caesia Tarantis - sure, that seems pretty crappy from where you're standing, but I say it can be just as awesome! So what if you had a crappy childhood? You can teleport, you're super smart and you're technically one of the most powerful people in the entire kingdom!"

Eris watched with a gleeful smile as Caesia's glum face slowly lit up. Ever the ray of sunshine, she had quite a talent for finding light in the darkest places. It was insufferable at times, but in moments like this she was exactly what Caesia needed.

"You're right," Caesia smiled, stiffening herself in determination. "All this time spent worrying about my past, about my powers, it's done nothing but hold me back... For better or for worse, I am Caesia Tarantis, and that won't stop me from living my life!"

She thrust up her arm and clenched her fist in defiance. She would not let who she was hold her back any longer, but it would instead make her stronger. Her name carried power and she intended to use it for good, as it always should have been.

"Thank you, Eris," Caesia grinned. "I had no idea how much I needed that."

"Hey, that's what friends are for!" Eris chirped, patting Caesia on the shoulder. "So, you get anything from your mum?"

"I did. She's surely pursuing her own nefarious goals, but she nonetheless gave me the information we needed."

Caesia presented the roll of parchment, sealed with red wax imprinted with a coiling serpent, sigil of House Lacroix.

"Remember how you said last week you wanted to go to Aldreichen?" Caesia asked as Eris' eyes burst with excitement. "It seems we've a murder mystery on our hands."

"Then what are we waiting for?!" Eris gushed, burning with excitement. "We've got a world to save!"

Chapter Three - Where Innocence Burns

Caesia looked back once more at the gorgeous spires of Abenfurt, in hope once again that she would never have to come back. As beautiful a place as it was, she had far too many bad memories of it. At least today she had made some good ones and for that, she was thankful.

They headed back through the gate, where Caesia hired another carriage to take them to Aldreichen. Eris was asleep before they had even reached the Tarantis-Verden border, insisting that she needed to be at the top of her game when they arrived. That left Caesia to herself, spending most of the journey flicking through her books, toying with spells and pondering her powers.

The road trailed gradually out of the forest and back into lush, open fields, which rolled for miles up to a distant outcropping of hills. The Heartland, in the centre of which Aldreichen stood, was surrounded at the edge by a ring of hills that began on one side of Unity Bay and wrapped all the way around to the other. The passed by the town of Gerasberg and north along the bay, starting up the bordering hills of the Heartland.

"Eris!" Caesia whispered, prodding her slumbering friend.

Eris was completely unresponsive. Caesia had learnt quickly that while Eris was a very silent sleeper, she was also a very deep sleeper. Caesia snapped her fingers, charging them with energy and dug them into Eris' side.

Eris jolted in surprise as the searing shock woke her from her nap and Caesia smirked as her friend's glare fell upon her. She was beginning to wonder if she took too much pleasure in physically abusing her friend.

"Sorry," she smiled, shaking off her hand in an attempt to make the subtle stinging leave her bruised fingers. "Just thought you'd want to see the city once we get up this hill."

Eris relaxed her glare and sat up straight, still somewhat groggy. "We're here already?"

"Not quite, still a good… twenty minutes, perhaps?"

"Oh… so, you figure out anything new while I was out?" Eris asked, shaking herself off.

"I have made no more progress the past hour or so than I have in the past week," Caesia sighed. "What infuriates me isn't my inability to use my powers, it's my inability to find the answers! I'm so close, yet I've never felt further away!"

"Maybe you should just leave it," Eris suggested, despite already knowing Caesia's response. "Seems like it happens whenever you need it anyway, so why bother?"

"I can't do that, I could never let it go! My powers are utterly revolutionary, they could totally change our understanding of the arcane should I come to understand them! To simply forget about something so extraordinarily fascinating, i-it would be against everything I've ever stood for!"

Eris shook her head with a quivering smirk. Caesia seemed nothing short of a lunatic when she talked about these things, so obsessive and incoherent. Still, it was clear how much this meant to her, so Eris wouldn't try to stop her.

"You really think it's that revolutionary?" Eris asked. Obviously a yes, but she wanted to understand just how special Caesia really was.

"With no concrete evidence as to its nature, it's hard to say for certain," Caesia sighed. "This could be anything from simply an undiscovered school of magic to spatial translocation to full blown transdimensional warping! There are so many possibilities, each with their own unique sets of consequences and connotations. It's overwhelming sure, but I've never been so deeply fascinated!"

That string of incredibly long words did nothing more than confuse Eris further. That said, it was clear to her that no matter how one looked at it, the abilities linked with Caesia's essence were world shaking. Who knew what it would mean to introduce teleportation to the world?

The cart neared the top of the hill and Eris snapped out of her thoughts and stood up eagerly in the back of the cart. She watched in amazement as the gargantuan capital city came into sight.

The city was enormous, thrice the size of Tryzantopol. It engulfed a slender, long island a short distance off the bay's north coast, wrapped almost completely in an archaic wall that opened up to a vast dock on the south side. All across the city, buildings of various colours flew the red and white flags and banners of House Verden from their jagged golden rooftops.

"Wow!" Eris laughed. "This place is awesome!"

"Don't let the view fool you," Caesia muttered. "Most of the city is a run down cesspit, what with the couple of million peasants crammed within its walls."

"Couple of million?" Eris gasped. "That's insane!"

Trust Eris to turn a completely negative statement into a means to be excited. Caesia wanted to be brutally realistic with Eris, for her sake, but she sometimes wondered why she even bothered.

"What's insane is that they'd rather let people sleep on the streets than expand beyond the isle," Caesia sighed. "House Verden would rather maintain the city's novelty than improve its quality of life."

"And they say we hate cities," Eris chuckled at Caesia's constant criticism of the kingdom. It was just like home.

"Anyone in their right mind should resent them," Caesia sneered. "Cities are but a means to corral and control the commonfolk. The conditions are laughable and in many places worse than in rural settlements."

"Okay, okay!" Eris laughed. "Stars, you really need to lighten up. What happened to super happy, determined Caesia from back in Abenfurt?"

"She's still here… but, I'm just trying to be straight with you," Caesia sighed. "You're not ready for the things you'll see here."

"Oh, come on," Eris chuckled. "No way is it that bad."

"One word, my friend," Caesia sighed, leaning back in her seat. "Religion."

"Uh… what?"

"You'll see, but I warn you - you'll never unsee it."

The battered dirt roads transitioned to aged cobbles as the cart trundled down into the Heartland. They passed through the surrounding blanket of farms and over the Minaachen Delta. Soon they were at the Channel Bridge, the sole entrance into Aldreichen. The colossal red brick bridge was massive in width, having to accommodate all of the traffic in and out of the city. Its arched supports were draped with banners and red-armoured guards infested either end.

"Alright, girls!" Called the cart driver. "Bridge is people only 'part from deliveries, so 'fraid this is end'a the line."

Caesia handed the driver the rest of his pay and the pair hopped from the back of the cart.

It was easy to see why the bridge was pedestrian only, completely crawling with peasants moving in and out from the farms, as well as marching soldiers cloaked in House Verden colours and yellow robed priests going from peasant to impoverished peasant uttering rites and prayers. This, the most filthy and overpopulated place in all of Elaria, was the cradle of modern civilisation.

"Eergh, what's with the smell?" Eris gagged as a choking, pungent musk fell over them.

"That is the smell of civilisation," Caesia smirked. "Manure and unwashed commoners."

"Suppose I've smelt worse," Eris sighed, not wanting to give in to Caesia's negativity.

"Well, you haven't smelt the pyres yet." Caesia muttered sinisterly.

"Pyres? What do you mean?"

"Let's just say there's a popular saying amongst the commonfolk - 'In Verdenheld, only the innocent burn'."

"That's... ominous," Eris mumbled, not feeling the most welcome she'd ever felt.

"For good reason," Caesia said. "But enough of this morbidness, we've got places to be. Do keep an eye out for pickpockets, by the way."

They started over the bridge, weaving cautiously through the shifting tide of commoners. To Eris, it was a dizzying experience, chaos like she had never known. Caesia on the other hand, felt extremely uncomfortable being so close to the filthy commonfolk. As much as she was trying to shake off her noble roots, she couldn't help but resent their lack of hygiene.

"I'm sorry," Caesia yelled over the din of chattering peasants. "I know I'm being a bit of a downer, what with my constant droning about how crap everything is."

"Nothing I'm not used to," Eris smiled. She honestly found Caesia's cynicism entertaining most of the time.

Caesia chuckled quietly to herself. "I guess you are... I admit, all this nonsense with my powers is seriously stressing me out. I'm ready to let all this stuff with my family go, but I can't get this damned essence off my mind!"

Despite her little release back in Abenfurt, Caesia was clearly still teetering on the edge of sanity. Eris desperately wanted to help, but she didn't know a thing about magic.

"How long has your, uh, 'gift' been a thing?" Eris asked. "Were you born with it?"

"I don't- I don't know," Caesia wheezed, trying not to breathe in as she squeezed between two groups of peasants. "My parents seemed convinced that I was born with it, but I was never sure if I should believe them. I just know I had it by the age of four, given a portrait in the Citadel."

"So, you think it could've just... happened?"

"Maybe. That's the common issue - I have so many theories yet no information to back a single one of them! It's getting me absolutely nowhere."

"Hm..." Eris sighed, wanting to offer insight but having nothing of worth to offer.

"Look, just forget it. I'll be fine."

Eris had a feeling she wouldn't be. It was only a matter of time before Caesia cracked under the tremendous amount of pressure she was putting herself under.

The pair were waved through the towering gates and headed into the city. The buildings in the middle of the isle were far better maintained than most in the city, though the streets were worn by the feet of millions of peasants. Most of these structures were painted a golden brown with sloped black roofs, unlike the crude, patchy brickwork of the more recent buildings at the city's edge, hurriedly built to accommodate the city's spiralling population.

"Alright," Caesia muttered, unravelling the letter her mother had given her. "My mother's notes say that we are to meet this spy at 241 Victory Plaza."

"Victory Plaza?" Eris asked.

"It's a massive square at the centre of the city, not at all hard to find. There's this great big, golden statue of Aldrich Verden in the middle of it, taller than every building here. And don't worry, I shan't complain about it - I believe it is a rather suitable commemoration of such a hero."

"How big are we talking?" Eris asked eagerly. "Because I want one."

"I bet you do," Caesia smirked. "I only know it's taller than most other buildings in the city. So its pretty bloody sizable, at least."

"Well, there's no time like the present!" Eris declared, waving Caesia along.

The enormous main road from the gate led straight through to Victory Plaza, at the centre of the city isle. The Plaza was an enormous, open space of grey and red tiles, worn and battered over four hundred years. The square was throbbing with peasants, all gathered around an elevated wooden platform on the far side.

Rising from amidst the sea of peasants stood the colossal, glistening likeness of Aldrich Verden, the first king of Verdenheld and heroic slayer of Valkyr the Oppressor. The statue rose high over the surrounding buildings and further still rose Aldrich's sword, Warden, thrust triumphantly into the air. He was depicted in his legendary armour, forged especially to withstand the power of Valkyr's burning scythe. The armour was carved and ornate, the chestpiece styled after the eagle of House Verden taking flight, while his helmet bore slender, elegant wings on either side. It was designed for practicality, but the Forgemasters of Schardenhelm spared no effort in covering it head to toe with House Verden's iconography.

"Woah!" Eris laughed at the enormity of the statue. "You gotta be really cool to get a statue like that!"

"He was," Caesia smiled. "Never in Verdenheld's history has there been another man like him, who fought for the good of his common man rather than his own selfish ambitions. If we had more leaders like him, the world would be a much happier place."

A voice boomed from amidst the crowds and echoed throughout the square. It was a voice that oozed both authority and righteousness. Caesia sighed at the sound of it.

"Behold, righteous citizens of hallowed Aldreichen, an unholy beast - abhorrent in the eyes of our lord!"

"Ah, seems we've arrived just in time," Caesia groaned. "You wanted to know what pyres are, see for yourself."

"By the will of the Almighty and the righteousness of our hearts, we shall deliver holy judgement to this foul abomination, a vandalisation of God's perfect vision!"

"What is this?" Eris asked, trying to peer over the roaring crowds as she weaved her way to the front.

"Verdenheld considers beheading far too dignified for the 'abhuman' races," Caesia whispered, not wanting to be heard bad-mouthing the church. "They prefer... a more stimulating approach."

Caesia squeezed through the front row of the crowd and yanked Eris through with her. Before them was an elevated stone platform, on which stood a yellow robed priest and several silver clad knights, their tabards white and purple and bearing the roaring griffin of House Barethia. In their midst was an ulkar wrapped in a humming chain wrought with runes, tied to a stake cluttered with firewood, tears streaming down his ribbed, blue face.

"Why doesn't he just turn invisible and run?" Eris asked.
"See that chain? The inquisitors have different ones for each race, all of which are enchanted to disable the respective race's most potent properties."

"And what are they going to do to him?" Eris mumbled, becoming increasingly uncomfortable as the priest approached a burning brazier.

"They're going to purify him. With fire," Caesia said darkly. "If you don't want to watch, we can leave."

"No... I need to see," Eris murmured.

The priest yanked an unlit torch from a pedestal and thrust it into a brazier. Caesia turned her back as he presented a flame and moved to the pyre, while Eris continued to look on in apprehension.

The priest stopped. Blood spattered across the crowd, all over Eris' face and across Caesia's back, as a female ulkar materialised with a dagger thrust deep into the priest's throat.

Caesia cringed and stiffened, shivering in disgust. Eris stood wide eyed and bloody faced as the priest's corpse dropped to the ground, his horrified face staring into the distance as his throat oozed crimson. Eris moved for her sword but felt Caesia's hand clench over her wrist.

"Don't," she hissed, squeezing her hand tight.

The ulkar dropped the priest and ran for the unlit pyre, while the knights moved to surround her. They calmly drew their shimmering silver weapons - holy blades thrice blessed, maces ablaze with golden flame, halberds flaring with blinding light. These were no ordinary Barethian knights, Caesia had heard of these warriors before. They were Judicators, the finest abhuman hunters in the entire Inquisition. If they were here, this was more than a simple pyre burning.

The ulkar scrambled up the pyre and reached for the chain binding the other, only to scream in pain as it lit up with fiery red light. She reeled back, her raw hand shaking as she fought the burning pain.

"You are undone, demon," One of the knights declared heroically, sliding his burning longsword from its sheath. "Your sentiment for this wretch has drawn you beneath the hammer of God's judgement! By holy fire, you shall be cleansed."

The bound ulkar looked on at the other, teary eyed. "Thaola, go! Save yourself!"

Eris ground her teeth at her inability to act, desperate to intervene despite the odds. The female ulkar leant in and embraced the other in a final kiss, prompting roars of disgust from the crowd. She stepped away and vanished in the blink of an eye.

She lifted her hands, cloaked with a shimmering purple and stared at them in terror, turning to see one the knights' hand outstretched and humming with purple light.

"No…" she mumbled, returning to her visible state as the knights raised their shields in a wall of silver.

One knight retrieved the priest's torch and stamped out the flame it left behind, while the central knight lifted his blade towards her and advanced silently. She leapt at him and tried to slip beneath his raised arm, only for him to slam his knee into her stomach. He clenched his fist and battered her to the ground, toppling her onto the pyre.

"Thaola!" the male screamed, tears streaming down his contorted face.

The knight pinned her beneath his foot and flipped his longsword, slamming it down upon her shoulder. Caesia and Eris cringed while the crowd cheered at the harrowing crack of bone that echoed across the plaza.

"I'll meet you there," Caesia whispered tearfully, rushing off into the crowd, unable to even listen to the horrifying display.

The knight with the torch approached the pyre and turned to the crowd, raising it into the air for all to see.

"Pious and noble citizens of Aldreichen, before you lies no mere demon," he bellowed, clenching his fist. "By God's wisdom, I declare this abomination guilty of countless terrible crimes - murder, arson, espionage, all dealt with malice against the hallowed servants of the lord!"

The crowd roared with anger, all seething with utter hatred and calling feverously for justice.

"By the light of the lord, I banish these demons from this blessed ground!" he cried, casting the torch upon the pyre to the sound of triumphant cheers.

Eris watched in sheer horror as the fire surged up the pyre and engulfed the couple, their piercing screams of agony burning into her mind. Their pale blue flesh cracked and boiled, turning a volcanic black as they convulsed and kicked violently. The repulsive smell of melting flesh crept across the crowd, who only cheered louder with the tortured shrieks. Eris felt sick, not just from the smell and the sight, but the whole gut-wrenching scene. She turned and pushed her way through the crowd, hand over her mouth and tears in her eyes.

Caesia peered around the corner and into the alleyway, where Eris lay on her hands and knees coughing and spluttering over a misty green pool of regurgitated vegetable soup. In hindsight, it was cruel of her to subject Eris to that without warning. Perhaps she had gone a bit far in her attempt to teach Eris a valuable lesson about Verdenheld. That was a lesson learnt…

"You okay?" she sighed, walking over to Eris and placing her hand gently on her shoulder.

Eris looked up at her. Her face was still spattered with blood, diluting her tears to form pale red streaks down her face.

"W-why?" Eris stammered. "Why would they do that?!"

"Because they're different," Caesia said. "People fear what they don't understand and that fear is quick to manifest as hatred. The nobility need that hatred to blind the commonfolk from how unfair their existence is."

"They control people through… through murder?"

"Genocide morelike. Makes you think doesn't it? About what the dragon said - that the world is better off without humanity. From here, he doesn't look to be all that wrong."

Eris staggered to her feet, coughing and snivelling all the while. "Are we on the right side?" she whispered.

"There is no right side. One seeks human extinction, the other seeks abhuman extinction."

"Then what do we do?"

"The abhumans are few in number, the damage is already done," Caesia sighed. "All we can do now is try to prevent millions more innocent deaths at the hands of Valkyr."

"I guess I can get behind that," Eris said with a shallow smile. "I guess that puts us on the side of justice."

"Come now," Caesia chuckled. "That was far too cheesy, even for you."

Eris giggled and slapped Caesia on the back to prompt her to move on. "Aw, your back is covered in blood!" she scoffed, peeling her red smeared hand from Caesia's invisible jerkin.

The colour drained from Caesia's face as she shuddered at the very thought. "Why would you tell me that?" she gasped, her voice suddenly hysterical. "Could you… wipe it off?"

"Of course, my lady," Eris muttered.

After a quick scrub down of Caesia's back, the pair headed down the row of houses bordering Victory Plaza. Caesia, despite sounding a bit less glum than before, still seemed distracted. Her eyes were never fixed in one place and sometimes showed subtle episodes of sadness or irritation. Eris would have been concerned if not for being distracted herself, still processing the events she had just witnessed.

She was completely taken aback and utterly confused by the twisted motives and actions of the city dwellers. Everything her father had told her was becoming clear - Verdenheld, or at least those who controlled it, were evil. Despite that, she knew she had to take their side if she was going to save innocent lives. After all, that was what heroes did.

Caesia stopped outside a run down house at the corner of the square. The outside was painted to maintain the appearance of the square, but the windows were boarded with aged wood. It had clearly been empty for some time.

"241 Victory Plaza," Caesia announced. "This is the place."

"Stars, first you're putting that weird see-through stuff in your windows and now wood?" Eris scoffed. "This place is crazy…"

Caesia stared at her blankly for a moment as she processed those words. She had never considered the fact that Eris had never seen glass in her life, she couldn't imagine how strange it must have seemed to her. That was a conversation for another day, she decided as she approached the front door and knocked delicately.

"What was that?" Eris laughed. "You call that a knock?"

"Do my hands look in knocking condition to you?" Caesia snapped, waving her disgusting, bandaged fingers in front of her face.

"All right, fair point." Eris mumbled, approaching the door herself and hammering it with her fist.

In response, the door jolted out of the frame and steadily opened with an eerie, drawn out creak. The battered old interior was revealed, the wood dark and rotting with age and the walls laced with ancient cobwebs.

"I... didn't think it possible, but this place is somehow more unnerving than the tomb full of reanimated skeletons," Caesia whispered anxiously.

Eris shrugged and entered the house, the floorboards whining loudly as she set down her feet. Behind her, she heard a panicked squeal from Caesia. She span around, hand on her sword to see Caesia hiding around the doorframe, quivering with fear.

"What?" Eris smirked.

"There's a spider!" Caesia wailed, staring into the hallway with terror in her eyes.

Eris blurted with laughter. "Are you kidding me? You can shoot lightning out your hands and you're afraid of spiders?"

"Just kill the bloody thing!" Caesia spat.

Eris observed on one of the strings of cobweb, a particularly large spider lying peacefully on the web.

"No way, he's not hurting anyone!"

"Eris, kill the spider right now!" Caesia growled, her voice oozing malice.

"Okay, okay!" Eris relented, pulling out her sword swiping at the web. "There, gone."

Eris noticed too late the spider's trajectory. She could see on Caesia's blank face the moment the spider made contact - the twitch of her eye, the quiver of her body, the expression of absolute terror. Eris wasn't going to enjoy what came next.

Before Eris could even manage an awkward smile, Caesia let slip a deafening shriek. Violent bursts of green lightning exploded from her body as she flailed around erratically, shattering boards and scorching the doorframe. Eris threw up her shield in terror, just in time for a bolt of lightning to slam against it and send her staggering backwards onto the staircase.

The storm of electricity subsided and the last of the energy dispersed into the air. Eris peered cautiously over the rim of her shield. The doorway was scarred by scorch marks and the frame was crumbling into ash. Caesia glared up at her, electricity still coursing across her body.

"Sorry..." Eris smiled, ducking slightly further behind her shield.

Caesia glanced down at the black particles that once were the spider, floating gently to the ground. For a moment she looked inclined to kill Eris on the spot, but quickly composed herself with a deep breath.

"Second floor," She muttered, wiping her hair back into position. "You're going first."

Eris thought it best to obey, for her own sake. She turned back to the staircase and began trudging off.

The stairs bent and cracked beneath their feet. Caesia tensed at the chilling atmosphere of silence and darkness, drawing as close to Eris as possible without impeding her. Eris' presence was the only thing keeping her from freaking out completely.

Eris peered around the corner at the top of the stairs. "Hello?" she called as she stepped into the empty hallway. "You sure this is the right place? I was expecting some kind of secret password or moving wall panel or something."

Caesia didn't bother correcting Eris' absurd fantasies. "Look, that room at the end isn't boarded up, if our man's anywhere, I imagine he'll be in there."

They moved down the hallway, Caesia ducking squeamishly in a hope that the cobwebs would hit Eris first.

"Not to scare you or anything, but this reeks of a trap," Eris whispered.

"Please don't say that!" Caesia moaned.

Eris approached the unbarricaded door and pressed up her hand against it. Caesia stepped behind Eris, trying to pretend that she wasn't hiding as Eris gently pushed the door open.

The walls and floors were painted with blood. Books and equipment lay battered and broken across the floor and a fresh corpse lay slumped against the bed in the middle of the room. They stepped cautiously into the room and as they approached the body, Eris saw the brutal state it had been left in. Deep punctures cluttered the dead man's torso, holes the width of a man's fist and filled to the brim with pools of blood. His face was contorted in a perpetual scream of horror, tears clinging to his wrinkled skin.

Caesia peered past Eris and immediately bolted to the other side of the room, hands on her head in panic. While Caesia staggered off to the side, Eris knelt down beside the body, nauseous at the gruesome sight.

"I guess we found your spy," she muttered.

Caesia said nothing, standing head in hands in the corner breathing erratically.

Eris turned back to the man and looked him up and down. This seemed like it had been done by some kind of creature, such massive punctures would be impossible for any weapon she knew of.

"Whatever did this, it must be involved in this guy's investigation…"

Caesia still gave no answer. She was trembling violently and her ragged breath was rapid and hoarse.

"Caesia?" Eris called gently, standing up and approaching her slowly.

Caesia turned around and faced Eris. Her face was slick with sweat and her eyes were bagged and raw. She was trembling and twitching, hyperventilating, sparks of electricity spitting from her skin with her every tortured breath.

"W-we need to- we need to go!" Caesia urged, utterly incoherent. "It could still be here! I-it could come for us too!"

Eris sighed sorrowfully and gently took hold of Caesia's shoulders. "It's okay, we're fine," she whispered, a smile on her face.

"I'm scared," Caesia sobbed, her voice a raspy whisper. "I... I don't want to die."

"We're not gonna die," Eris smiled.

"You don't know that!" Caesia cried. "I don't want to end up like this..."

Eris smiled timidly, brushed back Caesia's sweaty, coarse hair and looked into her tired eyes. She cringed at the static touch of Caesia's electrified sweat, but hid the pain behind a sweet grin. "Don't worry, I'll protect you," she whispered, wrapping her hands around hers. "And you'll protect me. Just like always."

Caesia looked down at the floor, embarrassed at herself. Her breath was becoming steadier but tears still ran down her trembling face.

"You know, it doesn't take a shaman to know that this is about more than just dying," Eris sighed. " Stop trying to put so much on your shoulders. Please."

"Okay..." Caesia mumbled, burying her face in her hands and wiping off the tears.

"Great. You just sit a minute, take all the time you need," Eris whispered. "I'll have a look around."

Caesia stepped back and slumped onto a battered old dining table, watching as Eris turned away with a warm smile. She realised now that she was pushing herself far too hard, that she was putting an absurd amount of pressure on her shoulders. Perhaps she needed to give her mind a rest, give herself some time to breathe and come back to her powers with a fresh face.

Eris ran her fingers across the dust-caked bed as she approached the dead man again. It was clear that this man was assassinated, silenced for he knew too much. The question was, what did he know and about whom?

She looked up and down the room, analysing the scene. There were little signs of struggle beyond the area close to the bed, suggesting a quick and expertly executed kill. In such an ominously silent building, the attacker must have had incredible skills in stealth. That would line up with an ulkar, but that did nothing to explain the wounds. Eris simply couldn't think what could deal such incredible damage as to puncture almost all the way through the man's body.

"Hello, what's this?" she mumbled to herself.

The man's body lay on top of a book, narrowly visible below his back. Eris got down on one knee and carelessly shoved the corpse onto its side, drenching the floorboards with the blood that sloshed from its wounds like water from a bucket. The book's cover was blank and battered, presumably some kind of notebook or journal. Eris opened it and flicked through the last few pages, only to be greeted with the unwelcome sight of Elarian Common.

"Oh, yeah..." Eris muttered. "Can you read this for me?"

Caesia looked up from wringing her fingers, her eyes still a raw red. "Um, y-yes. Give it here."

Eris placed the notebook in Caesia's quivering hands. She flicked to the back and skim read the headings:

'02.10.411 - Anti-Human Graffiti'
'16.10.411 - Suspicious Packages'
'38.02.412 - Ulkar in the Slums?'
'14.04.412 - Missing Inquisitors'

Caesia read silently over the spy's investigation notes. They mostly explained what they already knew, but they also described the spy's intended next move.

"Alright, I... I've got it." Caesia mumbled, her voice still hoarse and quiet.

"Great!" Eris smiled, taking back the book and nonchalantly flinging it onto the bed. "How you feeling?"

"I've been better," Caesia muttered.

"You know, you don't have to do this if you don't want to. It's okay if you want to-"

"Leave you to your inevitable death? What do you take me for?" Caesia smirked. "I may be scared shitless, but I'm not going anywhere."

"Alright," Eris grinned. "Then let's get down to business."

"Okay, I... Sorry, can you just... move him?" Caesia asked, trying to keep her eyes off the corpse. "I-I really, I just can't."

Eris rolled her eyes and wandered over to the bed. She grabbed one end of the dusty bedsheet and flung it onto the floor, draping it over the body.

"Thanks," Caesia mumbled. "Anyway, the spy found a note left at the scene of the disappearance by the captain of the guard. He claimed to have vital information to the case, but didn't want to get the city guard involved."

"Why not?"

"It doesn't say. Corruption in the guard, perhaps?"

"Maybe… I guess we don't know what that information is?"

"No, but the spy was to meet the captain anonymously at a masquerade ball hosted by Lord Arrenni." Caesia smirked. "It seems our friend had a soft spot for clichés."

"Sorry, but what's a masquerade ball?" Eris asked. "Is it a sport?"

"It's… like a party, only with less partying and more masks. You'll hate it, I assure you."

"Huh. When is it?"

"This evening at six."

"Guess we've got some time to kill then," Eris sighed.

"On the contrary, my friend," Caesia grinned. "We've got no time to lose! If we are to attend this ball, we'll need to look the part!"

"Please, no…"

"Which means we'll need dresses!" Caesia exclaimed, suddenly bursting with enthusiasm. "And some nice shoes, maybe something to make you look pretty?"

"I don't want to do this anymore," Eris muttered.

"Come on, it'll be fun!" Caesia urged. "This is what girls do!"

"Can't we just-"

"No. Now come, we're going shopping!"

Chapter Four - The Masquerade

Eris impatiently rammed her foot into a slender blue slipper, which Caesia had insisted would complement her icy blue dress. Eris had picked hers immediately with no particular care, while Caesia had spent near enough an hour picking hers out. A draining experience to say the least. Eventually, she had settled on a purple dress, which Eris swore she had already seen her pass up half a dozen times.

"This is humiliating!" Eris yelled to Caesia, who was changing in the next room.

Eris resented the whole outfit. The dress was pretty but it was ridiculously tight and made her feel like the centre of attention even with nobody in the room. It was only made worse by the fact that she would have to wear some goofy mask.

"Quit your whining," Caesia laughed, appearing in the doorway.

Eris' jaw would certainly have dropped were she not trying to appear extremely discontent. Caesia looked incredible - she wore her dazzling purple dress like a second skin and her normally pasty, gaunt face was brought to life with makeup. The glistening green of her eyes was brought out beautifully by expertly applied eyeliner and her hair was tied back in a flawless, silky bun. This was a woman trained all her life for exactly this.

Caesia eyed Eris narrowly. "You're not wearing your corset," she hissed.

Eris' eyes grew fearful as she snapped from her trance. "Please!" she begged as Caesia slipped her corset from beneath the bed.

"The corset is the most important part of a lady's outfit!" Caesia explained. "Look, you're slouching."

"I am not."

"Yes you are. Go on, get the dress off."

"Give it here, I'll do it myself," Eris demanded.

"No you won't. For the inexperienced, the corset is a two-woman job. Off."

Eris sighed and turned away from Caesia, undoing the back of her dress. She wriggled out of the constricting sleeves and let the front of the dress flop away. Caesia handed her the corset, which Eris snatched off her with contempt.

"You see, *this* is humiliating," Caesia chuckled, as she watched Eris half naked, fiddling with the corset like a caveman.

Eris muttered angrily to herself as she wriggled into the corset. Caesia grabbed the back and began tying it up.

"Brace!" Caesia yelled, as she forcefully yanked the strings and tightened the corset.

Eris felt all of the air in her lungs be pumped out of her as the corset constricted her chest. Suddenly, she found herself barely able to breathe, locked into a fashionable prison.

"What sick bastard made these?" Eris wheezed.

"Clearly someone who took great pleasure in other people's suffering," Caesia smirked, watching Eris waddling around, stiff as a broom. "Else they'd be a bit more comfortable."

Eris wriggled her arms back into her sleeves and began doing up the back of her dress again.

"Alright, I reckon you could benefit from some blusher," Caesia mused. "Your complexion doesn't-"

"No way," Eris growled. "I draw the line at the corset."

"Fine," Caesia chuckled. "I suppose your pale complexion could complement the dress' cold colour palette. At least brush your hair, would you?"

"Yeah, yeah," Eris muttered, reaching for her bag to get the hairbrush.

"Careful not to pick up too much dust," Caesia warned. "You may not think it noticeable on your dress, but believe me - nothing goes unnoticed at these things."

"Why are you so obsessed with this?" Eris asked, running the brush through her frizzy hazel hair. "I know you were taught to be good at it, but you're such a... perfectionist."

Caesia smiled amusedly. "Do you really want to know?"

"Not another sob story, is it?"

"Kind of..." Caesia sighed. "See this scar?"

Eris peered closely at Caesia's cheek, just below her eye. For a time she could see nothing, until she finally made out a near-invisible line in her skin across the top of her cheek.

"Huh, I never noticed that."

"Didn't think so. When I was fourteen, I came to dinner with the King having botched my eyeliner in a rush. After the King left, my father struck me and told me I was worthless and an embarrassment to the family. So, every time since I made sure that I was flawless, because I was scared that he would hurt me again."

"Oh... sorry I brought it up."

"Ah, it doesn't bother me," Caesia sighed with a weak smile. "I've grown kind of numb to that sort of thing now. Course, that doesn't mean I hate him any less."

An awkward silence hung in the room as Eris finished dressing. Caesia sighed and wandered to the window, where she parted the shutters and peered between the crudely placed boards blockading the window. The crowds in the plaza were assembling once again into a great mass as a group of women were dragged onto the stage. She wondered what they had done to 'deserve' this. Were they abhuman sympathisers? Believers of a different faith? Obstacles in a noble's path? Did it matter? You could get burnt for anything in Verdenheld, so long as someone thought it necessary.

She remembered a time when a thief was burnt at the foot of the Arcana Citadel. They called him a changeling in disguise, when she knew for certain that he had picked her brother's pocket the day prior. Such was the pecking order.

"Whatcha looking at?" Eris chirped, snapping Caesia back to reality.

"Nothing," Caesia sighed, releasing the shutters as the pyre flared to life. "You sorted?"

"Yep."

"Alright, now that you're dressed there are some essential bits of etiquette and whatnot we need to go over."

"Oh, great…" Eris groaned.

"First off, you need to talk properly - keep contractions minimal and avoid informal words at all costs. Secondly, you must address everybody you meet by their full name and title, or at the very least 'my lord' or 'my lady'."

"Wait, then what's the point in the masks?" Eris scoffed.

"It's… a strange tradition. The masks aren't there to hide one's identity, but simply to serve as a novelty. The idea is that even the most acquainted lords and ladies introduce themselves as strangers. I know it makes no sense, but just go with it."

"Um… okay?"

"Anyway, it is also of vital importance that you obey at all times the rules of the ballroom. You will be offered to dance by a man and you will dance with him until a break in the music, in which you will move to a new partner. Most men will attempt to converse with you, in which case you must humour them, so get a persona figured out. Oh, and whatever you do, do not attempt to dance with another woman. You get all of that?"

"Just about, I think," Eris muttered.

"Good. Now, let's make sure you know how to walk."

"You've got to be-"

"Quiet!" Caesia snapped. "If you want to be taken seriously, you'll need to maintain correct posture and a confident stride. Follow my lead."

Eris threw back her head and heaved an exaggerated sigh as she stepped to Caesia's side.

"Shoulders back, lift your thigh like so," Caesia explained. "Relax your arms and point your hands down, keep your elbows close to your body.

Now, you must keep in mind the distance between your steps - about a foot will do, any more and it will appear too masculine."

Eris awkwardly positioned herself as Caesia commanded. "I feel ridiculous."

"Hush!" Caesia hissed. "Now, you want to step forwards ensuring your heel meets the ground first, like this. Then shift your weight forwards like so. Rinse and repeat, feet always slightly apart."

Caesia strutted up and down the room confidently. Eris thought she looked like an absolute prick, but that was in fact exactly what they were going for.

Eris walked across the room in a vague imitation of Caesia's walk, wobbling clumsily on her heels.

"Not awful..." Caesia muttered. "But it could use some work."

"I'll practice on the way there," Eris mumbled.

"Fine," Caesia sighed. "Let's move onto dancing."

"Oh, for-"

"Shut it you whiny... come here. I'll need you for this."

Eris staggered over to Caesia, who grabbed her wrists and pulled her in.

"Okay, I will be the man and you the woman. You must stand shoulder distance apart from your partner and place your hand on their left shoulder. Now, I will step forwards with my left foot and you will step back with your right."

Caesia stepped forwards and Eris backwards, Eris nearly losing her footing as the heel of her shoe went down between two floorboards.

"That's it. Your partner's left foot should always land besides your right foot. Now, we simply step to the side, like so. Then we put our feet together and repeat!"

"Wait, really?" Eris blurted, dropping her hands. "That's it?"

"Not quite, continue," Caesia commanded, pulling her back into the dance. "It is likely that your partner will occasionally perform an underarm turn, which is as easy as spinning on the spot for you. Or, if they're feeling a bit saucy, they may go for a dip."

"A dip? Like, in water?"

"No, like this," Caesia grinned, suddenly sweeping Eris off her feet.

Caesia nearly toppled over as she suspended Eris expertly, not having considered how poorly built she was for supporting the weight of a whole person. Eris fought to suppress an excited giggle as she hovered in Caesia's embrace, her long hair cleaving dust from the floorboards. Caesia swung Eris back onto her feet with a smug smile.

"You're scarily good at this," Eris laughed. "Do the dancing skills also have a tragic backstory?"

"Nope, I just had a lot of compulsory dance lessons. Besides, that was only the basic stuff."

"How advanced does it get?"

"A conversation for another time," Caesia smiled. "I think that about covers everything. We should get going, don't want our contact thinking we're a no show."

"Agreed."

"Wait!" Caesia demanded, stopping Eris with an outstretched hand. She pulled her close and sniffed her dress like a starving mutt.

"Please stop," Eris mumbled, feeling extremely uncomfortable.

"You've no perfume on," Caesia hissed.

"I hate you."

Eris and Caesia wandered through the streets of Aldreichen, their destination only a short walk from Victory Plaza. The golden brown buildings were bathed in evening light as the sun fell low in the sky and the locals had begun to disperse from the streets.

Eris had tried Caesia's fancy walk for a bit since leaving, but had since gone back to walking like a regular human being. Caesia however, insisted on maintaining it the entire way there, despite having to hold up her dress to stop it from dragging along the filthy cobblestones. Before departing, they had donned their masks. Eris wore a basic white mask with a blue accent around the edge, while Caesia wore an extravagant purple, gold trimmed mask with a plume of green feathers protruding at the side.

"Alright, the plan is simple," Caesia said. "I will make my way to the contact and find out what he knows. You must simply remain nearby should there be any trouble. You've got a weapon right?"

"Yep," Eris confirmed, patting her thigh.

Eris' dress depressed beneath her hand to reveal the shape of her sword against her thigh. Caesia was quite impressed that Eris managed to hide it so well in such a tight dress.

"Great!" Caesia smiled. "By the way, I know I've been rather critical, but you look good."

"I don't feel good," Eris smirked, still being crushed by her corset.

"Well you suit a dress phenomenally."

"Thanks, I guess?" Eris sighed. "I'd compliment you, but I know I'd mess it up."

"What do you mean?"

"I'm... not good at compliments. They always come off weird, you know?"

"I'm intrigued. Try me."

Eris screwed up her mouth in annoyance. She really didn't want to do this. "Okay... your eyes are really pretty?" she smiled with uncertainty.

"Alright, that was a bit weird," Caesia smirked. "But thank you!"

"You don't know the half of it." Eris sighed.

"Sounds like there's a story in this," Caesia said eagerly. "Do tell."

"I ever mention Jon?" Eris asked, garnering a confused look from Caesia. "Childhood friend. Best friend, that is. We kinda met through my rubbish compliments... When we were twelve, I approached him in the training yard and told him I liked his shirt. Next day, he showed up with a flower and asked me to be his girlfriend!"

Caesia burst into a fit of quiet laughter. "Aww!" she sighed. "That's so cute!"

"I know, right?" Eris laughed. "I said yeah, then we never talked to each other for the next two years. I'd totally forgotten when he showed up and asked if we were still a thing."

"And what did you tell him?"

"Well, er... by then I'd realised I wasn't really into... him," Eris muttered. "I told him he wasn't my type, but we could still be friends if he wanted."

"That has to be the most adorable story I've heard in my life," Caesia chuckled. "Something tells me you'll never let him live that down."

"Not in his life," Eris grinned. "But don't feel bad for him, he has stuff on me too."

"Like what?" Caesia asked, an eyebrow raised in intrigue. "Something scandalous?"

"That... is not for you to know," Eris mumbled, her eyes drifting aside.

"Oh, come on, you can trust me!" Caesia urged. "We're thick as thieves, are we not?"

"I'm not about to embarrass myself for your amusement," Eris smirked.

"Aw, but I love it when you do that!" Caesia laughed. She enjoyed nothing more than watching other people making fools of themselves.

"I bet you do..." Eris sneered.

They turned onto Phoenix Way, the street on which stood the Grand Royal Ballroom. The building was built close to but separately from the palace because the king of the time wanted a surrounding terrace for outdoor events. The flawless, golden building glimmered in the warm sunlight. All the way around it were stained glass windows depicting various kings, heroes and historical events in an array of vibrant colours. The raised terrace surrounding the building was covered with a vast variety of plant life from across not just the continent, but even overseas, as well a series of water features spewing glistening blue water.

Eris looked on at the magnificent building ahead. "Wow, this is..."

"Extravagant?" Caesia sighed. "Yes, the nobles really like to overdo it when it comes to parties and the like."

"I was going to say nice," Eris muttered.

"Oh. Well, my point still stands."

"So, how're we gonna get in?"

Caesia looked the building up and down. There was a guard at the entrance receiving invitations, a rather young man whose inexperience she intended to take advantage of.

Caesia looked back to Eris with a confident smirk. "Oh, that's easy - I'll seduce the guard."

"Seduce?!" Eris laughed. "Seriously? Your chest is flatter than the pavement."

"Anyone can appear smoking hot, so long as their movements and demeanour are expertly handled," Caesia declared. "Apart from teaching me to be an upstart prick, my mother also threw in a bit of subterfuge for good measure, Lacroix tradition and all that. I've got this."

"You're not going to…"

"I'm not going to sleep with him," Caesia groaned. "I have standards, you know."

"Alright then, super spy," Eris sneered. "Lead the way."

"Of course, but first I'll need you to grab the guard's attention for a moment."

"Can do."

Eris moved towards the guard while Caesia slipped off to the side of the building.

"Excuse me?" Eris called in a crude imitation of Caesia's posh accent. "Can you help me, sir?"

"Here for the ball, miss?" The guard asked, descending the steps to meet her.

Eris glanced over to Caesia, stiffening her jaw and trying with all her might not to laugh as Caesia unathletically scrambled onto the terrace. Caesia glared at her as she brushed herself off, before slipping into cover.

"Um, no," Eris smiled. "I am in need of some directions to, er, Victory Plaza."

"That would be back the way you came, miss," The guard chuckled.

"Ah, you have my gratitude, sir," Eris smiled, turning and walking away.

The guard turned around to see Caesia come staggering to the top of the stairs, pretending quite convincingly to be drunk.

"Oh, hellooo!" Caesia blurted. "Sorry, I-I think I musht be loss."

"Enjoying the party, ma'am?" The guard smirked.

Caesia purposefully tripped on the last step and fell dramatically into the guard's arms. At least she would have if the guard had not the reaction time of a sloth. Caesia collapsed onto the ground, landing hard on her bruised arms and letting slip a long, pathetic whine as searing pain shot through them.

"Oh my God!" The guard gasped. "Are you okay, ma'am?"

She slowly pushed her face from the cold ground and glared up at Eris, who was laughing hysterically behind her hands a short distance away. A scowl on her face, she looked around quickly and before the guard could react, thrust her hand out and loosed a crack of green lightning into his stomach. The guard was blasted several feet into a nearby bush, where he shook and convulsed as the electricity surged into his body.

Scrambling up off the ground and cradling her arms against her chest, she made certain to avoid eye contact with Eris as she approached.

"Wow, that was really impressive!" Eris chuckled, wandering over. "What section of the super spy handbook was that one from?"

"I got it from section *shut your trap*," Caesia hissed, followed with a defeated sigh. "We will never speak of that again."

"No promises," Eris grinned, gesturing to the unconscious guard. "What do we do with this guy?"

"Hm... we'll chuck him in an alleyway, make out like he's been drinking."

"I guess I'm doing the heavy lifting?" Eris sighed.

"Correct," Caesia smiled.

Eris groaned and grabbed the man beneath his shoulders. She wondered if the real reason Caesia wouldn't get her arms seen to was because it was an excuse to exclude herself from all the hard work. In fact, come to think of it, Caesia was perfectly capable of enduring the pain of casting her spells... so surely she was able to lift a man! Eris felt like an utter idiot - Caesia had been playing her for a fool.

She dragged the guard across the empty street and flung him into an alleyway, almost collapsing as she tilted dangerously far in her stupid shoes.

"So... how to we make him look drunk?" Eris asked.

"Don't look at me, I've never drank," Caesia muttered.

"I've had like, one beer ever."

"Huh. Surely you've seen your fair share of drunks back home?"

"You're stereotyping again," Eris smirked.

"Well... just leave him," Caesia sighed. "We shouldn't be here long anyway."

"Fine, but if he bursts in halfway through and we get arrested, I reserve the right to slap you again."

"That's reasonable enough," Caesia sighed. "Shall we?"

They made back towards the ballroom, Caesia ascending the steps with a confident smile. This was it - the occasion that she had trained all her life for, be it dance, etiquette, manipulation, everything! It was time to be the Tarantis she had always tried not to be.

Caesia pushed open one of the ornate double doors into the ballroom. The golden hall was wrought with mosaics and murals depicting Verdenheld's history, most of them obscured by the swaying crowds of nobles. The room hummed with slow orchestral music and subtle chatter, almost sending Eris immediately to sleep as she stepped in after Caesia.

"I take it back, this is extravagant," Eris chuckled. "You know how you'll find our man?"

"I will ask someone. And watch it with the 'you'll'. No contractions, remember?"

"Yeah, yeah," Eris groaned, sauntering off to the dance floor.

Caesia smirked and rolled her eyes. As Eris took a gentleman's hand on the dance floor and was whisked away, Caesia surveyed the room. With their masks on, it was difficult to tell who was noble and who was not and thus had no means to identify the captain. She had no choice but to ask around.

She moved towards the dance floor, where a surprisingly scruffy bearded man offered her his hand.

"A dance, my lady?" he smiled, taking her hand gently.

He was dressed formally like the rest of the men in the room, but he was far less so in appearance. His short ginger beard was ragged and untamed, his face rough and worn. Both his clothes and his simple black mask were old and battered, as if they had seen years of use and little care. He was surely an Ironhand, by their reputation for scruffy, unkempt appearances, likened often by men of the other houses to that of stray dogs.

"Of course," Caesia grinned, stepping onto the dance floor and placing her hand on his shoulder. "Balder Ironhand, I presume?"

"Close," The man chuckled. "I am his brother, Veldin."

"Apologies, Lord Veldin," Caesia smiled. "How are you finding the festivities?"

"Dull is a word that comes to mind. Such is the case with much of this business," Veldin groaned. "What I wouldn't give for a beer… but enough about me, perhaps you ought to introduce yourself?"

"Of course. Caesia Tarantis, daughter of Lord Edmund Tarantis of Abenfurt."

"Ah, I remember - the girl with the gift," Veldin mused. "Your old man often finds an excuse to slip you into conversations."

Caesia could hear the discontent in Veldin's voice. She expected as much, her father was very much the antithesis of the Ironhands - incredibly stuck up and when he needed to be, utterly emotionless.

"Oh, is that so?" Caesia asked with intrigue.

"Aye, in the same way one would speak of a prized catch," Veldin muttered.

"Like a trophy? That sounds about right," Caesia sighed.

"Yes, although he seems to have shut up about it recently. Thank God."

Caesia smirked knowingly. It was clear that her father feared to make the news of her disappearance public. He always cared more about his reputation than anything else, thus it was incredibly satisfying for her to know that she had put it jeopardy.

"Well, perhaps he has more pressing matters on his mind," Caesia smiled.

"Such as?"

"Oh, I would not know. What about your family? How are things in Schardenhelm?"

"We are still trying hard to find a new source of tricinium, what with our end of the Scar drying up. My father plans to propose an expedition into the Shattered Coast to scout more of it."

"Kranik must be getting desperate," Caesia said with concern. "He knows well the dangers of the Shattered Coast."

"He believes the arachni presence there is a myth," Veldin sighed. "Maybe he is right, but if not…"

"It could spell disaster. Disaster that could span not just the Iron Peaks, but the realm as a whole."

"Exactly," Veldin muttered. "Perhaps you would ask your father to knock some sense into him?"

"I would not count on it. My father and I have been… distant as of late."

"A shame," Veldin sighed. "I know the feeling. I have spent months now helping my father prepare the expedition… yet, I heard only this week that he favours Balder for the job of leading it. Balder - the oaf who could barely swing an axe when I drove the Vulkites back through the mountains."

"Maybe your father has other plans for you?" Caesia suggested, unsure of what else to say. She was never all that good at comforting people, for she had little experience with people in general.

"Maybe… but he knows I want this," Veldin growled. "Why would he deny me?"

"I'm afraid I do not know."

"Hmph... how do you cope with it?" Veldin muttered. "Having a father so cold to your feelings? Apologies if I am prying too deep, but..."

"You need not apologise," Caesia smiled. "If you want my advice, forget about it. I let my family rule me all my life, until I found out there was a life for me beyond them. Now... I have purpose."

"You think I should just go my own way?" Veldin scoffed. "What about House Ironhand?"

"Ironhand, Tarantis, they are just names. Powerful names to be sure, but they do not define who we are. Are you a name, Veldin, or are you a man?"

"Hm... that is deep, Miss Tarantis," Veldin smirked, his mood slightly lightening. "And a lot to think about. But, I apologise, this is meant to be a celebration!"

"Yes, what are we celebrating exactly?" Caesia asked.

"You do not know?"

"I... did not have time to ask my father."

"Ah. Jonas Arrenni decided to host this grand ball in celebration of Newport's success."

"But Newport was founded in all the way back in three-five-three, nearly sixty years ago!" Caesia scoffed. "It has been thriving for decades, what ever could be the occasion?"

"He says that the jungle tribes have been defeated, that they are on the run and all of Strausia is now ours for the taking."

"He should know better than that," Caesia said gravely. "There is no conquering that jungle, no matter how many trees House Arrenni cuts down."

"I agree," Veldin sighed. "For all we know, the tribes could be withdrawing only to prepare a greater assault. House Arrenni should be capitalising on the peace, not swaying in a ballroom."

The music began to calm and die down. Veldin slowly withdrew his hands from Caesia's shoulders with a smile.

"Well, would you look at that? It seems our time is up," he sighed. "I must apologise - I have turned this whole affair into a series of complaints about the realm!"

"Oh, stop apologising, would you?" Caesia smiled. "I for one enjoy political matters, especially complaining about them. I imagine it is the Lacroix blood."

"Well in that case, it has been a pleasure, Lady Caesia." Veldin said, executing a crude bow. "I hope we might continue our conversation at later date."

"Indeed!" Caesia chirped. "Good luck with your father, Veldin."

"And with yours," Veldin chuckled, joining hands with his next partner and disappearing into the crowd.

Caesia span around to the receiving arms of her next partner. She always found the younger members of House Ironhand to be quite good company, what with their nonchalant approach to the political scene. It was refreshing, yet she had sadly experienced the best of what she would find in this hive of merchants, noblemen and politicians. It would only be down from here.

Eris stepped away from her partner with a plastic smile. She'd had the unfortunate luck to be paired with Sir Jacques Duffant, resulting in her having to smile through a gripping tale of his latest knightly deeds. It had been a struggle not to gloat about her own mighty deeds while he enthralled her with his heroic saving of a damsel from some bandits.

She swivelled around to meet her next partner, a tall man with short, greying brown hair and a stern, immovable look about him - broad shoulders, weathered skin and behind his turquoise mask, dull grey eyes that made one shift in discomfort beneath their iron gaze.

"Greetings, my lady," he smiled, his voice conveying an unnerving authority despite his welcoming tone.

"Good evening, my lord," Eris grinned.

The man appeared offended for a moment, putting Eris particularly on edge. "Ah, you must not recognise me by the mask," he chuckled. "Edmund Tarantis, Lord of Abenfurt."

Eris had never frozen so suddenly in her life, colour draining rapidly from her face like she had seen her own ghost. Her mouth went dry, her throat tight and a fearful shiver jolted up her spine. "Ah! Of course, yes! I have heard much about you!" she stammered, utterly incoherent in her terrified state.

"And who would you be, my girl?"

"I am Lady Erisian... Severin," Eris smiled, trying desperately to suck in her fear and compose herself.

"Severin? That does well to explain your rugged appearance and lack of makeup, but I must say you have quite the... northern accent."

Eris screamed internally. Sir Jacques was an idiot, he had set her hopes so high, given her the notion that she could just bluff her way through this with ease. She should have known that Caesia's father would match his daughter's wit.

"Yes, I, er... was married into the house," Eris mumbled. "I am from Loftenheim originally."

"I see. I trust you are enjoying the festivities, Miss Severin?" Edmund asked.

"Yes, they are quite… festive," Eris smiled awkwardly.

She was beyond terrified, fearing for her every word. She was scared to say something she shouldn't, as she was often prone to doing.

"Say, how is your daughter nowadays?" Eris chirped. "I hear from Lord Severin that she is quite phenomenal."

"She is doing well," Edmund smiled. "Soon to enter her second year at the College. She will be fit for the royal court in no time, I expect."

It was scary how flawlessly Edmund hid Caesia's disappearance, more convincingly than most people spoke truths.

"Lord Severin says she has a gift," Eris inquired. "Green essence?"

"That she does, though the scholars have still made little of it," Edmund sighed. "Nonetheless, we believe it to simply be a matter of time before her essence reveals its true nature."

"And what do you think that nature might be?" Eris asked.

"It is impossible to say. For all we know, it could be a simple mutation, nothing more."

"A mutation?"

"It is simply a possibility," Edmund said. "If it is indeed a mutation, no doubt the Inquisition will try to snap her up like they did when she was born."

"You mean they nearly killed her?" Eris gasped.

"Nearly," Edmund smirked. "Luckily, we managed to call in some experts from the College to disprove the crazed notion that she was some kind of demon-child."

"And… you think they will try it again?" Eris mumbled.

"It certainly would not surprise me."

"Do you think they will succeed?"

"I will do what I can to prevent it, but if it comes to it, I may have to let her go," Edmund sighed. "Useful as a girl of her intellect is to me, it is better her than House Tarantis as a whole."

"You would really just… just let them take her?"

Edmund's eyes narrowed, his patience waning. "You seem awfully concerned with my daughter, Miss Severin…" he sneered. "Why might that be?"

Oh no - She pushed too hard, caught his suspicion. She bottled her panic as best she could, searching desperately for an excuse.

"I, er… I just feel sorry for her," Eris smiled innocently. "She has so much on her shoulders, I just worry that it might be too much for her."

"Hm. Well, I suppose you are quite right to worry. She… does not cope particularly well with responsibility," Edmund sighed. "Several pieces of rather expensive furniture have had to be extinguished and replaced in wake of her tantrums."

Eris smirked subtly. The thought of Caesia having a temper tantrum was quite scary, but equally amusing. She suspected that she had not yet witnessed a total meltdown, but was rather glad in that respect.

"Poor girl…" Eris sighed affectionately.

"Yes, but enough about my daughter," Edmund muttered. "Say, your movements are rather rigid, is something the matter?"

"Um, no, I am simply not used to this sort of dancing," Eris mumbled, trying to cover up her anxiety. "You can take the lady out of Norskar, but you cannot take Norskar out of the lady!"

"True enough," Edmund sighed. "Might I ask, how did you come to get that garish scar?"

Eris' heart skipped a beat. She had forgotten completely about the scar, the thought had never crossed her mind that she'd have to explain it.

"It is from a… domestic incident. Yes, I would rather not go into it."

"I understand. Though I must admit, I had never taken the Severins for the wife beating types, never mind wife slashing. Well, not aside from late Lord Viktor…"

"Oh, no, I… it was back home. In Loftenheim," Eris stammered. "My father, he was… he was *very* abusive. It is why I came to Verdenheld."

"Oh, really?" Edmund mused. "Who is your father exactly?"

"You would not know him," Eris said quickly. "He was the Jarl's… advisor."

"You mean to say you are not of noble birth?"

"Um, sort of… I am loosely related to the Jarl. A cousin's cousin."

"Hm, you have done well to come this far, Miss Severin," Edmund smiled. "I am sorry to hear about your father."

"Well, I suppose fathers can just be like that sometimes," Eris grinned. "Cold, unloving, abusive…"

The music began once again to die down and Eris withdrew her hands with a plastic smile.

"A pleasure, Miss Severin." Edmund grinned, a look that still made Eris uneasy.

"Thank you, Lord Edmund," Eris chirped. "And give your daughter my best when you see her."

Edmund watched with narrowing eyes as Eris glided to her next partner. Her entire body relaxed as she fell into another man's grip. Strangely, that had been a more harrowing experience for her than being both slashed across the face and plunged off a cliff. Such is often the case when first meeting your friend's parents.

Caesia had found herself in the hands of Geldus Verden, the notorious lady-killer grandson of King Friedrich. To be in such hands was the dream of many noble girls, yet Caesia did not share that sentiment - she was not fazed by his chiselled features and flowing black hair. She never cared for looks when it came to men. In fact, she had little care for romance as a whole, far more interested in her books. Maybe that was why she had no friends…

Geldus had leapt straight into romancing her, not even an introduction exchanged either way, such was his way. Of course, Caesia was not some dense, pampered noble raised on tales of damsels and knights, who seemed to be Geldus' target demographic.

"You move like a fair petal on gentle wind, my sweet darling," Geldus admired. "So elegant, so beautiful. Your eyes, like the glistening dew of spring's dawn, could hold my gaze for an eternity."

There it was - the poetic, over the top compliment. It was always her eyes, people paid little attention to anything else. It is why she tried so hard to make them pop with her makeup, they seemed to be her only asset. Gaunt faced, flat chested and all-round feeble, she had little else going for her.

Geldus flung his arm around Caesia and drew her into a dip, leaning in close and gazing into her eyes. So distracted by wooing her was he, that he had completely overlooked the uniqueness of her eyes and thus her identity as a whole. She wondered if his cavity of a head would even have taken the hint were he to notice.

"My, I am flattered," Caesia smiled. "Tell me, what else about me leaves you so stricken by love?"

She figured she might as well have some fun with this. She would play a game - how many compliments could she fish out of Geldus before the music stopped? If she was going to get anything out of this conversation, a bit of fuel for her self esteem would be welcome.

"Well, where to begin?" Geldus mused. Caesia could see the cogs in his hollow brain working to pick out anything else redeemable about her. "You are enchanting, my lady, your voice a silken symphony to my unworthy ears. You call to me, your skin fair like the winter snow, yet you melt my longing heart. You are an angel and your presence is my virtue."

Caesia simply stared speechless into his eyes. He was exaggerating, right? He didn't mean any of that, he was just trying to get into her undergarments! But if that was the case, why did his words make her feel so warm? He was lying, surely, yet he had touched her heart all the same.

"But enough about you, let us speak of *us*," Geldus whispered seductively. "I would buy you a drink. The finest wine, a bottle to share…"

His melting eyes felt as if they were burning her beneath her skin as she began to grow hot at his words. Wait, why was this happening? No, there was no way she was letting this happen. Not on her life!

"A-as… invigorating as that sounds, my lord, I am afraid I am promised to another," Caesia stammered, pushing herself a greater distance from him.

Geldus grinned, undeterred. Her heart throbbed at his smile, her body reacting completely opposite to her mind. She despised this man, thought him rude and disrespectful, yet her body was drooling over him.

"What does it matter?" He urged. "Who need know? A simple excursion to my quarters and a night of drink and pleasure. Nothing more."

Caesia's cheek were swamped with a rosy red behind her mask, her mouth falling slightly ajar and her eyes trembling as his words sank into her mind. It was happening - she could feel his masculine allure seeping into her mind like a seductive parasite. She had to end this conversation quickly, before she found herself in this belligerent arse's bed! Damn her body's wants and desires, she was smarter than this!

"I will imagine I did not hear that, Lord Geldus," she mumbled, swallowing her flustered inner self and grinning sinisterly. "What would Lord Tarantis think if his daughter's petals were plucked so… dishonestly?"

Caesia watched with a smirk as the colour flushed from Geldus' face and his confident grin fell to a look of utter distress.

"You… you are-"

"Yes," Caesia smiled, the power rush of manipulation overtaking whatever this was that she was feeling. "And I do not think I must explain to you the connotations of your improper comments."

Good, she could feel her control rushing back as Geldus reeled back in frozen terror. All feelings of attraction subsided - he was on *her* strings now.

"In fact, perhaps there is something your could do for me?" Caesia sneered as she span elegantly beneath Geldus' hand. "A favour, one that might convince me to overlook this transgression. I am looking for somebody, the captain of the city guard. Him and I have business to conduct and I would surely appreciate it if you could help me."

"Of- of course!" Geldus smiled uneasily, terrified to make the wrong move in front of Lord Tarantis' daughter. "That is him over there, with the shaven head."

Geldus nodded towards a quite muscular man, less dapperly dressed than the other men at the ball and rather large in stature.

"Thank you, Sir Geldus," Caesia smiled as the music faded into a break. "And when you next see fit to woo a damsel, do make certain that you know their name."

Caesia stepped away from Geldus and onto a new partner, leaving the young lord with a harrowed look on his face. She had felt some crazy emotions back there, emotions she did not think she even had, and she hated herself for it. Was that what attraction felt like? No! No, no, no, absolutely not. That man was disgusting, abhorrent! She would never even consider… would she? She was terribly confused - this was why she hated romance, so complicated.

As she linked hands with the next man, she cleared her mind and plotted a route through the ballroom, towards the waiting captain. It was best that she forgot that altercation ever happened.

Eris peeled off from the crowd, giving an awkward smile to her most recent partner before turning away and rolling her eyes with a heavy sigh.

The dancing here was far too simple and dull - it was just the same few steps repeated over and over again. Dancing in Norskar had no formula, no premeditation. You just flailed around and made it up as you went along. Anyone could dance in Norskar, pretty dress or not, and it would be nothing short of fun.

Eris wandered over to the bar, finally beginning to get the hang of walking in her shoes.

"Good evening, sir," Eris smiled as she shuffled into a seat.

"Evening, ma'am," the bartender called. "What can I get for you tonight?"

"Just water, please," she figured it was best she stuck with something basic, being on a covert mission and all.

The bartender grabbed a jug of water and began pouring. "Who are you here with tonight, ma'am?"

"Oh, um…" Eris looked around the hall trying to come up with a name. "I'm with Lord Wall… door… Waldor Severin."

"Waldor Severin?" the bartender asked with an eyebrow raised. "I admit, I have never heard of such a man."

"Yes, he is quite a new… person."

"I see…" the bartender muttered, shoving the water across the counter and moving to attend to the next patron.

"Ah, good to see I'm not the only one out of place here!" called a woman from behind as Eris swigged her water.

Eris turned around to a blonde haired woman no older than thirty, uncomfortably squeezed into a white dress and disguised behind a simple black mask that drew attention to her burning red eyes.

"What do you mean, out of place?" Eris muttered, eyes narrowed in suspicion.

The woman moved to Eris' side and leant casually against the bar. "It's obvious. You look like a Nord, sound like a Nord and you drink like a

Nord. Don't get me wrong though, you look pretty convincing to the untrained eye."

Eris looked blankly for a moment into the woman's mesmerising scarlet pupils, which seemed almost to shift and dance like a blazing fire. Her eyes fluttered as she shook off her hypnotic daze, before putting on a welcoming smile.

"I suppose you're from Norskar too then?" she assumed, happy to finally find someone she could talk to like a real person.

"Beer, please!" the woman called to the bartender. "I am. You are?"

"Erisian." Eris smiled. "You?"

"Hera. So, what brings a Nord to a fancy Verdenheld ball?"

"I could ask you the same question," Eris smirked.

"Confidential then, understood," Hera chuckled. "I'm just here… experiencing the culture."

"Pretty crappy isn't it?" Eris laughed.

Hera took her beer from the barkeep and drank a delicate sip. "Yep. Everyone in this city is a selfish prick, or someone being trodden upon by them."

"You're from the chiefdoms aren't you?" Eris whispered with a knowing grin, knowing that familiar disgust well.

"Where else can you have an opinion without being executed?" Hera laughed. "Ah, what a better world it would be if everyone could live like us."

"Then there'd be nobody for people to hate," Eris sighed. "And these people love to hate."

"Do you ever wonder why more people don't fight back?" Hera probed. "Why the world tolerates this kind of bigotry?"

"I don't know. Maybe people just think there's another way," Eris smiled. "Violence solves a lot of things, but I don't think it'll solve this."

Eris' usual optimism garnered a look of disappointment from Hera. "No meaningful change has ever come about through peace," she muttered. "You really think these self absorbed bastards would ever allow change?"

"You think all out war is the only option?" Eris mumbled.

"I'm just saying… the only way to mould clay is to first soften it over the fire," Hera said darkly. "But I digress! Do you drink?"

"Not really…" Eris muttered. "I could never really get into beer."

"Well, I guess you haven't tried the stuff from Vilandil…" Hera grinned.

"Ah, I shouldn't. I promised-"

Hera gestured to the bartender, who grabbed a bottle and began pouring. "Surely one couldn't hurt, right?"

Caesia slipped nimbly through the crowd as the music died down, approaching the captain as he stepped away from his partner. She slid smoothly between the captain and his next partner, who scoffed and turned away in disgust.

"May I have this dance, Captain?" she asked confidently. "We have much to discuss."

The captain's eyes lit up nervously. "You, er... of course!" he stammered, taking Caesia's hand. "Forgive me, I did not expect someone so... young. Or female."

"Well, sometimes espionage requires a more delicate touch," Caesia smiled. "Do you have a name, Captain?"

"Yes, Antony Levelle."

"A pleasure, Mr Levelle," Caesia grinned. "Now, I believe you had-"

"Not here," Levelle snapped. "Nobody must hear us."

"Then we head onto the terrace," Caesia suggested.

Caesia glanced over at Eris, a look that quickly turned to a glare at the sight of her laughing hysterically with a woman, a tankard of beer in hand.

"Oh, for the love of…"

"Who is that?" Levelle whispered.

"Wait for me outside," Caesia growled as she pushed him away.

She parted ways with Levelle and waded to the edge of the ballroom, passing up offers to dance as she marched across the room and made towards the bar with darkness in her eyes.

"And then I was like, 'hyaaah'!" Eris yelled, making a cleaving motion with her hands. "And the dragon was like, 'raaah'! And then- and then Caesia was like, 'oh my God, Eris, you're super cool and really, really attractive'!"

Hera smirked as she took another sip of her beer. Unexpectedly, she was quite enjoying Eris' company. Where she had expected to find a daring, heroic adventurer, she had simply found a childish girl out for fun. She watched with a sigh as someone far less fun stormed into view behind Eris, signalling the end of their fun.

Caesia ground to a halt and eyed Eris up and down. Her cheeks were slathered with beer, with suds culminating around her mouth. Her eyes had sunken half closed, one eyelid slightly below the other. The idiot had gotten herself drunk, and in record time.

Upon noticing Caesia behind her, Eris jolted in surprise, her drink sloshing out of her tankard and dousing her dress. "Caesiaaa!" she sang merrily. "How's my favourite… person?"

Caesia glared silently into Eris' groggy eyes, her temper boiling at the sight of her friend's gleeful smile.

"Hey, d-did anyone ever tell you how hot you are when you're angry?" Eris mumbled. Hera giggled as Caesia's face went a bright red. "Oh yeah, this is Hera!"

Hera composed herself and gave Caesia a playful wave, a cheeky smirk plastered on her face.

"Caesia, you gotta try this stuff!" Eris urged. "It's from Vilandil and it tastes like *rainbows*!"

Caesia closed her eyes and clenched her fists as she took a deep breath. "Eris, we are going." she demanded.

"What?!" Eris gasped. "Come on, can't we stay a bit longer? I made a new friend!"

"We. Are. *Going*," Caesia growled, thrusting her finger to the terrace door.

"O-oooh!" Eris laughed. "Yeah, the... the thing!"

Caesia, completely tired of this idiocy, grabbed Eris by her arm and yanked her from her seat. They stopped for a moment as Caesia wrenched the tankard from Eris' grip and cast it onto the counter, before continuing on their way.

"Bye, Eris!" Hera called with a smug grin. "Be seeing you!"

Hera watched as Eris and Caesia disappeared into the crowds. She swigged down the rest of her beer and slid from her seat, ready to get to work. It was a shame that those two had to get mixed up in this - she liked them.

Caesia dragged Eris along the edge of the ballroom, receiving several looks both from concerned and confused partygoers.

"What did you tell her?!" Caesia hissed as she navigated to the exit.

"I-I was jusht telling her how we killed the dragon..."

Caesia grumbled a series of insults and complaints under her breath. She supposed it didn't matter too much if Eris went around bragging about that - who would believe her?

"I can't believe you," Caesia growled. "You had one job! In fact, no, you had no job! All you had to do was dance and somehow, in some total deficiency of mental functioning, you managed to fuck it up! Why did I even bring you along?"

Caesia burst out onto the moonlit terrace, frightening Levelle with her explosive exit. Ignoring him, she escorted Eris to the nearest water feature, releasing her and letting her stagger clumsily into it. She threw up her hands and thrust Eris' head into the once tranquil pool of water, holding her down with all her might as she kicked and flailed.

"Excuse me?" Levelle called.

"One moment," Caesia sighed.

She yanked Eris out of the fountain and let her fall to the ground, wheezing and panting for breath.

"Next fountain I put you in, you're not coming out!" Caesia spat, yanking off her mask and slamming it furiously to the ground.

Caesia left Eris' side and took a deep breath to compose herself. Eris, now slightly more sober, peeled off her soggy mask and leant back against the wall in contemplation. She was beginning to understand that she had a serious problem with self-control.

"Alright, Captain," Caesia muttered, unravelling her bun and letting her hair sag to her shoulders. "What do you have for us?"

"O-oh, yes!" Levelle stammered. "We've had a bit of a… suspicious development in the missing inquisitors case."

"I'm all ears."

"Alright. Once we'd finished sweeping the sewers, one of the lads approached me, said he didn't recognise one of the guards."

"Is that unusual?" Caesia asked.

"The guards in each district are pretty tightly knit. I asked around and one of the boys said they knew him - man by the name of Cedric Bechard."

"And what does that mean to you?"

"Not much to me, but I'm told he lives at the edge of the Palace District, in an area the locals call 'Splutter Alley'."

"Splutter Alley?" Caesia scoffed. "Let me guess, there's a lot of illness going around there?"

"Yeah, but the same can be said for all the bad parts of town," Levelle sighed. "He lives at number four, Aven Road."

"Number four, got it," Caesia smiled. "Might I ask, why get a private investigator involved in all of this?"

"Well, with the suspect being so tightly linked with some of the guards, I don't want to risk making this public," Levelle explained. "It only takes one corrupt or sympathetic bloke to blow the whole thing."

"Makes sense," Caesia smiled. "Thank you, Captain."

"No problem, Miss," Levelle grinned. "Good luck with Cedric."

Levelle made back for the ballroom and Caesia recounted the information once more in her head, before wandering to Eris' side.

"Enjoy the party?" she smirked, leaning up against the wall beside her soggy friend.

"Sorry…" Eris mumbled.

"Forget it," Caesia smiled. "Just don't do that again, alright?"

"Yes, ma'am," Eris sighed. "Meet any interesting people?"

"A few here and there," Caesia muttered, shaking herself off as she became slowly flustered again. "N-nobody too stand-out, really. You?"

"Yeah… I always imagined your father would have a receding hairline," Eris said smugly.

"Wait, what? He's here?!" Caesia hissed. "You're joking."

"We danced, it was really uncomfortable. Funny though, he told me you were still at the College."

"I'd expect as much, he always cared more about his image than anything else," Caesia muttered. She wouldn't let his presence faze her, she was beyond him. "I'd best not think about it, we ought to get to work."

"Agreed," Eris declared, springing to her feet. "Let's go find this Cedric guy."

Eris sprang up and they headed across the terrace, towards the still unguarded steps. Eris stumbled as she started after Caesia, still rather tipsy.

"You absolute lightweight," Caesia chuckled. "What the hell got you drunk that fast?"

"Vilandil Brew…"

"No bloody wonder!" Caesia laughed. "That's the most alcoholic stuff in all of Verdenheld! I'm sorry to say, but you've probably just shaved several weeks off your life."

"Oh… worth it," Eris smiled.

"Moron."

Chapter Five - Under Prying Eyes

Eris came suddenly to a halt as they stepped into Victory Plaza. Caesia followed her blank stare to the spy's abandoned house, outside of which stood a man banging impatiently on the door. He was no peasant - his green tunic clean and wrought with patterns of yellow thread. Green and yellow however, were colours quite familiar to Caesia.

"Who's that?" Eris whispered.

"I don't know…" Caesia muttered. "But he's dressed in House Lacroix colours. Could just be a coincidence though."

"Guess we might as well go talk to him. It's not like he's gonna kill us or anything."

"Unless he's some kind of master pyromancer in disguise, I believe you're right," Caesia said. "Let's see what he has to say for himself."

They hurried across the square, which was nigh empty now that night had begun to fall. The last light of day was slipping behind the golden rooftops as the last few peasants hurried home for the night. Bar the distant patter of homebound footsteps, an eerie silence hung over the plaza.

As they approached, the man at their door turned to meet them, beckoning to them with a wave as he walked to meet them.

"Lady Caesia?" he smiled, receiving a begrudging nod from Caesia. "Package for you, ma'am."

The man hauled a bland, featureless box from his side and presented it to her. It was roughly the size of her torso, a size that had her concerned that she would topple over at the weight.

"Um… get this, Eris?" she said with a cheeky smile.

"Anything for you, your grace," Eris muttered.

Eris hauled the package out of the deliveryman's hands. It was quite heavy, but nothing she couldn't handle. Though, she supposed it might have snapped Caesia's brittle legs should she have tried to carry it.

"Lady Amelie sends her regards, my lady," The deliveryman smiled, handing her an envelope marked House Lacroix's seal before turning and hurrying away into the night.

"Great," Caesia groaned. "I suppose you'd best chuck that in the nearest alley."

"Oh, lighten up!" Eris laughed. "Your mum's giving us free stuff! What's not like?"

"I don't need her help," Caesia growled, flinging open the door with a whining creek and heading inside.

"Don't know if you noticed, but her help is kinda the only reason we're here," Eris smirked. "We're keeping this package."

Caesia glared back at Eris for a moment, before retracting her scowl with a heavy sigh. Eris was right, she was being petty. No amount of help would change anything between her and her mother, but that did not mean she had to reject it.

"Fine," Caesia growled, twisting back around and ascending the rickety staircase in a series of chilling creaks.

Eris followed her up the stairs with a triumphant smile and headed into the spy's hideout, where the pungent stench of rotting flesh was beginning to overtake the building.

"Oh, God!" Caesia gagged as she stepped through the door. "If it's all the same to you, I'd rather not come back here again."

"I-I'll second that," Eris spluttered, dumping the package onto the bed in an explosion of dust.

Caesia delicately peeled open the envelope and presented a folded sheet of expensive parchment, clearing her throat before reading it aloud.

"Dear Caesia, I could not help but notice how terribly underequipped you were for physical confrontation. I have provided more appropriate apparel for the occasion and wish you the best of luck. Yours sincerely, Amelie Tarantis."

"Apparel?" Eris asked eagerly. "That's armour, right?"

Caesia sighed in disappointment at Eris' lack of education. "Yes. Armour and clothes."

Within a split second, Eris was feverously shredding apart the packaging. After a series of lightning tears, she flung the box open and peered inside. Her face immediately dropped as she reached into the box.

From the package, she pulled an open face leather helmet. It was expertly crafted, slender and light yet nonetheless protective with sleek flaps falling from the sides.

"A helmet?" she groaned.

"What's wrong with a helmet?" Caesia asked.

"I don't like them," Eris sighed. "They're tight and itchy."

"There is no way you're going out there without that helmet," Caesia demanded. "You wouldn't have that bloody scar if you'd just worn one in the first place!"

"Make me!"

Caesia flicked up her hand and propelled a small, shimmering green disc into Eris' forehead, which exploded into sparks on contact. Despite the pain that shot through her arm in doing so, Caesia smirked as Eris stumbled backwards and nearly tripped over herself.

"Ow!" Eris hissed, staggering against the wall. "Asshole."

"Wouldn't have hurt so much with a helmet on!" Caesia grinned.

Eris grumbled beneath her breath as she lifted her helmet to her head and tried to squeeze it on. However, so perfectly fitted was it to her head that she could hardly cram all of her hair into it.

"Let's see what else we have here," Caesia muttered. "A few more things for you it seems - a pair of steel shoulder pads and… a knife?"

"A knife?" Eris asked, just as confused as Caesia. "What in the stars do I need a knife for?"

"Backup, I guess," Caesia sighed, shifting Eris' equipment aside.

Eris approached, yanking off her stuffy helmet and inspected her new gear. She liked the pauldrons - a set of segmented steel plates, just as slender and aerodynamic as her helmet. The knife too was incredibly light, a rather skinny, minimalist little thing designed only with practicality in mind. It was good to see that Caesia's mother understood her desire for agility over all things.

"You're mum is awesome!" Eris laughed, picking up the knife by its mahogany handle.

"She's just trying to make up for her failures," Caesia sighed. "It's going to take a lot more than this, I assure you."

"You sure you're not being a little hard on her?" Eris asked, toying childishly with the knife. "I mean, it sounds like she's really trying to make amends."

"I want to think that… I wish I could," Caesia muttered, turning back to the box. "But it's just not that easy. Lying is in her blood. She's a manipulator, probably Verdenheld's best. Taking her words at face value is idiocy at its finest."

"I still think you should give her a chance," Eris insisted.

"I will… but I won't make it easy for her."

Caesia peered back into the box and brought out an absurdly thick, battered, old tome. Its pale brown cover was totally blank, like was always the case with old books. As she turned the cover, a small slip of paper shot from the pages and floated to the dusty ground. With a heavy sigh, Caesia bent down and delicately plucked the slip from the ground.

'I expect this will come in handy, courtesy of the College's restricted archive, A.' Restricted archive? That either boded extremely well or extremely poorly.

"What's that?" Eris asked as Caesia flicked through the pages.

"I don't… wait," Caesia gasped, her eyes bulging from her head. "Bloody hell! This thing has every abjuration spell known to man in it!"

The first page read 'Encyclopedia Abjuria', a copy of the tome in which the scholars of the College of Arcana recorded every abjuration spell ever discovered. She was blown away that even her mother could get her hands on the thing!

"Every spell?!" Eris laughed.

"Right down to the forbidden ones," Caesia chuckled. "God, this is… this is unbelievable!"

"You sure your mum's all that bad now?"

"Don't push it!" Caesia hissed. "This changes nothing."

As Caesia slammed the old tome shut, she noticed the glint of Eris' knife out of the corner of her eye. She span around to see Eris hold her knife up to her face, a mass of hair in her hand.

"What the- what are you doing?!" Caesia snapped.

"Haircut," Eris smiled, cleaving the knife through her hair and reducing her fringe to a fraction of its size. "I can't fit my head in my helmet, so I'm getting rid of some hair."

Caesia watched in disbelief as Eris discarded a bundle of hazel hair onto the ground. "You'd think there would be room up there without all that brain matter…" She muttered.

"Oh, come on!" Eris groaned. "I know I have a lot of stupid ideas, but would it kill you to cut me some slack?"

Caesia sighed as another shower of hair floated to the floorboards. That girl was unbelievable. She thought it pointless to object, turning instead back to the package. She reached in and yanked out some kind of clothing, which unravelled before her as it rose from the box.

It was a slim, beige coat, extending to a length that would fall just above her knees. It was nigh-weightless and tight fitting, in order to keep her light on her feet. A glance into the interior revealed thin, flexible leather padding around the shoulders and chest, attached to the fabric exterior. Protective *and* stylish - she liked it.

"How do I look?" Eris chirped, wedging her helmet over her head.

Caesia turned again and looked at Eris with surprise. Despite her primal method of cutting her hair, she had in fact pulled it off quite well. Her hair fell only part-way down her forehead, the rugged, frayed ends of her fringe protruding from beneath her helmet. Elsewhere, the scruffy hazel mess barely escaped its leather tomb, some loose strands narrowly making it to her jawline. Crude as she was in appearance, she certainly looked the part.

"I… retract my abuse," Caesia smirked. "You look awesome."

"Yeah, who's got brain matter now?" Eris laughed. "I feel so cool!"

"You know you're still wearing a dress, right?" Caesia chuckled as Eris span around gleefully.

"That I am," Eris chuckled. "On that note, let's get out of these damned corsets before I lose circulation in my boobs."

"Um, yeah… let's do that."

Eris skidded into the silent streets of the Palace District, strapping the last of her pauldrons over her shoulder. Caesia followed closely, squeezing her coat tight at the frigid touch of the night-time breeze. They started towards the district's edge, destined for Aven Road.

Caesia had demanded that they stay as close to the streetlights as possible. Eris could tell how paranoid she was, watching every alleyway like a hawk and breathing exclusively through her nose in fear of disease. Someone clearly didn't get out much.

"Aven Road," Caesia whispered as they turned onto the next street. "I guess it could be filthier."

On either side of the road were crudely cobbled together houses, with wooden platforms, boards and posts inelegantly tacked onto the dull stone buildings. From some hung improvised washing lines draped with faded clothes, while others sported clusters of overflowing bins dumped in the midst of their dying, drab gardens. It was a mess to be sure, but it didn't quite scream 'Splutter Alley'.

"I think it's quite charming," Eris smiled. "I mean, surely it can't be-"

Eris was interrupted as a woman in rags sprang from the shadows and drew a crude, rusted knife inches from her neck. Before a word could leave her wrinkled mouth, a crack of green lightning blasted her off her feet and sent her skidding on her back into the alley from which she came. Eris turned to Caesia, utterly taken aback by the rapid transpiration of the situation.

"Um, thanks…" she mumbled.

"No problem," Caesia sighed, shaking off the pain in her hand. "Guess Levelle wasn't kidding about the bad neighbourhood. If I catch the plague, I'll be livid."

"I'm not sure bad neighbourhoods and plague go hand in hand," Eris muttered.

"Maybe not, but if I see even a single rat, I'm leaving."

Eris watched over Caesia's shoulder as a tide of rats washed over a toppled bin in the alleyway behind her.

"If you say so…" she sighed.

They came to a stop in front of a house no different from the rest - ramshackle and run down.

"Number five," Caesia groaned, looking the filthy building up and down. "God, I barely want to touch the place…"

"Stars sake, could you be anymore stuck up?" Eris snapped. "You're not gonna die, you're not gonna catch a disease and stars above, your not gonna dirty your pretty new coat!"

Caesia stared at Eris blankly for a moment, an awkward silence hanging between them. Her eyes slowly sank as her mouth fell open, totally speechless.

"What?" Eris asked, worried by the hurt look on her friend's face. "You okay? I didn't mean-"

"Sorry, I... I wasn't ready for that," Caesia mumbled. "Sometimes I don't realise how petty I'm being."

"It's not your fault," Eris sighed. "Just try and cut down on the complaining will you? I'm trying to have fun here."

Caesia chuckled under her breath. Any other person would have tried to remain serious in this situation, but leave it to Eris to consider fun her top priority.

"Loud and clear," Caesia smirked, her mood growing lighter. "I'll keep it to myself next time."

"Cool!" Eris smiled. "I don't mind it normally, venting your stress and all that, but it's getting a bit much, you know?"

"I understand. Does this mean I'm still allowed to complain *sometimes...?*"

"Long as you don't go spitting on the poor like usual, be my guest."

"Do I do that?" Caesia asked, strangely surprised.

"All the time!" Eris laughed. "Anyways, how we going about this?"

Caesia shifted her attention back to the house. The building was no different from every other house on the street - run down, leaking at the seams and constructed half of scrap. It was baffling to think that not long ago they had been standing under a statue made of pure gold.

"I'm... not sure," Caesia mused. "With the element of surprise, we should be able to apprehend him with little issue."

"I'll get the door!" Eris declared.

With an ecstatic grin, Eris thundered into the miserable garden and leapt at the door, slamming her foot against it and battering it open. She swept into the house, sword drawn, where a man, woman and child jumped up from a dining table. The man ushered his startled son behind him and tugged his wife close.

"You're under arrest, Cedric!" Eris declared, aiming the tip of her sword towards his neck.

Caesia skidded through the doorway after Eris, hands raised and crackling with energy. She looked the terrified citizens up and down. They stood beside a dining table littered with morsels and scraps. All three of them were draped in ragged clothing, each one malnourished and pale. This didn't seem right.

"Wait... are you Cedric Bechard?" Caesia asked with uncertainty.

The man shook his head erratically. Caesia glanced to Eris, who was already beginning to back slowly towards the door. The two of them edged awkwardly out of the building and Caesia gently shut the door behind them.

"Oops," Caesia whispered. "That was awkward."

"Yeah... let's not do that again."

"Definitely. I swear he said fifth house."

"I, uh, wasn't listening that hard," Eris smiled apologetically.

"Oh, for- you know, I'm beginning to think we're not cut out for this line of work," Caesia sighed, kicking dirt from the unkempt garden as they headed back into the street.

"Ah, we can just knock."

"Knock?!" Caesia hissed. "You want to get him some chocolates as well?"

"Okay, okay, jeez," Eris groaned. "I'll go look through some windows."

Eris trailed off to the fourth house, wondering all the while what in Elaria chocolate was, while Caesia followed reluctantly in tow.

"Do be careful!" Caesia urged. "You can't let him see you."

"So what if he does?" Eris jeered. "Where's he gonna run?"

"He'd have time to get a weapon..."

"And how would that help him against me?" Eris laughed confidently. "I killed a dragon, I think I can take some bloke with a sword!"

Eris slumped down onto one knee and glanced cautiously through the window of the next house. The inside was no reflection of the building's exterior - the dining room ahead was by no means luxurious, but was well maintained and homely. The furniture was clean and the table was crowned with a bowl of shiny apples. Her gaze suddenly met that of a man as he stepped into the room. The balding, middle aged fellow stared at her for a moment before bolting for the backdoor.

"He saw me," Eris sighed, shuffling hurriedly to her feet.

"What?!" Caesia hissed. "You bloody- what's he doing?"

"He ran to the back!" Eris declared, racing off around the house. "You go that way! I'll head him off!"

She had vanished around the side of the building before Caesia could utter a single word of objection. With a reluctant groan, Caesia thrust back her arms and ignited them with energy, cringing at the subtle burning pain in her bruised hands as she ran into the alleyway. Her face dropped at the sight of the foul state of the place - upturned bins, sewage spilling from the drains, it was a nightmare! As she considered retreating back into the street rather than braving the sickening gauntlet before her, Cedric appeared ahead of her.

"Stop!" she yelled, tip-toeing carefully across the islands of stone amidst the sea of sewage.

Cedric span around and stared at her with panicked golden eyes. Caesia gasped and sheltered her face as Cedric launched a bolt of misty yellow ice down the alleyway and winced as all feeling left her feet.

Ice exploded into around her feet, her abrupt halt toppling her forwards. She threw out her hands to catch herself, only to shriek in horror as they plunged into a puddle of sewage water. Withdrawing them in a knee-jerk reaction, she slumped further still and landed on her forearms, a sharp pain spreading up her arms as her head fell on top of them and dunked into the sewage.

"Eris!" Caesia wailed, the ends of her hair sloshing in the revolting sea below. "I-I'm freaking out!"

Eris slid around the corner ahead of Cedric, sword and shield drawn. Cedric jumped in surprise and ground to a halt, reeling back his arm and slinging another bolt of ice down the alleyway. The bolt exploded against Eris' shield and consumed its battered wooden face in shimmering yellow ice.

"Freeze!" she yelled, grabbing her shield by its rim and hurling it down the alleyway.

The shield hurtled through the air, clanged off the wall and rang as it slammed against Caesia's forehead. Eris's mouth fell ajar as shards of ice exploded off her friend's forehead, knocking her head straight back into the water.

"Uh oh," Eris whimpered as Caesia's whole body surged with green lightning.

Caesia let slip a deafening shriek of pure horror that echoed across several city blocks. Cedric turned around only to see a wave of energy explode from Caesia's body like a supernova. He gasped as the water beneath him surged with electricity, shooting up into his body and knocking him out cold in seconds. Eris watched the whole scene unfold, wide eyed and having taken cover a few metres away. The stone walls were blackened by heat, several discarded planks were ablaze with roaring orange flame and Cedric's clothes had been burnt to crisp, the skin beneath having warmed by several tones. Eris now understood why Caesia's father had made such a big deal of her tantrums.

Eris edged cautiously back into the alleyway. Caesia, who was clawing herself slowly up the wall beside her, glared suddenly at her with utter contempt. She was dripping with sewage, her hair congealed and sagged and much of her upper body was covered in slimy water and filth.

"My bad," Eris smiled innocently.

Caesia stared for a moment in silence, her temper boiling behind her hateful, bagged eyes. She couldn't feel her feet and there was sewage up not only her sleeves, but also her nose. "Eris?" She whispered, her voice hoarse from screaming.

"Yeah…?"

"Please remove me from this ice before I turn that fucking smile to ash," Caesia growled.

Eris dropped her smile and scraped her shield from the ground in a hurry. Caesia grew confused as Eris turned around and approached Cedric, clutching her shield in either hand. She gasped as Eris raised it over her head and cleaved it down.

"Eris, no!"

Eris slammed the face of her shield into the back of Cedric's head with a thud that echoed into the empty street. The ice around Caesia's feet turned suddenly to frigid water and rushed away into the cobblestones.

"Oh…" Caesia mumbled. "Is he okay?"

Eris knelt down and extended her palm in front of Cedric's face, feeling a subtle gust of warm air.

"Yep," She chirped, springing to her feet.

"Good… but please, don't do that again," Caesia muttered. "And for the record - you're on two strikes now. You've had the spider and the sewage, one more and I'll fry your brain and find a new friend."

"Yeah, like you could ever find another person who'd put up with your complaining," Eris smirked, before immediately shrinking away under Caesia's iron glare. There was something about her gaze that could be particularly menacing when she wanted, it must have been in the Tarantis blood. "Hey, er… what in the stars was that anyway?"

"You mean that thing I just did?" Caesia smirked. "When I lose control of my emotions, my essence tends to go a little… crazy."

"Is… that a green essence thing or do other mages do that too?"

"It's called volatilis disorder, commonly developed by mages who experience a great deal of trauma at a young age. It essentially causes a mage's essence to become linked to their emotional state. You probably noticed how my lightning bolts tend to blast people off their feet when I'm angry or scared, and how my shields were far more powerful when we fought the dragon."

"Huh, that explains a lot," Eris muttered. "Why'd you never mention it before?"

"It just hadn't come up in conversation. I didn't think it would be necessary to mention it, but today has proved otherwise."

"Guess so," Eris smirked. "Could you, uh… get his arms?"

"I would, but my hands…" Caesia mumbled.

"Oh, boo hoo!" Eris sneered. "Poor Caesia's pathetic little hands are too fragile! How will she cope? Grab the damned arms, faker!"

Caesia chuckled quietly. "Guess I could only keep up the charade for so long," she sighed, moving to grab Cedric's arms. "I just can't believe it took you so long to catch on."

They hauled Cedric up between them and began shuffling towards his house. Caesia gritted her teeth as her sensitive hands pressed against his cold skin. She may have used the pain as a means to avoid responsibility, but it certainly wasn't manufactured.

"I had a hunch, but I didn't want to say it," Eris muttered. "Because unlike you, I'm a decent person."

"Which is both your greatest strength and weakness equally!" Caesia smiled. "In that way, I like to think we compliment each other."

"By me being nice and you being an asshole?" Eris smirked, an eyebrow raised.

"Precisely," Caesia grinned. "Thus, we come prepared for every occasion!"

Eris sighed heavily. "How come you're so proud of that?"

"If I learnt anything from my parents, it's that it's important to be proud of who you are, even if you are a prick."

"Wise words indeed, Miss Tarantis," Eris chuckled.

"Don't call me that," Caesia muttered. She hated the sound of her surname, it sent chills up her spine.

Eris kicked in the door and carelessly dumped Cedric onto the ground. Caesia simply rolled her eyes and chose to ignore it, having little energy left for complaining.

The next ten minutes were spent by Eris crudely tied Cedric to a chair with a variety of clothes and belts pulled from his drawers. Caesia had retreated to the fireplace to warm up after washing the sewage from her hands and replacing the soggy bandages. She watched in amusement as Eris dismantled Cedric's well kept house bit by bit, breaking only one plate before stepping back to admire her handiwork.

"Please, my lady, don't overwork yourself," Eris muttered, rejoining Caesia.

"Hey, that man is heavy!" Caesia snapped. "And I'm not built for manual labour."

"True, you do have the body structure of a snake," Eris grinned.

"What's that supposed to mean?"

"Skinny and big-headed."

"Well played," Caesia smirked. "Shall we begin?"

"One moment…"

Eris reached across the dining table and plucked a glossy red apple from the bowl in the centre. A garish smile grew across Caesia's face as Eris admired it.

"What?" Eris asked suspiciously.

"Nothing… just amused at your poor choice of apple," Caesia mumbled, her mouth quivering as it tried to curl against her will.

"I can eat whatever damned apple I please!" Eris growled.

She bit stroppily into the apple, cleaving a huge chunk from its side. Caesia's smile grew ever wider as Eris' face gradually contorted into a confused scowl. Her senses were overwhelmed by a horrible bitterness, the likes of which she had never experienced. Caesia burst into hysterics as Eris spat a glob of chewed wax onto the floor, coughing and spluttering like she had taken in a breath of smoke and ash.

"Oh, my God!" Caesia blurted. "You absolute moron!"

"Wha- what was that?!" Eris gasped, still spewing chunks of wax onto the floorboards.

"That, my poor, naive friend, was a wax apple," Caesia chuckled.

"Wax?! Like candles?" Eris hissed. "What- I don't… why?!"

"They're for decoration!" Caesia laughed.

"I hate Verdenheld."

With a final chuckle, Caesia wandered to Cedric's side and ignited her fingers with electricity. "Ready?" she asked.

With a nod from Eris, she prodded Cedric in the side. A jolt of energy shot through him and he awoke suddenly from his slumber. Squirming erratically, he looked desperately around the room, before glaring defiantly at Caesia.

"I-If you think you'll get anything out of me-"

"Ah!" Caesia interrupted, jabbing him again with her electrified finger. "You'll talk when you're asked too."

"You-" Cedric cringed as Caesia's finger dug into his side again.

"Did I not make myself clear?" Caesia hissed. "Now, let's make this quick. We know you infiltrated the guard's investigation of the recent murders. Why?"

Cedric was silent. After a soundless moment, Caesia turned with a sigh to Eris, who was stalking around the room staring at the floorboards.

"Looks like we're doing this the hard way," Caesia sighed. "Eris, break something."

"Hm?" Eris mumbled, looking up obliviously from the floor.

"Break something!"

"Ah, my specialty!" Eris smiled.

She walked into the kitchen and surveyed her surroundings. After a lengthy time of indecisiveness, Eris shrugged and cleaved the entire drying rack onto the floor. Caesia winced as a myriad of plates, bowls and cutlery struck the ground with a deafening crash.

"I said break something, not *everything*!" Caesia snapped. "Whatever…"

She turned to Cedric, who glanced up at her with a careless expression. Caesia took a moment to consider her options. As much as she wished to go easy on the man, no agent of the Oppressor would budge under niceties. Perhaps it was time to get serious.

"Look, if you don't tell us what we need to know, things are going to have to get ugly!" she hissed. "What's going to happen is I'm going to paralyse you and render you numb from the neck down. Then, you'll watch as my friend here breaks every bone in your miserable body!"

Eris looked up from the floorboards with a startled look on her face. She didn't sign up for this.

"You're bluffing," Cedric growled. "You're obviously nothing more than a prissy noble girl. Hell, you'd probably cry at the sight of dust!"

Caesia paused in calculation. She had desperately hoped that he wouldn't see past her bluff. In hindsight, it wasn't a particularly believable one - he knew from her accent alone that she didn't have the guts for torture. She was beginning to realise that she wasn't as good at subterfuge as she thought.

Her thoughts were cut short at the sound of a loud bang behind her. She swivelled around to see Eris cast aside a shard of floorboard, which bowled down several pots and pans on the other end of the room. Caesia watched in disbelief as Eris yanked a thick stack of dusty paper from the ground.

"For you, my lady!" Eris smiled, presenting the stack to Caesia.

"How the hell did you find these?!" Caesia gasped.

"Rule of thumb - when somebody's hiding something, you always gotta check beneath the floorboards."

"You and your bloody stories…" Caesia chuckled, taking the stack and batting off the caked layers of dust. "Let's have a look at these, shall we?"

Caesia glanced up with grin, watching as Cedric squirmed in his seat. He was panicking, she could see it in his eyes. She looked back to the papers and began to skim read them one by one. As she progressed further into the stack, a disappointed frown soon began to take shape.

"Damn it… let him go," Caesia groaned, casting the papers aside.

"Seriously?" Eris scoffed.

"Yes. This man is part of some 'Resistance', helping abhumans escape the Inquisition. He's not our enemy."

Apprehensively, Eris slid her sword from its sheath and slit the clothes binding Cedric. She then paused in realisation that she had just cut several of Cedric's shirts in half.

"You're... letting me go?" Cedric mumbled, shaking off his hands. "No torture? No execution?"

"I suppose we didn't make our purpose clear," Caesia sighed. "We're not with Verdenheld, nor do we serve its interests. We couldn't care less about your Resistance."

"I see... so, you'll leave me be?"

"Soon. First, I need to know - what were you doing infiltrating the guard's investigation?"

"I can't say."

"You have to!" Eris urged. "We're investigating... well, it's more important than you could imagine."

"You're lucky enough that I don't call the damned guards after what you did to my house!" Cedric hissed. "You snapped my floorboards, trashed my kitchen, broke all of my plates and ate one of my bloody wax fruits!"

"Yeah... sorry about that," Eris mumbled.

"Look, all that aside, you have to help us," Caesia insisted. "I believe an abhuman may be responsible for a... rather gruesome murder, just off Victory Square."

"Murder?"

"Wait, wait, wait," Eris interrupted. "Since when did you jump to that conclusion?"

"I've been giving it a lot of thought. Those massive puncture wounds line up with an arachni, while the clear use of stealth could suggest either an arachni or ulkar. Either way, if word gets out about it, which it will, the Inquisition will scour this city clean."

Cedric was silent in contemplation. Caesia knew that he cared about abhumans above all, that he would have to help.

"Please, do the right thing!" Caesia urged. "If we can get to the bottom of this and bring in the murderer, we can avoid an inquisitorial purge."

Cedric sighed defeatedly. "You're right... I'll tell you what I know," he mumbled. "I was there to misdirect their search, keep the guards from digging too deep."

"You know what happened to the inquisitors?" Eris gasped.

"No. At least, I don't think so," Cedric sighed. "But, there are... things, in the sewers. Things that the guard can never know of."

"Cedric, we need to know," Caesia said gently.

"Arachni. A whole hive of them. The Resistance keeps them fed, alive, keeps the guard off their scent."

"A whole hive in the sewers?!" Caesia gasped. "If the guard knew about this-"

"They would slaughter them all," Cedric mumbled. "You... you won't tell anyone of this, will you?"

"Of course not," Caesia smiled. "But, what of the killings, the disappearances? You think it could be their handiwork?"

"I... I can't imagine why they would jeopardize their safety like this... it can't be them."

"Alright. Thank you, Cedric," Caesia sighed, turning to Eris. "We've got all we need. Let's go."

Caesia and Eris stepped out of the house, leaving Cedric looking blankly around his upturned kitchen. They wandered once again into the fiery hearth of the streetlights, and the cold breeze of night.

"Okay then," Caesia muttered. "Let's get moving."

"You've got a plan?" Eris asked.

"Slow down! First, let's just go over what we know. The arachni are presumably killing people in the sewers, which we can quite easily link to Valkyr, what with his appeal to the other races."

"So we're looking in the right place after all," Eris grinned. "One step closer to catching that bastard!"

"Yes, though the question now is how do we act on this information?"

"We could go see what's going on down there," Eris suggested.

"Are you mad?" Caesia hissed. "We'd be murdered in an instant!"

"Only if the arachni are responsible, and I don't think they are. Why would they live in peace for hundreds of years and then suddenly start murdering people? It doesn't add up!"

"Hm... that is a good point," Caesia mused. "Why would the arachni jeopardize the last safe haven for their race?"

"The only way to know is to ask," Eris insisted. "Maybe they'll be willing not to kill us if we show them we don't hate abhumans."

"I hate everything about that plan, but you're right," Caesia sighed. "We need to see the other side of this story."

"Yep, and I reckon the best place to start is right over there."

Eris gestured to a filthy, rusted sewer grate across the street. Caesia shuddered at the thought of what revolting stuff could have flowed through that grate. She watched apprehensively as Eris moved over and stuck her fingers under it without a care.

"Hold on, how are we even going to find the arachni?" Eris muttered as she wrenched off the grate. "I mean, they're not exactly gonna be seeping from the walls... I hope."

"I don't know, I guess we'll just have to hope we run into one."

"They've hid for hundreds of years, you really think we'll just run into one?" Eris asked doubtfully.

"Perhaps I should have put more emphasis on 'hope'."

Eris yanked off the grate, the removal of which released the choking stench of raw sewage into the street. Eris' nose nearly turned inside out as it scrunched up, overloaded by the potent stink from below.

"Eergh, that's revolting!" Caesia blurted, wrapping her hands around her mouth. "I can't believe I'm doing this."

"Yeah, your shoes are gonna be ruined!" Eris sneered, playfully elbowing her friend.

"Don't get me started."

"You sure you're okay with this?" Eris asked. "You seemed pretty spooked by regular spiders, let alone human sized ones."

"I might scream internally, but I'd like to think I can control myself," Caesia mumbled, little faith in her own words.

"If you say so," Eris sighed. "But I don't wanna have to drag your ass out of there if you faint."

"I'll be fine," Caesia smiled. "Well, not really, but fine enough."

Caesia peered cautiously into the manhole, into the complete blackness below.

"Uh... you first?"

"No way! You're the one with the light."

Caesia sighed anxiously and stepped onto the cold, rusty ladder, cringing at the frigid touch of the iron bars against her feeble skin. She moved gradually down it, checking her back with every step. Eris followed closely behind, sliding the grate back over them as she clambered into the darkness.

"This is just great," Caesia groaned, stepping off the ladder and into the lightless abyss. "It's cold, wet and literally stinks like shit. Bet you feel right at home."

"Alright, I'll give you that one," Eris chuckled.

Eris stepped off the ladder behind Caesia, who was stood trying to recall the right spell. Eris sniggered quietly at Caesia's glowing green pupils floating in the darkness, her eyes the only thing visible in the entire tunnel.

"What?" Caesia snapped.

"Ah, nothing," Eris smirked.

Caesia lifted her hand and opened her fist, igniting a dim, green flame in her hand and illuminating the aged grey stonework around them up to a couple of metres. So weak was it that it didn't even hurt her arms to maintain it.

"I thought that would be a bit brighter," Eris sneered.

"Oh, hush," Caesia snarled. "Just be happy I'm casting spells at all with these arms! Any brighter and it'll mean a constant burning sensation in my hand."

"We could've just brought a torch…" Eris muttered.

"Do you have a torch?"

"No, but-"

"Then zip it."

They started off into the darkness, wandering along the stone platform at the tunnel's edge with not a clue where they were nor where they were going. Caesia struggled to keep herself from complaining about their utterly filthy surroundings, which were internally freaking her out. She had to fight through it, to make do on her promise and resist complaining.

"So, what happens if the arachni just say 'yeah, we're working with Valkyr'?" Eris asked. "Because on scale of one to ten of things I want to fight, I'd place hundreds of arachni at a solid two."

"Well, that depends on if they let us leave," Caesia sighed. "Either we get out and alert the army, or we don't and get slaughtered."

"They must really hate you guys, huh?" Eris muttered.

"Yeah, that's just what happens when you launch a holy purge of an entire people. Doesn't make a great impression."

"You people are idiots," Eris smirked. "Hey, think fast!"

Eris plunged her foot into the murky water and kicked sewage into Caesia's path. Caesia let slip a squeal as sewer water splattered her coat, looking down at her quivering legs with her mouth ajar. Her gaze snapped quickly to Eris and turned foul as she reeled back her arm.

"You little-"

Caesia's words turned to a pathetic wheeze as the back of her hand struck Eris' arm with little force. Her fingers were overcome with a burning pain as the bruised skin battered the hard leather of Eris' armour. She span away from Eris in an attempt to hide the searing pain she was experiencing, clearly to no avail judging by her friend's demeaning laughter.

"That's it! Strike three!" Caesia growled, her eyes flaring bright as crackling light spread across every inch of her body.

"Woah, woah, that was barely anything!" Eris stammered. "That was at the *most* strike two and a-"

A lightning charged punch smashed Eris' shoulder and sent her spinning away into the wall. Caesia growled with fury and lunged after her, only to suddenly pause. The energy coursing through her body simmered away as the distant patter of water echoed down throughout the tunnel.

"You hear that?" Eris whispered anxiously, stumbling upright.

Caesia surveyed the tunnel to no avail. She ignited a flame in her other hand and hurled it down the tunnel, watching the walls carefully as it soared weightlessly along the water.

"Huh, guess we're fine," Eris smiled.

Caesia was unconvinced. She swivelled around to check behind them, where her eyes met a cluster of eight piercing red eyes in the darkness.

Within a split second of being seen, the arachni launched itself from the ceiling with a blood-curdling screech and lunged like a blur at Caesia. Caesia screamed in terror and went up spontaneously in green light, shrieking as she reappeared ankle deep in the sewage stream. Eris slid her sword from the sheath and swung in panic at the arachni, which crawled up the wall and vanished into the darkness of the ceiling before Eris could even get a good look at it.

"Get down here!" Caesia yelled to Eris. "We need to keep away from the walls!"

Eris leapt down into the stream, showering Caesia's coat with an explosion of water.

"Sorry!" Eris smirked, raising her shield in readiness.

"You complete and utter- There!" Caesia snapped, as the arachni launched itself again from the ceiling.

Rather than try and block eight scything legs, Eris reeled back to allow Caesia some space. Caesia swung back her arm and launched a feeble lightning bolt at the arachni, who sprang onto the wall and kicked off it, towards her. Caesia threw up a shimmering green barrier between them, which the arachni smashed into before retreating back into the shadows.

"Argh, that… that hurt," Caesia wheezed, her arms stinging at the sheer force with which her shield was struck.

The arachni descended from the ceiling directly above them, landing between them as they sprang out of its way. Eris leaned back, narrowly dodging a cleaving blow from the arachni's bladed arm, while a strike from its other arm sliced across the front of her shield, tearing a deep scar across it.

It drew back the eight spider-like legs protruding from its back and made a lunging strike towards Eris. Sensing Caesia's approach by the hairs on its legs, it ceased the attack and sprang onto the ceiling. A shower of dust and debris rained over them as the arachni slammed its legs through the stonework for grip.

"This is a battle of attrition," Caesia hissed, the energy around her hands beginning to crackle more violently as she became further agitated. "And we've no chance of winning it!"

"Then let's cut out the attrition part," Eris growled. "We've gotta make a decisive move!"

"I might have an idea, but I can't afford to say it out loud," Caesia whispered. "On my go, jump out of the water."

"And leave you alone with it?" Eris scoffed.

"Just trust me!"

Caesia and Eris waited in a nervous silence as the arachni stalked through the darkness. At the faint scratching of poising legs, Eris sprang out of the water. The arachni lunged at Caesia, who threw up her arms in fear and blinked a metre back. As the arachni looked up with irritation, Caesia slammed her arms into the water.

Faster than even the arachni could gauge, intense lightning surged into the stream, electrifying the water. Electricity rushed up the arachni's legs, who shook and convulsed at its touch. Caesia screamed in agony as she pumped more and more electricity into the stream, her arms on fire with searing pain. As the arachni staggered to its knees, Caesia withdrew her trembling arms and wiped the blood from her nose She winced at the stinging of her hands as they touched her face.

Despite her friend's fragile state, Eris launched into the water and held the tip of her sword to the arachni's neck. Finally, she could get a close look at the creature.

In the darkness of the sewers, most prominent was her ghostly white skin, giving way for jagged black chitin formed like crude blades all along her forearms and calves. From her back burst eight insectoid legs, armoured like her arms and legs and each wielding the piercing might of lance. As for her face, which looked up at Eris with an wobbly, apologetic smirk, she was fairly unremarkable. Her face was round and fairly plump, sporting a dishevelled mass of black hair formed like a bush around her head. The tangled mess obscured two of the eight blood red eyes strewn across her forehead, all of which stared wide open as she bore her maw of razor teeth in a smile.

"W-well played," she spluttered, her voice hoarse and words somewhat slurred. "Don't suppose you'd accept an apology?"

"I could be convinced to," Eris muttered. She turned to Caesia, who nervously approached. "You alright?"

"I'll live," Caesia mumbled, her arms still shaking.

"So, let me get this straight," the arachni smirked, propping herself into a sitting position with her hind legs. "You - two humans - are not gonna kill me?"

"We're here to talk," Caesia sighed. "We're investigating the death of some inquisitors in the sewers. Not that we're with them, I might add."

"Inquisitors?" the arachni muttered, shuffling clumsily to her feet. "Nah, I think I'd remember eating an inquisitor."

"So you're the one responsible for all the other 'disappearances'?" Eris asked cautiously.

"Guess so," the arachni grinned, shrugging nonchalantly. "Humans are like fine dining down here, considering I gotta live off rats. They're just... irresistible!"

Eris shuffled uncomfortably at the hungering look in the arachni's trembling eyes. "Right... and why have you just started doing this?"

"Well, long story short, I got exiled and then I got hungry. Figured I may as well eat humans since nobody's gonna tell me otherwise. And let me tell ya, you guys have no idea just how mouth wateringly delicious you really are!"

Eris turned to Caesia with a sigh. "So all the other disappearances had nothing to do with the arachni. It was just..."

"Maeve," the arachni smiled, happily baring her unnerving maw of razor teeth.

"So, the inquisitors aren't linked to the other disappearances," Caesia sighed. "I'm not sure if that makes things better or worse... If Maeve here knows nothing about them, maybe we ought to ask the other arachni. I imagine they keep close tabs on goings on in the sewers."

"But how do we find them?" Eris asked. "They could be anywhere and this city is massive!"

"I could take you there!" Maeve offered, springing up and down eagerly. "After all, I kinda owe you for not killing me!"

Caesia and Eris looked at each other in concern. It wasn't often that Eris shared Caesia's concerns for danger, which spoke volumes about how untrustworthy Maeve really appeared.

"Okay..." Caesia sighed. "But if you try anything-"

"Yeah, yeah," Maeve jeered. "Don't worry, I'll behave. First though, we gotta stop by my place. I need a drink!"

Caesia rolled her eyes. "Fine, but you're taking it to go."

"Okay, follow me!" Maeve exclaimed, skipping off down the tunnel and twirling with glee.

"Not so fast!" Caesia called. "We can't all see in the dark."

Maeve paused with a deathly expression on her face and came back trudging back, muttering angrily to herself. "Why are you humans so shiiiiit?" she groaned.

"You're weirdly energetic for someone who just got electrocuted," Caesia observed, watching Maeve's feet drag and her arms flail as she walked. "You're drunk aren't you?"

Maeve giggled playfully. "You can tell?"

"Are we seriously throwing our lot in with an alcoholic spider woman after she just tried to eat us?" Eris whispered to Caesia.

"What other choice do we have?" Caesia muttered. "And I wouldn't bother with whispering, arachni have heightened senses - she can totally hear you."

"Yep!" Maeve chirped. "And she wasn't wrong!"

"So, Maeve…" Caesia called as they started into the darkness. "How long have the arachni been down here?"

"Well, technically I'm not supposed to talk about it… but I don't care," Maeve said smugly. "I think it's been, like, three hundred years or something."

"Three hundred years?" Caesia scoffed. "That must mean they arrived at the end of the purge!"

"Purge?" Maeve asked, stricken for a moment with confusion. "Ah, you mean the war."

"No, the purge. Verdenheld's genocide of you people?"

"That what they tell you?" Maeve laughed. "Yeah, it was like, sixty years of war. Loada people died."

Caesia was utterly taken aback. "Sixty… I'm sure I've never heard of that war."

Maeve grinned mockingly. "Is it so crazy to think that the humans might've, you know…"

"Stricken it from history…" Caesia gasped. "No, that's impossible."

"Is it though?" Maeve chuckled. "I mean, I know I'd wanna forget the bloodiest war in history if I started it."

Caesia was blown away by this revelation, that such was the sheer power of Verdenheld that they could erase an event from history entirely. It was in no way a surprise, but it opened up so many questions - What else could they have hidden? How many more gruesome holy wars could they have waged over the past four hundred years?

"How bloody?" Eris asked, intrigued to know the extent of brutality that the kingdom was capable of.

"I dunno, do I look like some bookworm loser to you?" Maeve muttered, prompting Caesia to screw up her mouth in offence. "Ah, here we are!"

Maeve approached a small alcove in the tunnel wall and leaned over to a stubby candle. She scraped together the ends of two of her legs, lighting the candle with a spit of sparks. The candle swamped the alcove with fiery orange light, revealing a cluster of blood soaked webs. The ground was littered with half eaten, decomposing human remains and the walls were tinted crimson and spattered with oozing gore.

Caesia went immediately light headed, her stomach tumbling as she staggered back around the corner. Eris tried to avoid looking at any of the corpses, distracting herself instead with the intricate patterns of Maeve's web.

Maeve fished a bottle of cheap red wine from amidst her web and wrenched the cork off with her clawed fingers. She crouched down and lifted up the arm of a freshly deceased peasant, trickling some blood into the wine.

"Seriously?" Eris gagged.

"What?" Maeve scoffed. "I'll have you know, blood is quite nutritious!"

Eris had never felt so conflicted. One half of her mind wanted to kill Maeve on the spot, avenge all these innocent people. It was completely wrong to spare her, given her sick, murderous tendencies, yet the other half of her brain understood that her continued living was necessary to the greater good. It was a reality that made Eris sick, but one she had to accept.

Maeve threw back her head and swigged the wine piggishly. "Aight, let's go!" She chirped, smearing her hand over the wine dripping from her mouth and leaving a bloody trail across her cheek.

She snuffed the candle with one of her legs on her way out and strolled off into the darkness, humming a merry tune with no rhythm whatsoever. Meanwhile, Eris headed back around the corner to fetch Caesia.

"Caesia, we're going now," she said gently, turning the corner to find Caesia sat against the wall, arms around her knees.

"Okay, just give me one more minute," Caesia mumbled, not crying this time at least. "I'm never going to unsee that."

"Same," Eris sighed. "Don't know why I expected anything different."

"This has not been a good day for me, has it?" Caesia smirked, staring timidly at the ground. "How many times have I freaked out today?"

"Probably like, four?" Eris laughed. "I'm more worried that I *haven't* freaked out. What does that say about me?"

"That you're a whole lot more cut out for this than me…" Caesia muttered.

"Oh, don't you dare start this again," Eris groaned. "You know you're just as capable as me, just… in a slightly different way."

"I know," Caesia smiled. "I'm the brains, you're the brawn."

Eris pursed her lips in contempt. "You know, you really do have a talent for turning nice conversations into a means to insult people."

"You'd have it any other way?" Caesia grinned.

"Hey!" Maeve called from further into the tunnel. "Quit your whining and get moving!"

Caesia rolled her eyes and scrambled up, Eris patting her heartily on her back as they returned to Maeve.

"You guys talk too much," Maeve sneered, ushering them along with a sluggish wave of her hand. "Come on, we're not far."

Maeve guided them deeper into the sewers, until they came to a stop in the middle of a tunnel. Maeve scanned the walls carefully, scratching her head for a time before realising she was drawing blood with her claws.

"Am I missing something?" Caesia whispered anxiously. "If this is an ambush…"

"Yeah, there are hundreds of hungry arachni hiding in the bushes as we speak!" Maeve sneered. "Have some faith, girl."

Maeve shoved her hand down the back of her ragged pants and squirted a handful of slimy, wet silk into her hand. She glanced back at Eris and Caesia, who stared at her in disgust.

"Yeah, my webs come out of my ass," Maeve muttered. "I'm a fucking spider, what did you expect?"

She turned and hurled the glistening blob at a wall, causing it to shimmer and distort. The wall was engulfed with red light and dissipated, leaving a crumbling hole in its place.

"Clever…" Caesia mused. She had always appreciated illusion magic for its creative applications, but secret entrances always held their novelty.

"Where does it go?" Eris asked.

"Just some big ass cave," Maeve said. "Like, really big."

"I wasn't aware there were caverns beneath Aldreichen," Caesia muttered. "Another secret?"

"Yep, dunno why they covered it up though. I think they just forgot about by the time we moved in."

"Anything we should know before heading in?" Caesia asked.

Maeve swigged the last of her wine and hurled the bottle carelessly over her shoulder, shattering it against the wall. "Well, I'm… not very popular here, so they ain't letting me in. If you can get through the guards, you're on your own."

"Okay, but wait here for us, would you? We'll need a hand getting out of here."

"Fine…" Maeve groaned. "But if you're not back in an hour, I'll assume you've been eaten or something. Come on, I'll make sure they don't murder you instantly."

Maeve headed down into the narrow, rocky passage behind the wall, followed cautiously by Eris and Caesia. They worked their way through the winding tunnel and into an open cave, where two guards stood in wait with their spears already poised in defence.

The guards wore battered, ancient suits of black armour, crafted from chitin like that which coated their limbs. The armour, while worn and eroded, was finely crafted and fitted sleekly around the slender frame of its wearer. It was clearly designed purposefully for speed and agility, as were their spears of pure, glistening white - seemingly made up of hardened webbing moulded into sleek blades.

"Maeve?" one of the guards groaned. "How many times do we have to-" He paused in shock as Caesia and Eris appeared behind her with awkward smiles plastered on their faces. "Have you lost your mind?! You bring humans to our sanctuary?"

"You know the penalty for this, Maeve," the other guard snapped. "And the humans cannot be allowed to leave alive."

"Okay, okay! Chill out, Zavek," Maeve sniggered, clearly becoming increasingly tipsy. "My friends here just wanna talk to the Matriarch."

"Are you… You know that can't happen." Zavek growled.

"Why not? They won't tell anyone, right guys?" Maeve assured him, turning with a smile to Eris and Caesia.

"No, no, of course not!" Caesia stammered. "We don't want to bring your people any harm."

Zavek looked to the other guard and gestured him over to talk. Maeve looked up at the ceiling, pretending very poorly not to listen in on their conversation.

"You're not seriously thinking of letting them in, are you?" the other guard whispered. "They could endanger our entire race! Not to mention we'd be exiled…"

"If we let them in, there is no way they can escape should they prove to be enemies," Zavek explained. "We should let the Matriarch decide what to do with them."

"A sound plan. You know we can't let Maeve in though."

"I know, I know," Zavek sighed. "It's pretty hard to forget that little stunt she pulled."

Zavek turned back to Maeve and sighed. "We will grant your humans an audience with the Matriarch. Should they cause any problems, we hold the right to execute them."

"Great!" Maeve exclaimed, slapping Caesia and Eris on their backs. "Have fun, guys!"

Caesia shuffled nervously past Maeve as she skipped back up the passage. "She just gave them the right to execute us," she whispered.

"Yeah… she sure did," Eris sighed.

"You will follow me, humans," Zavek commanded. "Stray but a step from my path and I will cut you down. Understand?"

"Loud and clear," Caesia smiled anxiously.

Zavek turned with a hesitant nod and headed further into the cave. Eris and Caesia followed as perfectly as possible.

"If you don't mind me asking…" Caesia called as she caught up to Zavek. "What did Maeve do to get exiled?"

"She went against the will of the Matriarch and nearly revealed us to your kind… she has a talent for that, it seems."

"Is that why she drinks?"

"How should I know?" Zavek scoffed. "Though it seems she was drunk enough to lead you here. How did you come to know of this place anyway?"

"Cedric Bechard told us. He shared our worry about the disappearances in the sewers."

"Maeve…" Zavek growled. "So her responsibility for jeopardizing our secrecy is twofold. Typical."

"I assure you, we've no intention reveal your being here," Caesia urged.

"That remains to be seen. I find it hard enough to believe that you don't abhor us like the rest of your kind."

"Unlike most, we are not brainwashed by lies," Caesia said proudly.

"Perhaps," Zavek sighed. "It is not my place to decide. I leave that to the Matriarch."

The cave eventually ended at a crumbling ridge, giving way to an enormous cavern, somewhere near the size of Victory Plaza. Its every wall was draped with glistening sheets of silk, white as a Norskar winter. The whole cavern was littered with battered white pillars and ancient ruins, remains of a civilisation long past illuminated by flickering torchlight.

"Wow…" Caesia gasped, not only at the mesmerising walls of webs, but also the sheer amount of the well preserved ruins below. "These are Old Empire ruins! Aldreichen must have been built over another city! Th-this… this is the discovery of a lifetime!"

Her heart sank knowing that she could never speak of this to anyone, that she would have to live with knowledge that would shake the historical community to the core. It was commonly considered that civilisation in ancient times had never passed beyond the Bulwark Mountains, but this proved every theory of the Empire's territorial extent utterly wrong.

"Your people have many secrets lost even to themselves," Zavek muttered. "This isle was once the centre of the Empire's control over these lands. Now it commands the lands of an equally nefarious master."

"You know about the Old Empire?" Caesia asked excitedly.

"Our people remember a lot about your kind," Zavek sneered. "Nothing good."

Caesia shrank away, deciding it best to shut up. Her fascination with history wasn't worth igniting an argument.

Zavek led them down a narrow slope into the base of the cavern, to a crumbling building at its edge. The building's roof was collapsed but otherwise, was fairly intact. Caesia observed the pillared structure with intrigue, fascinated by the most well preserved piece of ancient history she had ever witnessed.

"You okay there?" Eris smirked, waving her hand in front of Caesia's face.

Caesia snapped back to attention. "Hm? Oh, I'm fine," she mumbled. "I'm just… a little excited, I guess. It's not every day you get to see ruins like these up close!"

"Right through here," Zavek commanded, ushering them into the building.

Eris and Caesia stepped into the ruined building, into a dark, empty room. The walls were battered and worn and a decrepit skeleton lay in its corner. Caesia winced at the loud clatter of a metal gate slamming behind them.

"You've got to be kidding me…" she sighed, burying her face in her hand.

"You will remain here until further notice," Zavek demanded.

Eris watched silently, a blank look on her face as Zavek wandered away and disappeared into the ruins. "Well, we walked right into that one."

"You don't say!" Caesia hissed. "Bloody hell, how could we have been this stupid?"

"You think Maeve set us up?" Eris asked.

"No, I think Maeve is an idiot," Caesia snapped, running her hands through her hair as she paced around the room.

"Huh. Well, what do we do now?"

"I'd say there's a fair chance we're going to be killed…" Caesia sighed. "Thus, I think we'd better make ourselves scarce. Fast."

"Couldn't agree more," Eris chuckled. "How're we gonna get out of here?"

"I'm not even going to bother trying to teleport," Caesia muttered. "We'll have to force our way out."

"You wanna melt the bars?"

Caesia approached the rusted, iron gate and peered closely through the bars, where there lay a faint, rippling yellow barrier.

"Pointless. There's an essence barrier projected around the cell," Caesia muttered, searching the cell carefully for a new solution. "We'll have to try something more unconventional."

Caesia paused as she noticed Eris becoming increasingly distracted. "What's wrong?" she asked, following Eris' gaze with a grin to the aged skeleton in the corner. "Are you… are you scared of that skeleton?" she laughed.

"Not scared!" Eris insisted. "Just… being cautious."

In truth, Eris felt incredibly anxious around the skeleton. After seeing them surge from the walls back in the tomb, she could never look at one in the same way again. She couldn't let another catch her off-guard.

"Right… anyway, I've got a plan. You see-"

Caesia was interrupted by a burning hiss. She swivelled around to see the barrier dispersing into yellow sparks. After a moment of confused staring, Caesia sighed in both relief and displeasure as Maeve's head appeared from above the door frame.

"Ladies," Maeve smiled, sliding clumsily down the side of the building.

"What are you doing here?" Caesia whispered. "I thought you were waiting outside."

"I was… but then I figured you guys were *totally* gonna get killed, so I came to save you!"

"What's with the change of heart?" Eris smirked. "You go soft?"

"Nah, I got lonely," Maeve sighed. "After two years, I forgot how much I like people."

"You got lonely?" Caesia laughed. "That's so sad…"

Maeve drew closer and narrowed all eight of her eyes menacingly. "Bold words for someone so edible," she grinned, bearing her jagged maw.

Caesia stepped back anxiously from the bars. Perhaps it was best if she didn't antagonise Maeve while at her mercy.

"Nah, I wouldn't eat you anyways. You've no meat on your bones," Maeve smirked, turning to Eris. "You on the other hand…"

"Don't even think about it," Eris warned.

"I'm kidding, I'm kidding," Maeve laughed. "Come on, let's go."

Caesia moved over to the bars and drew her hand to the bolt. As she charged her finger with lightning, a sharp pain jolted up her arm and she reeled back, whimpering quietly.

"Some mage, you are," Maeve muttered. "Allow me."

She yanked back one of her hind legs and slammed it down, cleaving through the bolt with a loud crack and severing it from the doorframe. She grabbed the gate and flung it open with the subtle squeal of aged metal.

"Thanks…" Caesia mumbled.

Maeve smirked as Caesia passed. She was enjoying how reluctant Caesia was to be kind to her - the girl was amusingly uptight.

"How'd you even get in here?" Eris whispered.

"I… might have beaten up the guard," Maeve smiled innocently.

"*What?*" Caesia hissed.

"It's fine!" Maeve smiled. "Zavek's busy with Lycoria, so he won't notice. Meanwhile, we can slip through one of the super secret exits!"

Caesia certainly wasn't optimistic. Maeve had sent them straight into this mess and she didn't feel particularly comfortable following her ideas again.

"I don't think we have any other choice," Eris sighed. She could see that Caesia was struggling to come to terms with the situation, but they needed to get going.

"I guess not," Caesia muttered, turning reluctantly to Maeve. "I suppose you'd best lead the way then."

"A wise choice indeed!" Maeve smiled. "How sneaky are you guys? Like, is it easier or harder with only two legs?"

"Eris is pretty nimble…" Caesia mumbled. "I'm not so sure about me though."

"She'll be fine," Eris smirked. "She weighs about as much as the clothes on her back."

"That is a *complete* exaggeration!" Caesia sneered. "But yeah, I guess I'm fairly…"

"Underweight," Eris grinned.

"Watch it…" Caesia warned. "Can we go now?"

"That we can!" Maeve declared, twirling around and strolling off. "Let's bounce!"

Maeve scampered through the ruins like a mouse in a maze, with no clear direction to where they were going. Eris and Caesia quickly began to wonder if Maeve actually remembered where the exits were, or even if she was so drunk that the exits were a nought but a fantasy of hers. Alas, they had little other choice but to trust in her.

"I'm sure we've seen arch before…" Eris muttered as they passed by another shattered building.

"You doubt me?" Maeve smirked.

"Yes," said both Eris and Caesia in unison.

Maeve frowned, appearing almost hurt. "Rude…"

"How do you know about these exits anyway?" Caesia whispered. "Are they not meant to be secret?"

"None of your business!" Maeve hissed. "Keep your nose up your own arse, not mine."

Caesia's eyes fluttered in shock as she shrank away from Maeve. What was it about those exits that could warrant such a rapid burst of anger? Perhaps it was just Maeve being mentally unstable, but Caesia couldn't help but feel like there was a much deeper story behind all this.

"Maeve!" called an approaching voice from behind.

"Uh oh." Maeve mumbled, avoiding eye contact with her companions as she swivelled around.

Zavek skidded around the corner and came storming after them, gripping a curved blade of hardened black chitin in his hand and scowling furiously.

"Maeve, you're under arrest!" he called. "Come quietly and the Lycoria might spare you!"

"Oh, come on Zavek!" Maeve groaned. "You used to be cool!"

"No I wasn't!" Zavek snapped.

"Yeah, he wasn't," Maeve sniggered to Eris and Caesia.

"You're not helping," Caesia hissed.

"Seriously, Maeve," Zavek urged. "Those humans could mean the end of-"

"Hey, they're not that bad!" Maeve insisted. "I mean, the brunette's a bit prickly but, you know…"

"Hey!" Caesia snapped.

"Case and point," Maeve smirked.

"Can you just take this seriously?" Zavek snapped.

"I am taking this seriously!" Maeve chirped playfully. "Last time I was this serious, I shat myself."

Eris and Caesia glanced at each other with smirks at the two arachni bickering like children.

"Alright, I'm taking you into custody," Zavek sighed.

"Why?" Maeve sneered.

"Because you're meant to be exiled!"

"But why though?"

"Oh no, we're not doing this again," Zavek growled. "I'm not taking your crap anymore."

"Really?" Maeve smirked. "You're doing it right now."

"Ugh, I didn't miss this…" Zavek groaned. "Please Maeve, you've got to see the bigger picture here."

"Zavy, I've got eight eyes!" Maeve laughed. "If there was a picture here, I'd know about it."

Zavek shook his head in pity. "What happened to you, Maeve? You went from the finest soldier down here to a drunken wreck."

"What happened to me?" Maeve smirked, before her face suddenly dropped into a scowl. "What do you think, Zavek? I got exiled. If the Inquisition hadn't broken me enough, your bitch matriarch decided to kick me out for saving all your skins!"

"By going out there you endangered all of us!"

"We were already in danger!" Maeve hissed. "Those psychos already had our scent! I had to do something!"

"And you nearly made things worse!"

"Nearly! *Nearly* made things worse!" Maeve snapped, her voice growing more and more hysterical. "But I didn't, did I? I saved everyone, but does anyone appreciate that? Noooo! They all say 'Maeve, you're a menace to society, you're totally insane'! I'm not insane!" she shrieked. "I just wanted to keep you assholes safe!"

"Maeve, the Matriarch-"

"Fuck the Matriarch!" Maeve growled. "You think I'm gonna answer to the bitch who threw me out in the cold after the humans practically skinned me?!"

"Maeve, please-"

"No, we're done! You can go tell Lycoria that if she comes after me, I'll rip every one of her goons limb from limb!"

Zavek sighed and screwed up his eyes in shame. "I'll pass it on... I hope you get better, Maeve."

Maeve watched with a scowl as Zavek disappeared back into the ruins. As he disappeared, her stiff posture sagged tiredly and she slumped pathetically against the wall.

"I need a drink..." she groaned, three of her eyes fluttering sleepily.

"Can I ask what that was about?" Caesia whispered.

"No."

"I've got water if you need some," Eris smiled, sliding her backpack down her arm.

"Not that kind of drink," Maeve muttered. "Actually, give that here."

Eris shovelled the waterskin from the backpack and forked it over to Maeve. Her smile slowly drooped into a frown as Maeve slid her finger along her arm and wrought a shallow, bloody incision through it with her blade-like fingers. Crimson droplets pattered into the waterskin, some rolling down the sides, before Maeve flung her head back and glugged down a mouthful of hazy red water.

"Thanks, I needed that," Maeve smiled, offering the waterskin back to Eris. "It's not quite wine, but beggars can't be choosers!"

Eris stared for a moment at Maeve, watching the revolting mixture trickle slowly down her chin. She knew that she should have been disgusted, yet looking at her she could feel nothing but sympathy after the altercation she had just witnessed. She understood now that Maeve was more than just some crazed weirdo - she was a genuinely decent person, broken and twisted by rejection.

"Yeah... you can keep it," Eris sighed.

Maeve looked herself up and down. "I got nowhere to put it."

Eris bit down on her lip as she cautiously plucked the blood soaked waterskin from Maeve's hand. She shivered at the cold touch of the blood and as Maeve staggered back up straight and turned to continue, she discarded it over her shoulder.

"I guess we'd best pick up the pace, since Zavek's being such a tight little bitch," Maeve muttered.

"Sounds to me like he was just doing his job," Caesia mumbled, her voice glaringly judgemental.

"Did I ask for your opinion?!" Maeve spat, before withdrawing immediately back into a cheerful state. "Anyways, the exit should only be around this corner. Or is it the next corner? Wait, was there a corner? Maybe..."

Maeve poked her head around the next corner with little caution in mind. She squinted all of her eyes and peered closely at the web cloaked wall of the cavern. The webbing was even harder for her to see through considering the octuple vision she had to deal with in her tipsy state.

"Are we here?" Eris whispered.

"Um... let's go with yeah," Maeve mumbled, slipping from cover and wandering to the cavern wall.

She stepped up to the wall and swept the webbing aside, revealing a shattered doorframe blockaded with a huge pile of fractured rock. She stared blankly for a moment at the blocked passage.

"Ah," Maeve mumbled, turning around with an apologetic smile. "It seems that after my... misuse of the exits, they removed them."

Eris turned with a frown to Caesia, who was biting down on her lip angrily, her eyes screwed up as she took several deep breaths in attempt to suppress her rage. Tendrils of energy arced between her fingers before she clenched them shut in an effort to suppress herself.

"Maeve..." Caesia growled, her eyes flaring brighter as she glared furiously at the innocent faced arachni.

"Don't worry, I can fix this!" Maeve urged. "I just need to-"

"No! I've had enough!" Caesia hissed. "You're not fixing anything! All you do is fuck things up, you're useless!"

"I was only trying to help..." Maeve mumbled, shrinking away pathetically.

Eris backed cautiously away as Caesia's skin began to subtly glow with green light. She wanted badly to interject, but feared that she would only push Caesia further over the edge - an act that could quite possibly have been the death of her.

"And now you're going to be the death of us!" Caesia growled. "We're going to die because we were stupid enough to trust a drunk, sadistic spider woman to be anything more than a thorn in our bloody sides!"

Silence fell suddenly over the three of them. Eris was in total shock at Caesia's brutality. Maeve was speechless, her eight eyes trembling and welling with tears and her legs drooping in defeat. As her mouth quivered in a struggle to produce a rebuttal, she span quickly around and hurried away into the ruins, tears pattering at her feet.

"Caesia... that was horrible," Eris mumbled ashamedly.

"That was the truth!" Caesia hissed, the light around her dying down as she calmed. "We're out here trying to save humanity and she's ruined everything!"

"She was trying her best!" Eris insisted. "You were way too harsh on her."

Caesia scoffed in disbelief at Eris' sudden jump to Maeve's defence. Up until now, she had shown just as much disgust at that creep's actions - Caesia had seen the horror in her eyes more than once. Yet despite all that, here Eris was fielding a totally opposite opinion to that which she clearly had just minutes before!

"What the- too harsh?" Caesia snapped. "We're going to die in here!"

"You didn't shout at me when I led you into certain death!" Eris growled. "Why is this any different from me leading you into that tomb?"

"The difference is that you're not a total buffoon!"

"No, the difference is that you just don't like her," Eris muttered, crossing her arms disappointedly. "You had a go at her because you find her annoying!"

"Yes, I do!" Caesia spat. "Who wouldn't? She's *disgusting*!"

"That she is," Zavek sighed, stepping from amongst the ruin.

Eris and Caesia fell silent as several soldiers clad in slender black armour filed out from the ruins, encircling them and levelling glossy white spears towards them. The girls stiffened as dozens of red, yellow and orange eyes fell upon them with glares of suspicion and hate.

"A shame, really," Zavek muttered. "She used to be the best of us, it's tragic to see how far she's fallen."

"Sounded to me like that's not her fault at all," Eris hissed. "You assholes abandoned her, left her to-"

Caesia's foot slammed down upon Eris', her minute strength dealing little pain to her friend but interrupting her all the same.

"For the love of God, don't make this any worse than it already is," Caesia whispered.

"I don't think any of us came here to debate ethics," Zavek said. "You wanted to see the Matriarch - she awaits your audience."

"Wait, seriously?" Caesia asked, utterly confused. "Then why the hell did you lock us up?"

"You are an unknown, a potential threat. It was necessary to detain you until we had the Matriarch's word on the situation. Now, you had best come with me, and remember - until proven innocent you are enemies of the arachni. Don't do anything stupid."

"Hear that, *Eris*?" Caesia sneered.

Eris gave Caesia a dismissive grunt before trudging after Zavek. How did nobody see what she saw in Maeve? Even Caesia was totally cold to her, although she supposed that came as little surprise - Caesia hated everyone. Eris knew that it was neither her business nor her place to persuade them all otherwise, but she had to. She felt an obligation deep within herself that she couldn't explain. Was it a sense of justice? Empathy? Heroism? All she knew was that she had to do something, and that was good enough for her.

The soldiers led Eris and Caesia through the ruins to the centre of the cavern, where stood the remaining ground floor of what had once been a far larger, marble structure. Cloaked in darkness and masses of silk, the building was a depressing sight indeed. Caesia wondered how these arachni could cope with living in such a dark, frigid environment, one that inspired such a feeling of emptiness. They stepped through the crumbling gate of the building and into a long marble hall.

The hall was just as drab and desolate as anywhere else. Webs sprawled across the shattered remains of the ceiling, connecting to the ground by decrepit statues far beyond recognition that lined the room's edge. Hundreds of narrow eyes watched them as they passed by groups of arachni soldiers, crafting and sharpening glossy blades formed of black chitin.

At the room's end stood a colossal, intricate web that dwarfed the rest by a large margin. The guards ahead stood to attention and Eris and Caesia were forced to a halt before the arachni matriarch.

"Matriarch Lycoria, the humans!" Zavek announced.

Lycoria, laid back casually on her web, stared at Eris and Caesia suspiciously. Like all the rest, she was pale and gaunt, sporting a cluster of serpentine yellow eyes and hair of pure white. She leant forwards and brought her hand to her cheek in thought.

"Zavek, when you told me there were humans asking for audience, you failed to mention that said humans were a pair of adolescent girls," she sighed, her voice smooth and silken. "Here you had me thinking it would be some kind of royal envoy or a-"

Lycoria trailed off and took a double take at Caesia, who shuffled uncomfortably on the spot. She tensed as the Matriarch slid cautiously from her web and edged towards her. Lycoria reached out apprehensively and took Caesia's cheek in her hand, staring analytically into her eyes.

"You…" she hissed, her claws digging into Caesia's face as she tightened her grip. "She has the scourge!"

Lycoria shoved Caesia away and every guard in the room drew their webspun spears in defence. Caesia's heart nearly burst from her chest as she froze in anxiety.

"I- I have no idea what you're talking about!" she gasped, barely space between her words as she panicked.

"Don't play me for a fool!" Lycoria growled. "Your eyes! There's no mistaking it!"

Caesia's eyes widened in shock, in realisation that they feared her green essence. She looked around the room - the guards' arms were visibly quivering, their eyes trembling. They were terrified... why?

"Look, I swear, you know more about this than even I do!" Caesia begged. "I don't know anything about it, all I can do is teleport and I can't even control that!"

"Liar!" Lycoria spat, throwing out her arm in anger.

"Ma'am?" Zavek whispered to his furious master. "I think if she were lying, we'd all be dead by now."

Lycoria growled under her breath and looked Caesia up and down suspiciously. "By all means, I should kill you where you stand," she muttered. "But I suppose if the secrets of your power are long lost... lower your weapons."

Caesia sighed with relief as the guards apprehensively withdrew. They truly feared her, feared a power that could do little more than translocate. There had to be more to this, more to her power that she was yet to understand.

"Please, Matriarch," Caesia urged. "If you can tell me anything-"

"Don't make me laugh," Lycoria hissed. "Those who came before you were power crazed tyrants, butchers! If you think I'd tell you how to wield power like they did, you're a fool."

Lycoria did not realise it, but in her words she had in fact been of help. As harrowing as it was to hear that her power could be used for such evil, Caesia now understood that it not only had potential to kill, but also that contrary to belief, she was not its first wielder. This information was of little use to her now, but it would surely be valuable.

"I'm not a fool," Caesia insisted. "I just... I've searched for answers all my life. Please, I'm desperate."

Lycoria smirked mockingly. "How is it that you humans have forgotten two whole millennia of your history?" she sneered. "If you've not a clue what I'm talking about, it's best we keep it that way. You seem nice, so I doubt you'd want the power anyway."

"But-"

"No buts," Lycoria demanded. "Now, I believe we may have gotten off on the wrong foot... I think names are in order."

Caesia screwed up her mouth in annoyance. From a possible wellspring of information on her powers, she had drawn little to nothing.

"I'm Eris, this is Caesia," Eris smiled. "We were hoping you'd be able to help us in our investigation."

"Hm... tell me Eris, how did you come to find this place?" Lycoria asked.

"Cedric Bechard, ma'am."

"Ah, Cedric... he didn't strike me as the loose lipped kind. You didn't hurt him, did you?"

Eris looked to Caesia with concern, the images of her slamming the back of his head with her shield repeating vividly in her head.

"Not apart from a few knocks upside the head," Caesia smiled, not eager to disclose how she nearly burnt him to a crisp. "We started off at a bit of a misunderstanding, but he came around."

"That's good, Cedric is a noble man," Lycoria said. "But why exactly did our friend deem it necessary to reveal the biggest kept secret in Aldreichen to a pair of girls?"

"Because if we don't succeed, the arachni will be insinuated in murder," Caesia said bluntly. "One that I expect will lead to some very thorough sweeps of the city for abhuman activity."

Lycoria only raised her brow, but was visibly concerned. "I think you ought to explain the situation in more detail," she demanded.

"Of course. A group of inquisitors have vanished in the sewers while investigating a magical anomaly. We found our informant on the matter murdered, covered in massive puncture wounds that I could only assume to be the work of an arachni. I've no sympathy for the missing inquisitors, but if you've any idea about this we need to know."

"Missing in the sewers," Lycoria smirked. "You know, I think you might've missed your mark there. You see, I've been getting some rather grave reports about Maeve..."

"We know about Maeve," Caesia sighed. "But she refused any knowledge of the inquisitors."

"And you're sure she was being truthful?"

"Would she have any reason to lie?" Eris asked.

"Hm, considering how open she seems to have been about her... habits, I suppose not," Lycoria muttered. "Zavek, have we anything on these inquisitors?"

"I'll check with the scouts," Zavek smiled, scurrying obediently from the room.

"Wonderful," Lycoria smiled, turning back to Eris and Caesia. "It is clear that this situation, should it go unsolved, will be a grave threat to our safety here. I will help you if I can, but I must be certain you won't tell anyone of our being here."

"Uh... what do we have to do?" Eris asked.

"A good question," Lycoria mused. "The two of you seem trustworthy enough, so let me ask you a simple question, a test of character if you would - why are you here?"

Eris looked at her blankly, trying to discern whether this was some kind of trick question.

"I assume you mean why we've chosen to pursue this lead, us of all people," Caesia deducted, intending to be cautious in her words - she did not know whose side Lycoria was on. "We're tracking a dangerous man and hope that this investigation will shed some light on his whereabouts."

"I thought so," Lycoria grinned. "And this dangerous man… might he happen to be a four hundred year old warlord back from the dead to burn Verdenheld to the ground?"

Caesia and Eris froze in fright. If Lycoria was with him, they had just been made.

"Yes, I was quite surprised when he of all people came knocking. Don't worry, I've already politely declined his offer," Lycoria smirked, amused as Eris and Caesia heaved sighs of relief. "He's not a bad man and I respect his cause, but I won't put my people through another war - not with Verdenheld."

"Maeve mentioned something about a war, one I'd never heard of," Caesia said. "She called it the bloodiest one in history."

"Hm, good to hear Maeve still remembers her roots," Lycoria smiled. "Yes, the Great Arachni War isn't exactly one you'll find in the history books. Sixty years of attrition, millions of human soldiers thrown thousands at a time into massacre after massacre. You see, there was once a time when Aldreichen had twice the population it has today, before Verdenheld cast every boy who could hold a sword to their bloody deaths."

Where Caesia was simply speechless, Eris' head was spinning. Millions of lives thrown away like they were nothing, all for the cause of senseless slaughter. One had to question at times like these whether it was right to try and save this terrible place, but she knew she walked the right path. Damn the genocidal maniacs who ran the kingdom, they could rot for all she cared - she was in this to save the little man.

The three of them stood in silence, nobody quite sure how to follow up such a harrowing tale. Lycoria lay back on her web and wringed her fingers impatiently.

"So… how's Maeve doing?" Lycoria asked, trying to fill the void. "Zavek was convinced she's been drinking quite heavily."

"Well, that depends on what she was like before her exile," Caesia muttered. "If she was already a drunk, homicidal-"

"Oh, shut up," Eris groaned. "Quit being so insensitive!"

"But she asked-"

"Matriarch, you have to help her," Eris urged, scowling as many of the guards broke into poorly suppressed laughter. "She's going crazy out there! Drinking blood, eating people, her head's not right!"

Lycoria leant forwards and stared for a moment at Eris, conflict in her eyes. "Look, I liked Maeve, she was… she was one of the better ones," she sighed. "But I can't so easily go back on my word and by what Zavek has told me, she's become somewhat irredeemable as of her exile."

"Exactly!" Eris cried. "It doesn't take a genius to see that the loneliness is tearing her apart!"

"Eris, she said no," Caesia whispered. "Respect her decision and-"

"No!" Eris snapped. "Matriarch please, she's not like that, I know it. You're all so distracted by how much of a mess she's become that you can't see past it! Beneath all that booze, Maeve is a good person and she needs to be shown that someone still cares!"

Caesia planted her hand over her face in embarrassment. Eris was kind, but she was naive. She was looking for something in Maeve that simply did not exist. Caesia had no idea where this notion came from, but it was totally idiotic.

"Can you vouch for this, Caesia?" Lycoria asked.

Eris looked to Caesia desperately, who glanced up between her fingers with a sigh into her palm. Of course she couldn't vouch for her, the woman was a lunatic… but she knew how much it would hurt Eris if she said no.

"I… yes, I can," Caesia sighed, withdrawing her hand and looking with guilt at Eris' smiling face. "Maeve… Maeve is an absolute freak of a woman and I find her nothing but obnoxious… but I've never known Eris to take so passionately to someone's defence. If Eris thinks she's redeemable, there's got to be something there to salvage."

Eris smirked at Caesia's disingenuous reply. She knew her friend meant none of that, but it was sweet of her to lie. As obvious as it was to her however, Lycoria seemed convinced.

"A lot of people do miss her…" Lycoria sighed. "She annoyed a fair few people, but she was always a ray of sunshine in our dark hole in the ground. You seem to understand her better than anyone, human. If I cease her exile, what then?"

"Then, you don't have to do anything," Eris chirped, smiling so sweetly that she could melt a glacier with its warmth. "Just let her back in, greet her with a smile and you'll have your sunshine back before you know it!"

Lycoria smiled warmly at Eris' reassurance. "You are particularly hard to say no to, human… Okay, you can tell Maeve that should she return, we'll happily receive her. So long as she behaves, of course."

Needless to say, Caesia was utterly boggled by the fact that Eris' begging paid off. She had no idea why Eris did that, but she was astonished all the same by how easily her infectious smile had managed to change the Matriarch's mind.

"I admit, it will be good to have her back, even if she has gone a bit crazy…" Lycoria sighed, turning to the doorway with a grin. "Ah, Zavek! What did the scouts have to say about our little problem?"

Zavek stepped back into the room, standing to attention, arms behind his back. It was amusing how formal he acted when his leader was lying back casually on her web beside him.

"Nothing on any rogue arachni, ma'am, but we have had some strange activities in the sewers. I believe the information may be of help."

"Great," Lycoria smiled. "You can brief our friends on the way out, no point in them loitering here."

"Yes, ma'am."

"Thank you for your help, Matriarch," Caesia said, making a subtle bow.

"And thank *you* for agreeing to keep our little secret," Lycoria grinned. "The two of you will always be welcome down here… no guests, of course."

"We're honoured!" Eris smiled, turning to Caesia with an eager grin. "Let's get outta here."

"Ah, yes. Back to the sewers…" Caesia muttered as they turned to leave.

"Hey, what did we say about complaining?" Eris snapped.

"I was not!" Caesia scoffed. "Just… stating the obvious for your pea brain."

Zavek hung back as Caesia and Eris strolled out of the room laughing and jeering. He edged cautiously to Lycoria's ear.

"You're sure it is wise to let the architect live, Matriarch?" he asked. "She could be beyond dangerous…"

"She doesn't know what she's doing," Lycoria smirked. "And who's going to tell her? The Empire is gone and the Lords want nothing to do with the scourge. She'll find no answers."

"I know, but… do we really want to risk another Cataclysm?"

"I'm well aware of the risk, Zavek," Lycoria sighed. "But the girl has no grasp of her powers, she'll never even get close to their might."

"I guess not," Zavek muttered darkly, trailing off after the girls. "For everyone's sake, I hope you're right…"

"What's taking him?" Caesia muttered, vigorously tapping her foot in impatience.

"Maybe he got lost," Eris smirked. "I mean, Maeve could barely navigate this maze."

"True, but Maeve was hammered," Caesia laughed. "Ah, here he comes!"

Zavek emerged from the battered ruins and waved to them as he hurried over. "Sorry about that," he called. "It seems the Matriarch liked you."

"All her," Caesia said, thrusting a thumb at Eris. "I don't know how she does it, everyone just likes her!"

"Maybe 'cause I'm actually *nice* to the people we meet," Eris muttered.

"Who can truly say for certain?" Caesia sighed with a knowing smile. "Anyhow, we've spent enough time here as it is, let's get to business."

"Indeed," Zavek smiled. "Our spies had nothing concrete, but they've noticed a pattern in strange activities late at night. Every day around midnight, a group of people assemble in the sewers."

"Any idea what they were doing?" Eris asked.

"No, they would scatter the moment our spies stepped into earshot."

"Strange..." Caesia mused. "It would take a fair bit of magical skill to detect something as far as arachni hearing range."

"Then how do we approach?" Eris scoffed. "There's no way they won't detect us!"

Caesia stared off into the air for a moment as she quickly processed and debunked various hypotheses.

"I can think of one possibility, though I can't say I'm a fan," she sighed. "Zavek, have you any sladium down here?"

"Sladium... yes, but what for?"

"I believe that we can use the essence nullifying properties of sladium to trick their means of detection into overlooking us. It's not foolproof, but I think it's the best we've got."

"Not a bad idea..." Zavek said, nodding slowly. "I'll be right back."

Zavek hurried off into the ruins, leaving Eris and Caesia at the settlement's edge. In the silence left behind, Caesia resumed looking at the various ancient ruins with intrigue. That was until she was interrupted by Eris seconds later, much to her displeasure.

"Caesia?" Eris chirped. "That sadium stuff, is it like moonglass?"

"Sladium," Caesia corrected. "And... moonglass? Never heard of it."

"It's like this weird white crystal, gave all the shamans headaches."

Caesia paused for a moment in thought. "Sounds to me like they're one in the same. Sladium is a white crystal that nullifies essence around it."

"Does sladium also come from the stars then?"

Caesia fought to suppress a snigger, not wanting to insult her friend's culture. "No, it comes from the ground... but by all means, it could've fallen from the sky long ago."

Excellent save, she told herself. As absurd as some of Eris' beliefs were, it would have been cruel to debunk them one after another.

"Right…" Eris mumbled. "Well anyway, if sladium is moonglass then are you sure we should… you know."

"You're worried it'll hurt me," Caesia smiled sweetly. "I'll be fine. So long as you carry it, I'll have only a headache to contend with. Just… don't hold anywhere near my head. Too close and I might black out."

"Gotcha!" Eris chirped. "And now if you're ever annoying me, I know how to instantly knock you out!"

"Good thing you're the annoying one then…" Caesia muttered.

"I guess… maybe I'll just hit you over the head with some whenever you're about to attack a person's beliefs, since you like to do that so often."

Zavek emerged from the ruins as Caesia shot Eris a sharp glare. For the sake of keeping it professional, Caesia retracted her hand behind her back and dispersed the electricity from her fingers. There would be plenty more opportunities to electrocute Eris, she was willing to let this one go.

"One chunk of sladium," Zavek announced. "Should be enough to mask you without causing you any serious harm."

Eris stepped forwards and took from Zavek a chunk of misty, white crystal. Caesia screwed up her eyes and took a deep breath as her head began to throb with a faint pain that steadily grew as Eris moved back to her side. She was going to have to live with it for a while - painful as it was, she had little choice.

Eris took a double take as the glistening green of Caesia's eyes began to flicker and die out.

"What?" Caesia mumbled, her voice pained and eyes squinted.

"Your eyes are going brown!" Eris laughed.

"Seriously?" Caesia gasped, the pain instantly washed away by excitement. "Oh my God, I have brown eyes! Do they look good?"

"Yeah, they're really pretty," Eris smiled. "You suit 'em."

"Awesome…" Caesia grinned, rubbing her temple as her headache began to more severely set in. "But I digress. If it looks like we're about to fight, I need you to hurl that thing as far away as possible, else I won't be able to channel essence. Got that?"

"Hold the shiny, lob it before we fight. Got it."

"Good," Caesia sighed, bottling her pain and standing straight. "Now, where are we headed exactly?"

"Overflow Chamber Forty-One," Zavek said. "You'll find it should you head right out the entrance and then take two left turns and a right."

"Okay. Eris, do you know roughly what time it is?"

"Dunno, about eleven maybe? Something like that."

"Then we've got a while to wait before our mystery group meets…" Caesia sighed. "Perhaps we should go there early, get an idea of the area and maybe pick up a clue of two."

"Sounds like a plan!" Eris smiled, juggling the sladium back and forth. "To the sewers!"

The last of the shimmering red light dispersed as the entrance was behind an illusion. All in all, that whole situation had gone surprisingly well - Caesia had absolutely anticipated violence and Eris, while optimistic, had been quite concerned about being eaten. Anyhow, they found themselves once again trudging through the sewers, Caesia holding her head in her hands as she fought through the pain of the sladium. It was becoming slightly more bearable the longer she was exposed, but it was never going to stop hurting.

"Hey, um... thanks for lying back there," Eris smiled.

"You knew, huh?" Caesia smirked, her voice still strained by the agonising presence of the sladium.

"Course I did, you don't like anyone," Eris laughed.

Caesia chuckled quietly to herself. "True. You know... as much as I detest Maeve, it was really sweet what you did back there," she smiled. "But I have to ask - what on Elaria happened down there that had you make such a complete one-eighty?"

Eris looked up at Caesia, who was looking at her like she was some kind of alien. Frankly, she was disgusted with Caesia and how she could not even fathom the possibility of Maeve being redeemable, even after all she had said in her defence.

"You heard what she said," Eris muttered. "All that drinking and craziness came from her being kicked out, even though she was just trying to do the right thing. If I went home next year and got exiled, I reckon I'd get pretty loopy."

Caesia could in no way relate. To her, Maeve had no redeemable qualities. She was a drunk, a psychopath and just generally annoying. It seemed that she was too far into the deep end, that Eris was grasping at straws that weren't even there.

"It seems to me like you see a bit of yourself in her." Caesia smirked, deliberately dodging a rebuttal for the sake of their friendship. "Not feeling homesick are you?"

It was blatantly obvious that Caesia completely disagreed with her, but Eris decided it best not to tear themselves apart in the midst of the investigation.

"No... I guess I just don't like seeing people sad. Not when they deserve to be happy."

"You think Maeve deserves happiness," Caesia sighed. "After all the people she's killed?"

"Everyone deserves happiness," Eris smiled.

Caesia stared for a moment at Eris' hopeful smile. Her view of the world was far too optimistic, but it was kind of nice. Caesia could only imagine how wonderful life would be if she could see Elaria through the same lens as Eris.

The two of them retreated for a moment into silence. Caesia didn't want to argue with Eris - she could not bring herself to shatter her friend's blissful little bubble. She figured it was good for Eris to be this way - her attitude helped her forge through the horrors of Verdenheld that other outsiders could never look past.

"Hey, can we just talk about what the spider lady said?" Eris asked. "You know, about your powers."

"You mean how she implied that I've the potential to wield incredible destructive power?" Caesia sighed. "Yeah, I'm not too happy about that."

"Seriously?" Eris smirked. "Because being all-powerful sounds pretty neat."

"If there's power to be had, I want nothing to do with it," Caesia muttered. "Ugh, why couldn't I have just been normal…"

"If you were normal, you might not have ended up out here…" Eris smiled, ever optimistic.

"Even so, what I'd give not to have this stupid essence," Caesia groaned.

"But I thought you wanted to learn more about it, not throw it away."

"I want to learn its secrets because I know I'm stuck with it. If there were a way, I'd be scrambling to be rid of it."

Eris supposed that was fair - Caesia's essence had done little more than make her life a misery.

"So… what happens if you get the chance to have that crazy power?" Eris asked.

"Eris, I don't care if I even turn out to be some prophesised chosen one - I'm not taking it," Caesia insisted, standing rigid in defiance. "I… I don't want my powers to define who I am. I just want to be me."

"And if the powers-that-be give you no choice?"

"Then I'll kick their arse-that-be," Caesia smirked. "Do you… think otherwise?"

"I mean, personally I wouldn't be so quick to turn down unlimited power… but I'll sure as stars support your choice," Eris smiled warmly. "We don't need crazy powers to save the world!"

"Exactly," Caesia grinned. "With our strengths combined, we've already got everything we need!"

"Careful, you're being optimistic again!" Eris laughed.

"Am I? God, what are you doing to me?" Caesia chuckled. "I swear, another week and I'll start smiling!"

"That'd be the day," Eris giggled, shoving Caesia playfully.

"I can't help but wonder though, what the extent of my power might be…" Caesia sighed. "By the way Lycoria talked about it, it clearly has the power to kill. That either implies a utility beyond translocation or simply the ability to kill through the means of teleportation…"

Here we go again, Eris thought as Caesia's eyes lit up and her voice quickened into unintelligible rambling. It was adorable watching her brainstorm - the excitement in her eyes, the crazed smile on her face, the way she flailed her arms back and forth in gestures. It was a sight to behold.

"I'd say the greatest likelihood is the latter, all evidence considered. It remains thus far as a utilitarian power of no destructive capability. Yet, on a larger scale it could theoretically be capable of mass genocide, shafting armies, perhaps entire towns into the sky and dropping them from a lethal height. The question is, at what scale is this power limited? That, I suppose, is more a question of human physical limitations. A master could no doubt be capable of translocating large groups of people with ease, but to be capable of mass teleportation one would have to move beyond that level of ability. That begs the question - were the past wielders of this power beyond the mastery of the greatest of our age or is this power of a nature that allows greater potential of its user? If the latter, there is clearly one, perhaps multiple properties that I am yet to discover-"

"Caesia!" Eris blurted amidst hysterical giggling. "Slow down!"

Caesia's eyes fluttered as her mind cleared and she settled down. "Yes of- of course. I should consider this later, it would be foolish to let it clog my mind right now…"

"Don't you ever worry your brain might catch fire when you do that?" Eris laughed.

"If it does, don't put it on my tombstone," Caesia chuckled. "And if somehow it makes it on anyway, consider it my last wish to make it read 'thought to the bitter end'."

"That was awful, even by my standards," Eris groaned. "I think you'd better leave the puns to me."

"Gladly."

As they rounded yet another corner of the winding sewer, a number forty-one painted in battered white paint came into view. On its right was a passage protruding from the main tunnel, into the overflow chamber. As they drew closer, a deep blue light became clear to see, its glow painting the walls of the lightless chamber with colour.

The stepped up to the ledge overlooking the large, square room built deep into the ground in order to fill up with overflowing sewage water. In case of massive amounts of overflow, another tunnel diverged from the room, a long tunnel that led to a grate through which moonlight beamed from the bay.

At the base of the chamber, a number of decaying corpses lay in a heap on the floor. They wore the studded leather coats and silver plates of the inquisitorial order. Their corpses were similarly wounded to the spy, wrought with deep punctures, having cut with terrifying ease through even their armour plating.

"More of the same wounds," Caesia muttered, descending into the chamber. "It's definitely arachni we're dealing with."

"You think there might be some rogue one's down here?" Eris asked.

"It is possible. If there are more arachni in the city, I doubt they all answer to the Matriarch."

"So we need to find these arachni before they kill anyone else."

"Not so fast. None of this explains the magical anomalies, which must have led the inquisitors to the arachni in the first place. Whatever they're doing, it must be beyond simple murder."

Caesia approached the pile of bodies apprehensively, from beneath which spilled a vibrant blue light. She held her breath, closed her eyes and rolled a body aside.

"What have we here?" Caesia muttered, picking up a glowing blue, ornate lantern. "This must be one of those seeker lanterns the Inquisition uses to detect magical anomalies."

"Is it just me, or is it getting brighter?" Eris said with concern.

Caesia looked down at the lantern, which was gradually brightening, the light beginning to pulsate more and more intensely. Her eyes widened and she cast the lantern down.

"They must be here!" Caesia hissed. "It's an ambush!"

Eris immediately reeled back her arm and sent the sladium shard sailing out of the chamber. Feeling as if a veil had been lifted from over her, Caesia's eyes flared back to life and she ignited her arms with crackling energy. Eris slid her sword from its sheath and held it defensively against her shield's rim.

"Well deduced, my diminutive human friends!" called the mocking voice of a man that echoed from the outlet tunnel.

A pair of arachni, a male and a female, stepped up to the ledge above. The woman sported ragged black hair and burning orange eyes, while the male's smug face was wrought with narrow, crimson slits and swamped by a blonde mop. The male folded his arms confidently, staring down upon them with a demeaning smirk.

"Kharmenia was right, Niria," he chuckled to his companion. "The brunette is a smart one."

"Oh, thanks…" Eris muttered with an insulted frown.

"We're not here to waste time showboating, Farenos," Niria groaned impatiently. "Let's just kill these idiots and get to work."

Eris grinned eagerly. This was her kind of bad guy - no boring speeches, straight to fighting.

"Of course, time is wasting," Farenos sighed. "And I was so looking forward to some slow, intimate death."

Caesia gulped down a sudden surge of anxiety as the two arachni poised in readiness. She looked to Eris, reassured by her intense grin. They killed a dragon, this was nothing.

The arachni descended upon them, Farenos falling upon Eris and Niria upon Caesia.

Caesia was immediately shunted out from under her assailant by her power, stumbling into a wall on the other side of the room. Getting a grip of where she'd ended up, she span around and launched a crack of lightning at Niria. The spell sent a piercing pain up her arm like she had been slashed with a sword, her eyes tearing up as she endured the pain.

Eris sprang back, shield raised as the Farenos pounced. He landed in front of her, his cleaving insectoid legs shattering the stone beneath him. Eris used that window to make a jab with her sword, immediately slicing a bloody gash across the arachni's cheek. She didn't expect that to work - he was sloppy, nowhere near as agile as Maeve. She held her confident smile for only a split second.

Farenos roared and threw himself at her, thrusting his legs out in front of him and knocking her sword and shield to the side. Her guard down, he swiped at her neck with his bladed arms. She threw her head back and ducked narrowly beneath his strike before kicking him away and lifting her shield again.

Caesia was approached steadily by Niria under a weak hail of lightning. Niria used the natural armour of her chitinous legs as a shield to absorb the electricity, which simmered away on contact.

"I expected you to be stronger," Niria laughed as another bolt struck her legs. "What's the matter? Not afraid are you?"

"Afraid?" Caesia scoffed. "Don't make me laugh!"

Caesia was terrified. Her lightning was only becoming more painful to use, thus she was holding back in fear of causing herself permanent damage. Niria was shrugging off her pathetic attacks with ease, there was no way she could win. She had to defend herself until Eris dealt with Farenos.

"Oh, don't worry…" Niria grinned, opening her shield and staring maniacally at her. "You won't be laughing when I tear your head from your shoulders!"

She flung herself at Caesia, swinging her legs one by one in an attempt to overwhelm her opponent. Caesia stepped back and cast out a tiny green disc of light, no larger than a plate, to catch the first strike. One by one, she deflected each of her assailant's legs with her shields, catching the last only inches from her stomach. As her final strike glanced off Caesia's defences, Niria growled impatiently and reeled back her chitinous arms.

"You think you're clever, bitch?!" she roared, swinging her arm-blades for Caesia's face.

A flickering green barrier stuttered into existence between them. The arachni's strike shattered the shield and sent them both reeling. Caesia screamed as her arms were set afire with a burning pain from absorbing the force of the arachni's heavy blow.

"Sounds like your friend's in trouble!" Farenos gloated to Eris as he poised to strike. "I wonder which of you will die first…"

"Funny, I was wondering the same about you!" Eris growled, thrusting her shield up in waiting for his strike.

Farenos lunged at Eris ferociously, slamming into her shield and sending her reeling back. She stumbled as her foot was snatched on an inquisitor's body, sending her toppling backwards onto the cold ground.

"Pathetic!" Farenos laughed, baring over her and pulling his legs back.

One of his legs swept by and battered her sword out of her hand with brutal force. She reached out desperately as her sword skidded out of reach. Farenos grinned as he fell upon her, slamming its uppermost legs down.

She threw up her shield and caught the legs, only for the both of them to shatter straight through the brittle, scarred wood. One raced to a halt just short of her chest, while the other sliced straight through the steel plates of her right pauldron like a knife through butter. Eris whimpered at the stinging in her shoulder as the tip of the leg dug deep into her flesh, shivering as the scraping of the chitin against bone quaked her skin.

"Aw, did that hurt?" Farenos sneered. He yanked his legs apart, splintering Eris' shield into a shower of broken shards. He grabbed her by the arms and pinned her to the ground, bearing his razor teeth in a dark smile. "Don't worry, it won't for long!"

Eris struggled in his grip as his gnashing maw open, saliva smacking her cheek as he leant down to sample her flesh. Her stalwart demeanour began to fail, fear overtaking as she let slip a pathetic sob, tears building in her eyes.

"Get off my food, you slimy prick!"

Eris' eyes snapped open as Farenos sprang up in fright, Maeve attached to his shoulders like a parasite.

"Nobody eats my friend but me!" she growled, scrambling up his back and opening her jagged maw wide.

Farenos cried in agony as Maeve sank a row of knifelike teeth into the base of his neck and ravenously slurped up the blood that burst out of the wound. He slammed the back of his armoured fist into several of her eyes, screaming as her teeth wrought crimson trenches through his skin before detaching and toppling from his back. He held his gushing wound, fear and desperation in his eyes as his breathing accelerated. Blood avalanched down his shoulder, creating a bloody trail as he staggered away.

"Man, he tastes good," Maeve wheezed, splayed out flat on the ground.

Niria glanced up as Caesia vanished from her grasp yet again. Her eyes widened at the sight of her wounded ally slumping against the wall.

"Damn it, Farenos!" she gasped, hurrying to his side. "Come on, they're not worth it."

She wrapped her four right legs around him and leapt onto the wall, scrambling up and disappearing into the outlet tunnel.

"Crap…" Caesia hissed, looking in defeat at Eris and Maeve, both totally wiped out on the floor.

Unwilling to let the murderers escape, Caesia steeled herself and ran after them. She barrelled up the stairs and leapt across the small gap between the entrance and the tunnel. The arachni were already closing in on the tunnel's end, faster than her even with one wounded.

"Come on, come on, teleport!" Caesia urged desperately, squeezing her eyes closed and concentrating with all her might. "Come on!"

Eris peeled herself off the ground, only now beginning to calm after such a brush with death. She stumbled to the top of the stairs and peered down the outlet tunnel, where she saw neither the arachni nor her friend.

"Is she dead?" Maeve chirped, peering over Eris' shoulder. "Please, tell me she's dead."

Caesia opened her eyes nervously, knowing she had done something, yet not sure what. She was met with a world forged of shimmering green light, a mirror of reality in every way.

"What is this?" she whispered, running her fingers cautiously along the walls of the tunnel.

Her fingers glided through the light as if it were liquid, leaving behind them a rippling trail. She span around and jumped at the sight of a pair of shimmering green shapes behind her. It was Eris and Maeve, only they appeared as featureless forms of pure light.

"Eris!" Caesia yelled, to no answer.

Eris couldn't see her, implying that this tunnel and by extension her powers transcended the physical plane. It was as terrifying as it was fascinating. She looked down at herself, curious as to why she did not appear like them.

To some degree she was scared, but her intrigue dwarfed all emotion. Whatever this place was, it wasn't common knowledge to the rest of the world - it was a revolutionary arcane discovery. Her mind flooded with possibilities, an endless wellspring of ideas and theories clouding any fear that might have gripped her.

"Hm... my arrival in this place seems to suggest that my abilities transcend the physical plane..." Caesia mumbled, scrambling for her notebook as she launched into her usual lunatic rambling. "All evidence points to this being a mirror of our world, perhaps suggesting that green essence makes up the fabric of reality, possibly meaning that I am capable of manipulating said fabric! Makes sense, maybe explains where I've been going wrong!"

A gleeful smile spread across her face as she thrust open her notebook and began making erratic amendments to her work.

"Yes, of course! I've been focusing on the idea of moving myself physically, where I should have been looking beyond reality!" she gushed, before pausing momentarily in realisation. "If my essence is that of the fabric of reality, perhaps I can do more than just move in and out of this plane... is it possible that I could shape reality at a whim? Thoughts for later, far too advanced to be considering now."

She moved gradually to the end of the tunnel as she scrawled pages of notes into her book. She had never been so excited, this was what she had waited for all her life! She reached out to open the grate and as she placed her hand on a bar, it exploded slowly into a cloud of green sparks. Caesia reeled back from the grate and narrowed her eyes in analysis. The bar was gone. She looked down at her hands and began hesitantly to giggle. She swept her hands through the grate and watched bright eyed as the bars dispersed into the air.

"Hypothesis confirmed," she grinned. She wondered if that had affected reality in any way.

She stepped out onto the seafront, surveying the shimmering green ocean. As her eyes met with the horizon, she gazed up to the sky in awe. It was an endless void painted with dancing colours - red, blue, yellow and purple. It was as if the whole universe had appeared before her eyes, which lit up as her mouth fell wide open.

Staring into the sky mesmerised, an excited yet apprehensive grin spread across her face. That was until her eyes met something in the dancing void. She felt cold, inside and out, as if she had been plunged into the icy waters of the North Sea. Her breath fell short and her eyes trembled as she struggled to close them, her gaze captured. Something was out there, something familiar, yet all she could see, all she could feel was nothingness.

A whisper hissed in the back of her mind, unintelligible as it echoed a hundred times. Her eyes widened in terror. The whispering grew, becoming harsh and raspy. It scratched at her the back of her head, drowning her thoughts and straining her mind. Then it began to burn. Her mind on fire with an overwhelming pain, she dropped to her knees, her breath short and panicked. A piercing jolt of pain shot through her brain and she screamed. She shrieked as her whole body convulsed with an endless agony, as if thousands of knives were being driven into her skull. Never had she known such pain.

"You guys aren't venomous, right?" Eris asked nervously, throwing off her shoulder pad to investigate the deep puncture in her shoulder.

She was incredibly disappointed in herself for letting such a mediocre opponent overpower her. She knew it could not have been helped what with his eight blade-like legs, but failure had never ceased to irritate her. Improvements had to be made, lessons learnt. She would not let that happen again.

"Nah, you're fine," Maeve muttered, licking Farenos' blood from her lips. "Here, use this."

Maeve shovelled some webbing out of her pants and hurled it to Eris, who caught it only to realise what it was.

"Ew, what the-"

"It'll plug the hole and stop the bleeding," Maeve smiled. "Just try not to think about where it came from."

"Right… thanks," Eris sighed.

Eris shuddered as she slathered the gooey silk over the wound and felt its cold, slimy touch sink deep into her skin. She took a deep breath and endured as she wiped away the shallow layer of blood left behind.

"Hey, what're you doing?" Maeve groaned, her finger still in her mouth picking bits of flesh from between her teeth. "You're wasting perfectly good blood!"

"There is no way you're having my blood," Eris laughed. "Go drink an inquisitor or something."

Eris paused as she glanced down the tunnel to an unusual sight. Maeve turned with her, to see that several bars had disappeared from the outlet grate.

"Were those bars always missing?" Eris asked, reaching cautiously for her shoulder pad.

"I don't think so…"

They watched around as Caesia flashed back into reality, staggering backwards out of the light and falling flat on the ground. Eris strapped her shoulder pad back on and rushed over to her - she looked like she had seen death itself, her skin a ghostly pale and her eyes wide with horror. Her body surged with green light that lashed and cracked the stonework around her.

"No, get back!" Caesia shrieked, throwing out her hand to stop them.

Out of Caesia's arm burst an enormous tendril of light that struck the walls around her with a deafening crack. Her disorder was acting up, her essence had become unstable. She was breathing erratically, her every panicked breath unleashing a violent, white-hot burst of energy that shattered the stonework into splinters at its impact. Maeve stared in total disbelief, Eris in sorrow, as Caesia slowly calmed, the storm of lightning gradually subsiding.

As the last of the energy dwindled and faded, Caesia slumped onto her knees, her essence completely dried out. Blood poured like a waterfall from her nose, her head span in a daze and the green glow of her eyes flickered and dulled. Eris hurried to her side, Maeve following very cautiously in tow.

"What happened?" Eris gasped, kneeling down by Caesia's side.

"I-I don't know," Caesia stuttered, her whole body trembling. "I w-went... I-"

"Shh, it's okay," Eris urged, grabbing Caesia by the shoulders and propping her up against the wall. "Just take it slow."

"I take it this doesn't happen often?" Maeve smirked.

"Depends if you mean the breakdown or the teleportation," Eris sighed.

"I kinda meant both…"

Caesia began to calm down and a hint of colour returned to her cheeks. She looked up at Eris with tortured eyes as Eris gently dabbed her bloody nose with her sleeve.

"You good now?" Eris smiled, smearing away the last of the blood.

Caesia nodded slowly, still shaking. "I… I accidentally left the material world," she mumbled.

"What?" Eris laughed. "That's awesome!"

"No!" Caesia gasped fearfully. "There was something in there with me. It looked into my mind, i-it hurt like nothing else I've ever felt!"

Tears began to pour from Caesia's eyes again and she began to shake more violently. Her eyes flared brighter and green sparks began to fall from her skin.

"It was like my mind was being torn apart!" she cried.

Eris scrambled onto the floor and slipped her arm around Caesia. "It's over now." She whispered, squeezing her tight and pulling her close. "Whatever it was, it can't hurt you anymore."

"I-It told me things…" Caesia mumbled, the shower of sparks subsiding in Eris' comforting embrace. "I could feel it talking, bu-but all I heard was the same one word over and over and over… Agris."

Eris looked at her blankly. That meant no more to her than it did to Caesia. She sighed and began to shuffle to her feet, only to feel Caesia's quivering hand tug on her sleeve.

"Wait," she whispered. "Can… can you just hold me a little while longer?"

"Not to play down all the emotional trauma, but don't you have like, assassins to chase or something?" Maeve asked.

"She's right," Eris sighed, turning to Caesia with an apologetic smile. "We need to figure out how we're gonna find these guys. You still with me?"

Caesia closed her eyes and pulled herself together. She had to keep going, afraid as she was. Whatever that thing was, it couldn't reach her here. She hoped so, at least. Now all that mattered was finding those arachni and stopping whatever they might have planned.

"Till the bitter end," she smiled, wiping the flood of sweat and tears from her face and shovelling herself off the ground. "Finding them should be simple. We'll use-"

Caesia took one step forwards and went up in a burst of green light, re-emerging on the other side of the tunnel and nearly stumbling head first into the wall. She looked herself up and down and turned in confusion to Eris, a look of epiphany on her scarlet face. She carefully took a step to the side, laying down her foot only for nothing to happen.

"Did you do that on purpose?" Eris asked.

Caesia was silent, staring down at her body. All of the fear and sadness was washed suddenly away by a momentous realisation. She now understood the nature of her power and her mind was already acclimating to the knowledge. She thought not of moving on the physical plane, but of transcending reality as she thrust herself forwards.

Eris watched excitedly as Caesia went up in green light and appeared near the end of the tunnel. She flung herself around to Eris with an eager grin on her face, light in her eyes that warmed Eris' heart.

"Stars!" Eris laughed. "How… how are you doing that?!"

"I-I figured it out!" Caesia stammered, a wide smile plastered on her face. "I understand how it works and now… now it's just clicked!"

Caesia went up again in light and burst back into reality with her arms spread with joy. Again she blinked, then thrice more, each time becoming more and more enthused by the exhilaration of jumping in and out of reality. Eris stared with a toothy smile and bright eyes as Caesia pranced and twirled around the tunnel like a ballerina.

"Caesia, this… this is amazing!" Eris gushed with pride. "Stars, I'm so-"

"Guys!" Maeve yelled over the echoing blasts of green light that polluted the tunnel. "Assassins!"

Maeve was right. As over the moon as Caesia was to finally begin making progress, the clock was ticking. She could gush about this later.

"Right, of course!" Caesia murmured giddily, skidding to a halt with a determined smile. "We can use the seeker lantern. I don't know why those arachni gave off anomalous signatures, but they did, meaning we can track them like the inquisitors did."

"Good idea," Eris said. "We might be able to surprise 'em if they're not expecting us."

"Doubt it," Maeve said bluntly. "Arachni have a sixth sense 'cause of these little hairs on our legs. They'll feel you coming."

"Thanks for the confidence boost," Eris muttered. "Still, they won't expect us. That's advantage enough for me!"

At that, they headed back down to the overflow chamber, where Eris picked up the throbbing blue lantern. Its glow now was far more dim, revealing the blue essence crystal within.

"I guess you ladies are off then," Maeve sighed. "I'd come with, but I'm pretty sure I'd be on a pyre within minutes."

"Well, thanks for coming back!" Eris smiled warmly. "You totally saved my ass, I owe you one!"

"Consider us even!" Maeve chirped. "I heard you what you said as I ran away… for some reason, you stuck up for me. I mean, nobody's been that nice to me in years!"

"Well, as Caesia told me - we compliment each other," Eris smirked. "She hates everyone, I love everyone. Thus, we come equipped for every occasion!"

Caesia chuckled at Eris' surprisingly accurate account of her words.

"Well, thanks for liking me," Maeve smiled, shooing them off. "Now get outta here! You assholes have stuff to do."

"Yeah, let's go… and hey, no eating people anymore," Eris urged. "You'll get all your people killed."

"Fine…" Maeve groaned. "But if you're ever in the area again, you're bringing me some damned meat. I'm not living off rats all my life."

"Deal," Eris smiled. "Oh, Maeve, there was something I-"

"What part of get outta here don't you understand?" Maeve laughed. "Tell me later, you know where to find me."

Time was indeed wasting, Eris knew she couldn't afford to stay and chat. She wanted to tell Maeve that her exile had ended, but she supposed it could wait until later. It wasn't like Maeve was going to get herself killed in the meantime. Right?

She and Caesia hopped across the gap and back into the outlet tunnel, where they made for the moonlight.

"Good luck!" Maeve yelled after them. "Don't get killed!"

Chapter Six - Gate Crashers

Caesia ran at the grate full pelt, vanishing in a burst of light and reappearing on the other side. She threw out her arms and twirled happily under the moonlight.

"Ah, I've never felt so alive!" she sang, staring up at the stars where once a vibrant void had danced before her.

It was getting onto midnight now. After several fits of crying and a whole day of stressing out, Caesia was running solely on adrenaline. It was certainly a good thing that Eris had slept on the road, else she'd certainly have been wiped out too.

Eris stepped out of the outlet tunnel, which brought them out at the far end of the harbour. The water shimmered under the moonlight, the whole bay bathed in glistening white. The docked ships floated peacefully, bobbing silently as the waves gently caressed their hulls.

"A beautiful night," Caesia observed, settled slowly down by the humbling view. "Looking out on the sea tends to make me wonder, what else could be out there?"

"I never thought about it," Eris said, strolling to her side. "I didn't even know there could be anything out there!"

"Really?"

"They didn't teach us much about the sea," Eris smirked.

She held up the lantern and scanned it across the port. The light flared up slightly at a specific point, towards which they continued.

"Huh," Caesia mumbled. "Yes, on a clear day you can actually see the other continent on the horizon."

"There's another continent?" Eris gasped. "What's it like out there?"

"They call it Strausia. Jungles and deserts mostly. A shame they stopped exploring once they found it, for all we know there could be so much more beyond our shores!"

"Maybe once we're done with all this Valkyr business, we should take a look for ourselves!" Eris exclaimed, a determined smile on her face.

Caesia chuckled and shook her head. "There is no way I'm going out there," she sighed.

"Why not? Imagine, it'd be the ultimate adventure!" Eris gushed. "To go where none have gone before!"

"I... well, I can't swim," Caesia muttered, rubbing her head in embarrassment. "Thus, there is no way you are getting me on a boat."

"You can't swim?" Eris smirked.

"Of course not, why would a lady need to swim?"

"Fair point," Eris sighed. "Maybe I'll have to teach you some time."

"I think I'd like that," Caesia smiled. "I suppose if I could get over my fear, I'd be all up for it."

"You mean it?"

"Yeah, it'd be fun! To discover lands never before seen - it's an exciting thought."

"Then it's a plan!" Eris said excitedly. "Next chance we get, I'm teaching you to swim!"

"If we get time. For all we know, this lead could send us straight onto another."

"I'm sure we'll find some time. If we've got time for breakdowns, we've got time for swimming."

Caesia sighed shamefully. "Yeah, sorry by the way…"

"Ah, it's not a problem," Eris chirped.

"It is though," Caesia insisted. "If I cry or scream at every single thing that comes our way, we'll get nowhere. What's more, I fear I'll end up killing you if I keep losing control. From now on, it'll be no more crying. At the very least, I'll save it for later."

"Fine, but you know it's normal to freak out at this stuff, right?" Eris chuckled.

"I know, but for the sake of the mission I need to toughen up," Caesia declared with a stiff upper lip.

"Well, by the sounds of what happened in that tunnel, I'd say you've been through the worst of it," Eris sighed. "You are going to be okay after that, right? You seemed pretty… traumatised."

"I am, and I won't easily forget what happened back there," Caesia sighed. "I can't get it off my mind, can't stop thinking about it! What if my powers are linked to it? What if by using these abilities, I'm letting that thing into my mind? I-I can't go through that again."

"Are… are you saying you're scared to use your powers."

Caesia gazed longingly across the water, a defiant grin spreading across her face. "Of course not," she laughed. "I've waited for this day my entire life, searched and searched for answers that were not even of our world! Some part of me wants to run, never use my powers again in fear of that… thing."

She stiffened herself and clenched her fists. Now was not the time for uncertainty - she had never felt so sure of herself.

"But I won't let some voice get in my way! I won't just accept my powers, I'll embrace them with open arms! And if that thing wants me, well, I'm told I have some rather destructive capabilities!"

So burning with determination was Caesia's smile that Eris was getting second hand adrenaline from merely looking at it. The events of the night had only worn Caesia further and further down and Eris had begun to worry as her emotions became unstable. Now though, this sudden genesis of Caesia's powers had wiped the slate clean - she was more confident now than she had been her whole life. Eris wasn't just looking at a renewed Caesia, this was a whole new person.

"And I've got your back every step of the way!" Eris declared, patting Caesia heartily on the shoulder. "We'll figure this out together."

Caesia grinned warmly. She was so lucky to have such a loyal and supportive friend. "Yeah… thanks, Eris."

"No worries," Eris smiled. "We're a team! I'll always have your back."

"Seriously though, I know I can be mean a lot of the time, but I… I really am grateful for all the support you've given me," Caesia mumbled, staring timidly at the ground. "It- It really means a lot."

"Hey, you did the same for me," Eris chirped. "That's what friends are for, right?"

"I guess so," Caesia smiled, staring again into the horizon.

Today, she was reborn. No more stressing, no more crying, no more whining about a distant past. She was Caesia Tarantis, daughter of Edmund and Amelie Tarantis, wielder of an essence that should not exist. That, despite all the pain it had brought her, was something to be proud of.

They headed deeper into Aldreichen, the lantern leading them back towards the city centre. The arachni could only have been returning to their lair or moving towards a new target. Either way, Eris and Caesia were prepared for a rather violent confrontation.

"Come to think of it, we don't really know much about what's going on here, do we?" Eris muttered. "We know the culprit, but we don't even know what they're doing, let alone why!"

"We don't need to," Caesia said. "What matters is the who and where."

"But what if they're good guys?" Eris urged.

"Eris, if I'm not mistaken, that guy tried to rip your throat our with his teeth."

"Oh yeah…" Eris mumbled. "But do you really think these guys are straight up evil?"

"No, I'm sure they have their twisted reasons - everyone is the hero of their own story. Still, I think the rather gruesome examples of overkill we've seen are reason enough to bring them to justice."

"Yeah, I guess good guys don't really punch fist sized holes in people…"

Suddenly, the lantern light flared up, momentarily dazzling Eris with a burst of blue light.

"I think we're here," Caesia whispered. "Have a scan, would you?"

Caesia watched carefully as Eris held the lantern high and swept it around. The light grew brighter, pulsating faster as it moved over one building after another. They shielded their eyes as the crystal burst with blinding colour, swamping their vision in blue.

"That one," Eris said, pointing to the building ahead.

It was a two-story structure built of grey stone, a massive golden eagle spreading its behemoth wings wide across the front. They hurried to the foot of the building, where Caesia stopped to read the inscription above the door. Eris stiffened as Caesia's eyes grew startled.

"This is the Hall of Glories!" she gasped. "It's where the leaders of the great houses meet with the king to discuss the affairs of the realm!"

"Then we gotta get in there!" Eris blurted. "Come on!"

Eris ran up the steps to the building and barged the doors open, stumbling into a large open hall. The walls were decked with friezes of glorious victories and memorials of unjust wars. Surrounding the room's supports were flawless golden statues of kings and heroes, trophies and tributes from a thousand battles cluttering their marble pedestals. Several groups of nobles and aristocrats backed away in fear as Eris and Caesia thundered into the hall. A group of scarlet cloaked House Verden knights stepped between them, hands on their swords.

"Hold it right there!" one of them snapped. "No entry without identification."

"King Friedrich is in danger, you must let me past at once!" Caesia demanded.

"Yeah, like I haven't heard that one before," the knight sneered. "Papers, or get lost."

"I am Lady-"

"You're nobody without identification."

"Let her through, you bloody fools!" called a familiar, gruff voice from across the room.

Veldin Ironhand, now changed from his formalwear and back into his armour, shoved his way through a group of aristocrats and approached the guards. Like most Ironhand armour, his matte grey suit was thick, rigid and extremely bland, impervious to many a blade yet also the heaviest gear one can find. His thunderous footsteps echoed across the room, the crashing of metal following him everywhere he went.

"Sir, we are under orders-"

"That's Edmund Tarantis' daughter, you morons!" Veldin growled. "You really want to piss him off?"

The knight looked to his fellows for approval, who all nodded anxiously. They stepped away and allowed Veldin to approach.

"Didn't imagine I'd be seeing *you* at this time of night!" Veldin laughed. "What brings you here, Miss Tarantis?"

"Are the patriarchs here?" Caesia snapped.

"Uh, yeah... they're upstairs."

"Veldin, there are arachni assassins in the building, I need to get to that meeting!" Caesia begged.

"Arachni?!" Veldin scoffed, before dropping his smile when Caesia's grim expression did not waver. "Wait, you're serious?"

"Of course I bloody am!" Caesia hissed.

"Shit!" Veldin gasped. "Then there's no time to lose, follow me!"

Veldin rushed across the hall with a deafening crash of armour plating, followed closely by Caesia and Eris. They sprinted into the hallways and charged up the stairs to the second floor.

"Something tells me you weren't at that ball to socialise!" Veldin bellowed.

"It's a long story!" Caesia exclaimed, sliding to a halt before the conference room door and igniting her arms with energy. "I'll get the door."

"Allow me," Veldin growled, drawing the battleaxe from his back and swinging it over his head.

Farenos crept silently across the exterior of the building, slipping nimbly to a window and peering through with an eager grin. Rubbing his burning, bandaged wound in his hand, he surveyed the room carefully.

The conference room was fairly toned down when compared to the rest of the building - red velvet carpets, cool mahogany walls and a banner denoting each house hanging from its walls. In the middle of the room, around a large, rectangular table, sat the house patriarchs. Alvus Severin and Edmund Tarantis on the far side, Ilias Barethia and Jonas Arrenni on the other, Kranik Ironhand at the end nearest the door and finally, King Friedrich Verden at its head. The gaggle of nobles sat around discussing matters of the realm, perfectly distracted from any silent entrance one might make.

He would have to be careful however, for they were not alone in the room. For every patriarch, there was also a member of the much feared Phoenix Guard. The guardsmen were each clad in a full suit of slender tricinium armour, elegant and streamlined yet heavily detailed with extravagant patterns and several depictions of the eagle of House Verden. A pair of wings spread from the centre of their helms and up the side of their heads, illuminated on one side by the throbbing yellow glow of their golden spears' crackling blades. Menacing as they were, they were a fact he had to cope with - they never left Friedrich's side.

"You're mad, Kranik," Alvus sneered, kicking back casually in his seat. "The realm is in a fragile state as it is after Jordenholm. We just can't afford it!"

"The realm needn't concern itself," Kranik muttered. "It'll be an undertaking purely by House Ironhand. I ask only the King's permission."

"I cannot help but feel as if you might be overstepping, Kranik," Friedrich warned. "The Shattered Coast is an untameable beast."

"Let House Ironhand worry about that," Edmund muttered. "The realm is in dire need of tricinium, drastic measures must be taken."

"Agreed," declared Jonas, steepling his fingers in calculation. "House Arrenni would be happy to support the endeavour."

"That's all well and good," Ilias hissed. "But Alvus is right, we can't afford to go throwing around our wealth after we lost a whole city! We need Schardenhelm's focus on rearming the Severin army!"

"Exactly," Alvus concurred with a smug grin. "I'm glad to see at least one of you have your head on straight."

"The forges are already hard at work getting your weapons, Alvus," Kranik muttered. "The expedition will draw no resources from the rearmament, I'll be funding it personally."

"I think we are overlooking the clear risks associated with you plan," Friedrich sighed. "It is all well and good funding this out your own pockets, Kranik, but what if it goes awry? Whatever you commit to this could be lost in an instant in such an unpredictable hellscape!"

"True…" Ilias mused. "Not to mention what manor of demonic hellspawn you could run into in your venture."

"Unless I am mistaken, Ilias, there is no proof of any such creatures in the wastes," Jonas sneered. "Simple myth and conjecture."

"Only because none have lived to tell of it!" Ilias insisted. "Even so, there are many more unholy threats out there that we know of for certain - arachni, Vulkites, ash drakes, *pyrewyrms*! Hell, even the Ashen Fleet's been known to roam the shores!"

"I mean this in the nicest way possible, Ilias, but you're being paranoid," Jonas sighed, tapping his fingers impatiently on the table. "Apart from the Anvilport incident those ten years ago, those sea dregs have never been of concern to the realm. As for the rest of your concerns… well, I do believe House Tarantis could be of service in that regard."

Jonas turned with a slender smile to Edmund, who simply glared coldly at him in a brooding silence.

"I… suppose not, then," Jonas mumbled.

"I am all for Kranik's little errand, but it will not waste my attention," Edmund said bluntly. "With House Severin so heavily crippled, my men must stand ready to respond to any manner of revolt in their stead."

"Reasonable," Kranik sighed. He had always respected Edmund as the only one with any common sense amongst the group. "Come on, Friedrich, what say you? My boys can handle a bitta fire, no problem!"

Friedrich shuffled uncomfortably in his chair, reluctant to possibly waste House Ironhand's time and attention. Something felt afoot after Jordenholm, he couldn't put his finger on it yet he feared that the city's ill fate was no coincidence. That alongside the sudden disappearance of resistance in the Strausian jungles left a certain air of tension, like the calm before a storm.

"I'll consider it, Kranik," Friedrich sighed. "But you must understand-"

Friedrich was interrupted as the door jolted under the force of Veldin's axe. The Phoenix Guard ignited their enchanted weapons with hissing golden flame and took up a defensive posture, watching the door carefully through their winged helmets.

Farenos grinned, confident that it was Niria who distracted their foes. He poised to strike from his position on the ceiling, pulling his legs from the woodwork and aiming them for Friedrich's frail, wrinkled neck. Finally, after a decade in the waiting, he would slay the tyrant king.

As the lock shattered under Veldin's mighty swing, Eris held up the lantern and scanned the room ahead. The throbbing blue light flared brightest as she held it up into the air.

"Ceiling," Eris hissed, buckling the lantern to her belt and sliding her sword from its sheath.

Caesia nodded and raised her hands in readiness, crackling electricity surging up her forearms. Eris and Veldin threw themselves against the doors, battering it open and staggering almost headfirst into a wall of golden spears.

Edmund leapt up from the table as Caesia skidded into the room, a look of utter disbelief on his face. Friedrich roared in terror, his guards turning instantly to face him, as a shadow descended upon him. He looked up at Farenos' bloodthirsty smile, his eyes wide with fear. The nobles cringed as the harrowing crack echoed across the room.

Blood spattered the floor as the tip of Farenos' leg scraped across Friedrich's shoulder, defeat on his face as a shimmering bolt of green light smashed into his chest with a deafening crack. Its sheer power blasted him to the ground, tumbling to the back of the room as he shook and convulsed. The patriarchs stared back and forth, mouth ajar, between Caesia and the assassin, while a guard rushed to Friedrich's side.

"There's a second one!" Caesia yelled, her voice strained as she clenched her arm, which had locked up under agonising pain after such a powerful blast.

She walked hurriedly around the table, ignoring her father's gradually darkening stare. She glanced to Alvus and returned his cheeky smile, only to turn back to Farenos to see a golden spear looming over him.

"No!" she shrieked as the guard drove his burning blade into the arachni's chest.

Her heart sank at the hiss of the blade, scorching Farenos' flesh as it cleaved through him like a hot knife through butter, snapping bones like twigs in a series of chilling cracks. He died instantly, a look of regret and failure on his tortured face.

"You idiot!" Caesia growled. "Who the bloody hell trained you? We could have questioned him!"

Edmund slammed his fist on the table, trying to mask his total confusion and surprise with his usual stoic demeanour. "Caesia, explain yourself at once!" he boomed, the other lords shrinking into their seats, apart from Alvus who planted his face in his palm.

Caesia continued to pretend her father was not present and looked around at the room full of startled lords, their expressions a mix of surprise and confusion. Her attention was caught at a faint pattering on the outside wall. She turned to see jagged shadow pass by the window and gestured to Eris, who nodded eagerly and sprinted after Niria.

"Caesia, do not ignore me!" Edmund demanded, circling around the table towards her.

Caesia ignored him, approaching Farenos' corpse with curiosity. Sparks of yellow light had begun to rise from his body like steam. Suddenly, he was engulfed by a shimmering cloak of yellow that lit up like the sun. Caesia gasped as she drew her arm away from her eyes, finding before her a pale, hairless man, his face featureless and eyes an empty white - a changeling.

"They aren't arachni at all!" she whispered to herself.

It added up - the magical signatures detectable by the lantern were the pulses of essence that changelings used to see. What didn't add up was why a group of abhuman would want to pin Friedrich's death on other abhumans. Nonetheless, this was a critical discovery.

She closed her eyes and breathed in as Edmund approached from behind and reached out to grab her shoulder. "Caesia! I will not be-"

Caesia flicked back her hand and created a wall of green light between them. The other lords sniggered as Edmund's head glanced off with a hiss and he stumbled back from the barrier. Making such a barrier burned Caesia's arms, but it was well worth the amusement.

She approached Friedrich, who was slumped back in his seat breathing hysterically as one of his guardsmen wrapped his wound. "Veldin, see that our liege does not leave his palace for the remainder of the night," she commanded, looking at the King with a plastic smile. "We'll handle this, your majesty."

"You are not going anywhere!" Edmund hissed, grabbing her shoulder forcefully.

Something in her mind told her in that moment to kill him, to fry his brain with electricity, but she was better than him. She span around and yanked her father's hand from her shoulder with a burning glare. Impulsively, she thrust her hand into his stomach, a blast of green light sending him skidding across the ground on his back.

"You are embarrassing yourself, Lord Tarantis," Caesia smirked. "You more than anyone should know better than to anger me."

"Your dull wit only makes you look a fool," Edmund growled, clawing his way slowly off the ground.

Caesia smiled, never before having the confidence to talk down to her father. "Declares the man being tossed like a ragdoll by his teenage daughter," she laughed. "Apologies, but I've got to run. I've a life to enjoy, if you don't mind."

She turned with a gleeful grin and approached the window, watching as Eris raced off across the road. As much as she would have loved to stay and taunt her father, she had business to attend to.

"Oh, and I can do this now," she smiled, tilting her head smugly as she vanished in a burst of green light.

Every jaw in the room dropped open in disbelief. Alvus snorted with laughter as he looked at Edmund's blank, defeated face. Edmund stared off into space for a moment, frozen in shock at what he had just witnessed. In near unison, everybody in the room turned to Veldin, who slowly raised his hands in defence.

"I… didn't know she could to that," he stammered.

Eris battered open the front door and skidded out onto the street, searching up and down the road, yet finding only beggars and the odd drunk in sight. Knowing that Niria couldn't have gotten far, she yanked the lantern from her belt and scanned slowly around her. The dazzling blue light slowly began to brighten as she moved it left. As it approached a ragged beggar, the woman glanced up with panicked eyes and after a moment of staring, leapt nimbly to her feet.

"Hey!" Eris yelled after her.

She didn't remember what Niria looked like, but she was pretty sure this wasn't her. Still, nobody would run if they weren't worried about getting their ass kicked. She thundered after the woman, easily tracking her around the corner by the sounds of her footsteps in the silent night.

As Eris headed for the end of the street, Caesia appeared outside the building in a flash of light, a passing drunk discarding his booze at the sight of her.

She glanced down excitedly at the fading energy coursing around her body - longer ranged translocation was exhilarating! She had felt the pure energy of creation rushing by as she leapt between realities. It was intoxicating!

She gave one last smug look at her father as he peered through the second floor window, sticking up her middle finger at his gobsmacked face before taking off after Eris.

Eris skidded around the corner and into the next street. Niria grabbed a drunk from the side of the road and toppled him to the ground in a heap. Eris smirked at the hilarity of the man writhing aimlessly on the ground before hopping effortlessly over him.

Caesia came around the corner and gasped as her foot slammed into the man's head. She staggered for about five metres before she slowly began to regain her footing.

"Sorry!" she called over her shoulder.

"Your welcome!" Slurred the drunk, stumbling to his feet in a daze.

Eris followed her target into an alleyway, weaving nimbly through a mess of boxes and bins. Caesia ground to a halt at the end of the cluttered alleyway and rolled her eyes at the sight of it, beginning to develop a hatred of alleyways. As Eris leapt over the last bin, Caesia ran at the first wall of boxes headfirst and in a burst of green light, passed straight through them. She giggled like a little girl as she burst from her tunnel of light, the sudden surge of air blasting her hair back as she leapt back into reality.

Niria slid to a stop and kicked the wooden blocks out from underneath a cart. Eris darted to the side of the street as the cart rolled into her path, a confident smirk on her face. She jumped up against the wall and kicked off it, landing clumsily on the driver's seat and springing back onto the pavement.

Caesia ran at the cart confidently and thrust herself forwards to blink through it. Her head slammed hard against the side of the cart and she staggered backwards, her head spinning. Rubbing her head and mumbling angrily under her breath, she threw herself at it again and appeared on the other side, quite disappointed with herself.

As she emerged, Caesia watched, panting for breath, as Eris turned into another alleyway. She really wasn't cut out for all this exercise.

"W-wait. What am I doing?" she scoffed. She was above running!

She thrust forwards and in a surge of green light, blinked several metres down the street. She leapt forth a second time and then a third, bringing her effortlessly to the alleyway. She threw out her arms as she launched a final time into the street, totally overwhelmed with excitement.

Eris ran out across the next street and into the adjacent alleyway, where Niria slid around the corner and into a small alcove. If the woman assumed to ambush her, Eris thought confidently, she'd be in for a surprise.

Her sword slid from its sheath as she skidded around the corner, coming face to face with five pale, hairless people. A sixth in their midst turned to face her, a woman not like them whose head flowed with blonde hair that parted around a featureless black mask. Eris froze, burning red eyes falling upon her as the woman's hand caught ablaze with crimson fire.

In an explosion of green light, Eris toppled to the ground at the other end of the alleyway, Caesia falling on top of her in a heap. She looked over her shoulder as the walls around her quaked, a colossal, inferno consuming the entire alley behind them. She cringed at the touch of the heat, the crimson fire barely caressing their bodies before it shrank away.

Amidst the towering flames, a shadow emerged. The woman appeared only as a warped, black shape in the dancing inferno, completely unscathed by the fire. Her arm rose towards them, cloaked in writhing flame and hung there for a moment. For seconds that felt like minutes, the glimmering specks of her red eyes stared into Eris'. Her fist clenched and the fire began to dwindle and flicker, her arm withdrawing hesitantly to her side. She stared once more at her would-be victims, before vanishing into the burning abyss.

Caesia rolled off Eris' back and onto the frigid cobblestones, laying there in silence and staring up into the sky. Eris scrambled onto her backside and glanced back down the alley, where the last of the flames gave way to nothing but blackened walls and charred rats. She turned to Caesia and followed her friend's gaze to a molten heap of slag on the ground beside them, a blue essence crystal lodged within the hissing mass.

"Oh my- I'm so sorry!" Eris gasped. "I-I'm such an idiot, I shouldn't have-"

"It's fine," Caesia sighed, a smile still plastered on here face. "We'll find a way around it, we always do."

"Yeah," Eris smiled. "You know you're bleeding, right?"

Caesia wiped her hand across her forehead, smirking as she dabbed a tiny speck of blood from the throbbing lump forming beneath her hair. "Ah, yeah. Hit my head pretty hard."

"No, I mean your nose."

Caesia looked down and wiped some blood from the small stream flowing from her nostrils. "Huh, it seems that my powers obey the basic laws of essence. Definitely something to bear in mind."

"Good, can't have you showing me up all the time!" Eris grinned. "I heard you laughing back there - I wasn't sure if you were dying or having the time of your life!"

Caesia's eyes lit up like stars as she surged suddenly with energy. "I- I've never felt such a rush!" she gushed, craziness in her eyes. "It's indescribable, I... I don't..."

Eris tilted her head with a sweet and gentle smile. The affectionate look in her starry eyes was like that which a mother gives her newborn child, one of love and pride.

"What?" Caesia laughed.

"I'm just... really happy," Eris smiled. "It means so much to see you so excited!"

"W-what do you mean?" Caesia mumbled shyly.

"You've just been so sad the past few days and... it hurt, I guess," Eris sighed. "It hurt because I couldn't do a thing about it! I just had to sit there and watch you go crazy over your powers... and now, seeing you really, truly happy... it just makes me smile."

Eris smiled the most heartwarming smile Caesia had ever witnessed. This entire time, Eris had been doing nothing but trying to make her happy as best she could. After the life she had lived, Caesia could scarcely believe it possible that someone could care so much more about another's life than their own.

"Why?" Caesia scoffed. "Why do you care *so* much?"

"I don't know... but I don't think it really matters," Eris smiled. "I just know that seeing you smile... it gives me the best feeling I've ever felt! I guess I just like to make people happy!"

"I... I always thought this was all about the adventure for you."

"Two birds with one stone, right?" Eris grinned. "Besides, as much as I wanna be an awesome hero, my best friend will always come first!"

Caesia chuckled quietly. When she had first met Eris, she thought her a selfish egomaniac obsessed with fame and glory. Only today had she begun to understand what kind of person Eris truly was. Between herself and Maeve, Caesia had seen Eris' true colours brought out, and they were beautiful.

"Eris... you're the best," Caesia smiled, a warm glow about her. "Wait, hold on a minute! You already have a best friend!"

"You can have multiple best friends!" Eris insisted.

"No, you can't!" Caesia laughed. "It's in the name - *best* friend. As in 'better than all the others'!"

"Well, I like you more anyway, so it's fine," Eris chirped.

"You like *me* more than your childhood best friend?!" Caesia scoffed. "How? You only met me a week ago and I just take the piss out of you all the time!"

"You might be surprised, but that's exactly what best friends do!" Eris smiled. "The more you insult each other, the better friends you are!"

"That makes no sense… yet I understand completely," Caesia smirked. "Alright then, best friend! Let's catch some assassins!"

"Now you're talking!" Eris declared, pumping her arms with excitement. "So, those guys were shapeshifters or something?"

"Changelings, yes. It does well to explain why the Matriarch knew nothing of them."

"And why they were nowhere near as good as actual arachni," Eris sneered. "Why arachni though?"

"Other than them being the ultimate killing machines?" Caesia sighed. "I've been thinking about that actually. You remember Lycoria mentioned that Valkyr offered her an alliance and she turned it down?"

"Valkyr had them pin it on the arachni and force them to join him!" Eris gasped.

"Yes, else Verdenheld would wipe them from the face of Elaria!" Caesia exclaimed.

"Great…" Eris chuckled. "Not only are we the only thing standing between the king of Verdenheld and certain death, but also the fate of an entire race is in our hands!"

"I know, terrifying isn't it?" Caesia laughed anxiously. "To think that barely over a week ago, I was sat alone in my dorm thinking I'd never make anything of myself. Now here we are, poised to change the course of history."

Eris enjoyed that notion. Daunting as it was, saving a king and a race all at the same time was a worthy deed of heroism to be sure. She hoped her ancestors were watching, because they would have to let her in after this!

"Well if we're gonna do that, we'd better come up with something fast!" Eris declared, determined as ever.

"Indeed, and I think I've a plan," Caesia grinned. "We know now that our enemy is greater in number, so I'd say it's safe to assume that they have a backup plan in place that will involve all of them."

"But why wouldn't they all go in the first place?"

"Simple - scare factor. If the king was killed by two arachni rather than five, it would paint them as a greater threat and warrant a more decisive action by Verdenheld."

"Makes sense."

"Anyway, it is likely that they will withdraw to plot their next move," Caesia said. "Which leaves us time to act."

"Then what's the plan?" Eris asked. "We take the fight to them?"

"Exactly, but first things first, we need another seeker lantern," Caesia sighed. "And there's only one place in Aldreichen that we can find one."

"I don't like where this is going," Eris muttered.

"Rightfully. We'll need to get one from the Inquisition, from their Aldreichen garrison in the Hallow District."

"And I guess they probably won't hand one over willingly?" Eris smirked.

"Yes, but worry not!" Caesia declared. "I've a cunning plan…"

Chapter Seven - The Lantern Heist

"Steal one?!" Eris hissed. "You want to break into a heavily fortified, heavily guarded military compound to steal a lantern?"

"Yes."

Eris' face lit up with an eager grin. "I'm in."

"Thought so," Caesia smirked. "Just don't fall asleep in the middle of the compound."

"Don't worry, I'm wide awake!" Eris declared.

It was well past one o'clock now, but they couldn't afford even a moment's rest. The stakes were high and they had to make every minute count. They were headed towards the Inquisitorial Garrison in the Hallow District, the area of the city centred around its cathedral that contained by far the most churches and temples. It was like an inquisitor's natural habitat.

"So, how do you plan on getting in exactly?" Eris asked.

"I'll figure that out once we're there," Caesia said. "I can't come up with much of a plan if I've never seen the place before."

"Fair enough," Eris sighed. "Hey, I know I've asked this a lot today, but are you doing alright? I know you were pretty worried about running into your father."

"Actually, it was quite a weight off my shoulders," Caesia smiled. "I may or may not have blasted him across the room."

"No way!" Eris laughed. "Go Caesia!"

"Yeah…" Caesia sighed. "I never thought I'd see the day where I didn't fear that man… but back there, I had the courage to look him in the eyes and treat him like he was nothing. Nothing has ever felt so good."

Eris was elated to know that Caesia was finally at peace with the darkest depths of her past. That was as much a weight off her shoulders as it was Caesia's.

"Why is it I never see you stressing about anything?" Caesia asked curiously. "It sounded to me like you were due to have a whole heap of responsibilities thrust onto you."

"Ah, I've had eighteen years to stress about that," Eris said dismissively. "This year, I'm just forgetting about it all. I want to experience the world, no commitments attached!"

"You just blank it from your mind?"

"Pretty much," Eris smirked. "Why waste my time worrying about the future when I could be living my life in the present?"

"Reasonable enough, I suppose," Caesia sighed. "What about all the blood, the gore, the life threatening situations, holding the fate of the world in our hands - how the hell do you stay so damn calm all the time?"

"Honestly, I just do everything I can to stop myself thinking negatively. I put on a smile, make jokes, tease people, anything it takes. If I never think about losing, I won't!"

"That's it?"

"I... I guess what I'm trying to say is that I tell myself so much that I can win, that I begin to believe it's fact. Knowing I can win makes me try my best, which in turn makes me win! It probably makes no sense to you, but that's how I keep going at my best and with a smile on my face!"

"You know, I think I do get it," Caesia smiled.

She had always admired Eris' carefree attitude and unbreakable drive, she even envied it to some extent. Now that she had come to peace with everything, maybe she would try and live that way too - put on a smile and quit complaining, maybe try to be more open to having fun once in while. That was an idea that she reckoned she could get behind, to finally let everything go and live a happy life.

"Find the girl!" Edmund commanded, his voice casting a daunting echo through the hall. "If she resists, and she will, use any force necessary to subdue her."

"And the other one, my lord?" asked one of the red clad knights.

"She is of no concern," Edmund muttered. "But should she get in the way, do not hesitate to kill her."

"Disregard that!" Veldin barked, storming across the hall with a furious snarl on his face. "You lot, get outta here!"

The knights exchanged confused glances and edged slowly away. Veldin turned to Edmund with a scowl and shoved a finger into his face.

"Friedrich is under threat of assassination and all you can think about is your bloody girl?!"

Edmund turned slowly to stare Veldin in the eyes, a tense silence hanging between them. His cold glare drew sweat from Veldin's brow and stiffened his shoulders.

"That 'girl' could be the key to a new era of arcane understanding," Edmund growled, drawing ever closer to Veldin. "*She* will save our dying kingdom, Friedrich will not."

"If the king dies there will be chaos!"

"If the king dies, there will be a replacement!" Edmund boomed. "There are systems in place to contain such events, to maintain order. Geldus Verden will succeed him and that will be that - a fossil traded for an idiot."

"Aldreichen won't abandon its king," Veldin said defiantly.

"Aldreichen may do as it wish," Edmund sneered. "If you insist on remaining blind, then so be it. I will deal with this myself."

"You'll jeopardize-"

"Friedrich is a dead man walking!" Edmund hissed. "I'll hear not a word more. Leave me."

Veldin opened his mouth in argument, only to shrivel away at Edmund's icy glare. With a furious sigh, he stormed off into the street, calling the guards to attention. As Edmund stood in contemplation, he sighed as Alvus Severin slipped to his side.

"Family troubles, Edmund?" he smiled.

Edmund both resented and respected Alvus equally. Brown of hair and sporting a finely trimmed beard, he was one of the younger breed, barely thirty. He brought with him a rather laid back attitude to politics, one that was often annoying yet made him quite reliable. He played the political game on one dimension, the only thing on his mind being crushing Verdenheld's enemies. Edmund liked that, despite Alvus' disrespectful attitude.

"Very funny, Alvus," Edmund snarled. "But I assure you, it is under control. My battlemages will have her by sunrise."

"Maybe I could lend some troops to your cause?" Alvus suggested. "Cut off some streets, blockade the bridge…"

"That will not be necessary. My men are far better suited to the task."

"If you say so…" Alvus sighed. "I'm not going to lie, Edmund, you're a bit of a laughing stock after the display your girl put on."

"It will be fleeting," Edmund muttered. "Once my daughter is returned to Abenfurt, we will learn much from her newfound abilities. The Council will not be laughing when I present to them the secrets of the arcane."

"And what will we do with these secrets?"

"Well, that all depends on what we find," Edmund smiled. "But whatever it may be, it will secure Verdenheld's dominance for centuries, perhaps millennia to come. Imagine for me, Alvus, a Severin battalion teleporting into an enemy army's rear flank."

Alvus' eyes widened as he stroked his beard deviously. "Now you have my attention," he grinned. "In that case, best of luck to you! I had best return to Tryzantopol, I've more problems to deal with than I have soldiers to deal with them."

"That is saying something…" Edmund smirked, an uncommon breach of his glacial personality. "Here I expected you to be running to Friedrich's aid."

"Kings rise and fall," Alvus smiled. "As long as it doesn't cause another Interregnum, I couldn't care less if we lose the old man."

"Well, long live the King," Edmund chuckled. "Once my daughter is dealt with, perhaps I could deploy some battlemages to help police the commonfolk?"

"Really?" Alvus scoffed, quite surprised that Edmund dealt in gestures of good will.

"Alvus, you know the stability of the realm is my top priority," Edmund assured him. "Such insurgencies cannot be allowed to persist."

"Well in that case, it would be appreciated," Alvus chirped. "Thank you, Edmund."

"Of course," Edmund said with a fledgling smile. "I will be in touch within the week. Good luck, Alvus."

He watched with a subtle smirk as Alvus disappeared into the streets, before turning to a nearby guard and assuming his intimidating stance once again.

"You there, boy!" he demanded, scaring the colour out of the guardsman's face. "You will run to my quarters and fetch my men. Ensure that they prepare for combat."

The red-clad young man nodded hurriedly and rushed off into the hallways. As he awaited the arrival of his battlemages, Edmund smiled in confidence. His daughter would elude him no longer and with her newfound powers, he would usher in a new age of magical understanding. He would not allow the kingdom to fall into irrelevance, Verdenheld would reign forever supreme.

Eris and Caesia headed deep into the Hallow District, at the far western reaches of the city. The buildings transitioned quickly from the sleek, golden brown structures of the Palace District to the rugged, red brick buildings of the outer city. As they came close to the district's core, the colossal, white spire of the city's cathedral came into view, towering over the surrounding buildings as a testament to God's glory. While it was nothing compared to the Grand Cathedral of Windspire, it was no less magnificent - the white stone was elaborately carved with patterns and tapestries and the stained glass windows displayed holy figures and scenes in an array of vibrant colours, including the featureless, yellow silhouette of God himself.

Across the square from the cathedral was the gate to the Inquisitorial Garrison. The wooden door, while large, would have looked fairly unsuspecting alone, if not for the two parallel rows of magically electrified spikes lining the top. Behind those walls laid a veritable battalion of inquisitors, sitting on a gigantic hoard of abhuman hunting equipment.

Eris and Caesia slipped into a dank alleyway across the square and took cover behind a pile of battered old crates.

"This is a terrible idea," Eris smirked, peering out and surveying the gate.

"Says the girl who dragged me up a mountain to fight a fire breathing lizard," Caesia laughed. "You have *no* room to talk."

"But they've got lightning spikes on the walls!"

"That may be, but observe - there are no guards outside the gate, meaning that they are undermanned. Thus, I'd hazard to say that much of the Inquisition's manpower has been shifted elsewhere, and that most of those remaining are asleep."

"Okay, so there are less of them, but we still need to get in and out without being seen."

"Hm… if I could get high enough to see into the compound, perhaps I could teleport in, grab a lantern and get out?"

"Still a terrible idea," Maeve whispered.

Eris and Caesia jumped in shock, both turning to Maeve with silent glares and receiving a quirky grin in return. The arachni's jagged yellow teeth were tinted red and morsels of chewed flesh still lingered within the gaps. She oozed a metallic musk that joined with the choking stink of sewage to launch a stomach churning assault on the senses.

"What the- what are you doing here?" Caesia spluttered breathlessly.

"I've been following you in the sewers, had nothing better to do with myself," Maeve smiled. "Then I heard you were gonna hit the compound and I just had to get in on it!"

"Why would you- hold on!" Caesia snapped. "You've been following us this entire time?!"

"Yup."

"Have… have you been listening in on our conversations?" Caesia hissed.

Maeve stared at her blankly, guilt written all over her face. It was hard to miss discomfort when the person in question had eight eyes to track.

"A little…" Maeve mumbled, turning with a grin to Eris. "You, by the way, are adorable. That was *so* sweet what you said about making people happy! I nearly cried."

"Um… thanks," Eris mumbled, looking away timidly.

"Ugh, whatever," Caesia groaned. "Anyway, why in Elaria would you want to break into a garrison full of soldiers trained to kill you?"

"I have my reasons," Maeve muttered. "Look, I know this place like the back of my legs and let me tell you - you ain't getting a lantern that easy. They keep their equipment in a secure vault."

"Okay, but why do you really want to break in?" Caesia asked, totally unconvinced.

"Fine, real talk - I've got a score to settle."

Caesia sighed impatiently. "Maeve, we can't just-"

"I'll be quiet!" Maeve urged, bouncing up and down excitedly. "I'm very discreet."

"And what exactly do you intend to do once you're in there?"

"Ah, I'm just gonna kill the Grand Inquisitor and be on my way," Maeve said. "Nothing too crazy."

"No way," Caesia said bluntly.

"How have we gone from stopping arachni assassins to helping one?" Eris smirked.

"Look, if you guys don't want my help that's fine," Maeve muttered, folding her arms and looking away in a clear attempt to guilt trip them. "But there is no way you can sneak in there on your own. You don't even know what's behind that wall!"

Caesia looked to Eris defeatedly. She felt extremely uncomfortable helping Maeve murder a man, but it would once again be an alliance of necessity. "Fine... but keep it quiet."

"Quiet is my profession!" Maeve grinned smugly. "Now, hold still."

She threw out her legs and wrapped her lowest pair around their waists with an innocent smile. The startled look on Caesia's face was priceless - she was so fun to mess with.

"What are you doing?" Caesia asked nervously, remembering well Maeve's reputation for eating people.

"All we can see from here is a wall, we gotta get a vantage point."

Caesia thrust Maeve's legs off her. "I can get up there myself!" she said stroppily.

"Go on then."

Caesia narrowed her eyes at Maeve and glanced up the wall of the ramshackle house beside them. She leapt up into the air and went up in green light. Eris and Maeve both smirked as she appeared a few feet into the air with a blank look on her face. Maeve flung out a leg and caught her by the collar as she fell back to the pavement.

"Woah, cool trick," Maeve sneered. "I bet the flying circus'll be *begging* you for an audition."

Caesia screwed up her face with contempt and let Maeve lift her up. Maeve slammed her legs into the stonework and lifted them off the ground, scuttling nimbly up the alleyway wall. Eris chuckled at the sight of Caesia, who had her eyes squeezed shut in an attempt to avoid getting scared.

"Man up, girl!" Maeve jeered, shaking Caesia around like a ragdoll.

"I hate you," Caesia groaned.

"Well you know what they say!" Maeve chirped. "You can't spell hate without hat."

Caesia's brain felt as if it had just malfunctioned in an attempt to process that statement. She simply hung there in confusion, not quite sure how to react to the sheer idiocy that had just graced her ears.

Maeve slipped onto the flat rooftop of the building and dumped Eris and Caesia onto the surface. She wandered to the edge, from which they could see across the square and over the compound wall.

"Much better!" Maeve exclaimed, lying down and peering down at the compound courtyard. "Now, you need a lantern, right? As I said, you'll need to get into the vault."

"And where is the vault?" Eris whispered, laying down beside Maeve. "In there, I assume?"

Eris pointed towards the monolithic, two-story building in the middle of the courtyard. The bland, grey block of stone and mortar was laden with electrified spikes and sladium-barred windows. Searchlights beamed columns of yellow across the compound, capable of magically revealing invisible foes, while a spattering of inquisitors patrolled around the building wielding crossbows loaded with sladium tipped bolts. The whole place was prepared against abhuman infiltration, yet it sported little defence against a simple human.

"Yep, that's the headquarters," Maeve explained. "You'll need to get into the basement to reach the vault, but first you're gonna need the key."

"Don't tell me, the Grand Inquisitor has the key?" Caesia sighed.

"That he does," Maeve grinned, an unnervingly fiendish look in her eyes. "Lucky for you, I'll be in the area to... procure it for you."

"I assume that's where we'll part ways?" Caesia asked.

"Yep!" Maeve chirped. "I plan to stay a while, so don't wait up."

"So, what's the actual plan?" Eris asked, itching to be done with the small talk on get on with the heist.

"Right, the plan..." Maeve muttered. "You guys have any paper?"

Eris turned to Caesia, who sighed reluctantly and shoved her hand into her shoulder bag. She shovelled out her notebook and flicked through dozens of layers of notes and equations until she reached a blank page. Eris smirked as Caesia crudely tore out a page, leaving a sizable chunk of the paper behind. Caesia looked it up and down, shrugged and handed it to Maeve, along with her inkpot.

"Um... a full piece would be nice," Maeve muttered.

"You'll live," Caesia said with a mocking smile. "Can you even write?"

"Pft, can I write..." Maeve scoffed. "Of course I can't! Luckily, pictures will do us just fine."

"Wonderful..."

"Alright, ladies, gather round!" Maeve said as she dipped the tip of her finger into the inkpot and began scribbling feverously. "Alright, you wanna go in through this side here, up there like that, take a right, then another right, then a left, then go straight into the hall, over there and… boom! Got your lantern."

"Maeve, you just drew a line," Caesia groaned, staring tiredly at the winding arrow scratched onto the paper.

"Yeah, and if you go in through the right door, you just follow the line! No need to overcomplicate things."

Caesia was too tired for this. She snatched the paper from Maeve, took a quick glance at it and tucked it away in her coat pocket with a sigh.

"Alright, I'm gonna slip into the grand man's quarters and get the key," Maeve declared. "I'll drop it out the window and you, teleporty girl, will teleport into the courtyard and pick it up."

"It's Caesia, by the way."

"Don't expect me to remember that," Maeve muttered. "Anyway, there's a blind spot right… there, where the searchlights won't see you. From there, you can make a break for the key. Then you'll need to get to the basement staircase inside the building. There'll always be a few guards, so you'll have to take em out, but then you'll have your lantern."

"Okay… might I ask, how it is that you know the interior layout of this place?" Caesia asked.

"Let's just say I had plenty of time for taking mental notes during my last visit," Maeve smiled darkly. "Wait here, I'll be back."

Maeve dug her legs into the rooftop and sprang up, silently moving across the rooftops. She reached the edge and peered over. It was laughable how easy it was to enter the compound, even for an abhuman. Sure, there were several anti-abhuman measures - doorways enchanted to disable ulkar invisibility, as well as wall-based traps to catch arachni, but once one knew where they were, they were easily avoidable. After all, she'd had plenty of time to memorise their locations from the comfort of various torture chambers.

Caesia and Eris watched from afar as Maeve launched elegantly from the rooftops and disappeared into the compound.

"I'm glad she showed up," Eris smiled. "We never would've figured this out."

"True, but I can't help but feel like she's going to do something stupid…" Caesia sighed.

Maeve landed nimbly atop the building and skidded slowly down the tiled roof. She glided to the edge of the roof and yanked down the back of her ragged trousers, attaching herself to the wall with a squirt of sloppy, wet silk. Upside down with her legs wrapped around her webbing, she crawled down the side of the building and to the second floor window. She peered through from above with a wide grin, particularly excited for her upcoming reunion.

Sitting away from the window was the Grand Inquisitor at his desk, working through the last of his paperwork for the night. The bald man was dressed in the usual studded leather armour of the Order, with golden accents on his silvered shoulders to signify his rank. Maeve smirked in reminiscence at the large ceremonial hat sat beside him - she remembered fondly how she so often made fun of it. Cone head, she would call him… good times.

Maeve tore off a few threads of her webbing and pressed it against the window, weaving her hand through it and gripping it tight. Her hand secured on the glass, she pressed the end of her finger against it and carefully slid it across the surface. Her jagged claw glided elegantly through the glass and as it came to a halt, she gently removed the transparent disc from the window.

The Grand Inquisitor was oblivious as Maeve pulled up her pants and slipped silently through the gap, expertly weaving her many legs through the small hole with the agility expected of an arachni soldier.

"Oh, I like what you've done with the place!" she chirped. "Could probably do with some better traps though."

The Grand Inquisitor jumped out of his seat and span around, his eyes growing wide at the sight of Maeve. "You!" he gasped.

As he turned to call for help, Maeve slung a handful of silk across his face, splattering over his mouth. She approached as he clawed fruitlessly at the silken trap, his muffled cries like music to her ears.

"You remember me! I'm flattered," Maeve grinned. "How's my favourite cone head? It's been a while, hasn't it?" she smiled, picking up the bucket-sized hat with a playful smirk. "I hope you've come up with better games since last time, I didn't find them all that entertaining…"

The Grand Inquisitor backed around the desk and bolted for the door. Maeve hurled another handful of webbing, which exploded against his hand as it grasped the doorknob. He yanked as hard as he could at the knob, which could barely even budge under the cloak of silk.

"I'll be needing this," Maeve whispered, sliding the key from his belt and placing the hat on his head with an excited gasp. "Perfection! Of course you're still the paragon of style that I remember!"

As Maeve turned away, Cone Head reached for his sword with his free arm and swung it at her in panic. Feeling the swing with the hairs on her legs, Maeve span around and grabbed the blade in her hand. Protected by the tough layer of black chitin coating her forearms, she heaved her grip down and twisted the blade from his hand.

"Now, now, play nice," she smiled, slamming his arm into the wall and taping it down with silk. "I'll be right back."

Maeve strolled over to the window and flicked the key out into the courtyard. She waved around Cone Head's fine silver sword as she returned to him, staring at the slender blade with intrigue.

"Is this new? I don't remember it," she mused. "Think I might keep it, consider it compensation."

Cone Head winced as she slammed the blade into his desk with a loud crack. She drew close to him, insanity burning in her eyes.

"Now, let's play a game, shall we?" she whispered, her voice suddenly coarse and crazed. "I think I still remember a few - hundred lashes was a good one… oh, what was that one where you sterilised me?"

Maeve slashed his hand free with one leg and flung him against a wall with another. She drew more webbing and as he scrambled up, pinned him to the wall by his arms, followed by his legs.

"I've been waiting a long time for this little role reversal," Maeve hissed, becoming slowly hysterical and more intense with her every word. "Every night I think about you, every time imagining a new and exciting way to make you wish you'd never been born!"

She leant into him, tears leaking from his eyes as her rows of serrated teeth drew close to his delicate flesh. His fear was a pleasure the likes of which she had never felt.

"What was it you said to me before you scooped out my ovaries?" Maeve whispered with a sinister smile. "I think it went something like 'the Lord will forgive you once you are cleansed'."

She ran her razor fingers up his body, slicing open his coat with one elegant stroke of her hand. Her thirsting eyes pulsating with her every unstable breath, twitching as a brutal lust for vengeance long nurtured burst to life like a blazing inferno.

"Where should we cleanse first?" she grinned, running her quivering hand gently down his face, his muffled screams flooding her with ecstasy. She was going to enjoy every gruesome detail of their happy little reunion.

Caesia watched as the key spiralled out of the window and landed in the dirt. "That's our cue." She whispered, shuffling to her feet. "I must warn you, I can only travel so far with this. Odds are, we'll appear at least a small distance off the ground."

"I appreciate the warning," Eris muttered, gripping Caesia's hand tightly. "What do you think she's doing in there?"

"Honestly, I really don't want to know," Caesia sighed. "Let's just get on with it."

Caesia stepped forwards and Eris watched in awe as a tunnel of green light blasted by, before exploding back into reality. They appeared about a metre above the key and dropped to the ground, Eris landing nimbly on her feet while Caesia landed clumsily on the side of her foot and toppled over into the dirt.

"Oh man, that's gonna take some getting used to," Eris whispered, holding her stomach as it settled back into place.

"Really?" Caesia smirked, holding her head high with a smug grin. "I'm fine."

Caesia scrambled to her feet and clawed the key up off the ground, slipping it into her pocket as they threw themselves up against the wall.

"So, we need to get into the building and find the staircase to the basement," Caesia recapped, unfolding Maeve's 'map'. "But how do we- Wait a minute."

"What?"

Caesia's face dropped, her hatred for Maeve boiling below her calm exterior. "Eris, Maeve's map says there should be a door right here."

Eris looked at the blank brick wall beside them, narrowing her eyes and staring closely in hope to find a secret door.

"That half-witted, spider bitch!" Caesia hissed. "What the hell were we thinking letting *her* give us directions?!"

"I guess we'd best find a door," Eris muttered.

While Caesia furiously scrunched Maeve's map into as small a ball as possible, Eris peered around the corner from where they hid. There were several guards dotted around the compound, mostly standing between the gate and the building. It seemed only logical to try around the back.

"Not this way," Eris whispered. "Let's see if there's a back door."

They crept around the building, hugging the walls and moving in and out of cover. The whole compound was eerily quiet and the back of the courtyard was utterly deserted. It seemed that the Inquisition were foolishly overconfident in their anti-abhuman defences. Never would they have expected humans to infiltrate their headquarters.

Eris spotted an unguarded back door and pointed it out to Caesia. They waited for a patrolling inquisitor to disappear behind the building, before moving carefully towards it.

"Hold on," Caesia warned. "We ought to check for traps."

Caesia looked the doorway up and down carefully. The left beam of the door frame was glowing an extremely subtle blue, presumably enchanted to disable biological invisibility. The crystalline upper beam was made of sladium, likely in place to force changelings into their original forms.

"I think we're clear," Caesia whispered, signalling Eris to move up to the door.

Eris crept up and carefully pulled down the handle. She moved the door slightly open and peered through the slit, where her gaze met an unlit room, completely empty from what she could see. Caesia slipped in behind her, a sudden pain jolted through her head, like someone had just shot her in the back of the head with an arrow.

"What's wrong?" Eris gasped as Caesia whimpered in pain.

"Nothing, just the sladium," Caesia mumbled, holding her head in pain.

She stepped away from the sladium and flicked her hand, a flickering green flame stuttering to life in her hand and illuminating the room. The pale green light revealed a network of large cages, all bearing the rosy tint of tricinium. Strewn across the room was all manor of strange equipment - a table bearing bolted straps, a steel vat of bloody water, crude prongs and bars leant against an unlit brazier. It was a torture chamber, cloaked in crusty, crimson stains and reeking of nought but death.

"Dear God..." Caesia gasped, her head becoming lighter and lighter as she took in her surroundings.

She surveyed the empty cages, the bars caked with dried blood and battered by hundreds of claw marks. Inside, they were almost totally empty, no bed, no toilet, just a layer of decayed faeces and a rusted dog bowl.

"What is this place?" Eris whispered, covering her mouth at the grim sight before her..

"This must be where they torture the abhumans before their executions," Caesia muttered darkly. "I figured the conditions would be inhumane, but this?"

They moved to the other end of the room, where a table sat between blood stricken walls. Surrounding it were several cabinets, laden with a whole host of brutal and horrifying tools, from red tinted scalpels to crude and jagged nutcrackers. The tools were not even cleaned, completely consumed by crumbling rust and decades of congealed blood.

Eris looked around in horror. Never in her life had she imagined such a sick, twisted sight. Every minute in this city had pushed her morality further and further past its limits. These were the people they were trying to save, these murderous sadists who knew nothing but hate. Were they doing the right thing by stopping these assassins, or were they really working with the bad guys?

"Can... can we just talk about something?" Eris mumbled.

Caesia glanced up at Eris' distressed frown with a gentle nod. "Sure," she smiled.

"I'm not so sure we should be doing this..." Eris sighed. "I mean, all of this, you know?"

"Seriously?" Caesia gasped, terribly surprised given Eris' general lack of objection.

She had never even thought about what effect today's events might have had on Eris, always so focused on her own problems. The cool and collected facade that Eris forced upon herself had totally masked her creeping concern about the morality of their cause. Caesia could only imagine what Eris must have thought of Verdenheld after what she had seen.

"We're trying to save a man who thinks this is okay! Caging people up like animals because they're different!" Eris sobbed. "Would it not be better to just… let him die?"

"If it were that simple, I'd happily leave Friedrich to rot," Caesia sighed. "This has been going on for over four hundred years, it won't stop with Friedrich. If we let him die, Geldus Verden will succeed him and believe me, we do *not* want someone like him in power if Valkyr comes knocking."

"I guess you're right…" Eris mumbled. "But I just feel wrong! I feel like by helping these bastards, I'm no better than they are!"

"You know that's not true," Caesia smiled. "You're an amazing person, Eris, far better than me. You always see the good in people where nobody else does, and you've no hates or prejudices, you just greet everything with that… that damned smile."

Eris smiled timidly at Caesia's admiration. She was right - as talented as Eris was with her sword, what made her truly special in this hellhole of a kingdom was her heart. Maybe that was how she would truly become a hero - not by slaying monsters or saving kings, but by finally bringing some good out in the world.

"There it is," Caesia grinned. "Come on, we'd be stupid to dwell in one place for too long. And quite frankly, I'd rather forget I was ever here."

"Yeah… me to," Eris sighed, putting on a tough face.

Verdenheld was a terrible place, festering with evil, but she could not let that blind her. There were still two million people living in this city alone, millions more throughout the world. She would protect them, she would stop the Oppressor because the world still deserved a chance. Despite the murder and hate that plagued its every corner, the people of Elaria were not evil. They just needed to be shown the light, and Eris would not let Valkyr snuff it just yet.

Maeve scooped up a bottle of Abenglade white wine from the side and rammed her claw deep into the cork. She kicked back on the Grand Inquisitor's desk and threw back her head, pausing just before the first drop trickled from the bottle. She lowered the bottle and peered shamefully at her faint reflection in the murky bottle.

"Look at you," she sighed. "People used to respect you!"

Maeve hurled the bottle across the room, watching as it exploded against the wall and showered the Grand Inquisitor's mutilated, blood drenched corpse with wine.

"Are you happy now?!" she hissed at her reflection in the window, her claws splintering wood as she shoved herself away from the desk. "You got your revenge, plucked out his intestines, fed him his own dick... but what now?"

Maeve stepped closer to the window and glared darkly at her reflection, disgusted by herself and filled with self-loathing. Only now that the deed was done did she see what she had become - a bloodthirsty, alcoholic psychopath who took sickening pleasure in mutilating her victims. How had it come to this?

"What does the world want with a murderous loser like you?" She sobbed, burying her head in her hands.

She had killed so many people, taken such pleasure in doing so. She was a monster, a freak. She wondered if the world would be better off without her, if it would rejoice were she to end it all. Yet, she knew deep down that the world was not yet done with her. Bleak as her life was, perhaps it wasn't irredeemable. Perhaps there was still a chance for her to make amends, to make a difference.

"No... no, no, no!" she cried, shaking her head back and forth as she turned her back on her reflection. "Shut up! Y-you're wrong..."

She glanced up through the slits between her fingers, at the mass of papers spread across the desk. An idea pushed through her crazed thoughts and nestled in her mind.

"You're wrong!" she screamed, glass exploding around her fist. She watched with ragged breath as the broken shards fell one by one from the window frame. "I'll show you... I-I'll kill them all!" she growled. "I won't let them hurt anyone again!"

With a crash of shattered glass, she withdrew her hand from the crumbling window and marched over to the desk. With renewed energy, she flung one sheet after another from the worktop, until she came to a stop with a crazed grin.

It was a letter, a correspondence from a House Arrenni official confirming the delivery of a large quantity of oil for the pyres. She began to laugh, a tortured giggle of joy and pain. She would burn this place, burn them all! Those animals would pay for the blood spilled within these walls - they would die by the holy fire they held so dear.

Perhaps Maeve was a monster, a remorseless killer with an insatiable thirst for blood, but that would not stop her for fighting for what was right. It was time to put her skills to good use.

Eris and Caesia slipped quietly through the torture chamber door and into the hallway. The dull grey corridors were deathly silent, the whole place felt like some kind of dungeon. To call it unnerving would have been something of an understatement, particularly after what they had just been through.

"Do we actually know where we're going?" Eris whispered.

"To the basement," Caesia said.

"Yeah, but how do we actually *get* there?"

"I… have no idea," Caesia sighed. "I'm sure we'll figure something out. I mean, this place is only so big, right?"

"Well, it's not all that small either…" Eris muttered.

"If we made it through that tomb, I think we can happily make it through this place," Caesia smiled. "So long as we don't run into another horde of skeletons, that is. I don't want to have to save you again."

"I was gonna get up…" Eris mumbled.

"The hell you were!" Caesia laughed. "You were crying you bloody eyes out!"

They reached the end of the corridor, where it split into two paths. Caesia groaned impatiently as they threw themselves up against the wall.

"Well, this is just grand," she muttered. "I reckon we go right."

"Why?" Eris asked.

"Why not?"

"Because I want to go left."

"Are you seriously doing this right now?" Caesia snapped.

"What?" Eris scoffed.

"You're being difficult for the sake of being difficult!"

"No, I just wanna go left!" Eris hissed. "Watch!"

"Eris, no!" Caesia gasped as Eris launched herself from cover.

She skidded around the corner and into the corridor and came face to face with a startled inquisitor. As he opened his mouth to yell, Caesia appeared behind him in a burst of light and sprang onto his back, throwing her arms around his face, squeezing her hands over his mouth and discharging an electrical current into his body. Eris watched with a bewildered smile as the vibrating inquisitor sank slowly to the ground, falling with a thud onto his face.

Caesia, who lay face down on top of the inquisitor, glared up at Eris, receiving in return a quirky grin. Caesia sighed heavily and scrambled to her feet, shaking off the pain from her hands.

"What the hell were you thinking?!" she hissed. "You could have gotten us caught, you bloody idiot!"

"Um... sorry?" Eris smiled, shrugging innocently.

"I swear, if I didn't have these bruises, I would slap you *so* hard right now," Caesia sighed. "Think yourself lucky."

"Yeah, thank the stars I don't have to feel the wrath of your twig arms!" Eris sniggered. "What are we doing with this guy?"

"We'll have to hide him," Caesia muttered. "Get one of those doors, would you?"

"What if there's someone in there?"

"There won't be, it's like... three in the morning."

"If you say so..." Eris mumbled, moving across the corridor.

She stepped up to one of the battered, old wooden doors on the other side of the hallway. Pushing her ear up against it, she heard nothing but the shuffling of the inquisitor's limp body.

"This one seems good!" Eris smiled, turning to Caesia. "What are- are you okay there?"

Eris watched with an amused grin as Caesia dragged the inquisitor behind her, both hands wrapped around one of his arms. Eris could see her skeletal wrists tensing and her cheeks growing red as she heaved him along.

"Totally fine!" Caesia gasped. "He- he's just... rather heavy."

"Weakling," Eris smirked.

She grasped the doorknob and thrust the door open. Wandering carelessly inside, she entered what seemed to be some kind of common room and glanced down at an inquisitor, playing a lonesome game of solitaire at a table in front of her. He twisted around to see the hilt of Eris' sword rushing for his head.

Caesia heaved the first inquisitor through the doorway and glanced over her shoulder. She froze in disbelief at the sight of Eris standing with an awkward smile plastered onto her face, beside another inquisitor who lay face down on the table.

"Now, I know how this looks..." Eris smirked.

"Are you kidding me?!" Caesia hissed. "I cannot believe you!"

"What?" Eris scoffed. "He was alone! How was I meant to know he was here?!"

"You could've looked through the bloody keyhole!"

"Looking through keyholes is a myth!" Eris insisted. "They're only big enough to see, like, a square foot of the next room!"

"Just... God, we are really not qualified to be doing this, are we?" Caesia chuckled.

"You only just figured that out?" Eris grinned. "So, what do we do with these guys?"

"I'm not sure…" Caesia sighed. "There's little space to hide them in here, but I don't think we should risk bursting into anymore rooms."

"I mean, unless you want to…"

"I'll pass," Caesia smirked. "Let's just chuck them in a corner and hope nobody comes in."

"Fair enough," Eris muttered. "It's the middle of the night, what're the odds-"

The door beside her jolted and swung open. As another inquisitor stepped into the common room and jumped at the sight of his fallen comrades, Eris scraped a book on beginner's solitaire off the table and thrust it into his head. The book slammed his forehead with a massive bang and staggered him into the doorframe. As he shook himself off, Eris grabbed him by the hair and hammered her fist into his nose.

The inquisitor stumbled to his knees and with a kick to the back from Eris, fell flat on his face. Eris carefully pushed the door shut and looked with a smirk at her bewildered friend.

"On the bright side, every inquisitor we clobber reduces the chance of another one showing up," she smiled.

Caesia stared in defeat at the new addition to their collection. Her body sagged and her shoulders sank as she heaved a massive sigh. Why did fate insist upon abusing her?

"Forget this…" she groaned. "Let's just go."

"We just gonna leave them here?"

"Fingers crossed, we'll be long gone once they're found. So long as someone doesn't go running down the hallways again…"

"Fear not, lesson learnt!" Eris declared.

"You mean the same lesson you supposedly learnt in the tomb?" Caesia laughed. "I'll believe it when I see it."

The door creaked open and Eris peered carefully into the empty hallway. The coast clear, Caesia edged out of the room and gently closed the door. That ordeal out of the way, they continued into the labyrinth of corridors.

From the common room, they gradually worked their way through the building. After several minutes of silent creeping and a lot of back-tracking, Eris edged open the door to the main hall. The massive room ahead was populated by about a dozen inquisitors, most with bags under their eyes and displeasure in their expressions, as night shifts will do to a person.

The girls took cover behind a cluster of barrels, tucked away at the edge of the room and dripping with thick, viscous oil. They must burn a lot of people to warrant this much oil, Eris thought, observing several other identical barrels littered around the hall.

Caesia tapped Eris on the shoulder and gestured towards a door at the other end of the room, which was attached to a sloping wall that could only contain a stairwell. She pushed her hand up against Eris' back and waited for a moment, watching the inquisitors carefully. She waited patiently for enough to turn their backs and then shoved herself and Eris forwards. They blinked across the hall and reappeared just short of the alcove in which the door was located.

Out in the open, Caesia looked back in panic, only to see that all of the inquisitors seemed distracted by something and were converging at the other end of the hall. There was no time to waste time finding out what they were looking at, they had to move.

"Go, go!" she hissed, scrambling around the corner and into the alcove.

Eris grabbed the door handle and yanked it down. It jolted and came to an unexpected stop.

"It's locked!" Eris gasped.

"Crap!" Caesia spat. "She didn't say we needed a basement key!"

Caesia peered back around the corner cautiously. There were no inquisitors in sight, but she didn't want to take any chances.

"I'll melt the lock," she whispered, pushing the end of her finger into the narrow slit between the door and the frame.

Eris shuffled impatiently on the spot as Caesia carefully blasted the bolt with a surgical beam of lightning. So focused was the energy into one place, that she was slowly losing all feeling in her hand. Suddenly, the door jolted out of place and creaked gradually open. Caesia retracted her hand, which went limp at her side.

"You need to see someone about that?" Eris sniggered at Caesia's floppy hand.

"It'll pass," she muttered. "Come on."

Behind the door was a flight of rickety wooden stairs leading into the basement. There was no hiding their entrance now, either they walked down the creaky steps or teleported down with a glaring flash of light. Caesia took a deep breath of forced confidence and started down the stairs.

As the wall beside them made way for an old wooden bannister, the vault came into view. Across the room was a wall of electrified bars, behind which sat an entire armoury of weapons, armour and equipment. Ahead of the vault, three inquisitors stood guard, dressed in thick, studded leather armour and sporting feathered, disc shaped hats on their heads.

They jumped to attention at the creaking of the stairs, hands on their swords.

"Who're you?" the leftmost inquisitor bellowed. "You can't be down 'ere."

"You idiot!" barked the central inquisitor. "They've got to be changelings! It's the only explanation."

"Sorry, we were just hoping you'd let us borrow one of those lanterns you got in there," Eris smiled. "We're investigat-"

"We ain't falling for your tricks, demon!" hissed the rightmost inquisitor. "Come on lads, let's fuck these creeps up."

"Worth a try," Eris sighed, sliding her sword from the sheath and reaching instinctively for her shield, only to remember it had been obliterated a few hours ago.

"These guy may be monsters, but the 'no kill' rule still applies," Caesia warned her, igniting her left arm with energy.

She flopped her right hand around frantically, in a vain attempt to wake it up. It seemed that she would have to deal with this one handed.

The inquisitors readied their fine silver weapons and prepared for battle. The leftmost inquisitor wielded a morningstar, the central a longsword and the rightmost a warhammer. Eris had never seen nor heard of a morningstar before, but the heavy silver ball laden with spikes could possibly have been the most brutal looking weapon she'd ever seen.

As they approached, one dipped his hand into a pouch and with a flick of the wrist, cast a blanket of white dust across the room. Caesia thought nothing of it at first, until her head slowly began to throb with pain. It was sladium dust. The energy around her arms crackled and fizzled out as she staggered back into the bannister, clutching her head and breathing harshly as the sladium pierced her mind like a blade.

"Huh, just her then," the central inquisitor muttered. "Stand aside girl, our quarrel is with the demon!"

"You won't lay a finger on her," Eris hissed, pulling her sword up in front of her.

"She's a slave to the bitch's will!" the leftmost inquisitor scoffed. "What do we do?"

"Kill them both," the central inquisitor growled. "A demon vanquished is worth a hundred wenches!"

The three inquisitors advanced towards Eris, who stepped defiantly between them and Caesia. She knew she had to make the first move, else they would continue to push her back to the wall.

She stepped suddenly to the left to challenge the morningstar wielder. Knowing he had little capability of blocking, she thrust forwards and forced him to stagger back. The sword wielder cleaved down at her arm with his blade as she pulled back. Her other arm found his and grabbed it tightly, buying enough time to withdraw her sword before she shoved him aside.

As he stumbled past her, the third inquisitor attempted to catch her off guard and take out her knees. He swung his warhammer low, the silver head spewing a shower of sparks as it skidded along the ground. Hearing the slow, heavy swing grind against the floor, Eris leapt into the air and let the hammer glide under her. She swept narrowly over the hammer and swung at the inquisitor's back as he brought his hammer around, spattering his leathers with blood as she slashed a narrow incision across his back. He grunted in pain and reeled away as the other two approached again.

"You'll have to do better than that!" Eris laughed, raising her sword in front of her again.

The other two inquisitors approached simultaneously. The central inquisitor lunged suddenly with a thrust at her gut, while his ally followed up with an overhead strike from his morningstar. Eris grasped her sword with both hands and swept it up, catching the inquisitor's sword with her crossguard and pulling it up into the air. She dragged her opponent's blade over her head and used the strength of both his sword and hers to stop the morningstar as it descended. She released the inquisitor's sword and pushed back against the morningstar, staggering the wielder away from her.

The swordsman stumbled away from Eris and collected himself. As Eris span around to meet him, he gripped his sword in both of his hands and swung a heavy blow at her neck. She ducked nimbly beneath it and grabbed him by the left shoulder. Eris smirked playfully as she mercilessly slammed her knee into his crotch. The inquisitor bent over in agony, opening up Eris to pull her sword's handle high above his head and smash it against the back of his skull. The inquisitor keeled over onto the ground, unconscious.

"Sorry," she giggled, confidently flourishing her sword. "That was dirty."

Eris could hear the heavy footsteps of the third inquisitor approaching behind her, heavier than the other by the weight of his hammer. She threw herself onto the cold ground as the warhammer flew overhead, a close call from being decapitated. She snatched up the unconscious inquisitor's sword as she rolled out of the hammer wielder's path, straight into the path of the other inquisitor.

She sprang up and span around, batting the morningstar out of her face with her steel sword and thrusting at his stomach with the other. The silver blade slid across the gap between the inquisitor's body armour and greaves, slicing a deep gash along the side of his body. The inquisitor roared in pain and stumbled away.

Eris swept back around to the hammer wielding inquisitor, who was reeling back his hammer for another swing. Before the hammer could pick up enough momentum, Eris pushed out both of her swords and battered it back, staggering her opponent and spinning him around with the weight of his own weapon. Before she could follow through however, the other inquisitor blundered towards her, clutching his wound and swung his morningstar at her clumsily. Eris effortlessly stepped around his strike and stuck out her leg. The inquisitor stumbled into her leg and toppled over, hitting his head hard on a nearby crate and falling still.

"Ouch," Eris smirked.

She turned to face the final inquisitor, who roared furiously and barrelled towards her. He swung his warhammer out in front of him, displacing Eris' fringe as she narrowly dodged backwards. She thrust out with her silver sword, only for the inquisitor to bat it away with the end of his hammer's handle. She jabbed again at his leg with her own sword, which the inquisitor sidestepped clumsily. He made a cleaving swing over his head and brought the hammer down, shattering the stonework and showering Eris with splinters of stone as she stumbled to the side. He suddenly dragged his hammer to the side, smashing Eris' legs out from beneath her as it swept into her.

A spike of pain surged through her foot as she was knocked off her feet, punctuated by the impact of his fist against her cheek. Eris toppled to the ground in a daze, barely catching herself before her head slammed against the floor. She rolled over sluggishly, her head spinning and ankle throbbing, as the inquisitor swung his hammer over his head. The looming shadow of his weapon cast darkness over her as it blotted out the lantern light.

His head barely flinched at the sound of a pathetic thud from behind him. He turned around, where he found Caesia withdrawing a dented book from his head. She smiled apologetically and backed hurriedly away as the inquisitor pulled back his hammer and advanced after her. Then he flinched again, more violently this time at a much louder clang against his head. He dropped his warhammer to the ground with a heavy crunch against the stonework and fell to his knees. The iron bar rang as Eris cast it to the ground with a cheeky grin.

"Nice save!" she gushed. "Course, I totally had it."

Caesia smirked at Eris' usual positivity, even despite the massive bruise emerging below her right eye.

"Sure you did," Caesia sighed, still cringing at the pain in her head. "Leave these guys some bandages will you?"

"On it," Eris declared, swinging her backpack off her shoulders.

She span around to the inquisitors as she stuck her hand into her bag, only to blurt a loud whimper as a sharp pain shot through her left ankle.

"You okay?" Caesia asked over her shoulder.

Eris glanced down at her foot with concern masked with a smile. "I'm sure it's nothing. I'll walk it off."

"You're sure?"

"Totally…"

Caesia sighed dismissively and stumbled over to the vault door, looking down defeatedly at the bent cover of 'The Best Defence: Getting Started With Advanced Abjuration'. That book was not easy to come by, though she supposed she no longer needed it what with this new encyclopedia of hers. She sighed and discarded the broken book onto the floor.

"How long have you been able to fight with two swords?" she asked as she shovelled through her pockets for the key.

"Since I was twelve. I just brought a shield to be on the safe side and say what you will, that thing totally saved us on the mountain."

"Still, you should consider doing it more often."

"Don't tell me your grace is impressed!" Eris sneered.

"I… will leave that up to interpretation," Caesia smirked, sticking the key into the door.

The vault door swept open with a shrieking whine and the crackling steel bars around it simmered as the electricity dispersed. Caesia stepped through into the armoury, followed closely by Eris, who deposited a roll of bandages beside an unconscious inquisitor.

The vault was brimming with all kinds of equipment. There were weapon racks cluttered with every manner of weapon imaginable, from knives to pikes, all forged from a flawless, glistening silver. There were trunks loaded with armour, mostly the studded leathers of inquisitorial uniforms or heavier variants of such, but also many cunning disguises for undercover operations. At the back of the vault were rows upon rows of shelves covered in a vast variety of equipment. Most interesting were the collars, such as those for changelings that prevented shapeshifting. The arachni shock collars were particularly advanced, able to be straightened out and thrown and designed to snap automatically around their targets upon contact. It was amusing, albeit concerning that Verdenheld's greatest innovations had come from genocide and oppression.

"Here we are," Caesia called, approaching a shelving unit full of lanterns of various colours. "Any preference as to colour?"

"Go for… purple. You like purple, right?"

"I *love* purple!" Caesia chirped happily, picking up and admiring a purple lantern. "How'd you know?"

"The purple dress and mask were a bit of a giveaway," Eris smirked.

"Oh, yeah," Caesia laughed. "What can I say, purple helps me focus."

Caesia stepped out from behind the shelves with the lantern, it's lavender essence crystal flaring with shimmering purple light.

"Perfect," she smiled, seemingly mesmerised by the glimmering light.

"Hey, wake up," Eris laughed, smacking Caesia playfully on the back. "I was thinking, maybe we should take some of this other stuff."

"Eris, I've no intention of… actually, that's a good point," Caesia admitted. "If we're going to take these changelings alive, we'd certainly benefit from bringing along a few of those collars."

At the thought of capturing the changelings, Eris came to a sudden realisation. "Stars, I just realised - if we catch these guys, they'll probably end up in that torture chamber!"

"I know," Caesia sighed. "Cruel as it may sound to say, I'd rather not concern myself with that. Their suffering will be necessary in preventing that of hundreds, maybe thousands."

"I guess so," Eris mumbled. "But that isn't gonna stop me from feeling bad."

"Same here, but we'll just have to deal with it."

Eris scraped several collars into her backpack, filling the room left by the roll of bandages.

"You know what?" Eris gasped. "We haven't eaten in ages!"

"Ah, I'll worry about eating later."

"Suit yourself, but I'm having a snack," Eris declared, shovelling a carrot out from under the collars.

"Leave it until you're outside, would you?" Caesia chuckled. "I don't want you to alert the whole garrison by crunching a carrot."

"Fine…" Eris muttered, dropping the carrot back into her backpack and slinging it back over her shoulders.

They stepped out of the vault and Caesia locked the door behind them, cringing as the sladium dust on the ground started drilling at her mind again. As they turned to head out of the basement, a horrified, bloodcurdling scream bellowed from upstairs, which was suddenly cut short and followed by a dull thud.

Caesia and Eris turned to each other, both of them equal parts concerned and furious. No doubt this was Maeve's inevitable feat of insanity that Caesia had so accurately predicted. Eris sheathed her new sword and strapped it around her waist, before they started cautiously up the stairs, worried about what they would find.

Eris and Caesia peered cautiously around the doorway and into the hall, where Maeve stood in the middle of the room, soaked head to toe in blood and surrounded by the scattered, mangled corpses of several inquisitors. She thrust one of her legs forwards and rammed it between the armour of another inquisitor, puncturing straight through his ribcage and erupting out of his back in a splatter of gore. She pulled him close and with a swift swipe of her bladed arm, slashed a deep incision through his throat. Laughed maniacally as the wound spewed blood all over her, she threw out her arms with glee and caught some on her tongue.

"So much for discreet…" Eris muttered as Maeve flung the inquisitor's limp body off the end of her leg and into another two, clobbering them to the ground.

"What is that bloody psycho thinking?!" Caesia hissed, her body becoming increasingly numb the longer she looked at the crimson drenched arachni.

"I don't know, but I think she's winning…" Eris mumbled.

Maeve side-stepped an inquisitor and slashed his knees with the serrated tip of one of her legs. As the inquisitor fell to the ground, she thrust her arms around his neck, rammed her arm-blades deep into his flesh with a harrowing crack and dragged her them back through his throat. Maeve giggled excitedly as his head toppled from his shoulders in a visceral explosion of gore that painted her face scarlet.

Caesia's face contorted in horror as Maeve plucked the man's bloodied head from the ground and dragged her tongue across the oozing stump. Caesia's legs turned immediately to jelly, her grip slipped from the doorframe and all went black. Eris span around as her friend collapsed to the ground with a pathetic thud, staring blankly at the ceiling, completely unconscious.

"Oh, stars above!" Eris groaned, peering back around the corner.

Eris watched as Maeve grabbed a wounded inquisitor by his collar and slammed him into a burning wall sconce. She held him there with a smug grin on her face as the inquisitor was set ablaze and began to scream hysterically in agony. Maeve dragged him away from the wall and skipped merrily towards one of the many collections of oil barrels scattered around the hall.

"Crap!" Eris blurted, her heart skipping a beat as she sprang into panic.

She slipped back around the doorframe, grabbed Caesia beneath her arms and heaved her scrawny body off the ground. Dumping Caesia over her shoulders, she leapt from cover as Maeve hurled the burning man to the ground beside the barrels.

Eris weaved between barrels and crates as she bolted for the exit. Every step sent pain shooting up her leg, but it was something she was willing to endure. As Eris skidded out of the door, Caesia was jolted into consciousness as she passed under the sladium beam.

"Wha- put me down!" Caesia hissed.

"No time!"

Eris slammed the door behind them and took off across the courtyard, towards the gate. The inquisitors in the courtyard jumped to attention as they fled by.

"Hey, stop!" one of them yelled. "In the name of-"

A colossal explosion shook the garrison as the oil barrels went up, the ground trembling beneath their feet.

"Jump!" Caesia commanded.

Eris leapt into the air and Caesia blinked them over the wall, the two of them falling a couple of metres into a crumpled heap on the other side.

The inquisitors turned to the building in terror as the walls of the garrison were blasted apart in a shower of brick and mortar. Enormous fireballs erupted from the garrison, engulfing every inquisitor in the compound in a towering inferno. As the foundations crumbled, huge swathes of the building gave way and toppled to the ground in an avalanche of stone, snuffing out the pained screams of droves of once sleeping inquisitors who had awakened to a world of fire. The horrified screams of a hundred men echoed throughout the streets of the Hallow District as their flesh melted from their bones and their blood was boiled beneath their tight leather armour.

Maeve hopped down from the crumbling remnants of the rooftop and pridefully observed her handiwork. Having single handedly slain almost every inquisitor in Aldreichen, she stood amidst the flickering flames triumphant, gleefully watching the last of the inquisitors writhing around on the ground. She spread her blood soaked arms victoriously and took in a deep breath of the choking ashen air.

"Fear not, my friends!" she yelled happily across the courtyard to the blackened husks of her oppressors. "The Lord will forgive you, for you have been cleansed!"

Maeve pranced and skipped through the scorched courtyard like a little girl, spinning in circles and leaping merrily over piles of burning rubble. She threw open the gates of the garrison and strolled confidently into the square, where Eris and Caesia lay panting on the ground.

"Ah, great!" she chirped. "You guys survived! You had me worried for moment."

"What the hell was that?" Caesia hissed. "You just murdered all those people!"

Maeve's face dropped and her legs retracted shyly. "I thought you'd be happy…" she mumbled. "Those people were monsters!"

"That doesn't matter, I watched you behead a man!" Caesia snapped. "You just killed a hundred people and walked out with smile! You're sick, Maeve!"

"You entitled bitch!" Maeve growled, her legs poising offensively as her expression darkened. "How many arachni do you think they've executed in Victory Square? How many abhumans do you think they've gutted, burned and tortured in there?! That, Cassie, was justice!"

"No, Maeve, it wasn't. It was a massacre," Caesia spat, her voice growing hoarse in the heat of the burning garrison. "You just sank to exactly the same level as them! You've become the monster yourself!"

"I was already a monster!" Maeve screamed, her pale face growing crimson. "I didn't kill those people in the sewers because I was hungry, I did it because it was fun and because it made my own pain go away!"

Tears trickled from all eight of Maeve's eyes and her voice became shaky and tortured.

"But that's not why I did this!" Maeve sobbed. "I killed those inquisitors so that other people won't have to feel my pain! If that makes me a monster, then I'll wear that label with pride!"

Caesia didn't know what to say. Maeve did things to those men that were simply unforgivable, butchering like animals those who she didn't leave to slow, fiery deaths.

Maeve stared for a time at Caesia, waiting to receive either further revilement, yet getting nothing but silence. Blood trickled from her lip as she bit down upon it and turned away. Her whole body quivering, she stormed off towards a nearby sewer grate.

"Maeve, wait!" Eris called. "I didn't get chance to say... You... you can go home now."

Maeve froze in place just short of the grate, her breath rushing from her lungs. "What?"

"I talked to Lycoria," Eris smiled. "They're going to let you back in, they want to help you."

"You," Maeve gasped, turning to stare at Eris with trembling eyes. "You did that for me...? Wha- why would you... I don't-"

"Everyone else said you were a monster," Eris sighed, glancing back disappointedly at Caesia. "But under all that killing and eating, I know you're a good person. Maybe you did kill all those people, but that just proves how much you care, what you'll do to protect your own!"

"You mean that?" Maeve mumbled. "You... don't think I'm a monster?"

"Of course not," Eris smiled, gently wandering closer to her. "You're just a little messed up is all, and I don't think that's a totally bad thing. I mean, crazy doesn't have to mean-"

Maeve lunged at Eris and threw her arms around her. She buried her face in Eris' shoulder and squeezed her so tight that the chitinous blades on her arms bore incisions into her armour. She didn't say a word, only breathed shakily into the fur of Eris' armour.

"For a human, you're pretty nice," Maeve mumbled with a smirk into Eris' shoulder. "Hope you're taking notes over there, bitch."

Eris looked back at Caesia's startled face with a smug grin. Caesia was red with embarrassment in watching the scene unfold, having retreated into silence as her prejudices were gradually disproven.

"Come on, you can get off me now," Eris laughed, trying to peel Maeve off her. "You're embarrassing yourself!"

"Aw, but I like it here…" Maeve groaned. "I've never touched fur in my life, it's so cosy!"

Eris heaved Maeve off her with a roll of her eyes. "Alright, let's compromise," she sighed, lifting off her slender steel pauldron with a clatter of metal plates.

Maeve wiped her face down and fluttered her eyes, before nimbly catching a handful of fur.

"There you go," Eris smirked. "Something to cuddle at night."

"Aw, hell yeah!" Maeve laughed, juggling around the fur in her hands. "I, er… I guess I'd best go home, then. Thanks, Eris."

"No problem! I'm told it's what I do," Eris smiled. "Now, you'd best behave down there or so help me, I'll come down there and sort you out myself!"

"Hmph, what if I want you to stop by?" Maeve grinned deviously. "Break a few things, eat a few people…"

"I'm serious!" Eris chuckled. "But yeah, I'll visit. Promise."

"Awesome!" Maeve sang, kicking open a nearby sewer grate. "And don't worry, I'll behave. Next time you see me, I'll be a new woman!"

"I'll hold you to that," Eris sneered. "See you 'round, Maeve."

"I hope so…" Maeve smiled. "Later, girl."

Eris took a breath in satisfaction Maeve scrambled into the sewers and dragged the grate back into place behind her. That had to have been the best feeling of her life - helping someone get the life they deserved. It only confirmed that this is what she wanted to do with her life, that she wanted to help the people who deserved better than they had, to see their smiling faces. Neither slaying a monster nor saving a king would ever come close to that feeling of warmth. This is what being a hero really meant.

"It's not your fault," Eris sighed, turning back to Caesia. "Don't kick yourself about it."

Caesia was sitting slumped against the wall, twiddling her thumbs in shame. Eris had been totally right about Maeve and it had made Caesia realise just how terrible a person she really was. She had long acknowledged many of her flaws, but this was a situation that simply made her feel cruel.

"Why not?" Caesia mumbled. "You were right… and I just spat on her like she was nothing."

"You did, but it's not like you knew any better," Eris smiled. "You were just raised this way. You know you can't expect to walk out of a life like yours and not bring any of it with you."

"That's just it!" Caesia growled. "I hate that I knew no better because it means I'm just like my parents, and that pisses me off!"

"Yeah, but it'll wear off!" Eris insisted. "Give it a few months and you'll be all smiles and sunshine!"

Caesia's face shifted gradually to a smile as she shook her head in disbelief. "Ugh, can you stop being so positive?" she laughed. "All I want to do is wallow in self pity and every time, in you come with all your damned optimism!"

"Yeah, and I'm not gonna stop till you forget how to frown!" Eris declared.

"So be it…" Caesia smirked, shuffling to her feet and stretching her legs. "Alright, you've once again cheered me up. Now come, we'd best get out of here before someone realises the Inquisitorial Garrison just exploded."

Ephaeus stepped into the dimly lit chamber, his every step staining his trousers more and more with splashes of sewer water. This was a humbling moment - the massive pillared room had been his home for a decade. It was a shame to think that these were his last moments in this place.

"Niria!" he called. "What happened?"

Niria turned to Ephaeus, her mouth trembling in hesitation. She stalked over to him, the white eyes of her companions glued to her as she walked her path of shame. As embarrassed as she was however, she stiffened herself and faced her leader with certainty, a stern look on her featureless face.

"We were intercepted," she spat. "It was the human girls Kharmenia warned us about… we should have taken her more seriously."

"We had no cause to," Ephaeus said. "Why should we have believed that a pair of adolescents could stand in our way?"

"If we had listened, Farenos would still live," Niria growled.

"I… had heard of his fate," Ephaeus sighed. "And in his death, our cover is lost."

"What do we do now?" Niria whispered, her usual stalwart demeanour wavering in her uncertainty.

"We fight," Ephaeus smiled. "This is far from over. The arachni may not meet their due, but King Friedrich still lies within our grasp. We must simply reach out… and rip him from this mortal coil."

Niria grinned eagerly, her faith rapidly returning. "Yes… Aldreichen will run red with Verden blood."

Ephaeus smiled in acknowledgement and passed Niria by. As he moved into the centre of the room, the empty eyes of his brothers and sisters fell upon him and they turned to attention. For years they had prepared for this day and they were long ready. At his word, the King Friedrich would die.

"My friends… the time has come," Ephaeus smiled. "For years we have waited in the darkness, for years we have planned and plotted and today… today we-"

Ephaeus fell silent as Avelin Kharmenia slipped from behind one of the pillars and leant casually against it. He could imagine the frown on her face just by the disappointed, crimson eyes that broke her featureless black mask.

"Please, continue," Hera sighed, waving her hand in a careless gesture.

"What do you want, Kharmenia?" Ephaeus growled, stiffening in defiance.

Hera rolled her eyes. Ephaeus hated humans with a passion and despite their alliance, treated her just as he would any other. She supposed she couldn't blame him, but it was a jarring change to the fear she usually commanded.

"You know exactly what it is," Hera hissed. "There were *ten* of you! Ten! And you sent in two?"

"We were attempting to instil terror."

"Terror? Don't you think killing the King would be terror enough? What happened is you fucked it up!" Hera snapped, her gaze growing dark with anger. "Do I have to do this myself?"

"That will not be necessary," Ephaeus smiled. "We have our quarry cornered, a rat in a trap."

"Same as last time, yet you still failed."

Ephaeus' face dropped at Hera's insolence. He detested the woman, so high and mighty. She thought herself in control, that she would unassailable. It was high time that somebody taught her otherwise.

"Watch yourself, Kharmenia," Ephaeus spat, clenching his fists. "I am not one of your toadies to be pushed around!"

Silence hung across the room, several changelings looking to one another with concern. Hera narrowed her eyes and stepped closer.

"Ah, I see," Hera smirked, shaking her head in amusement. "You think you're above me. You think this little operation couldn't exist without the virtue of your presence." Her voice grew more mocking by the moment, the situation becoming increasingly hysterical to her. "How cute."

Ephaeus' mind burned with fury, Hera's mocking gaze fuelling a rage he so wished to conserve for Friedrich. "Listen here, sorceress!" he hissed, looming over her with a hateful glare. "I don't care who you are, nor do I care for your cause! You and your master are but a means to an end, a tool and nothing more!"

Hera stared at him for a moment, her eyes blank and careless. The changeling had a great deal of nerve talking down to her like this, it almost tempted her to vaporise him on the spot. No, she preferred to keep things diplomatic, at least where possible.

"Then I'm glad we share a mutual opinion of one another," she muttered, backing away from Ephaeus and turning to leave. "I couldn't care less how you feel about me, nor my master. Just do your damned job."

"Oh, we will," Ephaeus grinned, a sinister darkness creeping over him. "I'm afraid however, that we will be terminating our arrangement here."

Hera stopped in her tracks and turned slowly to face Ephaeus again. She looked at him not with the contempt he expected, but with an eyebrow raised in amusement behind her mask. He could see that she took him for a fool.

"Nothing personal, truly," Ephaeus smirked in confidence. "The fact is that we no longer need you. You have fulfilled your purpose and now you must die, as I have so desperately yearned for since the moment we met."

In a dull purple flash, a fly took a humanoid form behind her and drew a silvered blade. Hera flicked out her wrist as the changeling thrust the dagger into her back, the steel turning molten in his hand and slumping to the ground. As the changeling shrieked at the burn of the melting metal on his hand, he burst suddenly into crimson flame. Hera clenched her fist tight as the fire roared ever more intense, before plunging the twin blades of her staff through his stomach in a visceral eruption of gore that splattered the spectating changelings.

Ephaeus revealed a slender arkansteel sword, the blade slick with poison that danced with colour in the light of his burning ally. He thrust it at Hera, who batted it aside with the end of the staff's shaft and battered him away. As the other changeling fell limp, she cast him from her staff's end and flung it around, its blood drenched blades igniting with scarlet fire as she levelled it towards Ephaeus.

"I took you for many things, Ephaeus, but not an idiot," Hera sneered. "Valkyr does not tolerate betrayal."

Even surrounded, the witch still antagonised him. His blood boiled at her venomous words, yet he remained calm and pushed his anger deep within himself.

"You can't kill us all," Ephaeus smirked, looking around at his allies, who approached drawing blades of their own..

Hera gazed across the room, a smirk behind her mask. She turned back upon Ephaeus with mocking eyes. "I don't have to," she grinned.

Ephaeus' face dropped as the crystal nestled between the blades of her staff flared suddenly with green light. Before he could manage another word, Ephaeus was struck by a violent blast of green energy, obliterating his every atom in a blinding flash. The changelings watched dumbfounded as the last remaining particles of their leader dissipated into the air.

"Should I expect any more disobedience?" Hera growled, slamming her staff on the ground.

She was met with silence. The dancing flames enveloping her blades simmered away and the light of the essence crystal flickered and died out. The awe stricken changelings knew who held the power here, she trusted that they would fall in line.

"Good. Now, it seems that a leadership role has just became available. Any volunteers?"

Blank looks were exchanged amongst the changelings. They had followed Ephaeus for near enough a decade now, most felt lost without him. Eventually, one stepped forwards - he was equally as pale and pathetic as the rest of the sect, yet held an air of stern authority.

"I will lead us," he declared. "I will spill the tyrant's blood where Ephaeus could not."

"Cereth, you bastard!" Niria hissed. "He was a great man! How could you disrespect-"

"Niria, is it?" Hera sighed, twirling her staff in her hand as she drew closer.

Niria shrank away at her approach, fearing the same fate as her leader. She did not answer but simply stared attentively, afraid to utter the wrong words.

"I understand your distress," Hera smiled, turning with a glare to Cereth. "A little empathy goes a long way, you know."

"You respected him?" Cereth sneered.

"Respect... is a strong word. He was *insufferably* uptight, but I admired his drive. Either way, try to show some respect for the dead."

"As you command, General," Cereth muttered.

Hera smirked and retreated back to the centre of the room, raising her voice for all to hear.

"Now, listen up - Cereth will lead you to the palace where you will kill King Friedrich according to the established plan. Failure will not be tolerated, are we clear?"

"Yes, General! Loud and clear," Cereth declared.

"Wonderful... you there!" Hera called to a changeling at the back. "What's your name?"

"Devren, ma'am."

"Tell me, Devren - How are your skills in combat?"

"Good enough, I think you'll find," Devren sneered.

"Is that bravado I hear?" Hera wondered. "I guess we'll find out... Go to Victory Plaza and project your essence as greatly as you can. You have the honour of being our distraction."

"Do we need a distraction?" Niria asked. "Together, we can handle anything."

"Evidence suggests otherwise," Hera muttered. "From what I've seen, I don't think you can stop those girls. The best you can do is slow them down long enough to secure the kill."

"No offence General, but you underestimate us," Cereth smirked.

"And I think you underestimate *them*." Hera insisted. "If they get past Devren, try to work around them - keep your focus on the target."

In truth, Hera was unsure whether those girls were a match for the changelings. The fact was that they could happily complete their objective without killing them, which she much preferred to do. They didn't deserve to die, nor did she want them to.

"Of course, General," Cereth sighed. "Shall we move forwards with the plan?"

"One more thing - if you see any other Verdens, kill them. Killing the King is one thing, but crushing the ruling house would be catastrophic," Hera commanded with a cunning grin. "Now get out of here, you've got a monarchy to topple!"

Chapter Eight - Out of the Shadows

Veldin surveyed the soldiers before him as he stepped onto the dining table, the wood bending under his bulk. A legion of soldiers had crammed themselves into the royal dining hall to hear their orders. Their faces were wrought with terror and anxiety, looks of suspicion being passed between them in the fear that their enemy could have been standing in their midst. They fell suddenly silent as Veldin's gaze fell over them.

"Now, I'll admit I'm not much for speeches - I prefer to let my axe do the talking," Veldin smirked. "So, I'll keep this brief. We're not just the last, but the *only* line of defence that stands between the abhumans and our king. We can afford no mercy, no quarter… Many of you, I'm afraid, are about to lose your lives fighting for a man who couldn't give two shits about you."

Friedrich shuffled uncomfortably behind his Phoenix Guard, trying to avoid eye contact with the crowd.

"So, don't fight for him. If we let these creatures win, all of Verdenheld will be plunged into anarchy and our enemies will rise to the occasion. Millions will die - women, children, innocent people! Don't fight for the king, don't fight for the kingdom! Fight for the lives of those you hold dear!"

The anxious frowns of the crowd grew slowly into cautious grins, a gradual roar of cheers rising. Veldin looked upon the crowd with an ecstatic smile, knowing he was exactly where he always should have been.

"Verden and Barethia, I want you lot on the ground floor! Arrenni and Ironhand, second floor! Severin, third!" Veldin commanded, the soldiers before him shifting into action. "Defend your king, defend your country, defend humanity!"

The crowd of soldiers rapidly dispersed, thundering to their positions in the wake of their respective captains and commanders. Veldin hopped down from the table with a crash of armour plating and approached Friedrich with a grin.

"Did you just tell my men not to fight for me?!" Friedrich hissed.

"Nobody wants to fight for their king," Veldin smirked. "People fight for what they care about and I'll be damned if any of those lot care about you. No offence."

"Offence taken!" Friedrich spat. "And what am I meant to do in all of this?"

"You just bunker down in your quarters while the situation is dealt with. The Phoenix Guard should be protection enough in there."

"You want me to hide?!" Friedrich scoffed. "I need to be out there, inspiring the men!"

"Believe me, you won't be inspiring anyone," Veldin chuckled. "All you'll be doing is opening yourself up to assassination. You're staying hidden."

"I don't have to take orders from-"

"Do you want to live, your highness?"

"Yes, but I-"

"Then do as I say!" Veldin snapped. "I won't hear another word elsewise!"

Friedrich growled furiously, signalling his guards to follow as he trailed off down the hallway. Veldin chuckled quietly to himself - Friedrich was just a dim-witted as his father had always described. Concerning as it was for the realm, it was quite entertaining.

"Veldin!"

Veldin's brow furrowed and he turned to see his stocky father waddling hurriedly into the dining hall, panting for breath after barely a jog.

"Father?" Veldin scoffed. "What the hell are you doing here?!"

"Don't worry, don't worry, I'm not here to fight!" Kranik laughed. "I heard you'd taken command over the palace's defence, had to come and see for myself!"

"Because you didn't believe it?" Veldin muttered. "I'm sorry it couldn't have been Balder."

Kranik's eyes widened, totally taken aback. "Is that what this is about?" he gasped.

"No..." Veldin sighed, hanging his head low. "Well, maybe a little. I guess I just wanted some recognition of my own for once."

"Veldin, you mean no less to me than Balder."

"Then why make him heir?" Veldin hissed. "I'm twice the man he is! I drove back the Vulkites, I quelled the rebellions, I-"

"Exactly!" Kranik boomed, shaking Veldin by the shoulders. "Which is why I didn't want to tie you down with all this diplomatic nonsense!"

"Wha- really?"

"My boy, you're a great general and an incredible leader of men!" Kranik smiled. "You belong exactly where you are right now, taking the fight to the enemies of Verdenheld!"

"You... do you really mean that?" Veldin mumbled.

"Of course I do!" Kranik laughed. "Tell you what - the king has approved my expedition and I can think of no better man to tame the Shattered Coast!"

"I-I'm honoured," Veldin sighed. "But... I'm not sure I'll be coming back."

Kranik tilted his head affectionately at Veldin's glum frown. "Veldin, you shouldn't-"

"No, I... I think I might stay a while," Veldin smiled, his saddened eyes lightening. "This city needs me."

Kranik's face dropped, confused but not entirely hurt. "Schardenhelm needs you, son. It won't have me forever."

"Then it'll have Balder. Who does Aldreichen have? Friedrich? Geldus?" Veldin laughed. "The Verdens have neglected this place long enough - it's time to show these prissy pricks how we do it in the Iron Peaks!"

Kranik chuckled merrily, patting his son heartily on the shoulder. "Perhaps it *is* finally time for House Ironhand to start doing their part in the Heartland," he sighed. "You're sure you want this?"

"Positive," Veldin grinned. "Last night, at the ball... someone told me that I had to walk my own path, wherever it might take me. I realise now she was right."

"Then the best of luck to you, son!" Kranik smiled, a hint of pain in his eyes. "And once this place is ship shape, we can see about this expedition."

"Father, you don't need to-"

Veldin was cut short as a monstrous roar echoed through the halls of the palace, followed quickly by frantic crashing and panicked shouts and screams. He glanced apprehensively down the golden hallway, his hand reaching for his axe.

"I think you've got company," Kranik grinned. "Go, son. Give those shapeshiftin' pricks a taste of Ironhand steel!"

Veldin grinned and thrust out his hand to meet his father in a final, hearty handshake. Kranik watched pridefully as Veldin drew his colossal axe from his back and thundered off into the hallways ahead. Aldreichen was in good hands.

Eris and Caesia departed hastily from the Hallow District before the city guard could arrive at the scene, not particularly keen on having an act of terrorism pinned on them. They followed the lantern back into the heart of the city, to confront the assassins once and for all.

"Now, I know we killed a dragon last week, but are you sure we can take a bunch of these guys?" Eris asked. "Not that I'm scared or worried or anything."

"I'd say we've a fair chance. If our fight in the sewers was anything to go by, these changelings perform rather sloppily in combat."

"Maybe they just don't, um... *be* arachni very often?"

"Hm, I guess that's certainly a possibility. It would be reasonable to think they'd be more adjusted to particular forms."

"Forms that they could happily use now that their cover is blown…"

"We'll cope," Caesia confidently smiled. "We tend to be rather adaptable."

"Yeah, like the shapeshifters aren't," Eris muttered. "I assume we're still doing the 'no kill' thing here?"

"Where you can, but with the lives of an entire race riding on this I'm more than willing to look the other way if you really have to… snuff one."

"Alright, I'll see what I can do. About *not* killing them, that is."

"Good…" Caesia sighed, before glancing down suspiciously at Eris' feet, one of which seemed to be dragging behind the other. "You're walking funny. Seriously, what's going on?"

"Ah, my ankle just hurts a bit."

"You're practically limping!" Caesia hissed.

"I know, but what am I meant to do about it?" Eris snapped. "I don't exactly have time to give it a rest, do I?"

"Well, I guess not… just don't put too much pressure on it, alright?"

"You know I can't do that." Eris smirked. "There's no way I can fight if I do."

Caesia growled under her breath. Eris was right - if she tried to focus on not putting pressure on her foot, it would probably get her killed. They were simply going to have to hope that she didn't deal herself any irreparable damage.

They turned onto the main road by which they had travelled from the city gates to Victory Plaza. Eris tried to hide a yawn at the thought of how long it had been since they stepped through those gates, her mouth trembling as she forced it shut. It was getting close to four o'clock now and both of them were becoming particularly worn out.

Caesia looked curiously at the lantern as it subtly flared up and intensified. "It seems our target is straight down this road."

"In Victory Plaza?" Eris groaned. "Stars, I don't wanna see that place ever again."

"It is possible that the target is beyond the Plaza. I don't see how they could hide there."

"Don't know about you, but I think this reeks of a trap."

"You think?" Caesia mused. "Hm, I suppose it would make sense, no doubt they're expecting us."

"Maybe we should just wait for them at the Palace. That way, they'll have to come to us."

"We can't risk letting them close the gap. We need to take them out here."

"Yeah, I guess it would be pretty hard to keep all of them away from the King at the same time," Eris sighed as they started down the road. "Alright, let's do this!"

The magnificent, towering statue of King Aldrich came into view as they turned onto Victory Plaza. The Plaza was completely deserted, the raised platform near the centre no longer sporting a pyre but a massive guillotine. The manner of execution was often changed up in order to keep the commonfolk entertained. This guillotine in particular was specially designed for executing arachni, as was evident by its unusual size and multitude of arm restraints.

Standing on the platform was a pasty bald man, dressed in battered and aged clothing like those often worn by peasants. He was looking the guillotine up and down with intrigue.

"Oh yeah, definitely a trap," Caesia confirmed. "Shall we?"

"Let's kick this guy's ass," Eris grinned.

They moved across the Plaza towards the platform, where the waiting man turned to meet them. His eyes were empty and white and his ghostly skin had not a hair on it - a changeling in its true form.

"Such a barbaric contraption," Devren sighed. "They truly allow us no dignity in our deaths. Collars, branding, public execution… does the cruelty of man know no bounds?"

"Well, this is quite clearly a diversion," Caesia muttered to Eris, garnering a defeated look from the changeling. "He's clearly trying to hold us up, the rest must have already departed."

"Should we just teleport outta here?"

"No, he'll just transform and catch up," Caesia sighed as she ignited her arms with energy. "We'll just have to make this quick."

Eris grinned eagerly and unbuckled both of her sheaths, drawing her steel sword with her right hand and the sliver with the left. Logically, she should have used the far superior silver sword in her dominant hand, but she was far better adjusted to the weight and shape of the steel sword.

"Sorry if you had a speech lined up," Caesia smirked. "But we've places to be."

Caesia couldn't be bothered listening to another monologue after Xeracrir. She doubted that humouring him would get her anything but exposition about why Valkyr was right and she was wrong.

"Very well," Devren smiled, a bloodthirsty grin spreading across his face. "Then I shall waste no time in slaying you!"

The changeling stepped to the edge of the platform and spread out his arms, which throbbed with pulsing yellow energy as he drew them into one another.

"Your people call us changelings, you blindly attribute us to a common gimmick! Let me prove to you that we are defined by more than mere parlour tricks."

He flung out his hands and the yellow light slipped to his sides, floating weightlessly along the width of the platform like a cloud adrift in a gentle breeze. The energy gathered in various spots, where it stretched and convulsed into identical shapes. In a blinding flash of yellow light, the energy took the forms of five identical copies of their caster, completely indiscernible from the true changeling in their midst.

"Oh, this should be easy," Eris smirked. "We just gotta find the one who we can actually touch."

"If only..." Caesia sighed. "Changelings normally use evocation to give their illusions physical forms."

"Wait, you mean-"

"Yes!" Caesia hissed. "Now shut up and fight!"

Devren and his doppelgangers leapt from the platform and grouped together, the true Devren merging into the group as they approached.

Eris raised her swords readily in front of her and moved into a defensive stance ahead of Caesia. Caesia pulled back her arm and whipped it forwards, propelling a crack of lightning across the Plaza. The bolt of energy smashed straight into the face of one of the doppelgangers, which barely flinched as his head warped and rippled with yellow light.

"I think I just fed it more energy," Caesia mumbled as the doppelganger's face reformed with a patronising smile.

"Do I have to do everything around here?" Eris sighed. "Just do... shield stuff."

"Can do."

Caesia lunged forwards and blinked across the Plaza, reappearing in a burst of light atop the platform. As Eris advanced aggressively towards the mob of changelings, Caesia thrust up her hand and raised a shield within their ranks, splitting the group and barricading two of them against the platform. Not about to be defeated by some wall, the doppelgangers pushed themselves up against the shield. Being made of pure energy, they could happily wade through it, albeit slowly.

While Eris clashed with the other three, Caesia stepped back into the middle of the platform as one of the changelings ascended the steps towards the guillotine. She flung herself forwards, blinking straight into his path and thrusting her foot into his gut with as much force as she could muster. As she blinked back behind the guillotine, the winded changeling staggered furiously after her.

Eris kicked out at one of the changelings, knocking him away as she simultaneously clashed blades with her other two assailants. She withdrew her silver sword from the leftmost and swung it at the other's blade, battering it aside and it's wielder with it. As the leftmost brought his sword back around and slashed at her head, she whipped her head back and let the blade glide past her face. His sword behind her, Eris took advantage of the vulnerable changeling and drove her steel sword straight through its chest. She shoved it away and shielded her eyes as it burst into a shower of shimmering yellow sparks.

Caesia reeled back from the guillotine as the changeling made a clumsy swipe across it. He leapt onto the massive contraption and hopped down beside her, sword held high over his head. The sword slammed into the side of the guillotine as Caesia reappeared on the side from which he had just come. He clambered angrily back onto the guillotine and swiped again at her.

She already had this changeling figured out - his ego was enormous. Having spent a week with Eris, she had begun to understand exactly how to push the right buttons.

"You're embarrassing yourself," Caesia smirked as she stepped back effortlessly from the strike. "You should really consider a different profession."

Becoming increasingly impatient, the doppelganger thrust out his sword at Caesia's neck, only for her to vanish and reappear at the end of the guillotine.

"Magician would suit you well," she sneered, leaning playfully against the frame of the guillotine. "The children would adore you!"

The doppelganger roared with anger and stampeded along the length of the guillotine. As he drew dangerously close, Caesia stepped casually back and flicked a lightning bolt into the mechanism of the guillotine. The doppelganger looked blankly at her in defeat as the massive blade came crashing down and cleaved straight down the middle of his form, dispersing him in a glittery yellow cloud.

Caesia sighed in relief that he was not the real changeling - that could have been beyond brutal. She looked around the Plaza in her moment of safety. People in the surrounding houses were stepping out onto their balconies and peering through their windows, curious as to what noise had woken them at this hour. It seemed their fight had caught a lot of attention, they had an audience watching them intently.

Caesia whipped around as she felt her shield shatter. The changelings closed in towards Eris, through the settling green particles left behind by the broken shield.

Devren stepped forth and spread his fingers as wide as they could go. His hands began to pulsate with yellow energy and a solid disc of light formed in either of his hands. Eris jumped in terror as the changeling launched a disc in her direction. It slammed into the ground and accelerated towards her like a loose wheel, a torrent of yellow sparks spewing in its wake as it wrought a black scar through the stonework. Eris threw herself off her feet as the disc sliced past her feet and tore off down the main road.

"You fight on the side of evil!" the changelings simultaneously declared. "Are you so blind to their lies?"

"Oh, I see the lies alright!" Eris hissed, regaining her footing and flourishing her blades. "I also see a white-eyed prick who's gonna get thousands of people killed!"

The changeling hurled his second disc before stepping back into his gaggle of doppelgangers. Eris ducked under it narrowly, the sweat on her brow evaporating as she slipped by. The disc whipped over her head and sliced effortlessly through the ankle of Aldrich Verden, like an evoked knife through warm butter. The disc soared into the distance, spewing yellow sparks and shaving off a chimney as it skidded over the rooftops.

Caesia watched as what little remained of the statue's ankle gave way with a thunderous crack. The stump leg slammed down onto the foot with a colossal thud and the statue began to careen over. The spectators on the east side of the Plaza began to step back anxiously from their balconies as the statue gradually veered towards them.

People screamed and wailed in terror, bolting indoors as the statue toppled from its pedestal. Caesia knew that they couldn't make it out in time. She looked back at Eris, who was being slowly encircled by the changeling and his doppelgangers.

"Don't die, Eris," she mumbled, launching into a sprint towards the eastern Plaza.

In a flash of green light, she skidded to a halt in the looming shadow of the statue, daunted as it descended towards her. In her weak state, she had no hope of holding it back - she had to use her disorder to her advantage and amplify her power.

She clenched her fists and drew all the essence she could must into her arms. The pain was immediate, only increasing as her bruised arms strained to contain the surge of power. With a scream of agony, she thrust out both of her hands and projected a glistening green shield ahead of the statue.

The statue slammed into the shield with a chilling crack that sent a surge of piercing, debilitating pain through her body. The pain only reinforced her shield, as she grew stronger and stronger with her emotions. A hail of green sparks showered the Plaza as the statue ground up against the barrier, the beautifully detailed armour being violently eroded by the crackling heat.

Caesia felt as if she had been ran through with a sword. A sharp, searing pain pulsed through her body and as she continued to hold the barrier in place, she felt as if every cell in her arms were on fire. She whimpered in pain, her breath shaky and hoarse, yet despite that she remembered Eris' words of wisdom - Caesia didn't believe that she could do this, she knew that she could. Through the burning agony, she forced a trembling smile across her face and reinforced her barrier with all her might.

Eris span slowly on the spot, working carefully to pick a suitable target from the four changelings. They encircled her like sharks, holding a sword to either side of her. She didn't falter - she was never one to believe in bad odds.

"For hundreds of years, the arachni have hid in safety and left the other races to fend for themselves!" the changelings boomed as one. "They will get for their betrayal what they deserve. One way or another, there will be a reckoning!"

As they closed in around her and raised their swords, Eris lunged at the fourth changeling with her steel sword and as he battered the blade aside, thrust at his neck with her silver sword. The changeling dodged backwards, opening a gap in the circle. Eris swept her swords to either side of her. The blades flashed narrowly past the heads of the surrounding changelings, warding them off as she leapt through the gap after the fourth changeling.

Amidst a storm of green sparks, Eris moved to engage the changeling. She battered his sword aside with both blades. Pinning the sword at his side with one blade, she flipped the other and swung it back across his neck. The doppelganger warped and convulsed as Eris' sword glided through his form, dispersing in a violent flash of yellow light.

"You know Valkyr wants the arachni as allies, right?" Eris smirked. "He won't let them die."

"Valkyr is but a means to an end - a tool that enabled our vengeance. He is a fool to think the arachni could survive Verdenheld's wrath! King Friedrich will die and the all of Verdenheld will come down upon this city!"

Caesia peered over her shoulder and watched as the last family fled from their home. The area clear of innocents, she dropped her arms and staggered to the side, blinking clumsily out of the path of the statue. As the statue's blade exploded through the roof of a house in a shower of planks and tiles, Caesia stumbled to her knees and watched the people fleeing the Plaza to safety. Her whole body was on fire with terrible pain, but it was worth it so long as everyone got out unscathed.

The ground shook as King Aldrich toppled to the ground with an enormous crash, followed by a massive crunch as he obliterated a row of houses with his blade. The ground trembled and threw a few of the changelings off balance, Eris leaping into their midst to take full advantage. Dipping below the strike of the first changeling, she slashed its ankle as she slid past.

As he stumbled off to the side, Eris thundered toward the fifth changeling, who was just regaining his footing. As he raised his sword from his side, she slammed her silver blade down into his wrist. The hand and the sword in its grasp dissipated into the air as she cleaved through his arm. He grabbed her other arm with his free hand, trying desperately to restrain her, only for her to ram her other blade deep into the his gut, causing him to spontaneously explode in a flash of yellow light.

Eris staggered back from the explosion, dazed by the sudden burst of light. Two remained, one of which she knew for sure to be a doppelganger after it's ankle wound had mysteriously disappeared.

She approached cautiously, both swords raised.

"Every second we fight, my brothers and sisters draw closer and closer to your king," both changelings sneered in unison. "Your cause is hopeless."

"I dunno, I'm feeling pretty good about this," Eris grinned.

"Then you are a greater fool than I had estimated."

Devren flicked out his arm and the world around Eris was suddenly swept into blackness. The Plaza, the changelings, everything was consumed by a thick shroud of darkness, like an impenetrable arcane mist. Barely able to see even a metre in front of her, she held up her swords defensively, monitoring the veil of shadow carefully.

At the sound of a footstep, she swivelled around and caught the blade of the doppelganger, shoving him back into the shroud. Devren lunged from the shadows behind her, his sword pricking her back as she thrust her body forwards in evasion. She swung around and batted his sword aside, slicing across with her silver sword and catching his forearm, carving a bloody incision across it and spattering the pavement with his blood. Devren turned tail and retreated back into the shadows, grasping the gushing wound.

"Oh, no you don't!" Eris growled, reeling back her swords and leaping into the abyss after him. She cringed at the chilling contact as the tips of her swords cleaved through his flesh.

The shroud vanished as fast as it had appeared and Eris covered her eyes as they readjusted to the light. Devren stumbled to the ground, moaning in pain at the two parallel, crimson gashes wrought down his back. As Eris approached, he scrambled around to face her, his face defiant yet contorted with pain.

"You fool," he gasped, his voice weak and hoarse. "Humanity… will never-"

Eris smashed her hilt against the changeling's forehead with a blunt thud. His empty eyes rolled up into his head and he flopped onto his side, unconscious. The spectators in the buildings, who Eris had scarcely noticed in the heat of battle, roared with triumphant cheers and hoots at her victory.

"Yeah, yeah, nice try," she sneered. "Give me a spooky one-liner then turn into a bird and fly away, I know how it works."

She sheathed her swords and threw her backpack off her shoulders. Shovelling through a mass of carrots, she yanked out one of the collars from the compound and flicked it open.

"You bad guys need to get some better tricks," she chuckled as she locked the sladium-laced steel collar around the changeling's neck with a powerful snap.

Their audience erupted into thunderous applause as she leapt up, their praise echoing all throughout Victory Plaza. Eris span around excitedly, her ego alight as she embracing her cheering fans. This was it - she was living her dream. The reality only now struck her completely, how far she had truly come from her little village in the mountains. She had gone where none of her people had gone before and not just survived, but thrived. It was like she had always dreamt when she had gazed out upon the world, the crazed fantasies of an ambitious little girl made reality.

Caesia, who sat panting breathlessly with blood trickling from her nose, gazed across at Eris with a warm smile as she watched the joyful tears roll down her friend's cheeks. Eris had done so much for her today, it was a pleasure to see her have a moment of her own.

While her friend stood in an ecstatic trance, she turned to survey the hundreds of smiling faces gazing upon them. She realised that despite her usual fear of audiences, she felt no such fear in that moment. Maybe the Caesia of old really was dying out.

"This is more like it!" Eris called, skipping to her side as the applause died down.

"I guess you've got the glory you were looking for?" Caesia laughed, smearing her bandaged arm across her bloody nose.

"Oh, I'm just getting started!" Eris smirked, turning and scrambling onto the base of the shattered statue. "I'll have a giant statue of my own in no time!"

"What are you doing?" Caesia laughed, assuming that Eris was about to give some kind of victory speech.

Eris waved her hands back and forth, the din of the crowd dying slowly down. "Alright, we gotta go and save the kingdom!" she yelled across the Square. "It would be great if you guys could hand this bloke to the city guard for us!"

She leapt down from the statue, gesturing Caesia to follow. As she landed, she gasped at a sharp, burning pain that shot up her left calf. In the chaos of combat, the adrenaline had totally drowned out the agonising pain in her ankle, which had been gradually growing the entire time. As excruciating as it was, she simply bit down on her lip and powered through it. There would be time to rest it later.

"I guess that's a good enough way to save time," Caesia smirked. "We'd better hurry, we're running against the clock and the clock is a bloody athlete."

As spectators poured from their houses to apprehend the blood sodden changeling, Eris and Caesia rushed off to the north side of the Plaza, destined for the palace.

"I don't understand..." Eris muttered as they barrelled out of the Plaza. "How did we detect him but none of the others?"

"I read that powerful illusionists can mask their essence entirely, or instead amplify it. He must have masked that of his allies and amplified his own to trick us. Very clever..."

"Huh. Well, I just hope we're not too late."

"Fingers crossed," Caesia sighed, glancing down at the small, bloody incision in the back of Eris' chestpiece. "Hey, you've got a, er..."

Eris glanced down at her back, at the slit where the changeling had jabbed her with his sword. She had barely noticed it at the time and now that the adrenaline was simmering down, it suddenly began to sting.

"It's just a scratch," Eris smiled. "I'll live."

She winced at the burning pain of the wound. It was little more than a papercut, the issue being that paper cuts hurt like hell. She had no time to tend to it though, they couldn't afford to stop now. Besides, it certainly hurt no more than her ankle.

"I've no doubt you'll live, but you're clearly in pain!" Caesia urged.

"I'll forget it's even there once we get fighting again. Really, it's not a problem."

"Fine, but I don't want to hear a word about it," Caesia sighed.

"Yes, ma'am!" Eris chirped.

Caesia rolled her eyes. Dire as the situation was, Eris was still treating it like some elaborate game. How Caesia wished she could do the same, although she supposed it was important for at least one of them to keep a serious mindset.

Eris' brow furrowed at the distant sound of humming. "Um, Caesia?"

"Yeah?"

"What's that-"

A wall of blue light swept across the street ahead. As Eris and Caesia skidded to a halt and readied themselves for a fight, the barrier careened around and encircled them in a shimmering dome. Several silver armoured soldiers stormed into the streets, turquoise hoods cast over their heads - Tarantis battlemages.

"Bloody hell," Caesia spat, grasping Eris' arm and yanking her along. "I don't have time for this."

The two of them went up in a flash of green light. Caesia's face burnt with pain as her face slammed abruptly against the barrier, deflecting her back in a daze as they staggered back into reality.

"Your intuition was correct, sergeant," Edmund sneered, stepping out into the street with his men. "Essence blocks essence, as always."

Caesia composed herself and turned around with a growl. Eris shrank away behind her, deciding that this was best left up to her.

"If it's all the same to you, I'd rather not do this now," Caesia muttered.

"What, so you can 'save the kingdom'?" Edmund chuckled. "No, I think you will be coming with me."

"Like hell," Caesia hissed.

Edmund sighed impatiently. "You do not understand the gravity of what you have achieved," he insisted. "What this could mean for the future of mankind…"

"As a matter of fact, I am not actually an idiot," Caesia spat. "My ability to transcend reality is revolutionary from an arcane standpoint, I'm well aware of that."

"Then you must understand why you absolutely *have* to come with me!" Edmund urged. "By studying your abilities, the College could unlock countless arcane secrets! It could be the beginning of a new age!"

Caesia glared for a moment at her father. "That's all you care about, isn't it?" she hissed. "It's all you ever cared about, always trying to better the realm without thinking about how anyone around you might feel!"

"This is beyond any of us! This is the future of-"

"Fuck your future!" Caesia snapped. "I'm not about to give myself up so a bunch of decrepit old farts can probe me for the rest of my miserable life!"

"Put your petty feelings aside and look at the big picture," Edmund growled, composing his menacing demeanour. "The Thyresians are surpassing us more and more by the day. If Verdenheld is to keep up with their technological strides, we *need* this advantage."

"Have you ever considered that Verdenheld's time might be up?" Caesia sighed. "That maybe it's time to share the world with others rather than kick the shit out of everyone who defies you?"

"You do not understand…"

"I do, funnily enough," Caesia sneered. "I understand this world *far* better than you. I understand that the only enemies Verdenheld has are those that it baselessly declares to be so! The realm is in decline because your ideals are archaic, because a kingdom built on hate can only go so far before it drowns in its own prejudices!"

"Your outlook is naive, blind! You do not see the powers of this world for what they truly are. Thyresia is no better than us, Norskar too."

"Perhaps so, but what I do see is a realm teetering on the edge of annihilation. The world is rising against you and you're too blind to see it. The people you've oppressed for hundreds of years have finally had enough and today, it's all began to culminate. Open your eyes, father, Verdenheld has reached its tipping point."

Edmund glared narrowly at his daughter. She had a lot of nerve trying to preach to him such naive ideals. She was a fool to perceive the world through such an optimistic lens, failing so dramatically to understand the cruelty of men. Perhaps the world was not all born of hate, but it needed Verdenheld as the holy bulwark against evil that it had always been. Edmund would ensure its survival, for the sake of humankind.

"I will not hear the council of a child," he hissed. "Verdenheld will stand, crush its enemies as it has done time and time again. We will endure."

"You're making a terrible mistake," Caesia said gravely. "This is far bigger than-"

"You have diverted this conversation long enough!" Edmund snapped. "I will hear no more of it. You will return to Abenfurt with me."

Caesia narrowed her eyes and stood stiff in defiance. "Not a chance."

"I expected you would resist, that you'd be beyond reason," Edmund sighed, turning away from her. "Apprehend them."

One of the battlemages outstretched his hand and the dome of light began to steadily shrink. Eris watched with concern as Caesia searched frantically for a solution to the situation. If she didn't know how to deal with the magical barrier, they were practically hopeless.

"Wait!" Eris urged. "What about the King? We need to help him!"

She knew that he would not care, but she had to buy Caesia time. Caesia was smart, she would come up with something, Eris just knew it."

Edmund smirked and glanced over his shoulder. "I couldn't care less what happens to that oaf. Frankly, I would say it is about time."

Caesia glanced up at her father, a subtle smirk spreading across her face as she eyed a sewer grate just outside of the dome.

"I'll be sure to let him know how you feel," she grinned.

"Oh, will you?" Edmund chuckled, crossing his arms patronisingly. "And how do you intend to do that?"

"I imagine it to be… something like this."

Caesia stepped back and grabbed Eris' arm. Before the battlemages could react, the pair went up in a flash of green light. The glow of the streetlights was stripped away as they plunged from a rushing tunnel of light and into the ominous darkness of the sewer.

"Nice!" Eris laughed, rubbing her eyes as they adjusted.

"Come on!" Caesia urged, grabbing Eris and tugging her along.

Edmund's eyes fluttered at the sight of the empty dome, utterly speechless. His patience for his daughter was beginning to wane.

"Sir!" called one of the battlemages, throwing out a finger to the nearby sewer grate, from which came the pattering of footsteps in water.

Edmund growled as he was struck by reality of what had happened. She could move through surfaces, he knew that! How could he have been so foolish?

"Well, what are you waiting for? Get down there!" Edmund barked. "You three, you're with me."

With three battlemages in tow, Edmund marched off down the street, while the other three made for the next sewer grate.

Eris flinched as the grate ahead of them exploded in a burst of yellow fire and crashed into the water below. Just as they passed beneath it, the first battlemage dropped into the sewer behind them in an explosion of filthy water.

"Halt!" he boomed, pulling back his arm and slinging a purple bolt of lightning after them.

Caesia swung her arm over her shoulder and thrust up a shield the size of her palm, dispersing the bolt with a deafening crack into a shower of sparks. She dragged Eris around the corner as another exploded against the stonework.

Eris gasped as another battlemage dropped into the sewers ahead of them. He drew up his fist and the water around him began to ripple and rise - a hydromancer.

"Out of my way!" Caesia growled, throwing out her arm and thrusting it aside.

The battlemage's eyes widened as he was shunted away in a burst of green light, reappearing behind them and slamming hard against the cold, stone wall. Eris looked back gobsmacked as he staggered back and toppled into the water.

"I didn't know you could do that!" she gasped.

"Neither did I!" Caesia laughed. "Over there!"

She thrust out her arm towards a ladder, dimly illuminated by the moonlight seeping through the grate above.

"We're going back up?" Eris mumbled.

"Unless you want to remain in a sewer all your life, then I'd say so!"

Eris ran ahead and leapt from the water, skidding to a halt at the foot of the ladder. She crouched down and as Caesia approached, put out her hands and thrust Caesia up onto the ladder, then following closely behind. As she scrambled up, the battlemages appeared around the corner, the frontmost mage slinging a whining yellow firebolt down the tunnel. The fire exploded against the ladder just as Eris pulled her legs up.

"Step aside," Caesia insisted, moving to the top of the ladder.

She crouched down and poked her head over the top to see two battlemages already on the ladder.

"You fellows must be exhausted!" she smiled. "Allow me to provide you some energy."

The battlemage nearest the top glanced up, suddenly stricken with terror. Caesia grinned as their eyes met and slammed her hands down on the top of the ladder. Electricity surged down the length of the ladder, the pair of mages trembling violently as energy coursed into their bodies. They fell from the ladder, onto the third, toppling into a crumpled, twitching heap in the darkness.

"Awesome," Eris smiled, throwing up her hand. "High fi-"

"Crap!" Caesia hissed, pulling Eris along once again.

"There they are!" bellowed a battlemage as he skidded into the road.

"Then stop them, you dolt!" Edmund snapped, emerging after him with the other two mages.

Caesia threw up a shield between them as a hail of fire and lightning was let loose with a deafening roar. The barrier hissed and crackled as their attacks met its surface, eventually shattering into a cloud of green sparks under the tremendous pressure.

The battlemages made chase and thundered after them. Caesia may have been slowing Eris down, but Edmund was also hindering the battlemages. So long as Caesia could keep up her defence, the mages would not close distance.

"This way!" Eris hissed, dodging left into an alleyway as a purple fireball streaked between them.

Following her friend closely, Caesia ducked into the blackness of the alleyway. Eris led her nimbly around the various piles of discarded rubbish and around a confused homeless family. Caesia looked back as they reached the alley's end, watching as the battlemages barged the men and women aside. She was flooded suddenly with contempt as a mage thrust an oozing barrel aside and unwittingly battered it into a small peasant child. As the boy toppled clumsily into a pile of decaying food, Caesia reeled back her arm and furiously slung a lightning bolt down the alleyway.

Edmund rolled his eyes as the frontmost battlemage staggered back, his arm limp at his side and coursing with green sparks.

"What in God's name do I pay you idiots for?" he scoffed. "You're a bloody waste of tuition!"

The mages piled out of the alleyway and into the street, where they caught a glimpse of Caesia and Eris disappearing around the next corner.

The girls stepped out into the main road. It was totally straight, not a single alleyway to turn to - they had to run, fast.

"Take my hand," Caesia commanded, Eris obediently grabbing her palm as they ran.

Caesia thrust her body forwards and yanked Eris along as she exploded into green light. The world rushed by like a hurricane and before Eris knew it, they were halfway down the road. She struggled to keep her footing as her feet hit the road once again, the sudden transition back and forth having been quite jarring.

Edmund skidded around the corner to see them go up in light again and flash back into reality almost an entire street down from them.

"You call yourself mages?" he snapped. "Do something!"

Eris' feet met the cobblestones again as they leapt from the vortex of light. The stirring of her stomach was but an afterthought as an agonising, sharp pain spread throughout her ankle. Ignore it, she told herself, there would be time from pain later.

She glanced back over her shoulder to see one of the distant battlemages winding back his arm, his hand throbbing with icy blue energy. A tendril of electricity surged after them, streaking down the road at incredible speed. In the split second she had to react, Eris did the only thing she could think to do. She let her grip slip from Caesia's hand, who turned around with a startled gasp.

Caesia watched as the bolt of energy slammed into the back of Eris' thigh, blasting her off her feet and pumping her legs full of electricity. She crashed to the ground on her back, her legs quaking erratically. Caesia slid to a halt and rushed to Eris' side, her eyes wide with panic.

"Eris, come on!" she begged, grabbing Eris' sides in a struggle to pull her to her feet. "We have to go!"

"I- I can't feel my legs!" Eris gasped, her eyes wide with terror.

Caesia looked her friend up and down. That must have been a weak lightning bolt to only disable her legs - no doubt the battlemages were being careful in fear of injuring Lord Tarantis' daughter.

"It'll wear off in no time," Caesia whispered. "Just-"

Caesia was cut short by the thunder of footsteps ahead. At the end of the road assembled a unit of ten Severin crossbowmen, lining up in a wall of fiery orange tabards. Sharpened white crystals at the end of their weapons glinted in the light of the streetlamps - sladium tipped bolts.

Edmund and his battlemages skidded to a halt as a man, heavily clad in a suit of battered schardenum armour, appeared behind the line. His armour was dull and blackened by years of conflict, his tabard filthy and scorched. On his belt hung a jagged mace laden with stubby, brutal spikes built for crushing bone.

"Well, what timing!" Alvus called, stepping between his men and out into the street. "I was worried I'd be too late!"

Caesia's face dropped in defeat, she felt her heart sink as if it were drowning in sorrow. She glanced down at Eris with fearful eyes, yet somehow received back a warm, reassuring smile.

"It'll be okay," Eris smiled, even despite the tears trickling from her eyes. "The good guys always win!"

Caesia clenched her teeth down upon her lip as she fought to suppress her fear. She couldn't go back, not after all she had been through - adventure, excitement… friendship. She had only just begun to truly live her life.

"I have this under control, Alvus!" Edmund boomed. "Your assistance is not necessary."

"You do, huh?" Alvus smirked. "Because from where I'm standing, it seems otherwise…"

"Excuse me?" Edmund scoffed.

Alvus grinned behind his helmet and turned to his men. "Open fire!"

Caesia grabbed Eris and pulled her close as the harrowing cracks of bowstrings echoed into the night. At least this way, she would die free. In that, she could take a final solace.

"You conniving brat," Edmund spat, his words punctuated by the clattering of armour against the ground.

As Caesia glanced up cautiously from Eris' shoulder, Alvus yanked off his helmet and gave her a cheeky grin. He gestured to his men, who locked new bolts into their crossbows and moved to encircle Edmund, who stood with a scowl amidst several silver armoured corpses.

Eris peeled herself away from Caesia in a confused daze, wiping away the tears from her eyes as she looked up at her friend's smiling face.

"Who's the crybaby now?" Caesia smirked shallowly, her face drenched only in sweat.

Caesia released Eris from her grip and let her slump gently to the ground. She tilted back her head and heaved the heaviest sigh of her life, releasing the culminated stress of the most hard-fought day of her life.

"What just happened?" Eris groaned. "Who in the stars is this guy?"

"An old friend," Caesia grinned, scrambling onto her feet.

She stood up straight, crimson faced but finally holding a handle on her emotions. She greeted Alvus with a warm smile, speechless under the overwhelming weight of her relief.

"My, you've grown into quite the strapping young woman!" Alvus laughed. "It's good to see you, little one."

Alvus chuckled in delight as Caesia flung her arms around him in utter joy. He rarely enjoyed a warm welcome as commander of the kingdom's foremost military force.

"Thank you, Alvus," Caesia whispered. "It… it's good to see you too."

"Don't mention it. I'm here for Friedrich's sake as much as yours."

Alvus patted Caesia heartily on the shoulder and continued towards Edmund. Caesia pulled Eris up off the ground, who settled on quivering, numb legs, and followed after him.

"Sorry about this, old friend!" Alvus called, spreading his arms apologetically.

"What is the meaning of this, Alvus?" Edmund snarled.

"Well, I'd been considering intervening from the moment you mentioned chasing the little one…" Alvus sighed. "But when you showed your willingness to kick Friedrich to the curb, I figured I had to do something."

"Yet you supported the idea yourself!"

"What can I say, I'm a good liar," Alvus smiled cheekily. "A simple but effective tactic - play along and get 'em to cough up the secrets. You my friend, showed a rather treasonous hand… but now remains the question - what are we to do with Edmund Tarantis?"

"A good question indeed…" Caesia smirked. "It's my understanding that treason is punishable by death."

Edmund glared at Caesia, despising the enjoyment she took from the situation.

"Do you have a preference, Caesia?" Alvus asked.

Caesia stared for a time into her father's contemptuous eyes. Her mind was telling her to choke the life out of him, but she knew she couldn't bring herself to it. She was better than him. She was not her father's daughter.

"Let him slither back to Abenfurt," Caesia spat. "He doesn't deserve the dignity of death."

Alvus signalled for his men to lower their crossbows and step away. They withdrew back to the end of the street to await their lord.

"Let's just make one thing crystal clear," Caesia growled, stepping closer to her father. "I'm not yours anymore. You don't control me and you never will, and you can tell the College that if they want to dissect me for research, I'll happily dissect them first!"

Edmund stared at her for a moment in silence. "Defy me all you want, girl," he spat. "You can't escape me forever."

"Is that what you think?" Caesia hissed, drawing face to face with him. "If I *ever* see you or your men again, I'll kill you all!"

"You could never kill me," Edmund smirked. "You're too soft. You always have been. Just a pathetic little girl who-"

Edmund staggered back as Caesia's fist collided with his jaw. It was a fairly weak punch, but took him completely off guard. He barely had time to form a glare before Caesia grabbed him by the tunic and pulled him in close.

"I don't think you understand how close I am to blasting a hole through your head," Caesia hissed, crackling energy lashing from her arms as her anger boiled. "Belittle me one more time and I will pump *so* much energy into your body that I could serve you on a platter!"

Caesia waited for a moment, allowing her father an opportunity to consider her threat. She wasn't going to kill him, but deep down she was longing for a reason to hurt him. Alas, he was silent.

"Nothing? No snide remark? No clever retort?" she spat. "Then listen closely - I have a life now. I finally have someone who gives a damn about me, finally I have a reason to live! So, you can be bloody sure that there is *nothing* I wouldn't do to keep it."

Edmund smirked mockingly. "Look at you. You've let that savage brainwash you," he chuckled, prompting an even greater scowl to grow across Caesia's face. "You've let her cloud your mind with these childish notions of fantasy and adventure."

"Yes, I have," Caesia sighed, pushing her father away. "And maybe I'll die for it... but I'll die happier than I've ever been."

"You're in over your head," Edmund sneered.

"I know," Caesia smiled. "And I love it."

Caesia turned her back and with a deep breath, started down the road. Eris looked back at Edmund and crudely imitated a curtsey before following in tow. Edmund turned with a scowl to Alvus, who returned a cheeky shrug.

"Girls..." he sighed.

"You've just crushed the only hope of Verdenheld's survival," Edmund snarled. "You will pay dearly for this."

"Not as dearly as you, my friend," Alvus smiled smugly. "Fare thee well, Lord Tarantis!"

Alvus strolled off to rejoin Eris and Caesia, leaving Edmund to dwell on his contempt.

"Did you really mean that?" Eris asked as they stepped between the ranks of the crossbowmen. "When you said you'd kill them all?"

"Of course not!" Caesia laughed. "But I think he got the message."

"Ah, good," Eris sighed. "Are you… are you okay after that?"

"Better than ever," Caesia smiled.

It was a colossal weight off her shoulders. While she knew deep down that she hadn't seen the last of her father, she finally felt truly free. It was relief like she had never felt before.

"Good to hear!" Alvus called, approaching them with a smile. "You did great."

"Thanks, Alvus," Caesia sighed. "I'd love to catch up, but…"

"Duty calls," Alvus grinned. "And it sounds like you ladies could use a ride."

Caesia glanced back at Alvus' horse nervously. "I… don't really do animals."

"Oh, come on!" Eris groaned, grabbing Caesia's arm and tugging her towards the horse. "We've got places to be!"

"Right you are, Caesia's friend!" Alvus concurred. "Mount up, ladies!"

Chapter Nine - The Tyrant King

Alvus' horse thundered onto Verden Street, where the Grand Royal Palace stood. The beautifully carved, golden structure loomed menacingly over the lush gardens surrounding it. On either side of the palace gates stood a pair of colossal towers from which the white and red eagle banners of House Verden fluttered all down the towers. Atop each tower flew the flag of Verdenheld - a white phoenix rising from yellow flame amidst a black background, spreading its wings to take flight, symbolic of Verdenheld's birth in the fires of war.

Around the perimeter of the Palace Gardens, hundreds of soldiers rushed about, throwing together makeshift barricades using anything they could get their hands on. Many soldiers were going door to door requesting temporary access to household furniture, while some pulled bins and discarded boxes from alleyways.

"What in Elaria is this?" Alvus scoffed as his horse skidded to a halt beside the barricade. "They call this a barricade?!"

"Sorry sir, the palace is off limits," a guard called from behind the barricade. "We have orders not to-"

Alvus slid from his horse and landed with a crash of heavy plate before the guard. "I am Lord Alvus Severin! I demand you let me pass!"

"Oh, er, of course!" the guard stammered, signalling the guards to move aside a number of bins.

Eris leapt from the horse, while Alvus extended his hand and gently helped Caesia down. They moved through the barricade and into the gardens, the vibrant paradise of stolen, foreign fauna awash with chaos.

"The last barrier I saw that was this shit was put together by peasant rebels!" Alvus hissed to the guard. "You can't just cobble together a load of crap!"

"Um… apologies, sir," The guard mumbled.

Alvus sighed impatiently. "Alright, what's the situation?"

"There's fighting throughout the palace, sir. Loads of the buggers in there, cutting up our troops by the dozen!"

"Then what are you doing out here?" Caesia hissed. "Shouldn't you be in there helping?"

"Veldin's orders, ma'am. We were to form a perimeter and stop the assassins from escaping."

That made sense, she supposed. These rank and file soldiers would be torn apart in there. She had to wonder why it was Veldin who commanded the defence of the palace and not one of the house patriarchs, nor even Friedrich himself. Perhaps he took her advice after all and volunteered.

"Do you ladies think you can handle this?" Alvus asked.

"Why…?" Caesia asked concernedly.

"Someone needs to get this barricade in order and I don't see anyone else qualified to do it."

"We can take 'em!" Eris grinned, jogging on the spot like a hyperactive child.

"Yes, we'll kill them with confidence," Caesia sighed.

"Not with that attitude…" Eris muttered.

"I will… take that as a yes!" Alvus smiled. "It's been a pleasure, Caesia. If you're ever in Tryzantopol, feel free to stop by, I'd love to catch up."

"I'll be sure to," Caesia grinned. "One more thing, actually - How'd you survive Jordenholm?"

Alvus smirked smugly. "Well, I wish I could say I fought my way tooth and claw from the rubble, but I'd actually just headed out to inspect the Norskar Gate. They'd informed me that some of the troops had been abusing travellers, so I thought it an excellent time to launch a surprise inspection! Oh, the look on my face when a dragon flew over my head only minutes out!"

Eris smirked in knowing that she had inadvertently saved Alvus' life by breaking a guardsman's jaw.

"Hm, what luck," Caesia said. "Well, that out of the way, I guess I'll see you later, Alvus."

"Here's hoping!" Alvus laughed as he retreated back to the gardens. "Best of luck to you!"

As Alvus disappeared, Eris and Caesia stepped up to the towering door to the throne room, where a soldier who moved to heave it open. The ground quaked as they stepped close and a number of muted thuds and crashes could be heard behind the door.

"What's that… rumbling?" Eris muttered anxiously.

"Ah, I figured they'd have sorted that out by now," sighed the soldier. "One of the fuckers got a bit… big when were on our way out. Guess I should've mentioned that earlier."

The gate careened open and the guards assigned to it quickly bolted for the barricade. Eris smirked, while Caesia nearly keeled over at the sight of the scene before them. Several House Verden knights were taking cover behind various pillars across the throne room. At the centre of the hall was the object of their fear, crushing pews and battering down golden pillars with its colossal tail. It was a dragon, negligible in size compared to

Xeracrir yet still standing an entire two stories tall on its hind legs. The serpentine, green scaled beast wrapped its neck around a pillar and thrust open its mouth, unleashing an enormous torrent of vibrant blue flame that consumed and utterly vaporised a helpless knight.

"Are you kidding me?" Caesia spat, to the further amusement of Eris. "I am *not* doing another energy beam."

"Yeah, I know… but it's fine, we know what we're doing now, right?"

Caesia mumbled a series of unintelligible complaints to herself as the dragon withdrew from around the pillar, leaving a smouldering mass of molten metal in its wake. It gaze snapped to Eris and Caesia as it caught the open door in the corner of its eye. A toothy grin stretch along its snout as it reared its head high.

"I sure bloody hope so," Caesia muttered, raising her arms ahead of her.

The dragon curled back its neck and a throbbing blue glow shot up its throat. It thrust its head down upon them and a column of blue fire exploded from its mouth. The blast crashed against a shimmering barrier, Caesia's arms burning with pain as she fought against the tremendous pressure.

"On my signal, I'm going to teleport you!" Caesia commanded. "You need to stab the roof of its mouth!"

"Its mouth?!" Eris scoffed.

"Just do it!"

Caesia pulled back her arms and thrust them forwards, propelling her barrier with a into the dragon's snout with a deafening crack. The beast ceased his attack as his own flames consumed his vision. The dragon stunned, Caesia poised her legs and issued her command.

"Now!" Caesia snapped, slapping Eris on the back.

Eris went up in a burst of green light and reappeared mere inches from the dragon's snout. The tip of her steel sword caught the roof of its mouth as she reached the peek of her launch and made a deep incision. The dragon roared with pain, throwing back its head as it wailed.

"Now what?" Eris asked, staggering to the ground and bottling the sharp bite of pain in her ankle.

"Now, I hopefully don't get swallowed," Caesia muttered, focusing carefully on the dragon's head as it curled into the air.

"What?!"

Caesia leapt into the air and vanished in a flash of green light. Eris watched in as much awe as terror as Caesia reappeared in the air above the dragon's mouth, dropping onto the end of the snout and planting one foot firmly on either side of its jaw. Caesia immediately began to regret her decision as she wobbled back and forth, staring fearfully into the endless blackness of the dragon's gullet.

Her arms crackling with lightning, she cupped her hands and thrust them into the dragon's throat. A slim, sustained beam of green energy shot ferociously from Caesia's hands, nowhere near as powerful as the last time she attempted the spell. It was however, powerful enough. A bloodcurdling roar from the dragon drowned out Caesia's screams of pain as electricity arced through its skull. Experiencing nothing close to the lethal voltage used against Xeracrir, the beast's serpentine blue eyes rolled up into its head.

Eris watched dumbstruck as the dragon's head careened to the ground. She was snapped out of her trance as Caesia staggered and slipped, unable to keep her footing on the dragon's toppling snout. Eris leapt after her with a gasp, arms outstretched. Caesia wailed as she plummeted to the ground, falling into Eris' arms and toppling her forwards. The pair tumbled into a heap on the scorched red carpet, both panting raggedly.

"Thanks!" Caesia gasped breathlessly, soggy with sweat thanks to the humid breath of the beast. "How was that for knowing what I'm doing?"

"That was the coolest thing I've ever seen!" Eris giggled, burying her face exhaustedly in Caesia's stomach.

Caesia rolled her eyes and shoved her friend off her, rolling onto her front and scrambling to her feet. "That's what you said about the last dragon," she laughed, extending her hand and yanking Eris off the ground.

Eris shrugged smugly. "Well, maybe you should stop kicking their asses so hard."

"I'll try, but… no promises," Caesia smiled.

The dragon was gradually cloaked in shimmering blue light, fading away to reveal an unconscious, featureless woman with a bloody gash in the roof of her mouth. Eris shovelled a collar out of her bag and crouched down beside her. It was sad to think she was condemning this woman to torture and execution, but their 'no kill' rule meant she really had no choice.

"Darling Caesia!" called an insufferable voice that sent a chill up Caesia's spine. "You have returned to me!"

Caesia swivelled around, a look of contempt on her face, to see Geldus Verden strutting across the hall, opening his arms.

"I knew from the moment our eyes met that our fates were intertwined!" he gushed. "Embrace me, my fair petal!"

Caesia was struck for a moment with an overwhelming sense of panic - she was terrified that her body may begin taking over again, that she might fall into his arms and be whisked away like a fairytale damsel. She would not let that happen.

As his arms wrapped around her, so did hers. Geldus' eyes widened at the static shock of her touch, suddenly beginning to quiver and shake.

Caesia held him tight as he gradually slumped to the ground, convulsing erratically as energy coursed into him. As he fell to his knees, Caesia cast him aside and sprang back up with a grin on her face.

Eris' eyes fluttered in shock. "That was…"

"Necessary," Caesia smiled. "And rather satisfying."

She turned to a steel clad knight, dressed in battered silver plate and bearing a blackened, red and white tabard, and waved him over.

"Ma'am!" he barked obediently, standing to attention.

"I don't suppose you know where we could find Veldin, do you?"

"He headed back towards the King, ma'am," the knight said, gesturing to a nearby hallway with his sword. "You'll want to head down that corridor, take a right then a left, head up the stairs to the third floor and down the first hallway on your right."

"That's a bloody long walk…" Caesia muttered, nodding in acknowledgement to the knight. "Thank you, sir knight."

As the knight turned away with a nod, Eris looked curiously around the hall. Despite the shredded carpets, smashed tables and collapsed pillars, the throne room was quite magnificent. Much of the room was painted in white and golds, while the carpets and banners were House Verden's blood red. The shimmering golden throne was styled to resemble Verdenheld's flag, the base of the throne carved as roaring flames and its massive rear a glorious golden phoenix, its wings curled around the throne as if to protect the king from danger.

As they moved for the hallway to which the knight had directed them, Caesia began to slow as her attention hung on the alcove beyond the throne. She remembered being here, those ten years ago, when Alvus had told her of the terrible evil that lay behind those doors. Where she had once heard whispers on the wind, there was nothing, yet she felt cold, as if something watched her. Wordlessly, it urged her to step closer, to throw open the doors and bring it freedom… but she made a promise.

She turned and took a deep breath, before forging on. Whatever that orb wanted, it would get nothing from her.

The hallway was littered with the fresh bodies of soldiers, mutilated and torn apart by the vengeful changelings. Several corpses, their faces contorted in screams of terror and agony, had their arms and legs torn from their bodies and flung across the hallway, leaving behind a crimson trail of blood. The walls were splattered with visceral sprays of gore, dripping down and saturating the carpet. Eris stepped into the hallway, her foot sinking into the blood sodden carpet with a revolting squelch.

"Close your eyes," she snapped, thrusting out her hand to stop Caesia before she reached the hallway.

"What? Why?" Caesia asked, tensing impatiently.

"Just… you don't want to see this."

"What do you… oh, um, I see," Caesia mumbled.

Caesia closed her eyes and held out her arm. She winced as Eris grasped her bruised wrist and pulled her along. As she was dragged around the corner, her senses were swamped by the potent metallic stench of blood and a shiver shot up her spine as her foot sank into the carpet.

Eris tried desperately not to look directly at any of the bodies as she dragged Caesia along, their wounds far too gruesome even for her to stomach. She could handle a few cuts and bruises, but gaping chest cavities and uncoiled intestines were a step beyond her limit.

As she stepped over another corpse, one of the bodies ahead feebly turned its head to her. She could see through the knight's visor, terrified, trembling eyes pouring with tears.

"H-help…" the knight gasped, clutching his small intestine in his bloody hand.

There was nothing Eris could do for him. Even if she could, she couldn't afford to stop. Trying to avoid eye contact, Eris continued past the whimpering knight, as if he were some beggar on the street.

"Did you just ignore a dying man?" Caesia hissed with disgust.

"What was I supposed to do?" Eris scoffed. "Do I look like a shaman?"

"You could have at least consoled him."

"In any other situation I totally would've, but I'm not letting these assholes slip away so I can tell a dead man he'll live!"

While a quite brutal way of looking at it, Caesia figured that Eris had a point. When every second counted, they couldn't afford such a triviality.

"That is… fairly morbid," Caesia sighed. "But you've got a point."

As they reached the end of the hallway and passed the last of the bodies, Eris unhanded Caesia and gave her a light slap on the back. Caesia opened her eyes and batted her eyelids as she adjusted to the light.

Peering around into the next hallway, where she beheld a fight still ongoing.

"I think I found your friend!" Eris called back to Caesia, who stepped up beside her and took a look for herself.

Her gaze followed the clashing of steel some way down the corridor, where a group of men fought with a pair of arachni. Caesia recognised one of the arachni immediately - Niria, the one who had attacked them in the sewers. Along with a new male companion, she battled against a trio of House Barethia knights, clad as always in flawless silver plate accented with golden patterns and holy sigils. Amidst the fray, Caesia could make out the ever recognisable fiery beard of Veldin Ironhand, wrestling Niria with his battleaxe as she tried to overpower him.

"Come on, we've gotta help them!" Caesia commanded, rushing fearlessly down the hallway.

Eris smirked, ever amused by Caesia's sudden changes between timid and fearless. She launched off down the hallway after her friend, unbuckling her sheaths and sliding out her swords.

Veldin shoved Niria back and smirked as she landed on her rear legs, hissing furiously at him. As he raised his axe in defence, he laughed triumphantly as Eris and Caesia came rushing down the hallway

"Better late than never, Lady Tarantis!" he bellowed.

"Stop calling me that!" Caesia hissed, hurling a bolt of lightning at the male arachni.

The arachni sprang onto the wall and turned with a glare to Caesia. He leapt nimbly across the width of the hallway and onto the opposite wall. As another bolt of lightning cracked towards him, he launched himself onto the ceiling, drawing ever closer to his prey.

Niria battered two of the knights aside with her legs and slammed one through chest of the third knight, punching effortlessly through the thick plate and scything deep into his heart. As the knight slumped to the ground, she turned to Veldin, who looked her in her many eyes with a cheeky grin.

"What's a pretty girl like you doing in a place like this?" he chuckled, raising his axe eagerly.

"Delivering justice!" Niria growled, lunging at him and thrusting her legs forward.

Veldin span his axe out in front of him, battering aside the legs. He swung it over his head and cleaved down upon her, the changeling reeling narrowly from its path.

"Come on, you bloody insect!" Veldin boomed. "Fight like you mean it!"

As the male arachni sprang onto the floor, Eris stepped out in front of it, swords raised. Her defensive jab sailed beneath him as he leapt elegantly into the air and kicked off the ceiling, landing in front of Caesia with a bloodthirsty hiss. He hissed in anger as his prey vanished before his eyes and turned around, met by Eris lunging after him.

Eris swung both of her swords overhead and slammed her opponent's topmost legs aside before making a rapid jab at its chest with her steel sword. The sword cut a shallow gash below his shoulder, prompting him to lash out in pain. Eris stepped back cautiously as the arachni thrust all eight of its legs around her like a pincer. She lunged backwards, flinging her swords up and clashing them against the legs, stopping them before they reached her.

A smile spread across her face as she noticed the fleshy gap between his legs' chitinous armour. She slammed her steel sword down upon it and in a shower of ichor, cleaved her silver blade straight through the arachni's slender leg.

As the arachni screeched in agony and reeled away, Eris stepped aside. A bolt of green lightning slammed into his chest with massive force, blasting him off his feet and sending him skidding along the carpet. Unconscious, he went up in shimmering red light, revealing the featureless changeling beneath, a shallow wound in his chest.

"Ladies, if you don't mind?" Veldin called.

Eris and Caesia span around to Veldin, who was confidently warding off the Niria despite clearly being at a disadvantage. As she lunged, Veldin thrust out his axe and shoved her back into the wall. A lightning bolt sailed across the room and smashed into the side of her shoulder, sending her staggering away in a daze as Eris thundered towards her.

She sprinted down the hallway and sidestepped Niria's bladed arm as she struck out clumsily. Eris thrust her silver sword between the changeling's legs, slicing a deep gash across her side. Niria backed off from Eris, shaking off her daze and coughing as she gripped her oozing wound. She bared her razor teeth and poised for a final attack, passionate tears in her eyes. As Niria's feet left the ground, she violently convulsed at a harrowing crunch, Veldin's axe burying in her back and snapping her spine in two.

"Haha!" Veldin roared heroically, kicking the wide eyed changeling off the blood soaked blade of his axe.

Eris and Caesia's faces dropped as Niria's limp, lifeless body slumped to the ground, a look of sheer horror in her empty eyes and a massive gash indented in her back. Veldin leant his axe up against the wall and prodded the corpse with his foot as it rippled with yellow energy. From the light emerged the broken and bloodied body of Niria, drenched in crimson and flushed of all colour.

"So much for 'no kill'…" Eris muttered, glancing with shame at Caesia's blank, pale face.

"Oh, were you wanting to accost the buggers?" Veldin stammered, rubbing his head awkwardly. "Damn, you should've said."

"Don't worry about it," Caesia sighed, shaking herself off and struggling to erase the image of Niria's face from her mind. "It's more of a personal thing, I just don't kill."

Veldin signalled the two remaining knights to take their dead comrade back to the throne room. "Suppose death is a mercy compared to inquisitorial custody…" he muttered. "Anyhow, I figured we'd be seeing you two again. The dragon guy give you much trouble?"

"Nothing we couldn't handle," Eris smiled, crouching beside the live changeling and locking a collar around his neck.

"Yes, we're rather experienced in the field," Caesia concurred. "Far more than most, at least."

"Really? You're turning out to be quite an interesting woman, Lady... Caesia," Veldin chuckled. "It'll be good to have someone competent to work with, as opposed to these idiot knights."

"Then let's get to work," Caesia smiled. "What's the situation?"

"The bastards are everywhere. Friedrich's held up in his chambers with his guard, while we're left to scour the place. It seems we've cleaned up most of 'em, but I think a few mighta slipped onto the third floor. I was just headed there when I ran into our friends here."

"Third floor then?" Eris asked, eagerly clenching her hands around the hilts of her swords.

"Aye, stairs are this way. You see anyone on that floor that ain't us or the King, they're probably not human."

The trio barrelled down the hallway, turning onto the stairwell and ascending the pristine marble steps.

"How is it you two got mixed up in all of this anyway?" Veldin asked. "You don't exactly seem the likeliest of duos."

"As I said back at the conference hall, it's a long story," Caesia gasped, panting as she ran out of breath running up the stairs. "W-we..."

"We ran into each other near Jordenholm," Eris said, taking over from her breathless friend. "Then we went and killed the dragon that burnt it down."

"You're kidding," Veldin chuckled. "Right?"

"Nope! Then it told us..." Eris trailed off, looking to Caesia for confirmation and receiving and approving nod. "It told us that Valkyr the Oppressor was back to kill us all."

"Truly?!" Veldin gasped. "And you trust its word?"

"Well, it tried to kill us after it let that slip, so probably," Caesia said.

"This is grave news. Course, no one'll believe it."

"That's why we're taking matters into our own hands," Caesia muttered. "We came here pursuing a lead."

"You mean to say these assassins are linked to the Oppressor?"

"Yes, as was recently confirmed by one of their own."

"Dear God..." Veldin mumbled darkly.

They leapt onto the third floor from the colossal flights of stairs, Caesia leaning breathlessly against the golden bannister rail. The halls of the third floor were eerily silent, the hallways cluttered once again with bodies, only this time their wounds were far more clean. There were no gaping cavities, deep punctures or torn limbs, rather there were surgically precise incisions and flawlessly clean stab wounds. The knights had been despatched with laughable ease.

"This doesn't look like arachni wounds," Eris acutely observed.

"Of course not," Caesia muttered. "After their exposure as changelings at the conference, they would happily be using any form at their disposal."

"The question is, what form?" Veldin mumbled, crouching beside a body and examining its wounds.

"The wounds would suggest blades or perhaps claws," Caesia analysed. "If it were claws, the creature's fingers must be opposable to achieve such precision."

"I think I know," Eris said from beneath her cupped hand.

"Really?" Caesia laughed.

"I can know things too, you know!" Eris snapped. "Hunters would sometimes get dragged back to the village with wounds like these. This is the work of a jorgheist."

"A what now?"

"Never seen one myself and the few victims that survived never got a good look at it. All I know is it's really fast, really deadly and uses clicking to see."

"That sounds… unpleasant," Caesia sighed. "We ought to be on our guard."

"Good thing they won't have the reflexes of a real jorgheist," Eris sighed. "Or else we'd be dead before we knew what hit us."

"So, how we planning on doing this?" Veldin asked. "I reckon we'd best sweep the place as a group, take this thing on together."

Caesia nodded in agreement. "Eris, you said this thing sees with sound?"

"Yep, like a bat."

"Then it'll know we're coming, probably wait for us in ambush. Be on your guard."

They stepped over the bodies and advanced through the deathly quiet halls. Eris tried to strike up a conversation but was quickly hushed by Caesia, who much preferred to listen out for signs of the creatures approach. As they stalked silently around the next corner, Caesia's ears pricked at the faint sounds of skittering, clawed feet echoed through the halls.

"It's close," Caesia whispered.

"Yeah, I got that," Eris muttered, lifting her swords ahead of herself.

The scratching of claws drew closer and closer until it was right on top of them and then suddenly, fell silent.

"That's unnerving," Veldin muttered stepping behind Eris and Caesia, back turned and axe raised. "You know how these things attack?"

"It sounded pretty hit and run the way they described it," Eris explained. "It almost always kept its distance, until the prey was-"

Eris was interrupted by a thunderous crack and a shower of debris as a tiny hole was blasted through the ceiling above them. From the hole burst a long, whip-like tail tipped with a massive, slender spike. The tail lashed down upon the jorgheist's unsuspecting prey, jabbing at Eris' head and slashing a gash through the side of her helmet as she leapt out of the way.

While Eris urgently patted down her face for damage, Caesia reeled back her arm and allowed energy to build up in her hand. She thrust her arm forwards with a pained scream, propelling a massive blast of lightning into the ceiling and blasting it open in an explosion of green light. Along with an avalanche of dust and debris, the jorgheist's slender, fur cloaked legs slipped through the hole, skittering and scratching as it tried to scramble back up. As it slipped back up onto the fourth floor, Caesia hurled another lightning bolt after it.

The bolt smashed into the jorgheist's leg, blasting it away from the ledge and onto their level. The creature landed on all fours, poised offensively. It was a horrifying beast, its barely humanoid body was yet far more slender scrawny and hunched. Sinister brown fur covered its body, adapted to the merciless cold of a Norskar night. It's head bore no eyes but rather a massive serrated maw that clicked and hissed erratically. The jorgheist crouched aggressively and let out a piercing shriek, poising its tail over its head like a scorpion.

"He's an ugly fucker!" Veldin laughed.

As Caesia loosed another bolt, the jorgheist sprang onto the ceiling and leapt immediately at her. The creature was like a blur as it soared through the air, Caesia barely managing to blink from its path as it plunged its tail down upon her. As the tail spike slammed into the ground, it punctured straight through to the floor below with a chilling crack. Eris swiped at the jorgheist with her silver sword, only for the creature to whip its tail from the ground and bat the blade aside. As Eris staggered to the side, it leant back on its hind legs and launched itself at her.

Caesia threw out her hand as the jorgheist pounced upon Eris, bringing up a shield of light between them. The creature screeched as if bounced back off the shield, its fur burnt a charcoal black by its contact with the crackling barrier. It let slip a high pitched roar as Veldin came in behind it with his axe. Easily sensing his approach, the jorgheist sprang to the side and as the battleaxe cleaved by, it turned upon him and leapt.

Veldin ducked with a chuckle as the jorgheist soared over his head, his amusement cut quickly short as the creature's tail whipped down around his arm and yanked him off his feet. Veldin crashed to the ground like an anvil as the jorgheist skidded back around, releasing its tail and preparing it to strike a killing blow. It sprang to his side in a bounding leap and thrust the tail down into his chest. The spike cracked his armour open like an egg, Veldin cringing at the snap of steel plate.

The beast staggered back against the wall, disoriented as it was swept away in a surge of green light. Caesia stumbled away from it, pulled her hands back and thrust them into the jorgheist's chest, hammering it point blank with a pair of lightning bolts. The blast exploded against the jorgheist's chest and sent it hurtling through an immaculate, stained glass window with a terrific crash.

Caesia leant against the wall, panting breathlessly and unable to watch as the jorgheist plunged to the ground with a terrified shriek. Its wailing was silenced as it slammed into the cobblestones below with a thud akin to hitting someone with a pillow.

"You alright, Veldin?" Caesia stammered as Veldin scrambled up.

"Well, I'll smell like wet dog fur for a few days," Veldin sighed, glancing down with relief at the unbloodied hole in his armour. "But I guess it's all just part of the job."

Eris really wanted to comment on the fact that he already smelt like wet dog fur, but decided that it probably wouldn't be too well received.

"Seriously though, you saved my arse. I owe you one," Veldin grinned.

"Forget about it," Caesia sighed, staggering to the window with bated breath.

She leant out of the window and gazed down at the twitching, mangled body of a female changeling. Guards approached cautiously from the perimeter barricade, weapons drawn.

"Is she okay?" Caesia called.

A few of the guards looked to one another for confirmation and a couple nodded their heads slowly with uncertainty.

Eris approached the window and uncovered another collar from within her backpack. "If she is, use this!" She yelled, dropping the collar out of the window.

She was certain that the collar would survive the fall, it looked practically indestructible. It rang as it clanged off the cobblestones, rolling to the changeling's side.

"Moving on!" Caesia declared. "What do you suggest we do next, Veldin?"

"No sign of any more of 'em, so I reckon we make for the King and secure the area."

"Sounds like a plan."

As they continued through the halls, the amount of slain knights strewn across the floor steadily decreased and the carpet began to dry of blood.

Amongst those final few corpses was a tricinium clad phoenix guardsmen, splayed out in a pool of blood with no weapon by his side.

"Takes some skill to bring down one of the king's golden boys," Veldin muttered. "Considering the mediocrity of the last few changelings, I'd bet there's another knocking about. One far more skilled…"

"Golden boys?" Caesia chuckled. "Do I sense a spot of jealousy, Veldin?"

"Not jealousy," Veldin sighed. "Those extravagant bastards are a waste of good tricinium, so much of it spent on those fancy patterns. We made less of that shit and we wouldn't be out of the stuff!"

"I doubt that'd be a problem if House Ironhand hadn't been blackmailed out of two thirds of their mines by House Arrenni," Caesia sneered.

"True, bloody Arrenni pricks stripped the whole mountain range of the stuff and what did they use it for? Building a fucking tower!"

"Yep, nobody flaunts their wealth like-"

Caesia's attention was suddenly drawn as a figure darted around the corner up ahead.

"You guys see that?" Eris whispered, readying her swords.

"What are we waiting for?" Veldin bellowed. "Let's get after it!"

Veldin thundered down the hallway, followed eagerly by Eris. Caesia rolled her eyes and set off after them, not pleased that the amount of reckless idiots in her company had once again doubled. Veldin slid around the corner and came to a small room that branched off into two corridors.

"Shit," he growled. "Alright, I'll take the right. Caesia, take the left."

"What about me?" Eris hissed.

"Eris, is it? You're gonna head 'em off," Veldin commanded. "Head back into the hallway, take a left, then a right."

Eris nodded and sprang off energetically into the hallway. Veldin barrelled into the rightmost corridor, leaving Caesia alone before she could even raise an objection.

"Oh yeah, don't let the voice of reason have a say…" Caesia muttered, starting down the corridor. "Let's just split up and leave each other completely vulnerable! What a *grand* idea!"

Eris skidded around the corner and up the hallway towards the next turn. As she approached the upcoming corner, a female changeling stepped out into the hallway ahead of her. She jumped as she sensed Eris thundering towards her and fled in a panic back around the corner.

"You're not going anywhere!" Eris declared heroically, sliding around the corner to see a completely empty corridor. "Oh… okay."

Caesia moved cautiously down her corridor. It would have been idiotic of her to run about the place like the other two, she could have ran straight into a trap were she not careful. She picked up the faint sound of footsteps, seemingly echoing from one of the connecting corridors up ahead. She raised her hands and slowly ignited them with energy, stepping silently towards the corridor.

"Woah!" Eris gasped, a bolt of lightning cracking past her head as she emerged around the corner. "Careful where you're aiming that!"

"Sorry, you scared me!" Caesia stammered. "You didn't find it?"

"I did, but I lost it," Eris sighed defeatedly. "Turned into a bird."

"I see," Caesia muttered, continuing to advance down the corridor. "Well, watch my back would you? I-"

Caesia raised her arms in defence as Eris skidded around the corner of another corridor further ahead. She turned to the Eris beside her and sighed deeply.

The second Eris' shoulders sank as she rolled her eyes. "Oh, for…"

"Seriously? Are we really doing this?" groaned the first Eris. "This is the oldest cliché in the book, just blast her!"

"Hey, up yours!" the second snapped. "Caesia, we haven't got time for this."

"Which is exactly why you should shoot her!" the first insisted.

"Wha- no!" the second growled. "Come on, Caesia! I can't believe you're even-"

"What's my middle name?" Caesia snapped, folding her arms impatiently.

The first Eris exchanged a devious smirk with the second's blank expression. "Anais," she confidently declared.

A lightning bolt smashed into the second Eris' gut, blasting her off her feet. She tumbled onto her back and slid motionlessly across the floor, drawing a delighted giggle from Caesia.

"Great!" the Eris beside her laughed. "See, I told you-"

Caesia flicked out her hand to the side and battered her into the wall with another bolt. She slammed hard against the wall, slumping down it and shaking violently until she finally fell into unconsciousness. Caesia grinned with pride in herself as the doppelganger went up in a flash of blue light and transformed back into a changeling.

"I never told her that," she said smugly. The fool had read her mind on the spot, as she expected they might.

Caesia wandered with a sigh to Eris' side, who lay twitching on the ground with her face fixed wide in surprise.

"Well, well… haven't the tables turned?" Caesia sneered. "Do you have karma where you come from?"

Eris was completely unresponsive. Caesia could feel the contempt in her eyes despite their blankness. She enjoyed it, perhaps too much.

"Plunged me off a cliff, forced me in front of a crowd, hurled a shield at my head… the list goes on," Caesia smirked as she crouched beside her friend, revelling in the reckoning she had brewed since Abenfurt. "Call me petty, but I couldn't resist the opportunity to avenge my many woes at your hands. Next time you put me through hell like that, you may want to consider who *really* holds the power here."

Once again, Caesia was taking genuine amusement from torturing her friend. She definitely had a problem, but she could not help herself. Her vengeance had been a long time coming.

She grabbed Eris' arm and rolled her over onto her front, flinging open her backpack and rooting around. She pulled another collar out from under a mound of carrots and turned back to the changeling.

"I know I'm laughing, but I really am sorry," Caesia chuckled, locking the collar around the changeling's neck. "This was incredibly cruel of me, even by my standards!"

As Caesia got up from beside the changeling, Veldin came jogging hastily down the corridor.

"I see you found the changeling…" he muttered. "What happened to her? Not dead is she?"

"No, she… got zapped by that changeling," Caesia smiled, looking cheekily back at Eris. "Quite embarrassing, really. Luckily, I showed up in time to save her from certain death!"

"Ah, great!" Veldin laughed. "Well, I think that takes care of all of them. We'd best retrieve Friedrich."

"Indeed!" Caesia chirped. "Would you mind…"

"Carrying your friend?" Veldin smirked. "On it."

Veldin picked up Eris' swords and shoved them back into their sheaths before hauling her limp body over his shoulder. They started off towards Friedrich's quarters, Caesia trying all the while to avoid eye contact as Eris continued to stare at her contemptuously.

They headed down a series of corridors until they reached the King's quarters, marked by an ornate red double door gilded with elegant golden patterns. Veldin dumped Eris to the floor, her limbs beginning to shift as she slowly regained movement.

"How you doing?" Caesia smiled down at her.

"I hay you," Eris murmured, her mouth still slurred but her eyelids flickering enough to display her anger.

Caesia smirked smugly and withdrew as Veldin banged his meaty fist against the door.

"Friedrich?" he called. "It's Veldin Ironhand, the assassins are dealt with."

"Can you stand?" Caesia asked Eris, extending out her hand. "Don't want you in such an embarrassing state in front of the King."

Eris shuffled stiffly up the wall with Caesia's help. Her movements were rigid and she was still suffering violent fits of twitching, but she could at least move.

One of the double doors creaked open and the winged helmet of a phoenix guard appeared in the gap.

"Prove you're not changelings," he hissed, his voice muffled by his tight golden helmet.

"The King's a dick," Veldin boomed.

"That, er… checks out. You two?"

"Green essence," Caesia declared, igniting her hand with crackling green lightning.

Eris looked herself up and down confusedly, before sluggishly shovelling a collar out of her backpack and snapping it around her neck.

The guard nodded and swung the door open. "Come right in."

The trio stepped into the King's chambers, an ornate and extravagant room, even by the standards of the rest of the building. The curtains and bedding were fine and silken, the walls were carved with expertly crafted murals and laden with incredible art from across the world. Friedrich himself stood anxiously at his desk, surrounded by four of his personal guard. He was toying nervously with his ragged, silver beard, bags under his eyes from his sleepless night of worrying.

"I didn't appreciate that comment, Ironhand," Friedrich muttered. "But I'll let it slide in recognition of your service. Those… things, they are all dead?"

"Dead or captured, yes," Veldin said proudly. "Course, the ones that we captured'll be executed come the end of the week."

Caesia turned to a phoenix guardsman with narrowing eyes as he tensed at Veldin's answer.

"Excellent," Friedrich smiled. "Despite your utter lack of respect, you've done fine work here today. I'm sure your father-"

"With all due respect, my liege…" Veldin interrupted. "I think your praise would be better placed in-"

The roar of flames saw Veldin freeze on the spot as one of the Phoenix Guard threw back his spear, the shimmering golden blade igniting in a burst of yellow fire. The blade cleaved down upon Friedrich, his guards only now drawing their weapons in defence.

Friedrich came crashing down as Caesia blinked beside him and barged him to the ground. The spear soared past his head, hissing as it rent a massive, burning gash through Caesia's back and spattered the King's startled face with blood.

The Phoenix Guard drew their weapons, spinning them in chauvinistic flourishes as Veldin hurried to his king's side. The changeling backed away hesitantly as a wall of burning golden blades was arrayed against him. He stopped before the gilded golden wall, a look of cunning within his ornate helmet. As the phoenix guard closed in around him, he leapt into the air and in a flash of blue light, transformed into an eagle. He swept over their heads, effortlessly dodging their swings as they cleaved their swords and spears through the air. Having passed the guards, he darted for the window, narrowing his wings.

Eris screwed up her face at the pain of abandoning her friend and sprang after him. She barrelled across the room, weaving nimbly between the guards' flailing spears. The eagle swept through the window and after him came Eris, leaping against the window and bursting through it in an explosion of shattered glass. She soared from the window and flung up her hands, grabbing the startled eagle and yanking it suddenly towards the ground.

The two of them glided clumsily to the ground, Eris skidding along the cobblestones as she was deposited and gasping in pain as her left foot burnt like she had landed on hot coals. As the soldiers in the courtyard rushed to apprehend the changeling, he transformed into his original form, casting out a storm of icy wind that blasted them back against the building.

"And here I doubted Kharmenia's words when she declared you a formidable foe," Cereth sneered. "You have done battle with every one of my brothers and sisters, yet you've still the strength to challenge me. I'm impressed."

"Well I hate to break it to you, but your 'brothers and sisters' were honestly a bit crap," Eris jeered. "Almost as crap as your plan! Sending two assassins when you got a bunch? Not a great strategy."

"You are stupid to think this the end. King Friedrich will die," Cereth growled. "Kharmenia will claim his head and fell this tyranny once and for all!"

Eris smirked confidently. "If this 'Kharmenia' is so cool, why does she have you doing all her dirty work? Ever think she might be too scared to do it herself?"

"Naive girl…" Cereth grinned. "I'm afraid you will die before you understand!"

A vortex of glacial wind rushed suddenly from the palm of his hand. All that Eris could think to do was spin around and shelter her head in her arms. The wind blasted across the courtyard and drew within grasping distance, before dispersing as fast as it had gathered. Eris peeled away her arms and looked back in confusion - the sladium collars in her backpack had dispelled the wind before it reached her.

"Very clever…" Cereth growled.

"Um, yeah!" Eris laughed, happy to play along with having done that on purpose. "Guess you didn't expect me to be more than just looks."

Cereth glared at her for a moment in contemplation. After a short time, a grin grew across his face and he loosened his arms in preparation.

"If I have failed, so be it. I will not return to my masters empty handed," he smiled, casting out his hand and conjuring a sleek blade of crackling blue light. "You have been a thorn in their side, I hear. Perhaps your demise will ease their fury!"

"Oh, I'm sure they'll be over the moon," Eris smirked. "Look boss! I didn't kill the most powerful man in the world, but I killed this teenage girl!"

"We will see if you mock me when my blade is at your throat," Cereth grinned.

Eris smiled eagerly and slid her silver sword from its sheath. "You guys sure have a flare for the dramatic," she jeered.

"Enough juvenile quips, die!"

Cereth lunged after Eris, who raised her slender blade in defence. She had picked the silver sword for a good reason - the Inquisition's blades were likely enchanted to withstand magical blows. Where the evoked blade of her opponent would easily have cleaved her steel sword in two, the silver blade would be able to block his attacks. She knew that it would be her only defence, for her armour was worthless against such raw energy. She had to play this safely.

The crack of energy against metal rang across the courtyard as Cereth's blade crashed against Eris'. He withdrew it with lightning speed and jabbed at her stomach, only to be batted aside. He had not expected such quick reflexes from her, surprised as she countered yet another strike and cast his sword away.

Eris blocked another blow, then another, then another. The changeling was fast, she could barely make a move of her own. As well defended as she may have been, she was dancing to his tune. That needed to change.

She swept around as an avalanche of wind rushed over her, letting the backpack absorb his magic. At the moment it subsided, she span around once again and met her opponent's blade.

"You're as fast as you are predictable!" Eris laughed as she swept his sword aside.

His blade out of her way, Eris flung out her leg and pounded Cereth's stomach with a kick. He staggered back, allowing her a moment of reprieve that she intended to use well. She slung her backpack from her shoulders and weaved her left arm through both straps. Tightening them around her forearm, she raised her backpack as a shield in front of her.

A gust of frigid wind blasted from Cereth's hand as he stumbled upright. Eris crouched down and let the wind part around her sladium packed bag, before leaping to her feet and bolting after her assailant. She flung back her sword and clashed with the shimmering blade once again.

A final few tears pattered to the ground as Caesia clawed her way desperately up the wall. She staggered to her feet, hunched by an agonising, burning pain and her legs quivering violently. Tendrils of light cracked the air around her as she fought to keep her essence stable and emotions in check. Her bloodied coat sleeve swept across her gaunt red eyes before she wriggled hurriedly out of it and cast it to the ground. Veldin glanced up as she gritted her teeth and began to hobble her way towards the window.

"What the- what are you doing?!" he gasped. "Caesia, you're bleeding badly! We need to get you to a biomancer!"

"No!" Caesia demanded. "Not yet…"

"You're in no condition to fight!" Veldin urged.

"I- I don't have to fight," Caesia mumbled, her voice a contorted rasp. "But I have to do something… We're a team."

Veldin sighed and retreated back to Friedrich, he knew better than to waste time questioning her. Caesia shuffled over to the shattered window, igniting her hands with energy and whimpering at the stinging of her shoulder. She slumped against the window ledge and peered into the courtyard.

Eris was holding her own remarkably, countering the changeling's every strike with relative ease. Yet, it was clear that she was constantly on the defensive. As impressed as Caesia was by Eris' masterstroke idea of her sladium bag-shield, it was only a matter of time before the backpack would be cut loose and leave her terribly exposed to her opponent's magic. Caesia had to ensure that this battle was resolved sooner rather than later.

Eris staggered back as Cereth battered her blade aside. She whimpered at a sudden jolt of sharp pain as she went down on her left foot with a spine-chilling crack, before bringing her sword back around to block his strike. The pain had been greater than previously and left her leg feeling strange, almost numb.

"You are injured," Cereth grinned, flourishing his blade.

"It- it's… it's nothing…"

A sudden spell of dizziness fell over her and her ankle began to throb with pain. In her daze she felt as if her stomach had turned upside down, her vision blurring and eyes fluttering. Her control of her body waned as her mind slipped in and out of consciousness in a desperate struggle to keep fighting. Not now, she begged. Please…

The crackling blue blade of her assailant swept high, its blurred form engulfing Eris' vision. She flung out her sword drunkenly, cleaving nought but air as she staggered back. The blue blotch in her sight grew closer, intensifying rapidly, its heat swamping her skin. As her sword slumped to her side, she could do little more than watch.

Light crashed against light as a flickering green wall flashed into reality between them, hissing as the changeling's blade fell against it. The crack of the sword against the wall was like a splash of cold water, Eris' eyes fluttering as she was jolted some way back into reality. The changeling glared upon the barrier and cleaved his blade through it, ripping a massive tear down its centre and dispersing it with little effort.

As the barrier parted, Eris glanced up at Caesia slumped against the shattered window above. The haze of Eris' vision began to fade as they exchanged determined grins. She drew up her silver blade once again and met Cereth's sword overhead, sweeping it aside and slipping past him. Every step upon her left foot now rang with burning pain, but that was an afterthought. It was time to finish this once and for all.

"I… I may be injured," Eris growled, levelling her sword to her face. "But that won't stop me from kicking your ass!"

Eris launched herself at Cereth, battering his sword down with brutal force and again from the side. He stumbled away, where his back slammed against a shimmering green wall. He deflected back towards Eris, who swept her sword down upon his and cleaved her fist into the side of his head.

He staggered aside, flinging up his sword and narrowly blocking Eris' as it rushed up from the ground. From his crouched position he jabbed quickly at her leg, his blade glancing off a disc of green light that flickered into reality ahead of it. Eris' knee collided with his chin as he withdrew his blade, sending him reeling further back towards the building.

A quick gesture from Eris to Caesia issued a final command. Eris flung open her bag and yanked a collar from her collection.

"Go!" Eris yelled as the changeling staggered back upright.

She reeled back her arm and bowled the collar along the cobblestones, spitting sparks as it bounced by Cereth's feet. In an eruption of green light, Caesia leapt into reality and swept the collar off the ground. She cringed at the piercing pain in her mind as the sladium made contact with her hand, pulling it up to her shoulder and thrusting for the changeling's neck.

Sensing her presence from the moment of her appearance, Cereth flung his blade around. Caesia staggered backwards as the sword sailed over her arm and clipped her nose with its crackling tip. A spatter of blood stained her cheek as she stumbled over herself and fell back against the wall, shrieking as her open wound scraped against the brickwork.

"Caesia!" Eris gasped as Cereth repelled a desperate strike from her blade.

He pushed Eris away and turned upon Caesia, raising his blade high. She flung out her arm in desperation, the sladium collar at her side causing little more than sparks to spew from her fingers. She could only cradle her head in terror as the sword plunged down upon her.

A chilling crunch echoed throughout the courtyard, plunging it into deathly silence. Caesia, her arms spattered with blood, withdrew her arms from her face. Cereth stared back at Eris in horror as he staggered to the ground, clutching the knife in his neck as it slipped from her quivering hand. Eris watched mortified as he fell to his knees, blood spewing from the wound that was meant only for his back. They stared each other in the eyes, him with total fear and her with utter horror. She watched helplessly as he silently expired, his face contorted with terror and sadness.

Eris looked upon his motionless body wide eyed and stricken with regret. Her arms trembled and her breath shortened as she came to terms with what she had just done. She had just killed a man. She had felt the skin puncture, the flesh tear. The chilling crack of the knife breaking flesh rang in her mind, as did the image of the desperate, white eyes of a man who knew nothing but fear in his last moments.

She looked down at Caesia, who lay there in equal shock. She glanced up at Eris in a silent exchange of emotions. Both knew what the other felt, yet neither could conjure words appropriate to describe it.

"You killed him..." Caesia whispered finally.

"I- I don't... it was meant to go in his back, I-" Eris buried her face in her hands, shaking erratically it in denial of what she had done. "Stars, what have I- I'm a murderer!"

"It's okay," Caesia smiled shallowly, her voice tortured with pain. "You were only trying to save me."

Eris wiped her eyes down and breathed deeply into her hands. Horrible as that was, it was the right thing to do - that man was a cold hearted killer and he was about to take a life that in Eris' mind was worth a hundred.

She glanced up as Caesia gasped with pain, finally coming down from the adrenaline of the battle. "Are you... are you alright?" she mumbled.

"Is it bad?" Caesia whimpered.

Eris looked grimly at the enormous red and black streak of bloody, burnt flesh carved across Caesia's back. It may have covered half of her back, but the spear had at least cauterised most of the wound in its wake.

"It's... big," Eris mumbled, stumbling over herself as Caesia began to panic. "B-but at least it's not bleeding, right?"

223

"It still hurts!" Caesia hissed shakily, before retreating to a feeble, fearful tone. "Am I- am I going to die?"

"No!" Eris chuckled. "You'll walk it off."

"Eris," Caesia sighed with a subtle smirk. "You are unbelievably shit at this."

"Cut me some slack, I've consoled you more times today than I can count."

"Can't argue with that," Caesia spluttered as she shuffled up the wall, her wound stinging harshly as it bent. "Argh, crap!"

"You need a hand, potty mouth?" Eris grinned.

Caesia made a shallow smile at Eris' calm expression. As terrible pain as she was in, the reassurance did well to sooth it.

"I-I'll be fine. It just stings when a move. A lot."

"That might take some time to heal," Eris muttered gravely. "There's no way I'm waiting a month to get back out there."

"Should be able to speed it up to a few days if I get it looked at by a biomancer," Caesia mumbled, cringing as she stood up relatively straight. "Of course, the scarring won't go away."

"Ah, who cares? You'll just look cooler, like me!" Eris declared, gesturing to her facial scar.

"Oh, of course! How cool I will look with a scar on my back!" Caesia sneered, still very much capable of sarcasm despite her terrible pain. "Whenever I'm bathing, all the passers by will stop to tell me how awesome I look!"

"Half the skin on your back missing and you're still giving me shit," Eris smiled, patting Caesia on her unscathed shoulder. "That's my girl!"

Veldin heaved a sigh of relief as Eris and Caesia shuffled back inside, jesting and giggling between one another. He withdrew from the window and dropped his axe to his side with a ragged breath.

"Is it done?" Friedrich mumbled, slumped onto his bed picking at his nails nervously.

"It's done," Veldin sighed. "He's dead."

"Hm... those girls have some spunk," Friedrich chuckled. "I'd consider them knighthoods if we weren't trying to keep this under wraps!"

"You know, you don't seem particularly fazed by all this."

"Ah, there was nothing to be afraid of. Just another bunch of conniving demons trying to bring the realm low, nothing we haven't dealt with before."

"They were more than that," Veldin growled. "They were beyond the common terrorist, we lost at least two hundred good men today!"

"That's it?" Friedrich smirked. "Pft, and I thought them a threat."

"*That's it?*" Veldin scoffed. "You're a real bastard, Friedrich."

"Excuse me?" Friedrich gasped. "It is a soldier's duty to give their lives for me, die in our place! They should be honoured."

"Honoured?" Veldin growled. "How far up your own arse-"

The thunder of a fist against the door drowned his words. The room fell deathly silent apart from the clatter of tricinium boots as one of the Phoenix Guard edged their way to the door. He reached out for the handle and slowly slid open one of the double doors, peering cautiously through the gap.

An explosion of green light obliterated the door and blasted a shockwave of heat across the room. The golden warrior toppled to the ground, the front of his body vaporised and smouldering with green embers. Veldin looked upon the corpse in horror - the front of its skull gone, the brain exposed with no frontal lobe in sight. In the bloody cavity of his chest, his organs were reduced to shrivelled black husks and his bones were all but smouldering ash.

A shadow crept across the room and in its wake came a figure amidst the cloud of rubble and dust. A pair of burning red eyes pierced the veil, illuminating around them a dark, featureless mask. A throbbing green crystal at the tip of a twin-bladed staff washed slender black robes in fading light as the figure approached.

"Sorry, that looked expensive," Hera smirked. "So good to finally meet you, your majesty…"

"Who the hell are you?" Veldin snarled, raising his axe in readiness.

"Of course, where are my manners?" Hera chuckled. "General Avelin Kharmenia. I doubt I need to explain much more."

"Kharmenia? That's impossible!" Friedrich gasped.

"What do you want?" Veldin spat.

"Oh, I was just in town and thought I'd swing by for a cup of tea with my old pal Friedrich," Hera sneered, an unnerving mix of sarcasm and menace in her tone. "What do you think? I'm here to kill your king."

"Your cronics already fucked that right up, what makes you think you've got a chance?"

"Observe that guardsman who I just blasted with the power of creation," Hera sighed. "See, you can't. You know why? Because I just blasted him with the power of creation. Now, I suggest you step out of that door and let me do my thing before I obliterate your entire being."

She made a convincing argument, but Veldin wasn't about to abandon his king and nor were the Phoenix Guard. They would fight to the end.

"What kind of general hides behind power like that?" Veldin smirked. "If you were truly powerful, you'd fight us proper!"

"Ah, yes! Let me just jeopardize my entire plan by letting you ram that axe into my spine," Hera laughed. "Or, I could do this."

Hera casually flicked her staff towards one of the Phoenix Guard. In a blinding flash, a mass of energy exploded from the crystal at its end, the sheer magnitude of the blast knocking paintings and vases to the ground. Veldin staggered back as the upper body of the guardsman beside him was swept away in an avalanche of light. The scorched pair of legs that remained slumped to the ground, spilling an ooze of blood into the crimson carpet.

Hera sighed impatiently as Veldin looked up defiantly from the body and clenched his hands around his axe.

"Wow, you're really not going to budge, are you?" she groaned. "You know what? I'm glad you decided to stay. Now that I think about it, leaving some bodies would up the scare factor a fair bit!"

The humming green crystal flickered and died out as Hera flourished her staff. Its twin blades roared with vibrant red flame and drew level with her face.

"So, I guess you'll have your fair fight after all," Hera grinned, tilting her head in mockery. "Lucky you."

Veldin glanced with a nod to the guardsman beside him before raising his axe. Together, they advanced upon the sorceress.

As her assailants approached, Hera reached out for the guardsman and clenched her fist. A dim red glow throbbed around his golden armour and it suddenly began to hiss. Immobilized in a fight against the escalating heat, the guardsman fell to his knees with a pained grunt and left Veldin alone to engage her.

"Fuck off with the dirty tricks!" Veldin roared as he swept his axe back to strike.

Hera stepped aside the sweeping blade with little effort. "You're right, that was unfair," she smiled. "Apologies."

Releasing the guardsman from her spell, she gripped her staff in both hands. As Veldin's axe came back around, the shafts of their weapons clashed. Hera ducked back and shifted her staff on its side, letting the axe slide along it and fall from the end. Her opponent's weapon swept aside, she thrust the blades of her staff up, its burning blades scorching Veldin's fiery beard as he staggered away.

With his target distracted, the guardsman lunged at Hera with his blazing spear. Her scarlet eyes darted to his blade and she smashed it aside with her staff, driving it into the floor in an explosion of sparks. Her fist cleaved around and smashed into the back of his head with a clang, sending him staggering behind her.

She turned again to Veldin's axe and as it clashed against the shaft of her staff, Hera ducked left and thrust him right. In the space created, she released the grip of one of her hands and swung the staff around by its end. The returning guardsman raised his golden spear in defence and before his eyes, the red flame dispersed from the staff's blades. Suddenly enveloped by unstable green light, the blades swept through the middle of the spear as if it were not even there.

Veldin had barely looked away for seconds before he turned back around to see the final guardsman's head fly from his shoulders in a visceral spray of gore. Hera drew her staff back to her side, the blood soaking her staff's blades dissolving into a red mist as the flames reignited.

"I have to say, I'm disappointed," Hera sighed, pacing up and down the length of the room. "I expected so much more from the famous Phoenix Guard. What a waste of tricinium."

"At least we can agree on something," Veldin growled. "You know, you're rather talkative for someone who wears so much black."

"Well, when you spend every waking hour intimidating underlings, these moments of relaxation are few and far between. I make of them what I can."

Relaxation? Is that what she called this? Was she simply overconfident or had she truly not broken a sweat behind that damned mask? Veldin would not let her words phase him, he was the last line of defence. He would not falter.

"I can be more serious if you want," Hera smirked. "I don't do monologues though, it's poor practice."

"How about we just fight? No need to overcomplicate things."

"You know, I couldn't agree more," Hera grinned, raising her staff in readiness. "Show me what you're made of, Ironhand!"

With a defiant roar, Veldin launched himself at Hera, cleaving his axe around and smashing it into the shaft of her staff. Again and again he swung his axe, met each time with the metallic ring of their clashing weapons. Hera blocked each attack with incredible ease and speed, yet made no attempt to strike back. She was either toying with him or testing him. Either way, he would ensure that she paid the price for her cockiness.

As the shafts of their weapons met once again, Veldin rammed his axe forwards and forced Hera back into a corner, before turning over his shoulder.

"Run, now!" he bellowed.

Hera watched in amusement as Friedrich bolted from behind his bed and rushed for the door. She flicked her hand beneath Veldin's arm and the carpet lit up with a streak of dancing fire. The wall of flame roared to life and towered before Friedrich, arching over him and cutting him off from the other half of the room.

"What's the rush?" Hera smirked, shoving Veldin away again. "We've still so much to talk a-"

Veldin's axe cleaved past again, easily dodged. As Hera looked up smugly from his weapon, a meaty fist drove hard into the side of her head.

His punch knocked her back in a daze, swinging her staff out in front of her to ward him off as she recovered. Veldin span around and swept a golden spear from amidst a puddle of blood. He thrust it forth, releasing it and sending it soaring through the air like a javelin. Hera grinned as the spear hurtled towards her and in a swift motion, swamped it in a torrent of green light.

"Inspired," Hera grinned as the spear ceased to exist. "Your initiative is impressive, albeit fruitless."

With Veldin having given up ground to attempt his gambit, Hera moved freely from the corner and flourished her staff again.

"Now it's my turn," she smiled.

Hera leapt towards Veldin, who met her staff with his axe once again. What remained of his confidence quickly began to wane as a series of lightning blows hammered his axe, staggering him further and further back as he struggled to keep up. She was wearing him down, fast.

Seeing a narrow opening in her flurry of attacks, Veldin swept his axe low. Hera leapt over the cleaving blade and span around elegantly on the tip of her foot, slamming the rear end of her staff into Veldin's forehead as he drew back his weapon. He lashed out at her sluggishly, his axe easily blocked.

As her staff slid from the end of the weapon, Hera glided around Veldin in but a second. He could barely turn around before the searing blade of her staff made contact with his leg. Hera rammed the weapon down into the unprotected back of his calf, hissing as it pierced flesh and shattered bone. Veldin roared with pain as his axe clattered to the ground and he toppled against the bed, his head spinning as he desperately clutched the scorched, bloody stump of his leg.

Hera was quick to capitalize on his incapacitation. She swept around and flung out her hand, grabbing Friedrich by his crimson robe and yanking him close. Her arm around his neck, she drew the burning blades of her staff to his trembling face.

"And just like that, it could all be over," Hera smiled, caressing Friedrich's cheek with the tip of a blade. "Are you afraid of death, Friedrich?"

Friedrich whimpered pathetically as the burning metal hissed against his frail, wrinkled skin.

"Are you afraid you'll be forgotten? That nobody will remember your name?" Hera hissed. "Because once we burn your kingdom to ash, once we tear this tyranny asunder... they will remember you. They'll remember a tyrant."

"W-w-why... are you doing this?" Friedrich gasped, his voice feeble and tortured.

"You're a rather poor listener, aren't you?" Hera sighed. "The age of Verdenheld is coming to a close, and we intend to give it an... explosive send off."

"You... you'll never win," Veldin mumbled, straining at the excruciating burning pain of his stump.

"Then what am I doing right now?" Hera sneered, before moving to Friedrich's ear. "Your life is in our hands, Friedrich. Try to keep that in mind."

Hera released her grip and cast Friedrich to the ground before Veldin, who gazed up at her dumbstruck.

"W-what is this?" Veldin scoffed.

"A message," Hera declared. "Valkyr is coming and you are powerless to defy him. So, be sure to enjoy the last fleeting moments of your lives... and if you feel like surrendering, look us up in Strausia. He'll be waiting."

Hera strolled away, hammering down her staff and tearing open an unstable green portal. She glanced with a devious grin over her shoulder as she slipped a foot into the vortex.

"Thanks for the fight, Ironhand," she smiled. "That was the most fun I've had in years."

"Maybe... maybe we should do it again sometime," Veldin growled.

Hera tilted her head with an eager smile not visible behind her mask. "I'd like that," she chirped, before turning to Friedrich and waving nonchalantly. "See you all soon..."

Veldin and Friedrich watched as Hera vanished into the dancing abyss of the portal. Veldin breathed a sigh of relief and slumped to the ground as it flickered and died. He did not understand - she had Friedrich exactly where she wanted him. All Kharmenia had planned had culminated in that single moment. Why then would she spare Friedrich after making such effort to get him in her grip?

As his vision blurred and head lightened, he glanced up at Friedrich who lay twitching and hyperventilating in a pool of his own guards' blood. Whatever Kharmenia's twisted plan may have been, the King was alive, albeit traumatised beyond imagining. The day had not been lost... but it undoubtedly had not been won.

Chapter Ten - Break of Dawn

Glaring light washed away darkness as Caesia's eyes drifted slowly open. The room around her quivered and quaked as she span in a nauseous daze. She peeled her face from the pillow and planted her hands delicately against the cold wooden table, when a sharp pain burnt suddenly across her back, sending her crashing back down and shattering her dizzied state.

"Woah now, take it slow," urged the calm voice of a man. "Here, let me help you."

Cold hands forced her shoulders to stiffen and retreat inwards, her raw skin so sensitive to the man's touch. Slowly, she was moved upright, until her blurring vision came to rest on a short, grey haired man who looked at her with a sweet smile.

"There you go," he grinned. "How are you feeling?"

Caesia rubbed her hands across her eyes and shook off her head as the nausea began to clear. She looked around the room, cluttered with medical tools and illuminated by a floating orb of shimmering light. It was a biomancer's practice, how did she get here?

"Wh- where's Eris?" she mumbled, her voice sluggish and incoherent.

"Outside. She brought you to me, said you blacked out halfway here. Begged me on her hands and knees to fix you up. Not that she had to, it's my job after all."

Caesia smirked shallowly. "Yeah… sounds about right. Is she okay?"

"Honestly, her leg is in a terrible state. In any other circumstances, I would have scolded her for putting so much pressure on a fracture… but from what she's told me, I suppose she had no choice."

"Can it be healed?"

"Yes, but it will require surgery," the biomancer sighed. "She's got a bit of a decision to make, hopefully you can convince her."

"I'll see what I can do," Caesia mumbled.

That was good to hear, she had feared the worst of Eris' injury, scared that too much damage could have put a tragic end to her adventuring career. Then again, she had to wonder if a defunct leg would even do a thing to stop Eris. Probably not.

"What about me?" Caesia asked.

"You… well, your flesh is healed. The new skin will take time to fully adjust and will be quite irritable for the coming days, and I'm afraid to say that it will leave a particularly severe scar. Of course, whether you consider that and issue is up to you."

Caesia sighed a breath of relief and peered over her shoulder, catching the very tip of her raw red flesh below her shoulder. It was then that Caesia was struck by the fact that she was topless, her face bursting with colour as she threw her arms around her chest.

"Don't worry," the biomancer chuckled. "I am both a professional and married."

"I-If it's all the same to you, I'd still like some clothes," Caesia stammered.

"Of course," the biomancer smiled, scooping her shirt and coat from the side. "I don't think I need tell you that your clothes are in a bit of disrepair…"

"Nothing a tailor can't fix," Caesia sighed, snapping up her shirt and hurriedly squirming into it, accidentally poking her head through the tear in the back as she scrambled for humility.

"Anyhow, there is one more matter we need to discuss," The biomancer said gravely. "I don't suppose you've had any recent contact with any… toxic materials?"

"Toxic materials? I mean, I did get dunked in sewage a few times," Caesia muttered, the cold touch of sewage still vivid in her mind. "And we did spend quite a lot of time in the sewer itself."

"Hm, just as I suspected," he sighed. "I expect you will soon see the onset of several symptoms, including vomiting, severe stomach cramps, diarrhoea… you get the picture."

"You're kidding," Caesia groaned.

"I'm afraid not. Come back and see me this evening and I will prescribe you a potion that should reduce the severity of the symptoms. With medication, you should be ship shape within a fortnight."

"Okay… thank you," Caesia sighed, pushing herself from the table and flinging her torn, scorched coat around her back.

Not only was she absolutely livid that she would have to get her coat stitched up, but now she would be stuck on medication for the coming weeks. Wonderful.

She waved the biomancer goodbye and stepped out of his surgery, into the golden hallways of the palace. Eris sat cross-legged on the floor beside the door, humming a merry tune while flicking through Caesia's Encyclopedia Abjuria.

"Hey, there's some really cool stuff here!" she laughed, thrusting the book in Caesia's face. "Check this out!"

She showed Caesia an example picture from the 'personal shielding' section. It depicted a man wearing a jagged suit of armour made up purely of light, it was bland and featureless yet nonetheless covered him head to toe.

"You totally need to learn this one, you'll look so cool!" Eris gushed excitedly.

Caesia chuckled and threw up her hands defensively. "I'm not nearly ready to attempt a spell like that, it's far too advanced."

"But you'll-"

"Yes, I'll figure it out some point down the line. These things take time you know!"

"I figured - this stuff makes no sense!" Eris scoffed. "I don't know how you even understand half of this crap."

"Maybe it would help if you could read it?" Caesia smirked.

"No, I mean the diagrams and stuff, it's all a load of nonsense! How do you make any sense of all this?"

"Practice, my friend," Caesia said smugly. "A lot of it."

Eris slammed the book shut and shoved it back into Caesia's bag. She forked the bag over to Caesia, who placed it carefully over her shoulder as to not irritate the new skin.

"You good?" Eris smiled. "You look good."

"Thanks," Caesia smirked. "The new skin is rather itchy against my shirt, but I'd say I'm feeling pretty good, all things considered."

"Cool..." Eris sighed. "You, er... had me pretty worried back there."

"I could tell, you bloody killed the man!"

Eris looked down shamefully at her feet. "I was just trying to protect you..."

Caesia smiled warmly. Eris did what she did because she cared, there was no way Caesia could fault her for that. Besides, in her shy, shameful state Eris was far too cute to be mad at.

"I know, I know. I can't be mad at you for that, you did good."

Eris grinned shallowly with reassurance. "I guess... but I did lose my cool a bit."

"It happens, forget about it," Caesia smiled. "Come on, I need some air."

Eris grabbed her crutch and with a hand from Caesia, clambered to her feet. According to the biomancer, she had fractured her ankle quite badly. He told her that it likely had been a minor fracture, but that she put so much pressure on it that it had worsened severely. Apparently, the recovery time could be sped up to but a few days provided they applied spells to the bone. Of course, that required surgery and Caesia wasn't quite sure how to break to Eris what that word meant.

They started off down the corridor and towards the stairwell. The hallways were deathly silent after the attack, the only sound echoing through them now being the clatter of Eris' crutch. The corridors were still stained with swaths of blood and the ornate, golden walls were battered with claw marks. The crimson carpet was saturated with blood and still produced a chilling squelch upon contact. Worst of all was the overwhelming metallic scent that only served to worsen the choking stench of rotting corpses.

"And I thought I looked a mess…" Caesia muttered. "This place is a bloody wreck."

"That doesn't mean you look any less of a mess," Eris chuckled.

Caesia looked as if she'd just woken from a week's sleep. The red bags under her eyes had bags of their own, her face was filthy with dust from the hole she blew in the ceiling and her fringe was swept across her face like a greasy blanket, her hair as a whole having become a ragged brown mop held together by sweat.

"Oh, I've not a doubt," Caesia laughed. "I must look like some kind of cave dwelling beast after all I've been through. If you think I look bad now, the biomancer said that I'm coming down with an illness!"

"Oh, for- please tell me you won't be stuck in bed," Eris groaned. "I won't survive another week off!"

"If I stay regular with the medication, fingers crossed I can stay on my feet. Believe me, I would no more like another week wasting away inside than you would."

Eris sighed begrudgingly, silently beseeching the ancestors to be merciful. "Okay… and on a scale of one to ten, how much are you gonna puke?"

"Suppose you'll have to wait and find out," Caesia smirked. "Though I expect at least a solid five…

They stepped out from the upturned throne room and into the Palace Gardens. Hundreds of soldiers were working quickly to disassemble their makeshift barricades, hurrying about in a rush to get back to their posts as day broke. A legion of medics armed with dozens of stretchers hauled countless dying and dead away from the scene, hundreds of dripping wounds leaving rivers of gore flowing amidst the stonework.

Light began to slip across the rooftops, the golden brown buildings shimmering in a fiery orange. The starry black sky began to fade into pinks and reds - day had finally broken, an end to the longest night of their lives.

"Ah, feel that morning breeze," Caesia smiled, throwing her hair back and embracing the cool air as she escaped the smouldering heat of the palace.

"Don't take it for granted," Eris chuckled. "The morning breeze back home gives people frostbite."

"Don't ruin this for me," Caesia hissed, relaxing in the soothing wind.

Caesia's moment of ecstasy was cut quickly short by the battering of heavy boots against the pavement as Veldin came hobbling out of the palace after them.

"There you are!" he bellowed. "Thank God you're alright, I was getting worried!"

"Alright... may be an understate- Oh my God!"

Caesia cupped her mouth in horror at the sight of Veldin's bloody, bandaged stump halfway down his right calf. His skin was a ghastly white and his massive form was being supported barely by a pair of crude wooden crutches.

"Ah, crutch buddies!" Eris smiled, receiving a burning scowl from Caesia.

"Yeah, I've... I've seen better days," Veldin mumbled grimly. "Did you know about Kharmenia?"

"One of Valkyr's old lieutenants, right?" Caesia asked.

"That last changeling mentioned her, I think she was their boss," Eris said. "He said she was gonna kill the King herself."

Veldin hung his head in shame. "And she nearly did," he sighed. "While you were gone, she burst in, killed the Phoenix Guard and kicked my ass hard."

"Stars!" Eris gasped. "Is the King okay?"

"She... she had him," Veldin mumbled, his voice shaky and incoherent. She could have killed him there and then but she let him go. I-I don't understand!"

"Fear, perhaps?" Caesia guessed, burying her chin in her hand as she thought. "Scaring Friedrich could be preferable to killing him."

"Maybe, but why do that when you could cause so much more panic by simply killing the man? Removing House Verden would send the kingdom into chaos, it doesn't add up!"

"I don't know what to say," Caesia sighed. "I suppose what matters is that Friedrich is alive."

"I guess so," Veldin muttered. "Though he's refusing to leave the palace anymore... which leaves what we do next up to me. You two'll have to fill me in on everything you know about this situation."

"No offence..." Caesia said. "But you don't look to be in much of a state to act."

"I'm in a better state than Friedrich, that's for bloody sure," Veldin smirked. "Now come on, I need some details."

"Okay, we can do that," Caesia smiled. "Let's take a walk, I need to stretch my legs."

The trio headed south towards the port. The city was at peace again, only the distant squawking of seagulls to fill the silence. It was nice, yet it felt almost unnerving after all they had been through.

"I must say, you're looking good as new, my girl!" Veldin chuckled to Caesia.

"I don't feel it," Caesia muttered. "I'm more tired than I thought humanly possible and my back is itching up a storm."

"I guess looks can be deceiving," Veldin sighed. "Nonetheless, I was nothing short of blown away by how well you handled taking a hit like that."

"Did you really think so little of me?" Caesia jested. "I think I've been in so much pain today that I'm starting to build an immunity."

"Hm, maybe once you ladies are done with this Valkyr business, you'll regale me with some of these epic tales," Veldin chuckled. "You two must get up to some crazy shit."

"Oh, you don't know the half of it!" Eris chirped.

"You can have a sit down with Eris at some point, no doubt she could gush about our adventures for hours on end."

"She's not wrong," Eris smirked.

"Anyway, I believe we had some important stuff to discuss?" Caesia said.

"That we do!" Veldin boomed. "I want to hear everything you've got on this Valkyr situation. I can make sure the realm is at least a bit ready for him."

"Alright, but I can't say we know much for sure," Caesia sighed. "We know he's trying to rally the world for another war against Verdenheld and that this assassination was a ploy to force the arachni to join his side."

"So, the arachni aren't with him? That's a relief."

"Indeed. What's more, Valkyr was seemingly behind the attack on Jordenholm, or at the very least his return prompted it."

"Makes sense, that attack bit a huge fucking chunk outta House Severin's manpower," Veldin muttered.

"Aside from that, we know little else," Caesia sighed. "Sorry we don't have much."

"You've not much, but it's enough for now. We'll be dealing with an army, which means I'll have to seriously whip this city into shape. I just hope I've got enough time…"

"You're staying?" Caesia smirked.

"Damn right, I am!" Veldin roared. "The guards in this city are morons, just about everything here needs some serious work!"

"And why is it your problem?" Caesia asked.

"Because if I don't make it my problem, who will?" Veldin sighed. "Besides, I remember what you said to me back in that ballroom and you were right - I need to spend some time away from Schardenhelm, forge my own path. I figure this is as good a place as any to get started."

Caesia smiled warmly at Veldin's recognition. "That's the spirit!" she chirped.

"It won't be the most glorious of jobs, nor will it be the most gratifying. When the time comes though, the people of Aldreichen will be glad ol' Veldin was here to put things in line."

"I can think of no better man for the job," Caesia smiled. "Is there anything we can do to help?"

"No, you two just keep doing what you're doing. Maybe you can get to Valkyr early and stop him before things get… out of hand."

"You can count on us!" Eris declared.

"I've not a doubt. By the way, a group of soldiers told me that the statue in Victory Square hit the deck not long ago, levelled half a block of houses. Don't know anything about that, do you?"

Eris made like she was thinking carefully. "Hm… nope."

"Huh, well hopefully I can convince the king not to waste resources restoring it, unlikely as that may be."

As they turned into the port, Caesia spotted a familiar figure leaning in waiting against the wall of a warehouse. Grom, cloaked sinisterly in shadow, gave her one of his signature, spine chilling smiles as their eyes met.

"So, where're you ladies off to next?" Veldin asked.

"I think we're about to find out…" Caesia muttered, maintaining an awkward eye contact with Grom.

Veldin followed Caesia's gaze to the tall, lanky man. "A friend of yours?"

"He's a… friend of the family."

"Well, I guess I'd best leave you to do your thing," Veldin sighed. "I'll be in touch should anything else Valkyr related crop up around 'ere."

"Great," Caesia smiled. "Thanks Veldin, couldn't have done it without you."

"Pretty sure you could've, but I'll take the compliment," Veldin laughed. "I've a hunch this won't be the last we see of each other, but good luck to you all the same!"

Veldin trudged off back towards the palace. As he disappeared into the city, Caesia reluctantly approached Grom, who peeled himself from the wall like the slimy man he was.

"You've done remarkably well for yourself, my lady," he smiled, unnerving as always. "Saved the King and the arachni in one fell swoop. Impressive."

"You expected anything less?" Caesia sneered.

"Your mother didn't, though I had my doubts," Grom sighed. "I felt that you were not cut out for my line of work, yet you proved me wrong time and time again."

"I appreciate the arse kissing, but can we just cut to the chase?"

"Indeed we can. As your investigation ran its course, I worked to compile a comprehensive list of places that may be of some interest. Seeing as you have no new leads to pursue, I would suggest investigating the places listed."

Grom revealed a roll of parchment, sealed with blank red wax, and handed it to Caesia with a smile.

"And what makes these places so interesting?" Caesia asked.

"They are points of significance to the Oppressor. Of course, it is entirely possible that they will yield no new information, but we've little else to work with."

"You don't think this is clutching at straws a little?" Caesia smirked.

"It is, but it will be a temporary fixture. I have every man, woman and child in my employ working tirelessly in search for leads, it is only a matter of time before this Valkyr rears his head again."

Caesia often forgot that Grom employed children to do much of his dirty work, or rather chose to forget. Of course, it was common practice for spies, yet it seemed far weirder when the employer was someone as creepy as Grom.

"Very well, I'll await your word," Caesia sighed, toying impatiently with the parchment.

"Wonderful!" Grom chirped. "Enjoy your adventure, my lady."

With a final, chilling smile, Grom slipped off into the shadows. His skin was so pasty that the darkness rendered him near invisible as he blended into the grey walls of the houses behind him.

"I think we'll have a read of this later," Caesia muttered, shoving the roll of parchment into her pocket.

"Yeah, I don't think my brain'll be able to process it," Eris muttered. "Too tired."

Caesia smirked as she wandered to the edge of the dock and looked out across Unity Bay. The port was near silent, the tranquillity disrupted only by the delicate brushing of the waves against the docks. The water glimmered as it did at night, only this time with fiery orange light as the sun slipped from behind the horizon, splashing the sky with a beautiful array of reds and pinks. It was a glorious sight, like a shining beacon calling to them across the waves - a call for adventure.

"You ever wonder how it gets over there?" Eris sighed, earning a grin of amusement from Caesia as she withdrew from her trance. "Like, how does it get from one side of the sky to the other? Where does it go at night?"

"I don't know," Caesia chuckled. "I always liked the really wacky theories. Did you know there are people out there who think the world is a ball and the sun goes round and round?"

"That's ridiculous!" Eris giggled. "If the world was a ball, then the people on the bottom…"

"Would just fall into the sky, exactly!" Caesia laughed. "It must have taken quite the imbecile to come up with that one."

"Well, maybe we need to go find out for ourselves!" Eris declared, clenching her fists with determination. "We can chase the sun to the end of Elaria!"

"You can never concentrate on one thing at a time can you?"

"Caesia, I've got a year," Eris smirked. "If I'm gonna do all this stuff, I gotta do it fast and without any planning whatsoever!"

"Fair point, but we ought to resolve this Valkyr business first," Caesia said. "Once all this is done with and I've figured out how to swim, I'll happily add 'sail off the edge of the world and die' to the to-do list."

"You promise?" Eris grinned.

"Absolutely," Caesia smiled. She had as much an itch as Eris to know what lay beyond the world they knew. Once Valkyr was dealt with, an adventure like no other surely awaited them.

They stood for a time in silence, Caesia watching the peaceful waves while Eris gazed out across the horizon, dreaming up ideas of what could be beyond.

"Eris?" Caesia mumbled. "Thank you… for helping me through all this family nonsense and all this stuff with my powers. I think now I can finally feel at peace."

"Ah, it's nothing," Eris smiled.

"Not to me," Caesia whispered. "You don't know how much it means, to finally have someone after all these years who gives a damn about me."

Eris smiled timidly, her cheeks rosy with embarrassment. "Alright, quit the sappy stuff," she laughed, shoving Caesia's shoulder playfully. "I've had way too much of that today…"

"You are absolutely right," Caesia smirked. "Tell you what - right now, I'll make you a promise. From here on out, I'll cut the crying, the complaining, all of it to a minimum. It's high time I started having some fun, wouldn't you agree?"

"Finally!" Eris gasped with relief. "We're still gonna make fun of each other, right?"

"You know I could never give that up," Caesia smiled. "After all, what would we talk about if we couldn't give each other shit?"

Eris reached into her backpack and routed impatiently through it, drawing a carrot triumphantly from its depths and handing it to Caesia.

"I'll eat to that!" she declared, raising another carrot high. "Here's to us!"

Caesia grinned with excitement while Eris engorged the vegetable, a whole world of possibilities ahead of her. So many things to see, so much to do, so much to learn! She had never been more certain that this truly was the life for her. Never had she known such happiness.

"To new adventures!" she smiled, thrusting her carrot into the air. "And to the best year of our lives!"

Epilogue

Ulfric's time in Strausia had been nothing but uncomfortable so far. Having to keep his heavy, fur padded armour on for appearance sake, he was absolutely drenched in sweat. He would easily have succumbed to heat stroke long ago had one of his shamans not laid a cooling enchantment upon the fur beneath the dense tricinium plates. Nonetheless, the humidity was unbearable, though he could not afford to show such weakness.

"And these 'xoctatli' are their rulers?" he asked, sweeping aside a cluster of vines from his path.

"Not just rulers," Maxim corrected. "To the Almanec, the xoctatli are the children of their snake god, Xoctatlacoatl. The xoctatli are revered as a race of demigods and were integrated into Almanec society as a sort of aristocracy."

"And the people happily accept this?"

"Indeed. They seem rather pleased with the xoctatli's rule. They speak of them as benevolent and kind."

"Good," Ulfric smiled. If the xoctatli cared about their people, they would surely see wisdom in his words.

They had trekked for hours through the jungle, escorted closely by a group of Almanec warriors, brown skinned men dressed in colourful feathered headdresses and crude clothes made up of tropical leaves and dull fabrics. Some wore unnerving, painted masks carved from animal skulls and in some cases, human skulls. Maxim Bassot, a researcher from Newport who Hera had convinced to come along with the promise of a closer look at the Almanec, had told him that they were taking them to their city. He hoped that Maxim spoke their language as well as he claimed.

"Two years ago, I had no idea this place even existed," Ulfric muttered, gazing into the midst of the jungle, a place so alien to a man from the tundra wastes of Norskar.

Home… it was but a distant memory. Two years had passed since House Verden raised Kalmansa to the ground. So much had changed, they had come so far - yet, he would never forget. In his time working against Verdenheld, this had come to be about more than petty vengeance, yet he would always remember where he began, fuel to drive his battle for freedom.

"Fascinating, isn't it?" Maxim smiled. "That these people can not just survive, but thrive out here."

"Doesn't surprise me, I'm from Norskar," Ulfric chuckled. "But, this place... so much life, so much colour. It's beautiful."

"That it is."

"And Verdenheld is ripping it all down," Ulfric growled, his fists clenched at the mere mention of the kingdom's damnable name. "Their greed will destroy this place, destroy those who call it home. Does that not bother you?"

Ulfric liked to probe people with this kind of question. He liked to know what drove them to accept Verdenheld's rule, finding both amusement and reassurance in how displeased people were beneath their tyrannical overlords.

"Well, I suppose it does..." Maxim muttered. "Not that I could do much about it. My best bet is simply to finish my work before the damage becomes too great."

"And you don't worry that the damage may already be too great?"

As Maxim opened his mouth to answer, one of their escorts spoke. His words were totally unintelligible to Ulfric, their language a jumbled mess of strange sounds.

"Our friend here says that their city is just through this treeline," Maxim declared. "Quetzacualcan, he calls it."

"Great," Ulfric smiled, despite already having forgotten the name. He did not need to know anyway, they would not be here long.

The warriors led them through a small gap in the dense treeline, Ulfric having to squeeze awkwardly through in his massive suit of armour. On the other side lay the city of Quetzacualcan.

The city was a strange mix of urban and rural, not as large and developed as the cities of other nations yet equally as impressive in its own right. Along the fringe of the city ran a river, upon which laid a blanket of rectangular plots growing all manor of colourful and exotic food. The ingenuity of their designs were impressive, so much more efficient and appealing than the rolling fields of farmland back home. As for the city, the buildings were equally as pretty - simple painted structures, decorated with beautiful patterns and cloaked in vibrant flora, as if a part of nature itself. From the centre of the city rose several colossal, golden pyramids, the central of which rose high above the jungle canopy. They were built up in tiers, with a sprawling staircase running all the way up one side. Ulfric was astonished that these seemingly primitive people were capable of building such immense structures - that kind of drive would serve him well.

"Incredible..." Ulfric gasped, earning a smile of approval from Maxim.

"I'd read reports on these places from Arrenni scouts, always described them as 'primitive'. Can you believe it?"

"We're talking about House Arrenni - I absolutely can," Ulfric sighed. "Verdenheld knows about this place then?"

"This one and a couple more. Of course, nobody has a clue how many more could be out there."

"You know what House Arrenni intends to do about them?" Ulfric asked, fearing the worst.

"Not a clue, but I know their encounters with the locals have been nothing but hostile," the translator sighed. "And I doubt that was the fault of the Almanec."

"Yeah, leave it to Verdenheld to start a war the moment they set foot on new land," Ulfric muttered.

"Indeed... and I suppose with all this business of deforestation and stripping the land of its resources, relations aren't likely to improve."

Ulfric smirked knowingly. Maxim knew he was helping him get support for a war against Verdenheld, a fact he agreed with happily for he had no care for the kingdom. What Maxim didn't know was what Ulfric intended to do with Newport.

"I don't think we ought to worry about that..." Ulfric muttered.

The warriors led them through the city, where the people went happily about their daily lives. Maxim had told Ulfric of the Almanec's tradition of human sacrifice, how a citizen would be randomly selected every week for what was viewed an honour. It was astonishing that these people, who lived with the constant possibility of being sacrificed to a sun god, were so pleased with their existence. That fact was that they lived as equals, that they were a united people not burdened by poverty and class divides. They were free, a shining example of what could be in a world without Verdenheld.

They came to the foot of the Great Pyramid, the colossal structure in the centre of the city that acted as both the seat of the Almanec Emperor and the centre of religious practice and sacrifice. The massive golden structure was subtly decorated with colourful patterns and depictions of gods painted onto the lower walls. Lush vines crawled down the stepped sides like mangled curtains, nature having been allowed to consume the pyramid completely.

"Why is every building in this place so overgrown?" Ulfric muttered as they ascended the endless staircase.

"I believe it is a sign of acceptance," Maxim explained. "The jungle is said to be a gift from their sun god, Teclahuitl. They allow the jungle to consume them, likened to being held within the sun god's embrace. Within his embrace, they find protection."

"So, would you say the jungle is… like a sort of shield?" Ulfric mused. "That without it, they would be in danger?"

"Essentially, yes."

"Interesting…" Ulfric smiled.

They scaled the colossal staircase, up to the pyramid's boxed peak. Ulfric had barely climbed so many stairs in his life and was left utterly exhausted. At the top was an open expanse, the floor stained with layer after layer of dried blood surrounding a simple, large slab of stone. As they approached the entrance to the throne room, a pair of guards thrust their spear into their path.

The Almanec 'Xoctecali' royal guards were both extravagant and menacing. They wore intricate stone masks carved as the heads of snakes, surrounded by a vibrant headdress packed with beautiful magenta feathers. Their clothes were strapped with leather pads, wrapped in the shedded skin of giant jungle snakes and painted with pinks and purples. One of their number stepped forwards and uttered an aggressive few words to their guide.

While the warrior secured their entry, Ulfric took a moment to take in the view. From the peak of the Great Pyramid of Teclahuitl, one could see beyond the dense canopy and gaze for miles across the flat expanse of Strausia. The whole continent felt like another world, the vast, peaceful jungles sprawling for miles with no sign of civilisation, a total antithesis to Athaea. He supposed that is why he liked it here so much - back on Athaea, no matter if he were in Norskar, Verdenheld or Thyresia, the open land left nowhere to go that did not remind him of the evils of civilisation.

"The Emperor is waiting," Maxim called as the Xoctecali stepped aside.

Ulfric span around with a smile and wandered back to Maxim's side. Together, they stepped into the throne room, the beating light of the sun swallowed up by searing torchlight.

"Any final advice?" Ulfric whispered.

"I know little of the Xoctatli, they rarely show themselves outside of the cities," Maxim muttered. "Just… treat him with the respect you would a king. Actually, perhaps that is a poor example."

"I get your point," Ulfric smirked. "Besides, I'm sure if I say anything I shouldn't, you'll set it right in translation."

"Of course," Maxim smiled.

Flickering torchlight illuminated the crude pink and purple banners that hung from walls of the throne room and cast the ominous shadows of the Xoctecali guards across the room like those of towering giants. Watched by eyes hidden within serpentine maws, Ulfric and Maxim marched to meet the most powerful man in all of Strausia.

Seated on a massive throne of beautifully carved gold, laden with purple essence crystals and decked with elegant pink feathers, was the Xoctatli Emperor of the Almanec. In all honesty, Ulfric had painted a very different image of the Xoctatli in his mind - when Maxim told him they were children of the snake god, he failed to mention that they were actual snake people.

His upper body was like that of a human, only with a hide of rough, weathered beige scales. At his waist began the long, winding tail of a serpent, thick enough to crush a man in its grip. Finally, atop his shoulders was the slender head of a snake, bearing a razor toothed maw and gazing upon Ulfric with piercing, serpentine eyes. He was built like a killing machine, one who's very appearance inspired fear. It was hard to believe that those like him made up this empire's aristocracy.

Maxim stepped forth and introduced Ulfric in Almanec tongue - "Your imperial majesty, I present to you Octavius Valkyr, Grand Warlord of the Elarian Alliance."

The Emperor stared for a time at his guests, evaluating them with narrow eyes. He replied in a series of strange, alien sounds, just like his underlings. His voice was coarse yet silky, his every sentence punctuated with a sinister hiss.

"The mighty Tezcahuitan, Keeper of Peace, Breaker of the Burning Horde, Lord of Quetzacualcan and Supreme Emperor of Almaneca greets you, Warlord. He is surprised by your arrival, but is most intrigued."

Ulfric smirked subtly at the grandeur of the Emperor's titles. Grand as they were however, they were fairly justified. Ulfric had done his reading on the 'archdemon', as Verdenheld called him - the behemoth monster who personally oversaw the shattering of a vast Severin army at the Battle of Hell's Maw. Tezcahuitan was not known to the kingdom by name, but his deeds in defence of his people were already legend.

"I need your help, your majesty," Ulfric declared. "I need your army. Verdenheld, the same tyrants who scour your lands of their resources, choke mankind of its freedom under their iron fist!"

Maxim conveyed Ulfric's message and received back a careless mutter. Tezcahuitan leant back ignorantly on his throne, resting his head in one of his clawed hands.

"Tezcahuitan fails to see how this is his problem."

Ulfric furrowed his brow impatiently. He knew that his proposal would be worth the Emperor's time, he just had to pique his interest.

"As we speak, Verdenheld tears down your jungle, your home," Ulfric said, trying to remain calm and composed for once. "And once it's gone, once you've lost the protection of your sun god, they will come for you… and Verdenheld is not known for its mercy, believe me."

Tezcahuitan seemed agitated at first by the Maxim's translation. He pushed his hand further into his cheek in thought, considering Ulfric's point carefully. He hissed a curious response.

"What do you suggest, Warlord?" Maxim conveyed.

"My offer is simple. I free your people and you help me free mine," Ulfric smiled. "You agree to help me take Aldreichen and I will help you destroy Newport."

"What?!" Maxim gasped. "You can't do that!"

"I will allow them to evacuate first," Ulfric calmly reassured him. "Tell him."

Maxim turned and uttered Ulfric's words hesitantly, earning a slow nod of consideration from the Emperor.

"We will free your people from Verdenheld's tyranny and save your home," Ulfric declared. "You have my word."

Tezcahuitan seemed intrigued by Maxim's words, leaning forward eagerly in his throne. Ulfric had his attention, it was time to hammer this home.

"He is interested in your proposition, but he must know how you expect to take on such power."

"I have an army of my own. Legions of soldiers gathered from across Elaria await my word - forces from Norskar, Thyresia, Novekhir. They all stand ready to march against the tyrant king. Together, with your armies at my back, we will be unstoppable."

As Ulfric spoke, a cunning grin grew across Tezcahuitan's narrow face, clearly becoming satisfied with Ulfric's answer. The Emperor leant back in his throne at uttered but a few words.

"The mighty Tezcahuitan is pleased by your proposition, but demands a tribute as a show of your good will."

"What does his majesty have in mind?" Ulfric asked.

Maxim asked Tezcahuitan, who leant forwards in his throne and hissed a single word. Ulfric watched with an eyebrow raised as Maxim stiffened at the Emperor's words.

"A sacrifice," Maxim mumbled.

Ulfric was eerily silent at the request. There was no greater force than the Almanec to stand by his side, both in size and strength. He needed to please the Emperor, yet he and Maxim had come alone. With a woeful sigh, Ulfric turned with a grave look to Maxim, who gasped at the sorrow in his eyes.

"N-no!" he cried desperately. "You-you can't be…"

"I'm sorry," Ulfric whispered. "I didn't want this."

"Then don't do it!" Maxim begged as Ulfric stepped cautiously towards him. "Please! I've got a family! My daughter-"

Ulfric placed his hand on Maxim's quivering shoulder, a weak smile on his face. "Once I'm done, they'll be free - we all will!" he urged. "Your sacrifice will free the world."

"No!" Maxim shrieked.

He span around to flee for the exit, yet the guards stepped out before him and crossed their spears, blocking his escape. Maxim breathed short and erratically, all he had to lose flashing before his eyes. He wasn't ready to die, he had so much yet to live for. He had barely gotten to see his daughter grow up.

Ulfric sighed shamefully, closing his eyes in disappointment with himself. This would hurt, but he was more than willing to go through with it. There was nothing he wouldn't do to achieve his goal. He looked to the guards and nodded, signalling towards the exit with his trembling hand. They lunged forwards, grabbing the poor, screaming man in their muscular arms and hauling him towards the exit. Maxim looked at him, a cry for help in his tearful eyes as he wailed and kicked in desperation.

"I'm sorry…" Ulfric mumbled.

Ulfric glanced to the corner of his eye as the Emperor slithered to his side, watching with a smirk as Maxim disappeared into the light.

"Worry not, my friend," he hissed with a cunning grin. "His death will grant us the might of the gods. In his sacrifice, we will be invincible!"

"You could understand me that whole time?" Ulfric muttered.

"I like to toy with foreigners, to test the extent of their ignorance," Tezcahuitan sneered. You though, you are worthy of my attention. I see that you respect my people and their culture and thus, *my* respect is yours."

Ulfric cringed as a tortured scream bellowed from the terrace outside. "Why did you need a sacrifice?"

"We christen our relationship in blood, so that the gods may look upon us in favour," Tezcahuitan smiled. "Now, tell me about this plan of yours. Newport, as your people call it - how shall we bring it to its knees?"

Hera waited anxiously at the bottom of the steps, watching a stream of blood trickle down the colossal staircase and into the dirt. It seemed she had missed something, hopefully nothing too violent - she didn't want to have to help Ulfric out of another diplomatic disaster. Her wishes were granted and she sighed with relief as Ulfric came trudging down the steps unscathed.

"Dare I ask?" she smirked.

Ulfric sighed mournfully. "We… can count on the Almanec's support," he muttered, raising an eyebrow as he noticed how tense Hera appeared. "Something bothering you?"

"Just figuring out a good way to break this to you," Hera sighed. "The Sect is gone. Every surviving member has been collared and prepared for execution."

Ulfric was silent, a blank and emotionless expression on his face. He ground his teeth and clenched his fists, trying particularly hard not to embarass himself in the middle of the city as his temper boiled.

"What happened?" he spat, his voice filled with malice.

"I think you know what happened - it was those girls again," Hera muttered.

"The ones who killed the dragon?"

"The very same."

Ulfric growled like a starving beast, itching to break something, "We should have killed them. I was a fool to let them go free after what they did!"

"We don't need to kill them, they're just girls," Hera said, trying her best to control Ulfric in his anger. "All we need to do is deter them, scare them off."

Ulfric thought carefully for a moment, his eyes narrowing in suspicion. "How is it you know these details?" he hissed. "You were following them again weren't you? Exactly as I told you not to!"

"We needed to know who we were up against!" Hera insisted.

"You were to continue your work on the Isles! Eliminating the Republic Fleet is vital to our plan! As long as it survives-"

"Preparations are complete!" Hera snapped. "I've been trying to tell you for days! Since you were so busy, I took some time off to do some research."

Ulfric sighed defeatedly, taking a deep breath and calming himself down. Hera was becoming worried about Ulfric's increasingly frequent outbursts of anger. Over the past two years his temper had only worsened under the weight that he placed on his shoulders and now that these girls had shown up and things had started to go wrong, it was reaching its tipping point.

"If you were there, why didn't you intervene?" Ulfric growled. "It was one thing leaving Xeracrir alone, but there was so much hinged on this plan!"

"Well, that would be the good news," Hera smiled. "I did intervene. I killed the King's guard and brought Friedrich within an inch of death. But I spared him... Coming that close to death can change a man - Friedrich, in his old age, will become paranoid in fear for his own life. Rather than lead, he'll run and hide and the realm will grind to a halt."

"And leave Verdenheld even more vulnerable than if we were to kill him!" Ulfric gasped, overcome with glee. "Hera, you're a genius."

Hera grinned in delight behind her mask. So uncommon was her brother's praise that it felt truly special to receive it. It warmed her heart knowing that he still cared for his sister.

"Oh, and I think we can expect a visit from the Arrenni Fleet in the near future," Hera said nonchalantly. "No doubt Friedrich will panic and throw all he's got at us."

"Wait... you didn't tell him-"

"I did. In his fear, he'll commit a vast force to Strausia. As it would happen, this continent is ripe for ambushes and guerrilla warfare, as the Almanec have proved time and time again. This is an opportunity for us to finally gain the upper hand."

Ulfric stared at Hera narrowly. This was an incredible risk, one far greater than any they had ever made - one that would make or break their entire plan. If Friedrich were to send an army, he would send more than just the Arrenni Fleet, House Severin would follow closely behind. What particularly worried him however was House Tarantis - they were extremely conservative with how they deployed their forces, but whenever they did it almost exclusively shifted the tide of war. Could it be that Hera had been overzealous?

"Hm... I hope you know what you're doing," Ulfric sighed. "Now tell me, what have you learnt from this 'research' of yours."

"Well, I learnt little of the girl with the green essence, only that her name is Caesia and that she is beginning to gain control over her abilities."

"And does that make her a threat?" Ulfric asked.

"Little more than she already was. Her abilities seem limited to short ranged translocation at the moment. She's special, but not by any significant means."

"And the other one?"

"I learnt quite a bit about her - she's an interesting one. Her name is Erisian, she-"

"Erisian? I know that name..." Ulfric muttered. "Yeah, Hestia had a daughter called Erisian. Whether she's the same one though..."

"Possibly, she was from the chiefdoms at least. She's sweet - only really seems to care about having fun, but I think there might be a little more to her than that... and she has a good heart, seems to hate the kingdom just as much as us."

"You think we could persuade her to see sense?" Ulfric mused.

"Maybe. It might be worth a shot," Hera smiled. "After all, she could be a valuable ally given her skills."

"Or it could be a waste of time," Ulfric muttered. "A waste of an opportunity to eliminate her."

"It's your call."

"Hm... persuading them to our side seems pointless. It would be far less risky to remove them from the equation entirely... but I don't know..."

Hera smiled sweetly, it was good to see that Ulfric was finally showing some heart.

"You know what? I'll trust your judgement on this one. Either way, we need to draw them out, for which we'll need something big!" Ulfric declared. "You'd best be off to the Isles."

Those words turned Hera's smile into a face-spanning grin. She had worked on Palindoscia for countless months now, it was to be her magnum opus. The concept of getting it started excited her to no end.

"Finally!" Hera sang. "Though... I'm not so sure the cult could handle those two. There's a lot more to them than meets the eye."

"It's unlikely, which is why I want you to personally oversee the operation. Ensure that it proceeds safely and successfully and should these girls rear their heads, deal with them."

Hera sighed reluctantly. "I'm not sure I'm comfortable with beating up young girls..."

"They're the greatest threat to our plans!" Ulfric snapped. "We must do whatever is necessary to ensure it's not jeopardized. We can't slip up now, not when we're so close!"

"I understand..." Hera muttered. "I'll send word to our men and assemble the cult. They say they have to do it on some holy day... first of Decima, I think. So if it's the thirty-ninth today... give me a month, should have things moving by the end of Imperith."

"Great," Ulfric smiled. "And don't worry, the Thyresians should be able to evacuate their innocents quick enough. We won't have another Jordenholm, not if we can help it."

"We won't have another Jordenholm, *period*," Hera demanded. "You can't just keep making excuses."

"We'll see," Ulfric sighed, flicking his hand dismissively. "Now, go. You've a lot to be getting up to."

Hera turned away with a roll of her eyes and drew her staff. Ulfric had taken the news about what Xeracrir did to Jordenholm far too well and it bothered her a great deal. She feared that he was becoming numb to the very people they were working to free.

"And what will you be doing while I'm gone?" she asked, focusing her mind and charging the essence crystal in her staff.

"We've just about checked off every candidate on the list," Ulfric said with an eager smile. "It's time our allies got to know each other a little better."

"Invading Newport, then?" Hera smirked.

"Exactly," Ulfric grinned. "The time is nearly here. Once Thyresia and Norskar are out of the picture, we'll be ready."

"I look forward to it," Hera smiled.

Ulfric turned away to take in the intriguing cityscape as Hera thrust up her staff high into the air, bringing it down and vanishing in a violent explosion of green light.

He sighed broodingly, lost in thought about those damned girls. Sure, ordering their potential deaths was regrettable, but he was long past remorse. He had already done so much that the common man would call terrible or vile, so many awful things in the name of freedom. He felt bad now, but it would be fleeting - they would be but another couple of lives sacrificed in the name of justice.

He would see peace reign, no matter the cost.

Eris and Caesia will return in
ELARIA: The Gathering Storm
Coming 2019

Other books by Jack Wright

ELARIA
Ashes of Verdenheld
Winds of Change

Printed in Great Britain
by Amazon